Cherry Ice

JILL LAURIMORE

PENGUIN BOOKS

Published by the Penguin Group
Penguin Books Ltd, 80 Strand, London WC2R ORL, England
Penguin Putnam Inc., 375 Hudson Street, New York, New York 10014, USA
Penguin Books Australia Ltd, 250 Camberwell Road,
Camberwell, Victoria 3124, Australia
Penguin Books Canada Ltd, 10 Alcorn Avenue, Toronto, Ontario, Canada M4V 3B2
Penguin Books India (P) Ltd, 11 Community Centre,
Panchsheel Park, New Delhi – 110 017, India
Penguin Books (NZ) Ltd, Cnr Rosedale and Airborne Roads,
Albany, Auckland, New Zealand
Penguin Books (South Africa) (Pty) Ltd, 24 Sturdee Avenue,
Rosebank 2196, South Africa

Penguin Books Ltd, Registered Offices: 80 Strand, London WC2R ORL, England

www.penguin.com

All characters in this publication are fictitious and any resemblance
to real persons, living or dead, is purely coincidental.

Published in Penguin Books 2004

1

Set in 11/13pt Monotype Dante by Intype Libra Ltd
Printed in England by Clays Ltd, St Ives plc

ISBN 0–140–00623–4

For Jon

JULY 1914

A Faerie Tale

Every family has its own mythology – those sagas which pass from parent to child, and in the retelling take on the substance of fable. One of theirs was the Tale of Gran's Cherry Ice.

Of course there was always an argument on the detail. Location for a start. Aunt Maev said it happened at Eastbourne, Aunt Prue claimed Worthing, but Gran was adamant it was Brighton. Brighton had a ring to it. Brighton, she always reckoned, added a necessary element of verve, and a certain jauntiness, to the overall picture.

And this is how she painted it.

Day One of the annual holiday. Driven out of the guest house by 9.30a.m. so as the maid of all work could get at the beds. A brisk sun shining on a beach just that bit too nippy for exposure of flesh – not that you did that much exposing in a time of striped woollen bathers hanging somewhere below knee-level. Ma and Pa set up camp on the shingle in the lee of the striped canvas screen: gazing out to sea (he), absorbed in the *Poulterer's Gazette* (she). The children let loose – set free, with sixpence each (in farthings and ha'pennies) and the Pier awaiting. Maev and Prue ran on ahead; Maev intent on fishing for a pair of toy binoculars with one of those remote-control grab machines – turn the handle, a ha'penny a go. Prue agape for Punch and Judy. Gran, then aged seven and a half, bringing up the rear – alone – seeing the kiosk on the promenade, all decked out with curlicues of gold around the counter – 'just like a little theatre' she said, and topped by a pennant fluttering in the breeze. 'Ices' said the flag – and down below, hanging on the wall, was the price list, just as you'd expect: no variety as to flavour, vanilla would have to suffice. But lots of gradation in size and presentation – cornets, wafers, even 'coupes' – and what could they have signified? And there, on its own separate board, were the fatal words – 'Cherry Ice Cream – 6d.' A *whole* sixpence? What sort of ice could demand a whole solid sixpence? Normal pocket money was a penny a week. The mixture of coins in her pocket was a special holiday allocation – something to blow, but only with a certain degree of caution.

She always said she left the kiosk then – wandered towards the Pier, thinking to catch up with her sisters – but the crowds were thick, and Gran was only three foot four. A vision started up in her head as she wound her way through bombazine skirts, soldiers' puttees, spats and plus fours. Cherry Ice. Something pink of course – very pink. Curved in a great ball, glistening with crushed whole cherries, rippling on the surface like half-submerged jewels, overflowing a cornet of unlikely proportions – a cornet as big as a trumpet for six whole pennies.

By the time she reached the Pier's turnstiles, the vision seemed to have taken on the stuff of reality, teasing her senses, so that she was drooling, tasting those cherries in anticipation, invisibly licking at the thick pink custard, now even seeing the very puffs of cloud out at sea, tinged with a rosy glow – though of course the saga got encrusted with such additions as the years went by. She was just about to hand over a coin to gain entrance to the Pier when she realized its loss would steal her only chance to change the vision into substance. And she made up her mind then, in an instant, and turned back through the crowds towards the kiosk to join the queue.

No one else seemed to be availing themselves of the faerie food. She had a good look, and person after person came away with just the usual, sad old normal vanilla, squashed between wafers, stuffed into cones. How strange these grown-ups were,

4

she thought, not to take their chance, ignoring the delight. Perhaps they hadn't seen the sign. Perhaps at a whole sixpence, it was too rarefied and special for the norm. When at last it was her turn, she had to stand on tiptoe to reach the counter.

'Cherry Ice please,' she said.

''ow many?' the man said.

'One,' she said, the mystique suddenly shaken at the notion that anyone could ask for multiples of such a treat. And the man had been distracted then – some boys had knocked into the kiosk with a football, and he'd yelled out, 'Watch what you're doing you little tykes!' and while he was still shouting after them, he'd handed her a large vanilla cone. She stood to one side, while the next person in the queue pushed forward, regarding the dollop of white cream already dribbling on to her hands.

'Please – please sir – ' she said, but felt her voice lost in the crowd and knew she'd have to make a firmer claim for her rights, the injustice she was suffering being perfectly clear even if she was only seven. And she in turn pushed herself forward.

''ere watch it you – just who do you think you're pushin' – where's your manners?'

But she forgot manners and thrust the dripping cone up. 'Please sir – I asked for *Cherry* Ice – ' and the man had peeked over the counter – 'What? Oh right – give it 'ere –' and for a moment the bad dream was going to come right, because he took the cone from her, and was surely about to replace it with the faerie food. Only it came back to her – exactly the same except for a large scarlet glacé cherry stuck in the top.

'There you are – there's your bloomin' cherry – now bugger off,' he said, and she did.

She always said she couldn't even eat the vanilla – that was part of the shame of it, wasting that whole sixpence on an ice worth only a penny. The glacé cherry itself would have choked her, so she went and buried the whole cone in the pebbles on the beach. And she couldn't appeal to her parents' sense of justice:

5

the horror in their faces if they heard of her careless profligacy would have been too hard to bear. She did tell her sisters – eventually; and how they laughed, though none of them ever forgot it, passing the tale on through the years – a symbol of disappointment, bravely, secretly borne. That sneaky, faithless Cherry Ice.

JULY 1964

Thursday

7a.m. British Summer Time

Somehow we miss the boat train. Somehow we manage to be late. Even with my idea of the taxi. Because M. was going to make us take the tube. She said it's only one stop to Waterloo and it'd be more reliable than trusting to traffic. But she gave in last night when she saw my pile of baggage, and that wasn't even all of it, because I still had my attaché case to pack, and my makeup bag. So she went down to the phone box on the corner and ordered a taxi for 7a.m. She said it wasn't meanness – not ordering one. It was experience – because they never come. And she's right. It doesn't. 'Isn't that typical?' she says. 'Your Gran's cherry ice all over again.'

So there we are, stuck out on the pavement surrounded by all my heaps of cases and stuff, only we realize the game is up after half an hour of waiting and looking hopeful. M. runs into Mr Christo's shop because he's just opened for the morning delivery, and asks to borrow his telephone, only when she gets through to the taxi company the woman is completely vague about timing – totally hopeless. And I can see Mr Christo through the window, standing in the middle of his display of plantains and lady's fingers, shaking his head and urging a more direct approach. Which is how M. comes to send me running along Bissett Street to Kennington High Road, to see if I can flag down a passing cab, while Mr Christo tries to ring his brother-in-law to organize a lift. By the time I reach the corner my carefully coiffed Tom Jones is all skew-whiff and there isn't a cab in sight. Well of course not. I could have told them that. Anyone would have known.

In the end it's Mr Christo's brother-in-law who comes up trumps, though it means squeezing into the front of his Bedford van and heaving the baggage into the back along with all his sacks of sand and cement. Nevertheless, by the time we get to Waterloo, the boat train we were supposed to take has already left. M. by now is red in the face from worrying whether we'd make it, and I'm pretty hot and bothered too because, well after all, can you believe it? I mean we've had weeks to plan this thing but even so.

M. frantically rushes ahead to quiz the guard on the platform, while I keep watch on the bags and try to brush the brick dust from the Bedford van off the back of my skirt. Honestly, it's such a struggle to keep any sense of grace and glamour when you're me and not (for example) Jane Asher or The Shrimp.

Once we get over all the breathless panic, our lateness turns out to have some advantages, because there's another boat train, the First Class one, and they let us take that instead. It's called 'The Cunarder', a Pullman – talk about luxury. Once we're off, I go to the bog and re-do my Tom Jones, and by the time I get back to the compartment, we're nearly out of London and most of the indignities of the early morning are beginning to fade. Nevertheless, I try not to catch anybody's eye in case I'd been spotted getting out of the Bedford van, along with kind Mr Christo's brother-in-law in his white singlet and tattoos.

Despite the grandeur of its name, this train is as packed as a day excursion. There's a heavy scent hanging in the air, rich people's scent, so I start playing this guessing game from trailing round the Perfume counters in Selfridges and/or Arding and Hobbs on a Saturday, and I reckon maybe a mixture of Arpège and Chanel No.5 – though there might be a dollop of Mitsouko in there as well? The two women opposite me have mink wraps tossed across their knees just as carelessly as if they're bath towels, even though it's summer. And when I went to the bog, there was a woman in the corridor wearing an ocelot hat. Everyone so far looks really rich and rather old – in their thirties at the very least.

Most of the seats in our compartment had been reserved so M. and I can't sit together. I'm on the corridor side and she's diagonally across from me, still looking anxious and tired, though the redness has worn off and now she's rather pale. Next to her is one of the mink women with tanned skin, smooth as a glacé kid glove, while M.'s looks softly puckered like tissue paper. I feel funny looking at her – funny and a bit sad somehow. It would be nice to reach out a hand and touch her, but she's too far across the compartment, too distantly lost in her own dreams. I have a real case of the butterflies – all mixed up and excited and nervous and wary, but also I think a bit guilty, because M. isn't going to be part of this adventure. M.'s got to stay at home.

There's a general stirring as we reach Southampton. The train slows right down as we get near the docks and even the mink women look excited. I'd love to jump up and have a good look, but my seat's on the wrong side from the ship and it would mean stepping on everyone's toes to get to the window. All I can see is just this brief glimpse of the very front tip of the bows, but of course it's the *Queen Elizabeth*. It has to be, because it's so enormous – just this sheer black cliff of steel – so high you can't see the white bit at the top where the name would be painted, not from this angle. You can't even see the sky: the ship blocks it all out. You can hear a gasp escaping from all of us, except that already the vision of the ship disappears as we're sliding into the Ocean Terminal.

Having arrived with all the First Class passengers, we can't get back to where we're supposed to be, with all the Tourist Class people; we're sort of stuck in the wrong place. The First Class boat train has its own First Class waiting room. It's upstairs, so we're more on a level with the ship, and it's very luxurious with lots of marble, and creamy leather sofas, shops, bars, even banks. If we weren't still a bit panicky it would be fun to explore, but M. is jumpy and that means I can't settle. In the end I'm just longing to go on board and get on with it.

You can see more of the ship from up here – but still only in bits through the windows; just oblongs of white steel with portholes here and there, like clues to help with identification. There's a balcony running the whole length of the terminal, but even from there you can't see the whole ship in one go and you have to crane your neck to look up to the top decks. So we just stand there staring. The ship isn't moving with the swell or anything, it looks absolutely rock solid. I suppose it's too big to bob about, and more and more I begin to get a real sense of how completely enormous it is, and wonder how I'll ever find my way around it. Then we go back inside and M. spots the W. H. Smith kiosk and asks if I want anything – if she can buy me *Vogue* or something – but I tell her I've already got the new one, the August edition, with Paulene Stone on the cover. And she says, 'What about something else – *Honey*? *Boyfriend*? A newspaper even?' And I say 'No thanks – I'm fine.' And she says, 'Yes you are Ella – you're fine,' and she reaches out and touches my cheek and looks really sad. 'You're just fine.'

2a.m. Eastern Standard Time – Point Harbor, Massachusetts

It's a hot, sticky night and the baby is kicking. Lynn rolls on to her side, trying to relieve the pressure, using the mattress to support the weight of her belly. If only she could divorce herself of this load for a while – put it aside, just for the night, but take it back into her care and responsibility in the morning. Now there's pressure against her bladder. Is it the baby arching its back, stretching out its legs, trying to unbend its knees? And then a tumble of movement so strong she can feel it from the outside, through her abdomen wall. If she put the light on she knows she would see it too – bumps which reveal themselves from within, sliding across her belly skin, bumps she imagines formed from a tiny heel, an elbow, a hand.

Is it ever hot – and August not even here yet. The windows are all wide open but there's not a breath of wind. She fancies she hears moths fluttering at the screens in the brief pauses allowed by the background scratching choirs of crickets. They should have put air conditioning up here, but Jack wouldn't have it. In an old New England stone house like this he claims it would be ugly, with its ducts and window units, and he says he won't have ugly: though more than likely it's the budget that won't extend that far, and he doesn't want to admit it. You never know for sure with Jack. The one certainty is his excitement with the house: its chimneys and shutters, its clear brook snaking through its land. His own private dream come to life.

In half-sleep she stretches out her leg across the bed but he's not here. Yet again. His bed, his unborn baby, his wife. So where is Jack? Still at work, or once more on a secret razzle? Does she drop off into a doze at last – or does he slide into the bed in the dark, even as she's thinking of him?

Whatever. Now he's here, hands cradling her belly, feeling the pressure of those tiny limbs within.

'Are you awake?' he murmurs into her neck.

'No,' she says, smiling into the dark.

'I thought so,' he says.

'What's kept you?'

'I went into Boston – had to see some people – business. A new supplier and we had dinner . . .'

'Yes?' but she knows better than to expect any more.

'I've just been looking at Ella's room – '

'Yes?'

'You're doing a great job – did the drapes come yet?'

'Yes – I collected them this morning.'

'She'll love it.'

'I hope so . . .'

'I've just been thinking – she's on her way . . . right now.'

'Yes?'

'The ship will be leaving any time now . . . I wonder how's she's feeling.'

But do you wonder how *I'm* feeling, thinks Lynn, easing herself sideways, seeking relief. And in my own world of hope and expectation do I need this now? My husband's daughter – not mine. A cuckoo in my nest.

'It's kind of exciting isn't it?' he says.

'I guess so . . .'

'You only guess?'

And seeing there's no point now in exposing her doubts, she adds, 'No Jack. I'm sorry. I know so. I do.'

11a.m. British Summer Time

I think they talk about the 'bowels of ships' don't they? And that's where I am on the *Queen Elizabeth* – down on D deck, deep in her gut.

Because of our unexpected journey on the Pullman, we still hadn't been slotted into the right group, and the covered gangway led us straight into the First Class entrance hall on Main Deck, which was big and glamorous and all lined in silky wood panelling. It was absolutely whirling – talk about a hubbub. Masses of stewards in white coats, and a great mixture of passengers, some of them really blasé and some of them in a terrible flap and everyone caught up in finding out where they belonged. A steward came forward to take my cases and looked very surprised when he saw my ticket. 'Miss Eleanor Feast,' he read out loud, *'Cabin D9?* – well I never did! Follow me ladies.' Then he winked, and shot off through the crowds with my biggest bag stuck under his armpit, and M. and I tried to keep up. He got to some stairs, told us that the lifts would be too busy, and started going down and down – and then the silky wood walls changed to ordinary paint and steel bulkheads, with pipes and cables running across the ceilings and just the faintest whiff of fuel oil. Obviously Tourist Class is a different kettle of fish. M. was really surprised – she said this wasn't the way she remembered the great *Queen Elizabeth*. Not the way at all. But then the last time M. was on this ship was eleven years ago when she was leaving Dad and America for that last time, so maybe she's not recalling it that well. I can just about remember it – sometimes. Though sometimes I think that what I'm remembering is just the story the way she's told it – and not my own real memory at all. I was barely four then, and what I *do* remember is being really excited about the voyage – only maybe I didn't realize that I'd never be coming home. Or not until now. But then America's not 'home' any more is it? To me it's 'abroad'. Funny really. And I remember I was in patent leather bar shoes like Eloise in that book. And oddly enough I'm in patent leather shoes today – sling-back winkle pickers with Louis heels, 29/11 from Dolcis and I love them.

It seemed to take forever, but at last the steward opened this narrow door and said, 'Here we are then – D9,' and there we were. And here I am. It's a tiny space, but all fitted out, tight and tidy as a picnic basket. Two sets of bunks in opposite corners, one washbasin, cream plastic water flasks and glasses lined up inside chrome rails fixed to the walls, little cretonne curtains up by each pillow which I suppose will give a bit of privacy. The porthole is sealed shut with a metal cover, so the light is artificial. The cabin we had that time before was much grander and was called a 'stateroom'. M. says it had real twin beds with satin bedspreads, a window on to A Deck and a basket of fruit covered in crackling cellophane to wish us Bon Voyage. And she says there was also a bouquet of long stemmed red roses sent by Uncle Sally and Aunt Bea, and that Dad had wanted to read the card, but she tried to keep it from him, hoping he might think they were from a lover and that he'd be jealous, even a little bit. And now she says that maybe, just maybe, if he'd stopped her then, caught her by the hand and begged her to stay, then maybe she would have done – and we'd have skipped the ship just like that – left our bags and fruit and flowers and run back down the gangway to New York. Only he didn't ask, so we didn't stay.

So anyway, once we've found D9, the steward leaves, and M. is kind of immediately determined to look on the bright side – so I do too, and I start opening all the drawers and the two tiny wardrobes, all empty, so at least no one else has turned up yet, which means perhaps I'll have it all to myself. Only M. says it isn't very likely because it's high season and the ship must be fully booked, because when Dad sent the ticket he'd written it was really hard even to reserve my one berth. Also, she says a lot of people come aboard at Cherbourg. Still, I reckon at least I have the pick of the bunks and I choose the bottom one on the outside wall because the porthole is at the end of it, and once it's uncovered I'll be able to see out while I'm in bed – it'll feel great to be all safely tucked up, yet watching the Atlantic Ocean right outside.

Then there's this banging on a gong and someone calling, 'All ashore that's going ashore!' and the door is flung open and another steward pokes his head in and says, 'All visitors ashore now please – ' And M. says, 'Just coming – on my way,' – and the steward says, 'Those that don't have to swim for it – ' and you can tell it's one of those jokes he's told a hundred times before – and then he says, 'You don't want to get that nice titfer wet do you?' M. blushes like she always does when someone pays her a compliment and pulls at the brim of her white straw hat so that it comes down over one eye, and the steward winks at her and goes. And that just leaves us.

'I'd better go now my honeybun,' she says and gives me a hug, and I hug her back – a great big mother-and-daughter bear hug. I close my eyes and smell her – this cloud of Floris Stephanotis which she only wears for best occasions – but then what could be more 'best' than this I suppose, this saying goodbye? Only I don't think 'goodbye' is a strong enough way of putting it. This is 'bidding farewell' like in Georgette Heyer – me going off on my own across the Atlantic on the largest liner in the world, the largest liner *ever*. And M. says, 'Give my . . . regards to . . . well, you know, to everybody.' And I think she was about to say 'love' not 'regards', but she sort of stops herself, and she doesn't say their names – not 'Jack and Lynn' – so I suppose 'regards' will have to do.

Once we get back up on deck – and this time we take the lift (only everyone calls them 'elevators' – American already!) – M. is caught up in all the whirl again and disappears down the covered gangway. I lose sight of her for quite a bit and then I see her again, on the balcony of the Ocean Terminal. She really stands out because of her straw hat – and then she pulls it off and starts using it to wave. She's waving and waving as the band strikes up 'Auld Lang Syne'. Then the gangways are pulled back, the lines are cast off and the gap between the ship and the shore is widening – wider and wider and the ship lets out this great blast on its horn. I can feel its vibrations right in the middle of my bones. And just for a moment I'm choked, just suddenly feeling – I don't know – a bit empty? And I nearly cry. But it only lasts a moment, because then the ship is reversing out into Southampton Water and it's exciting to watch.

Kitty, still clutching her hat, also has a feeling of emptiness, though hers lingers. She stands on the balcony of the Ocean Terminal for a long time, watching the ship's progress. After the initial slow reversing away from the dock, the *Queen*, with her retinue of tugs in attendance, is now moving forwards, towards the sea. Her tiered rails are packed with a fringe of waving arms. Goodbye, goodbye – snatches of music cross the widening gap mixed with shouts – what's that tune? Then the mighty blast of the siren – goodbye! As the liner moves away, improbably huge, her bulk entirely blocks out the hills and factory chimneys on the far side of Southampton Water. The other ships moored across the dock look like Dinky toys in comparison. Scattered statistics have lodged in Kitty's memory from when she too made this voyage, but in reverse. Isn't the *Queen Elizabeth* something like a fifth of a mile long, so long that if she was standing up on end she'd be taller than the Eiffel Tower – her rudder alone, heavier than the whole of the original *Mayflower*? Odd facts and figures, but the sort of thing every cross-Atlantic habitué always knew back then, when this was, almost literally, the only practical way to travel.

It doesn't seem that long ago that Kitty herself was the waving figure on Main Deck, holding the tiny Ella firmly by the hand, Jack already lost to view on the Manhattan pier, amidst a sea of trilbies. But then maybe he hadn't hung around to wave – whereas now Kitty waits till the yellow of Ella's linen suit fades into a distant tiny smudge, then disappears. Even so she remains standing at the very end of the Ocean Terminal, her eyes fixed on the two famous red funnels moving quite quickly now down towards the Solent.

All the energy required to get Ella this far, the subtle process of negotiation with Jack, the organization, has drained her, leaving a void, so that now she's slightly nauseous. And after all, it's Ella's adventure, not hers, so that she feels suddenly pushed aside and of no account. Ella is to break into a new world, while she is left behind.

Over the loudspeaker, visitors are being urged to leave the terminal. The special train is not, it seems, to return them to Waterloo, but taxis and buses are available to take them to the main Southampton station. Kitty goes to board a bus, but still feeling sick, and put off by the crowds, decides instead to walk. After all why hurry? There's no one at home now to hurry for: nor will there be, not for the whole rest of the long summer. By the time she reaches the station, the returning ship's visitors seem to have dispersed and the next train for London looks gratifyingly devoid of passengers. She finds an empty compartment and flings herself into the window seat facing the engine, feeling drained. She closes her eyes. A few minutes later she's irritated to hear the sliding of the compartment door, and wearily opens them again. A man is standing there. Quite tall, quite fair.

'Are any of these seats taken?' he asks. It's a cultured voice. BBC Home Service.

'No,' she says, her instincts already wary. Nearly the whole train looked to be vacant, so why has he chosen this carriage? Why can't she be left alone? And if not alone, why have her space invaded by a man? Instantly any sense of security fades.

'Thank you,' he says, and takes the seat on the corridor side, also facing the engine. So now there's just an empty space between them, along the scratchy British Railways velour. She shifts her legs uneasily, tucks her feet more firmly under, crosses her ankles. She'd intended to drift off to sleep – at the very least close her eyes and let her thoughts wander, the last few days have been exhausting – but now she's got to make an effort not to sprawl. Keep her eyes open – not allow herself to be caught unawares in front of this stranger. Perhaps she snores when she's asleep, perhaps her mouth hangs open. No, sleep won't do. She stares out of the window as the train moves off, itchily aware of his presence. Could she just get up and move to another compart-ment? It would look rude wouldn't it, but who cares – except it would be worse than rude; it would be revealing. Any move would betray her foolish unease.

He coughs, then clears his throat. 'Excuse me, but didn't I see you earlier – down at the dock – the *Queen Elizabeth*?'

'Yes,' she says, warier than ever.

'I thought so – recognized your hat . . .'

That hat – what an issue it's turned out to be. I'll never wear it again she thinks. There's a silence in the compartment. She doesn't want to add to his information: she stares out of the window.

'Do you think that was all a deliberate ploy to wring our withers?' he suddenly says, though he doesn't seem to be addressing the comment particularly in her direction.

'I'm sorry?' she's forced to ask.

'That music. I mean, for heaven's sake, "Auld Lang Syne" – !'

'Oh is that what it was – I couldn't really catch it – '

'Might as well give us "We'll meet again" don't you think? My God, for a nation brought up on stiff upper lips we're suckers for sentimentality aren't we? As if we couldn't be trusted to *feel* – I don't need cheap music to make me feel, thank you very much – cheap music, potent stuff – '

'Noël Coward,' says Kitty, recognizing the reference. 'Strange how potent, etcetera?'

'*Private Lives* that's right – what was the song in that . . . Gertie Lawrence sang it in the London production – '

'"Someday I'll find you" – I think that was it . . .'

'There you are then – perfect example. Moonlight and all that – potent in its way . . . touches you on a nerve somehow, doesn't it? Not like all this "yeah, yeah, yeah" stuff – '

'Oh I don't know. I rather like all that – '

'You do? The Beatles, the Rolling Stones and all that?'

'When I hear it. I've got a daughter – she loves it. It was her I was just seeing off – ' and then Kitty stops herself sharply. She hadn't intended to let herself be drawn into conversation.

'With a school trip?' he asks.

'I'm sorry?'

'Your daughter – travelling with her school?'

'No. No she's alone. She's off to see her father.'

'*Ohh* . . .' said in such a knowing fashion. He's drawing conclusions right enough. Why hadn't she kept quiet. 'He lives there – or just working?'

'Lives.' Shut up Kitty.

'Divorced?' he goes on.

'Yes.' What can have possessed her to say so much?

'Me too.'

'Really?' but that sounded far too relieved – even eager.

'I've just been doing the same thing I suppose – only in reverse. Sort of. I know about daughters too. Actually I have three. I've just sent them back with their mother. They live in Georgia. I won't see them again for another year. You see what I mean – we don't need music to remind us of the sadness of goodbyes.'

'No,' says Kitty, staring out of the window, but regarding the reflection of his profile in the glass, 'we don't.'

12 *noon* – RMS Queen Elizabeth

We've picked up a bit of speed and the shoreline of Southampton Water slips past quite quickly. Here on A Deck everyone else seems to *be* with someone. Everyone else seems to know what they're doing. I don't, so I stick to my place by the railings. They're crammed with people hanging over the sides, watching what's going on. Everyone seems excited – that feeling of being off at last – and I eavesdrop like mad. I hear we're heading down towards the Solent and I wish I'd looked at a map before I left because then maybe it would make more sense. Then this girl next to me starts shouting in an American accent, 'Goodbye England, little *old* England.' Then the girl next to her, another American, shouts into the wind, 'Goodbye for *ever*!' – and the first girl says, 'Not necessarily – I may come back – one day . . .'

and the other one says, '. . . with a husband and six children . . .' and they start shrieking with laughter and saying they're so excited, that they'll be back in Chicago in a week and they don't know how they've *survived* it, and they're shrieking again. I'm dying to know what it is they've survived: I mean, can it have been that bad in little *old* England? I actually feel quite defensive about it – as if maybe I could explain whatever it is to them, whatever it is that went wrong. Only I can't butt in, though I do try smiling to catch their attention. It doesn't work though.

They're so similar – like Sandra Dee only with auburn hair, all pert and pretty with dazzling teeth, and you can tell they're just smiling into their futures. Glowing American girls. I wonder if I'd have been a real American girl if we'd stayed. It's hard to imagine. There's something about American girls – at least the ones I know. English girls like me are sort of, well – pale and sooty. We've got soot in our souls. I've certainly got soot in mine. American girls never seem to have come across soot – or coped with geysers. You have hot-and-cold-running everything if you're an American girl. Or boy – I suppose. If only I can manage to break in somehow – make myself known. Otherwise it's going to be a very silent five days. I'll have to try and squash my awful shyness, but it's difficult. I can already feel I don't belong. These two girls seem so much like a unit – certain and safe with each other – while I just stick out like a sore thumb.

Then I hear them say they'd better go and unpack before lunch – so at least that gives me a clue, and I do too.

Only it's not that easy to find your way around this place – it's as strange as trying to get to grips with a new town. I mean, I've got a pretty good sense of direction, but even so. I'm down at the stern of the ship (I'm picking up the lingo already), and it takes me for ever just to get anywhere near the bows – because at least I do know that D9 is *in* the bows – but I can't find that first staircase or the lift. I seem to be wandering around for ever, so I take another lift and get down to D deck, only it's an entirely different part and there aren't any corridors through to my bit (the stewards call them 'companionways' – oh, and the ship is never a 'boat' she's always a 'ship', and she's always a 'she' too, never an 'it' – Vera the bedroom stewardess filled me in). So then I have to ask directions and go all the way back up to R Deck and muddle my way forward and then back down again. So it's a lesson learned. Vera says the ship is so huge and so complicated, that it takes her twenty-five minutes to walk briskly from her quarters at the stern on E Deck (so there is more even further down below us) to the bit of open deck at the bows which the staff are allowed to use for fresh air. That's much further than Bissett Street to The Oval!

Anyway, eventually I do get back and that's when I meet Vera. She wears a uniform with a white cap like a nurse, and calls me 'Miss Feast' which makes me feel *sooo* grown-up. She seems very friendly and asks whether I want early morning tea or coffee – oh the luxury – and I've plumped for tea – decisions, decisions. And she says we'll have lifeboat drill before lunch and shows me my lifejacket. I ask her if anyone else is coming into my cabin and she says she'll have to check the passenger list and would I bear with her – and then she disappears, before I can ask her to uncover the porthole.

I unpack everything I reckon I'll need for the voyage. All the big baggage has gone into the hold. There's a room down in the other bit of D deck where you can store your cases, but it's awkward to get to from here, so even though you could get out more stuff later if you need it, Vera doesn't advise it. She says to unpack as much as you can, so I have. It's fab to have so many new clothes all in one go like this. Only because of the trip of course. Well I had to. M. says that of course it's going to be very hot and humid in New England at this time of year – and that bit I can really remember from when I was a child. Those summers were so hot and steamy – such a contrast to the winters with lots of snow. I remember winter always looking like a Christmas card in Sproughton, NY, before we left – and then when I got to England the weather seemed more or less the same all the time, not very much one thing or another. Anyway, I've packed lots of really summery things in the suitcase that's in the hold, but M. says the mid-Atlantic can be quite spiteful, even in July, so I've kept out my jacket, several sweaters and the wonderful red mac we got in Marshall & Snelgrove's sale. I think it's the same one Caroline Maudling's been spotted in – there was a picture of her in the *Evening Standard*. I wonder what it's like to be the daughter of the Chancellor of the Exchequer and live in Downing Street? I wonder what sort of bedroom she's got? Mine isn't much bigger than this cabin, just a slice off the top of the landing, so really I should be feeling at home already.

There's only a washbasin here in the cabin, so I slip out to explore the facilities. They consist of three ladies' bogs down the corridor, round the corner past the stairs. And there are also a couple of bathrooms along there. The tubs have seawater taps, and Vera's already said she'll give me special soap so I can get up a lather.

After all the hubbub and noise it's gone really quiet. There's no one around and I don't know what to do next. I've got this booklet they gave me with the ticket, called *General Information for Passengers*, so I lie out on my bunk and read it all through. Lots of stuff all about baggage masters and New York Customs; vaccination certificates (no entry to America without one – mine's stuck inside my passport); the Purser's Office; British Currency Control, with a reminder that we mustn't take out more than our £50 travel allowances (as if M. could afford that much – she's given me £30 which should be heaps); hire of deck chairs, rugs and cushions; Fire and Lifeboat Stations – and there are interpreters on board (hopefully I won't need one of them) and hairdressing salons and something called 'beauty culture' (I could do with a bit of that). There's a fully equipped operating theatre (I really hope I won't be needing *that*!) plus a physician, a surgeon and several state registered nurses. I'm just thinking this would actually be quite a useful place to drop down dead if you have to, when a bell starts ringing. I stick my head out into the corridor. People are lined up at the end, wearing lifejackets. Vera's ushering them along – 'Follow the signs – up the stairs to the Boat Deck – don't take the elevators – the stewards will direct you to your Muster Station.' I grab my lifejacket and join them. It's a peculiar thing – made of padded cream canvas like a large baby's bib with another bit at the back like a hump. We file up the stairs – it's a long way, I think I counted fifteen flights. Nobody's making much by way of conversation, and the lifejackets make us look so stiff and peculiar, not exactly the latest thing.

The lifeboats are as big as fishing smacks and are strung up on hoists, ready for action. We're gathered under one of them and given instructions about what to do in case of a disaster. I listen carefully, but lots of people don't even look up, as if they've heard it all so often and it's way beneath them. There's a group of boys like this, talking all through the drill. One of them has a long, dark Beatle haircut – gorgeous. I try smiling at him, but he doesn't notice me. Really it's a bit stupid of them not to listen – they'll regret it if we have a disaster. Like the *Titanic*. Only I must say it seems impossible to imagine a real disaster. I try. I look down at the sea and try. But we're still in sight of the Isle of Wight with the sun shining and the ship seems so immense it's hard to imagine her being defeated by anything.

The train is stuck outside Aldershot. Broken down? Points failure? They've been waiting over half an hour.

'It's too bad,' the man says. 'Too, too bad. You'd think they'd send someone along with some information. Do they think we have all day?'

'It's been a long day already,' says Kitty, thinking of last night's sleeplessness, her mind etched by anxiety and anticipation. Then their lateness and the taxi that didn't come. If they'd missed the final train – then what? *Could* you actually miss an entire passage on the *Queen Elizabeth*? The notion of 'missing' something so huge seemed laughably unlikely, but presumably people do. 'Where's the conductor I wonder?' she says aloud, managing to inject the right degree of bored irritation into her voice, drowning out the bubbles of doubt.

'Never there when you want one. Like policemen,' he says. 'I think it's known as Murphy's law.'

'What is?'

'You know that thing – bread always lands butter-side down. Law of averages.'

'Oh that – if things *can* go wrong . . .'

'They always will – yes. Not that I'm an adherent myself. On the whole I'm a born optimist.'

'Are you?'

'And you?'

'Oh no – not me.'

'Are you sure?'

'Quite certain.'

'How disappointing.'

'Why?'

'I'd thought perhaps – if we're in the same boat – forgive the pun – said goodbye to our children – bit of a gap – lonely moment. Well – I thought perhaps you would join me for a late lunch – though at this rate I'm afraid it might have to turn into that abomination called a high tea . . .'

'A "high tea" – I haven't had one of those in a long time.'

'Neither have I. Shades of "Nanny knows best."'

'Up the wooden hill to Bedfordshire,' says Kitty, who in reality has never had a nanny who knew best.

He laughs. 'So you see, I'm disappointed.'

'I'm sorry.'

'Of course, pessimist or no, you could perhaps change the habit of a lifetime – if it's been a lifetime that is . . .'

'Perhaps not quite so long . . .' and Kitty laughs too. What harm could there be? 'High tea', for heaven's sake! 'I'd be delighted to share your high tea,' she says, smiling.

'If we ever get back to London,' he says, looking out.

'Oh yes – there's that of course. If we ever get back.'

1.30p.m. – RMS Queen Elizabeth

Lunch time and it's getting easier to find my way – up to R Deck, past the Purser's Office and the Bank, turn right and there it is, the Tourist Class Dining Saloon. For a moment I feel absolutely terrified, going in alone, because it looks pretty full with hundreds of people already eating. I haven't a clue where to put myself, but then a waiter comes forward, looks me up on a list and tells me I'm on Table 54, and that from tonight on I'll be Second Sitting – and that's it. He just leads me past all these other tables full of chattering people, and takes me to one right in the middle, with six chairs, only one of which is currently occupied – by this man with a purplish face and a gingery moustache. He jumps up as the waiter is seating me, and holds out his hand. His name is Sydney Maxton-Bligh which sounds very posh, though his voice isn't posh at all. It's a bit like Kenneth Williams in *Hancock's Half Hour*. He must be as old as – no probably *older* than – Mr Christo. The waiter pulls out the chair right next to him, so I have to take it, or it would have looked rude and peculiar. I tell him my name and he says, 'Eleanor – Eleanor Feast – what an apposite name in view of the feasting to come. A nice old fashioned name.' Old *fashioned* – I ask you?! So then I tell him most people call me Ella, but he says, '*I* shall call you Eleanor – *Miss* Eleanor.' And then he asks if my parents are on their way or have they decided to give lunch a miss. So of course I explain I'm travelling alone. I mean, honestly, do I look like the sort of person who's travelling with their parents for goodness sake? Then he asks if it's my first voyage, and I tell him no, that I'd done it as a child. And he says, 'Many moons ago –' and laughs. So I tell him I don't remember it all that well, that it was years ago, and he laughs again and says, 'Years and *years*' – so I think he's actually laughing at *me*. I don't know why – what's so funny? I have a quick look around and there are lots of other tables full of much younger, snazzier people, so I don't know why I've got stuck with Mr 'Call me Sydney' Maxton-Bligh – talk about my luck. *Honestly.*

Meanwhile I'm trying to concentrate on the menu. It's a thing like a large birthday card with a picture of ballet dancers on the front and today's date and 'Luncheon' printed on it, which I think is quite impressive because that must mean they print it specially for each meal. M.'s always told me about the amazing food on these ships – it's one of the things I've been looking forward to – but Sydney M-B gets all extra chummy and says, 'Shall we perambulate through it? Together?' I'm trying to put him off, so I say coolly that I can manage, but he says, 'Of course you can my dear, but why not allow me to guide you through? I'm something of a regular you see – twenty-seven return trips, this'll be my twenty-eighth – part of my work as a gentleman's gentleman with various employers over the years. Now what's it to be – Broccoli Polonaise – what would that be when it's at home?'

Honestly, there's no stopping him. So I just say, 'I don't like broccoli,' and he says, 'Who does little lady, who does? But are we limited – are we heck. How's about Salad chiffonnade then . . .?' and he starts reading off all this stuff from the menu: salsify Florentine, carrots Crécy, pommes de terre Lyonnaise or persillées – Idaho baked, sour cream or butter, with chives or without, Jersey Royals – 'and that's just your root vegetables

– you see what I mean?' he says. 'Of course in First Class choice is well nigh infinite – in fact if it's not on the menu you've only got to ask. They like that in First – set them a challenge. Service is what it's all about.' Then he asks if I've ever travelled First. I tell him I don't know. That other trip might have been I suppose, or maybe it was Cabin Class – M. never said, and I didn't know to ask. But I don't think he's all that interested because he just rushes on, telling me that he's travelled First quite a lot 'when I was with my Dowager – not a literal one you understand. She was my shampoo heiress out of Philadelphia – I used to call her the Duchess. She liked that. She knew how to treat a fellow. Oysters. Caviar – you've never seen the like. Now what's it to be?'

I'm just about to tell him I'll have soup, hoping that might shut him up, when I hear a warm American voice saying, 'Well hi there – this looks just *beautiful*,' and there's a couple being brought to our table by the waiter. They're young – well young*ish*, especially next to Sydney Maxton-Bligh, and called Laura and Ken Wagenburg. They're from New Rochelle, and they're on the return leg of their honeymoon. They came over on the *Queen Elizabeth* too. They'd loved it so much that they booked the same cabin to go home in. Isn't that romantic? And they order from a special kosher menu, which has Sydney M-B going into extra ecstasies about the glories of the *Queen Elizabeth*'s near limitless catering arrangements.

Laura Wagenburg is really pretty – like another one of those Sandra Dee girls, only older – but with that same shiny auburn hair and gleaming straight teeth. (I wonder how – how can they seem so alike – is it the orthodontists or maybe the hairdressers? English girls aren't so alike I'm sure. I mean I don't think I'm like *anyone* – that's my problem.) Though Laura isn't very fashionable – she's wearing a pink gingham dress with lots of puffed petticoats, so obviously she doesn't know this is the season for the shift. But perhaps the shift hasn't got to America yet – and then after all, we've got Mary Quant and Mods and everything, while America's got . . . well, not a lot really – Elvis Presley and the Ronettes I suppose, so maybe it's not so with-it as we are?

Anyway, Laura's got this huge wide smile, and she beams at Sydney M-B, and tells us she loves the seating arrangements and the way we're all just thrown together by the luck of the Head Waiter's table plans – 'It's kind of like getting a box of Crackerjack' – and of course Sydney M-B doesn't understand, whereas I remember Crackerjack perfectly well from when I was little and living in America. It's funny how just one word like that can bring it all back – of me actually being American and feeling like an American, because I really was – with the accent that got me teased when I went to school in England, and how I thought maybe the English had a different language because they called their 'pinkies' their 'little fingers' and said 'Say when' if they poured you a drink. I haven't thought about Crackerjack for years, but I know just what Laura means, because you never knew what was going to be in those Crackerjack boxes – you just had to take pot luck. Only personally I wish my particular pot luck had landed me on a different table. The one just in front of ours and a little to the right is packed with these really gorgeous looking boys, including the one with the Beatle haircut I saw at the boat drill.

Laura asks Sydney M-B if he's from London, and he says, 'No, Basingstoke.' So then she asks if that's near London.

'Not far,' he says, 'although I'm only based in Basingstoke. I tend to drift where the work takes me – my current employer is in fact American. I'll be accompanying him to Arizona.'

And Ken Wagenburg joins in with, 'That's a little far from New Rochelle.'

'Well, it's a big country as they say. He's travelling First Class – taken one of the suites on Main Deck. I'll be driving him across from New York.'

'That's one helluva drive,' says Ken, 'over a couple of thousand miles?'

Sydney M-B says his employer doesn't like flying, and that even though money's no obstacle he prefers to sail and drive. Then he says, 'Not as if we haven't got the right car for the job though – loaded aboard this morning, Bentley Continental – ' and suddenly Ken Wagenburg looks weirdly alert, as if someone has wired him to a 13 amp plug.

'That wouldn't be the SII drophead coupé would it? The Park Ward?'

'Most certainly would – ' says Sydney.

And now Ken goes berserk – 'Is it lefthand drive? – oh my God they hardly made any of those things – did you hear that Laura? – it's the one with the straight-through wing line – hooded headlamps – V8 – give you what – sixty in ten-twelve seconds?'

And Sydney M-B is nodding proudly. 'That's the little baby – quite the bee's knees – '

'What colour?' Ken is almost shouting.

'Rolls-Royce Garnet with tan hide upholstery,' says Sydney.

'My God – you couldn't arrange for me to get a look at it could you?'

'Not in the hold I don't think – but maybe when we reach New York you could take a peek?'

It turns out that Ken has a car dealership in New Rochelle. It sells Volkswagens but his big dream is to move to Rolls Bentley if he can 'effect an amelioration in his client base' – that's literally what he says. Actually, you do wonder if we share the same language sometimes – and all this time Laura's looking into his eyes with a dazzling smile on her face, as if he's her own personal deity. Amazing. I suppose that's what love could do to you? I wonder if M. ever felt like that about Dad.

Laura asks if Sydney's employer lives in Arizona, and Sydney goes a bit mysterious and says, 'He's a citizen of the world. Ex-service – very senior. I was just about to tell Miss Eleanor here – retired naval commander, only we keep it under our hats if you know what I mean,' and he taps his left nostril and winks at me.

'We did consider flying – quite seriously – ' says Ken, who's calmed down now and gone into a 'quite seriously' sort of voice, 'but I gave it a lot of thought – made a pretty balanced judgement – it's so much more expensive – and then on top of the fares with such a long trip Laura needed a lot of clothes – and the cost of excess baggage is prohibitive with the airlines – and then we knew we wanted to shop really quite extensively while we were in Europe – '

'We bought wonderful glass in Venice,' says Laura. 'We've got a real chandelier for the family room – it's down in the hold right now – and we bought a beautiful Limoges dinner service – '

'We must have saved at least twenty-five per cent on what we would have paid at Bloomingdales,' says Ken, 'and that's quite some saving, even with the duty.'

'If we have to pay duty . . .'

'We'll have to pay duty sweetheart – I explained that to you.' He says this slowly, as if she's a slightly backward child, and turns to scan the room. 'Now, where's that waiter – we had to leave the hotel so early this morning we missed out on breakfast. I could eat a horse.'

In the end we all nearly eat a horse. Sydney Maxton-Bligh keeps telling us that lunch on the first day is a pale shadow of the banquets to come, but nevertheless we all seem to munch through appetizing mountains of food. I settle on vichyssoise, grilled sole and a huge slice of blueberry pie. It's all scrumptious. I haven't seen or smelt a blueberry since I left America. The taste, even cooked in a pie, throws me instantly back to being a tiny child. Food was the first big shock when I came to live in England. As I've always remembered it, food in Sproughton, NY was this most wonderful colourful mixture of Italian and Chinese and German with lots of good old American of course: corn muffins and angel food cake and Swiss cheese on rye. Whereas England seemed to throw up (sometimes literally I'm afraid) all these wishy washy horrors like boiled parsnips and Brussels sprouts and tapioca pudding. Except, of course, there were the goodies I gradually discovered, like toad-in-the-hole and buttered new potatoes and Huntley and Palmer's iced gems and Rowntree's jellies in cubes you could suck if you were being really wasteful. I think about all this while I work my way through my huge lunch, and otherwise I keep quiet, because all the conversation is about percentage savings on cashmere and the cost of leather goods in Florence, so I really have nothing to contribute. And all the time I can see the table with the Beatle boy over Sydney M-B's left shoulder, and they all seem to be having such a laugh. I bet they aren't deep into a comparative study of v-necks versus turtle necks.

In the middle of coffee, Sydney Maxton-Bligh looks at his watch, and tells us we'll be coming into Cherbourg in about an hour. He says it can be a bit of a circus, 'Shall we perambulate?'

'"Perambulate",' says Laura. 'Oh Sydney, you're so wonderfully *English*.'

We all get up then and Sydney links her arm. 'Shall we go and promenade on the Promenade Deck?' he says.

'There you go again – so *English*,' says Laura. Only *I've* never heard anyone in England say either 'perambulate' or 'promenade' – far too old fashioned. And I should know. But then Sydney links my arm too, and Ken's on my other side, and Sydney starts singing: 'We'll "Prom Prom Prom Tiddly Om Pom Pom",' and that's how we leave the dining room, which by now, thank heaven, is nearly empty. Otherwise I'd have died – well *honestly.* I *ask* you.

Only once we get up to the Promenade Deck, which is the glassed-in one which goes right round the ship, about three or four decks up from the restaurant, it turns out to be mostly First and Cabin Class, and we can't reserve steamer chairs there. The place for Tourist Class seems to be the Sports Deck, and Sydney says we ought to go up and get ourselves all sorted out before the Cherbourg people come on board and bag all the best spots. So that's what we do.

The Sports Deck is right up at the top between the two funnels, which act like wind breaks. There's yet another 'lounge' up there and a bar and bogs. We get ourselves settled on these long steamer chairs, and stewards come along and bring us rugs and cushions, tucking us up like babies, and then charge us £1 each. That's for the whole voyage of course, but I do hope there aren't too many things like that, that we have to pay for, because my total allowance is £10 for the whole trip, which M. said would be masses. The rest of my £30 she's changed into dollars for when I arrive, so I mustn't break into those on board. But you have to pay for drinks too, and anything you want from the shop, so it'll soon go won't it? Anyway there's no point in worrying about it yet I suppose. So we're all stretched out and enjoying the sun and the fresh air and feeling we're just whipping along, when some more stewards arrive and start taking orders for tea. And we've only just finished lunch!

Laura says her waistline will have disappeared by the time she reaches Manhattan, and she's pulling at her tight belt. I wonder if I should tell her it really doesn't matter because waistless shifts are the thing now, but I think maybe it would be a bit tactless. So instead I just lie back and pretend to close my eyes, only I keep them open just a slit so I can watch the other passengers. Some of them are playing deck tennis already – they can't have eaten as much lunch as us. It's a funny feeling – spying like this, and just like me too, watching from the outside, looking in – and I know I'm not yet with the people I want to be with on the ship, but at least I'm not alone any more. I've found some sort of place and if the worst comes to the worst I can spend the whole voyage up here on the Sports Deck reading my O-level set texts can't I? Trust my luck. Still, if it does happen, maybe I'll have finished *Middlemarch* by the time we reach New York.

Laura wants to know if I've done this trip before, and so I tell them about that other time – and that I'm really an American too – and they all start to laugh, and Ken says, 'With that accent?

Never!' and Laura says, 'More British than the British!' – only I've heard that before. And I tell them I've been in England for a long time, and Sydney M-B interrupts with 'Years and *years*' and starts laughing again. But I'm getting a bit fed up with being laughed at and I explain it's easy to pick up an accent when you're tiny, and that in any case my mother's English. So then they want to know all about visiting my father and Laura says, 'But that's so *exciting* . . .' (She seems to find lots of things exciting – I must try and develop some of her enthusiasm.) 'And he must be so excited too – here you are, all grown-up. He'll be *thrilled.*'

Well I hope so – I do hope he'll be thrilled, but I wouldn't bank on it. Thinking about it makes my stomach turn and I feel sad and alone suddenly, so I get up and go over to the railings. The French coast is clearly visible, although it had just been a smudge on the horizon when we came up after lunch. I can see people on the lower decks gathering and pointing, so it seems a good time to slip away from the rest of Table 54.

'See you at dinner,' Laura calls after me.

'We'll have a little treat,' says Sydney M-B, 'something special . . . wait and see . . .'

I go down to the Boat Deck and make my way towards the bows. There's a narrow curved deck right at the very front, high over the pointed triangular prow of Main Deck, and it's crammed with sightseers. Below us are the first actual seafarers I've seen since I came aboard. Up till now the only staff I've noticed seem to have been waiters and stewards, as if somehow we didn't need real, actual seamanship to get us across the Atlantic – just a nifty knack with silver service. But down there now are quite a lot of sailors doing whatever it is they do with cutlasses – no I mean windlasses don't I – or is it capstans? That nautical palaver anyway, ropes and chains and hatches and stuff.

There's a mood of excitement up here as we head into Cherbourg. I feel it too, only I still don't have anyone to share it with.

It seems impossible to break into any of these exclusive-looking groups, even though we're all squashed together. I wonder if perhaps I look as unapproachable as they do, and I have another bash at smiling, trying to catch somebody's eye – but it doesn't work, so, as I can't see much over everybody's heads, I wriggle towards the very front by the rail.

From further off, the land looked too low-lying, too countrified – just a streak of brown and green – to be about to dock this monster. But now I see almost dead ahead a stone harbour wall with the town looking as if it's miles away in the background across the water. There's a gap in the middle of the wall with stone fortresses on each side. Only from here it seems an incredibly narrow space and, even though we've slowed right down, I just don't see how the *Queen* can possibly squeeze through, which is what I say out loud to no one in particular – 'We're never going to make it are we?' The woman on my right gives me a silent superior stare, but a voice behind says, 'Don't worry – it's only an optical illusion.' I look round and there's the lifeboat Beatle boy practically hanging over my shoulder – and then it's really infuriating because I can feel myself *blushing*. I mean, I must be turning puce I'm feeling so hot, but I manage to squeak out, 'What?' – and he says, 'The harbour wall – it's plenty big enough you know, it just looks too small from out here.'

He's got this northern voice – just like a real Beatle. And he's got Paul's little cherub mouth, only his cheeks are thinner – his cheeks are more like George. And his eyes are a bit close together like John, though he doesn't seem to have anything that's the least bit like Ringo. He's very tall so I'm having to stare straight up at him. I can see right up his nostrils.

'It's a fantastic bit of engineering, that breakwater,' he's saying. 'They started it back in the eighteenth century, Louis the fifteenth – hundreds of people died building it – it's just like an artificial island made of rocks.'

'How do you know all that?' I ask.

'It's just a sort of hobby-horse of mine.'

'Cherbourg?'

'Transatlantic liners,' he says.

'Have you done the trip often then?'

'No – my first voyage – how about you?'

'Second,' I say.

'Quite the little sophisticate then.'

'Me? No – I'm . . .' – a bit confused, that's what I am – 'The last time I did it I was only little.'

'You're a bit of a tiddler now,' he says.

'No, I don't mean I was short, I meant I was a tiny child.' I'm wishing like mad I had a northern accent too.

'I know what you meant,' he says, but he's looking away towards the breakwater. By now we're near enough to see people standing round the forts on either side. We're so high above them that they look like tiny figures out of *The Borrowers*, but you can see they're waving, and then I don't know what gets into me, but I go and start waving too. I mean I'm not the only one – quite a lot of people along the railings are waving – but when I peek at the boy he's got his hands in his pockets and he's sort of smirking at me, so I feel a fool.

He was right about the gap though – we glide through with plenty of space to spare. On the other side there are four tugboats waiting, and they start up this thing almost like a conversation with the *Queen*. They whistle and she answers with these huge blasts of her horn. I jump about a foot off the deck every time she does it, and she does it a lot as she edges slowly towards Cherbourg Terminal. It's actually rather amazing, the way all the boats work together and the ship is just eased in so carefully that the gangways stretching out from the terminal building are precisely matched up with the entrances to the ship. I realize that's something interesting enough to say to the boy, because all the time I've been watching what's happening, I'm totally aware he's just behind me and I'm feeling *so* self-conscious. So I work out exactly what I'm going to say and I turn round to say it – only he's gone. Which is really disappointing. Talk about missing your chances. *Honestly.*

So now what? I hang around for a bit, watching things happening on shore – passengers coming on board and cargo being loaded by cranes through the big hatch down on the triangular deck. But there's a limit to how long you can be all that keen on just watching, especially with no one to talk to, so I go back inside and start exploring. Pretty soon I'm back in the First Class entrance and it's in the same whirl it was this morning with all the new passengers arriving, except more so because there are even more Americans with a few French mixed in too. I've actually got the luxury of feeling a bit superior for once, because at least I know where I belong now, whereas here are all these new people rushing around looking panic-stricken again.

In all the hubbub I stop off at the First Class Writing Room at the top of the stairs and have a good look. It's as wood-panelled as everywhere else in First and it has little desks, each with its own table lamp and a supply of *Queen Elizabeth* paper. It's sky-blue with a picture of the ship sailing across the top, with matching envelopes. So I take some to write to M. on – I think she'll be very impressed. Then I go into the First Class Main Lounge which is absolutely cavernous, with a huge portrait of the Queen Mother in a ball gown and tiara looking down over all these sofas and tables. It's very calm and cool after all the frantic activity going on outside. There's a string quartet playing at the far end and I sit down on one of the sofas for a moment, looking around and feeling a bit of a fraud in the wrong class – except there's no one to tell you where to go, or where not to for that matter, everyone's far too busy. The ceiling is very high up. It's all like I'd imagine a ballroom, completely panelled in pinky-coloured wood, but with a thick carpet – very luxurious, as M.'s always told me, but also very old fashioned. Maybe it didn't seem old fashioned to M. back in 1953 but, although I wouldn't want to disillusion her by saying anything, to me it's a bit like the Odeon at Tooting Broadway – not my cup of tea at all. Which leads me to the little business of tea actually being served in the lounge and a steward coming past me carrying a cake stand stashed with pastries and asking if Madam would care to order? And this particular 'Madam' says no, feeling even more of a fraud, and gets out of there pretty darn quickly.

And now what – go back to my cabin, maybe start my letter to M., tell her what's happened so far? So here I am again, going down, down, down, back into the hot, enclosed guts of the ship, with the low ceilings closing in again, more aware of the contrast than ever this time.

4p.m. – London

They pull into Waterloo nearly an hour late. It was points failure after all.

'Definitely high tea,' he says, looking at his watch. 'Lunch at any self-respecting restaurant will have finished at least an hour ago. Lunch is "off"!' – which makes her laugh.

By now they know each other's names. His is Gilbert Denby, and she's already slightly disappointed. Gilbert – not a name to conjure up any echoes for her – too surprisingly dull, and not a lot you can do with it. Gil – too fishy? Bert – too low? He seems to like her name though – 'Katherine Feast . . . Kitty . . .' he says, seeming to roll it round his tongue. 'Scottish?' he asks. But she scarcely knows this man so keeps her counsel – just laughs and says, 'Not exactly . . .'

They go straight to the taxi rank. There isn't even a queue. He ushers her into the first cab in the line and tells the driver to take them to Fortnum and Mason. It's all so effortless. So easy. Another world, thinks Kitty as they cross the Thames. London looks so

different from inside this cab with a man taking responsibility –
for once. Even the Houses of Parliament, usually rimed with
grime, are glowing golden in the afternoon sun.

As they turn into Piccadilly he leans forward. 'Drop us at the
Jermyn Street entrance will you? We want the restaurant.' So
easy, so commanding, although she'd have enjoyed walking in at
the front and through the main shop with its crimson carpet and
frock-coated retainers.

In the Fountain Restaurant, she is seated at a banquette against
the wall and has a good view of the room. He is facing her.
He asks for tea immediately – 'Unless you'd prefer something
stronger?' But no, they agree they're gasping after the long train
journey and so Earl Grey it is – what else?

He orders Eggs Benedict. She a smoked salmon salad. It comes
with tender spears of asparagus and slivers of buttered brown
bread. Later there are tiny intricate cakes filled with cream, topped
with marron, laced with kirsch.

He talks of his three girls and of what they'll be doing this very
moment on the ship. He checks his watch – they're still running
to the same time. The ship's clocks probably won't have been put
forward yet – that one hour a day, so that by the time the ship
arrives in New York it will already be on Eastern Standard Time,
ready for the fray. He's familiar with it all, has done the trip
several times himself, and of course the girls and their mother
are regulars. Kitty's journeys however, the ones which have lived
so vividly in her mind until now, suddenly seem very long ago.
Coronation year, 1953, was the last, aboard the oh-so-symbolic
Queen Elizabeth – but then there was that other one, the voyage
she doesn't care to recall too closely, as a war bride crammed into
the *Queen Mary* with so many other hopeful girls, many with an
additional burden of babe at hip or breast. That journey seems
part of a wholly different life to her, one she'd prefer to forget.
Now more uncertain of the voyage as subject matter and not
wanting to betray herself, she tries to turn the conversation

towards his daughters – delicately, leaving a vacant space in the subject marked 'ex-wife'.

They're very young, his children, he tells her – twins of seven and another girl of four. Yes, a boy would have been nice, but there you are – who cares now? Who would care if only they could all be together. It's a deep sorrow, the failure of this marriage. He'd met his wife 'in 1953 funnily enough – there's a coincidence'. She'd come to London from Savannah, Georgia to see the Coronation. He'd bumped into her in The Mall – they'd both been camping out over night to bag themselves a good view. She'd never done such a thing before and was laughing with her girlfriends at the excitement and discomfort in the sopping English summer night – for could this *possibly* be June? Was there ever such a summer deluge? He'd never done such a thing either – had never felt the necessary excitement of blind Royalist loyalty before, though his parents had taken him to see the balcony of Buckingham Palace on VE Night when he was fifteen and he'd never forgotten it.

Kitty is already readjusting her perspective – so he's younger than her, by five years. He must have married pretty young – too young for a man really, too young to be forced into nest-building and the curtailment of wild oats.

'We were much too young of course,' he says, reading her thoughts. 'My Southern belle, she missed home terribly. Missed America and her parents. And it's not as if I could have gone to live there, not really. I'm in the Civil Service – Whitehall – not the sort of job which travels easily. So there you are, one of those things. A sad tale – and what about you?'

Well, how much can she, should she, say to this stranger? He's looking at her intently across the table and part of her takes fright, instinctively avoiding his scrutiny and the intimacy it suggests. But another part watches his steady brown-eyed gaze, and his mouth – imagines the sensation of his chin against hers, slightly rough like sandpaper, slightly aromatic like musk. Well, it's been a long time. She absorbs that thought for a second, then refocuses and sounds, she hopes, quite brisk.

'Well, not dissimilar I'd say, only the other way around. I met Jack here – at the end of the war, we married and I went to live with him in America.'

'A GI Bride?'

'If you have to consign me to a category I suppose that might cover it.'

'Oh I'm sorry – I didn't mean to denigrate . . . I wasn't . . . please don't take offence.'

But she does take offence. 'Labels are sometimes too convenient don't you think?' she says. 'Makes us sound like lemmings or sheep – whereas of course we were – we *are* – all complete individuals with our own unique lives. There was nothing blind about that time – the war just threw us all into different locations, gave us different opportunities. But I always resent the idea that we somehow weren't aware of what we were doing – most of us were. I know I was. I married Jack with my eyes wide open, but in the end it didn't make any difference.'

'So what went wrong?'

'Maybe you could blame it on our natures – and the lack of time we had to know each other – *that* I'd grant you was a product of the times. The war certainly didn't give us the luxury to linger did it? And then of course the distances were so huge weren't they? All that way across the Atlantic . . . it felt like another world. It *was* another world.'

'It still is,' he says.

'Perhaps less so? Don't you think?'

'I don't know so much. I go through this agony every year. My wife brings the children over – I have to pay for it of course, costs a fortune, though obviously it's worth it . . .'

'Why don't you go over there – just one fare to pay?'

'Stay in some hotel in downtown Savannah you mean? Take them to the "movies" as they call them, buy them ice cream?'

'No, I can see it wouldn't be ideal.'

'At least this way they get to see me in situ – in my own home. They get to see that *I* belong somewhere too. She always stays with my mother in Sussex – they're still very fond of each other – and I also get the chance to de-Americanize them for a brief while.'

'Ah of course – they adapt so quickly at that age.'

'They've practically turned into Huck Finn, they've adapted so fast.' He laughs, a bitter little sound.

'My ex is going to find that with Ella – my daughter. The last time he saw her she was Stars and Stripes American.'

'And now?'

'Now she's . . . well you'd have to call her very English.'

'How old is she?'

'Fifteen – just – but very young with it really – only child, convent school. She's not very sophisticated. Not yet. Thank God.'

'Hard to let go?'

'What?'

'For you? Hard to let her go?'

'Oh no, not at all – I'd never – I mean I'm not like that at all . . .' But feeling a familiar ache, a sense of loss looming, she lets the sentence trail away.

He deals with the bill so subtly that it's a fait accompli before she's even had a chance to offer a contribution.

'This has been fun,' he says. 'I'm glad I spotted you at the Ocean Terminal waving your white hat, Katherine Feast. I'm glad I saw you on the train. We should do it again some time – may I ring you?'

'I'll give you my number at work,' she says quickly, adding, 'you're more likely to catch me in then,' although in reality she has no other number – only the GPO phone box on the corner of Bissett Street.

Now they're walking up towards Piccadilly, and he's hailing

another taxi. 'Let me drop you home,' he says, as the cab is in the act of turning towards them on that proverbial sixpence, across the traffic lanes.

But no, that's the last thing she wants. She's revealed quite enough – too much perhaps – and with a shrug and a wave, she crosses Piccadilly and loses herself in the crowds heading back towards the station.

It's a hot stinking squash in the rush-hour tube. Kitty strap hangs on the Northern Line heading south for The Oval. Body odours do battle with chemical scents designed to mask them, and emerge victorious. Sweat prickles in her scalp and she can't wipe it away as it starts to descend her forehead, for one hand must keep its grip on the overhead ring and the other is trapped between her thigh and the buttocks of a bowler-hatted man crammed beside her. The back of his neck bulges pinkly, wetly, over his collar, and only an inch or two from her nose. City Life. The only way to survive is to let your mind rise up and away. Float above it. What could be a greater, more immediate contrast to the previous couple of hours – sipping Earl Grey in Fortnum's, inhaling a scent of peace, calm and plenty. City Life. Ho hum.

Yet City Life is what she's always yearned for – seems to have craved since babyhood. Where could such a yearning come from – and why hasn't it withered in the sad, stressed reality which has proved so very different from the dream?

The train stops at Charing Cross; the canned-fish packaging of people shifts and rearranges itself. Some get out, releasing pressure, but then even more get in. Kitty moves further down the carriage, grasps another ring, closes her eyes as the doors slide to again.

Once upon a time there was a girl from Norfolk who shouldn't have been there. Not according to her mother. But no – it starts earlier than that.

*

Once upon a time there was a mother who shouldn't have been in Norfolk in the first place. If you will go and give birth to a daughter in the King's Lynn hospital, then bring her up amid carrots and mangelwurzels in the Fens, you don't exactly offer a head start do you? Not if it's bright lights and city slickers you long for – and Kitty's mother Florence did. Always had. But then Life went and handed you the joker in the pack. Always having the last laugh. That's Life. According to Florence. Like that cheat of a cherry ice all those years ago.

It had started quite promisingly – Life. Father was the sub-postmaster in Blackheath, only a few stops by steam train from London Bridge. Mother, apart from being a mother, could almost style herself a milliner, had worked for Madame Julia in Baker Street and kept up her own little atelier for local ladies – a sideline in feathers and veiling once the girls, all three of them – Maev, Prudence and Florence – were born. But somewhere along the line, they began to turn their eyes away from London Bridge, south-eastwards towards Kent. A postmaster's skills could transfer to other places – and wouldn't it be best to take themselves and the growing girls away from soot, smoke and smuts, give them air and space? And if you liked feathers and hats then why not feathers and birds? And if it's birds you're after, why not be practical and go for chickens while you're about it? Talk about the rot setting in. Kitty never heard the last of that in her own childhood – of her grandparents' perfidy in dragging the children away from the noisy comfort of the Lewisham Road to the open spaces and damp woods of Little Wiston. The smell of those chickens, said Florence – of having to scrabble around in the laying boxes collecting eggs amongst the chalky-green gobbets of hen-muck – none of it had ever left her, or the mud, or the cold. So it was all the odder that she landed herself in Norfolk.

Though it's not as if she hadn't tried to break the spell in the most physical way possible by running away at the age of fifteen with Mr Sawyer's Seaside Saucies. She'd heard they were doing a week on the coast, split between Margate and Ramsgate, and that's when she'd gone. Left a note and took the bus – several buses in fact – via Canterbury, with the money she'd been saving for years from birthdays and Christmas. Nearly £5 she'd had – plus a nifty ability to do the splits and dance the can-can. Not that Mr Sawyer turned out to need these talents – not yet awhile – though a willing junior laundress, ironer and seamstress didn't go amiss, given the way his dancers shed sequins.

All around the coast they toured, as far south as Lyme Regis, as far north as Skegness. In winter they settled into various pier pavilions for the festive season. The first year it was Whitby, the second Hunstanton. By that time Florence had graduated from sewing sequins to high kicking in the back row of the chorus. If she'd only hung on, she'd probably have made it to the front – then who only knows what might have happened? The following year there was an illustrated article in *Titbits* about the Seaside Saucies – if *only* she'd hung on. But that's Life for you. Because it had another little trick up its sleeve – a trick called Percy Combs.

Percy Combs – with his black, slicked hair and his great farmer's hands. She'd been putty in them – that was the trouble. No one had really told her you see. Not really. And she'd liked him – of course she had. Thought she'd loved him – then – otherwise she'd never have let him. Well of course she wouldn't. And that was another of Life's little japes, because she never thought it was all that special – a grunt and a heave, something like a sneeze really. Cherry ice all over again – nothing to write home about. Though she had to write home once she knew she was going to have a baby. Four months gone she was before she'd cottoned on – four months and ready to begin the Easter season at Lowestoft. Only she was already starting to show, so that was the end of her dancing career.

At least Percy was decent enough in his way – offered to marry her without a pause. At any rate her parents thought so and were

prepared to forgive and forget, coming up to see her decently
wed in King's Lynn and settled into the small farmhouse near
Hockwold Fen. Except there was no baby – not that time. It died
inside her at near full term – a boy – leaving her to the exhausted
stress of labour without its saving reward. That perhaps could
have been her moment. Had she run off *then*, she might have
rescued herself. Chased round the coast – caught up with the
Seaside Saucies, had herself another go. Except for Percy, and
the sorrow of the man – and her sorrow too – and those hands
again. Wouldn't you know it, she'd fallen straight away, pregnant
with what turned out to be little Katherine May – known as Kitty
from the start, and imbued with city yearnings along with her
mother's milk. That's where it must have come from.

Next stop The Oval. Kitty goes up the escalator and crosses over
to Kennington Park Road, breathing in the warm summer evening
air – exhaust fumes and fried fish. City Life.
   In Bissett Street, Mr Christo is standing ankle-deep in the paper
wrappings from his fruit boxes, winding up his awning. It's a long
day for him. He closes much later than other shops: half his trade
is done during those hours when ordinary establishments are
having their lunch, or early closing days or going home to tea.
Mr Christo's is nearly always available if you happen to be running
short of potatoes or even that exotic stuff like green peppers or
tinned stuffed vine leaves, though lots of the locals regard him
and his stock with cockeyed suspicion for its foreignness.
   'You all right then?' he says, stopping his winding. 'Spiros get
you there all right?'
   'What?' says Kitty – for a moment she'd forgotten this morning
and the missing of the boat train. Well it's been a long day for
her too, and it's had its twists and turns, though with what result
she's not yet sure. But then of course it all floods back. 'Yes – oh
of course – will you thank him for me? Spiros? Because it was so
kind of him – and you, getting hold of him like that. We were

only just in the nick of time – I don't know what we'd have done if you hadn't helped.'

'And she got off then – on the boat?'

'Yes – we made it – she's on her way.'

'You going to miss her.'

'Well – '

'Mrs Christo tell me – she say that Mrs Feast she going to miss that Ella – what she going to do all summer . . .'

'Well – I expect I'll manage. There's lots to do and it's not for ever. It's only one summer isn't it . . .' and she tries to quell any tendency for her voice to sound wistful.

'You must come and eat with us.'

'Oh no – really – ' Mr Christo is landlord as well as neighbour. Thus far they've always maintained a respectful distance from each other.

'Mrs Christo make her kleftiko – ' Mr Christo kisses his fingers to the prospect of the dish, ' – and we drink to little Ella and her journey. Just you think, she going all that way alone – '

'Not so "little" Mr Christo – '

'But it make you think, don't it – the things these children can do? My own life – can I imagine it – that I go to America, to New York on the *Queen Elizabeth* – I should be dreaming I have such a chance.'

'Yes Mr Christo – and I should be dreaming too.'

6p.m. – RMS Queen Elizabeth

Back down on D Deck, I'm fiddling around in my handbag looking for the key as I turn the last corner to my cabin – only the door is already open and my bags are standing in the corridor. I poke my head in and find the whole space is filled up by one woman, two little girls and piles of suitcases. The girls are sitting on my bunk and the woman is squatting down in front of the chest of drawers, taking out all the clothes I'd stashed in there so carefully this afternoon. There's already a pile of them on the floor. One of the girls is up by the pillow end of my bunk with the covers pulled over her knees, and the other, bigger girl is down at the bottom, rhythmically kicking the metal porthole cover. No one seems to notice me, and I'm just stepping inside when the woman turns to the second girl and shouts, 'For crying out loud Eenie, put a sock in it!' That's when I clear my throat and take another step in. I can't get any further – there's too much stuff in the way.

'Hello,' I say.

'What?' the woman says, and now she looks up and sees me. She's solid and squarish, with fleshy brown arms sticking out of a blue cotton sundress. 'What?' she says again. Sweat is sprinkling her forehead and running down her cheeks. 'Eenie – what did I tell you? Cut that out.' The voice might be American but there's something else in there that I don't recognize, something guttural and perhaps continental?

So then I tell the woman that this is my cabin – and all the time I'm hoping there's some mistake, only the woman says, 'Join the club sweetheart.' Then she picks up the pile of my underwear she's removed from the drawers and says, 'These yours?'

'Yes,' I say, 'and that's my bed – my bunk I mean.'

'Uh-uh sweetheart – these are ours – booked. We reserved from New York – both the bottom berths and the top outer. Mo can't climb the ladder – her legs are too short – and I'm too heavy.'

Of course I didn't know you could book, and I tell her.

'I'm sorry about that. Tough. We knew. We always book. I'm Mrs Keropoulos – pleased to meet you. And these are my daughters – Eenie and Mo.'

So of course I introduce myself, and Mrs Keropoulos says, 'Hi there Ella. Now, we're going to need this bureau – okay? – because with two small girls we've gotta lotta stuff. I'm sure you understand,' and she empties the last drawer from the chest on to the pile she's already made.

'What about me?' I ask. 'What about my clothes?'

'Sorry sweetheart – Eenie Keropoulos what did I just tell you? – did I tell you to cut that out or what?' because the bigger girl is still kicking the porthole, then turning back to me, 'I'm sorry about that Ella. You could maybe put your stuff on the top of the closet. You see the problem I'm sure. With two children and all – they've gotta be able to reach – Eenie I'm not telling you again you've got that?' The child called Eenie gives another good hard kick on the porthole cover.

Mrs Keropoulos turns back to me. 'You'll have to accept my apologies about this Ella.'

'No,' I say, 'I mean I'm sure we'll squeeze in – a bit of give and take . . .' I'm actually a bit fed up, though. I mean, all that unpacking I'd done, and all that lovely sophisticated peace and quiet I thought I was going to have.

'What?' says Mrs Keropoulos. 'No, of course we will. We'll have to – there's no getting around it. You think I wouldn't like the cabin to myself? No, I mean about my daughter and the kicking – she's a sweet kid, but I have to tell you, the journey we've had you wouldn't believe. When I get back to Hoboken I'm telling Mr Keropoulos that's it! No more! Every year he makes me do this – take the kids to see his family on Rhodes. He won't trust Greek ships, so we can't sail from Piraeus like normal people – you have any idea what kind of a journey it is from Rhodes to Cherbourg? I have to tell you, I get in that bed tonight I don't move for five days I'm so exhausted. Eenie Keropoulos I tell you once more you'll get the flat of my hand – '

What I'd actually like is to get a word in, only there isn't any space in the conversation to put one – except that it turns out she has to draw breath like the rest of us and I get my chance.

'Actually,' I say, '*actually* I was going to find a steward and ask him to open it – uncover it I mean.'

'You what?' she says.

'If she could see out – Eenie – well maybe she wouldn't kick it – the porthole I mean.'

'You can't uncover portholes on D deck.'

'You can't? Are you sure?' She has to be mistaken.

'Sure I'm sure – you can trust me on that one. Mr Keropoulos is such a cheapskate he sends his own family practically in the *hold*. Does he travel this way when he's going to see his parents? Does he heck. Eenie you do that once more, you stand outside until dinner!'

'You mean we won't be able to see out the whole way over?' I don't like the idea of that at all.

'That's right,' she says. 'They would've told you that when you booked.' But of course M. and I didn't book the ticket. Dad did, which I go and tell Mrs Keropoulos.

'Too bad you've got a cheapskate for a father then – begging your pardon.'

'Oh no – I'm sure he didn't know,' I say, the implications of the closed porthole rapidly dawning, 'but that's awful – we're all shut in.'

'It's not so bad – it's only the same as inside cabins – and there are plenty of those, even upstairs on A Deck. You'll get used to it, unless you have claustrophobia.' Mrs Keropoulos looks up from where she's still kneeling on the floor and gives me a searching stare. 'You *don't* have claustrophobia do you?'

'Not as far as I know,' I say.

'Thank God – all I need after my journey is a crazy girl. You'll be okay – take a deep breath, and you'll be fine.'

I gather up my mound of clothes. Everything else I'd carefully laid out in the cabin this afternoon has now been put up on the top bunk of the inner wall, even my alarm clock and books. Talk about giving a hint. And I can take it – all right, so this tiny space, just the area of the bunk itself, is to be all I can call mine on this whole mountainous ship for the next five days. I climb the ladder and shuffle along on my knees, trying to make myself a place to sit. The ceiling looms far too near overhead. It's hot up here and stuffy. A bit smelly too. I lie back on one elbow and watch Mrs Keropoulos unpack. The child called Eenie has stopped kicking.

'That's my girlie – now,' says Mrs Keropoulos, 'you see what Ella's doing up there? This is a good idea Eenie – you can do that too – you just sit back and keep quiet and when Mommy's finished we'll go find the nursery.'

'I don't want the nursery,' says Eenie, raising a very pink face from the mattress.

'You know you like the nursery – and then you'll get to go to the party in a coupla days – and you'll get the nice balloons.'

'I don't wanna go to the party.'

'Of course you do – you'll get the balloons and the ice cream and Jell-o – and they'll give you one of those lovely pins like a little boat.'

'I don't wanna little pin – ' but now the other girl kicks out, catching Eenie lightly on the head.

'Yes we do,' she hisses.

'Mom, Mo kicked me.'

'Don't kick. What is it with my daughters they've got this mania to kick.'

'But we do want the pins like little boats – Mommy we *do!*'

'Of course you do – I *told* you you do – now shut up a while and let Mommy get some stuff put away will you.'

'Toy-toy Mommy,' says Mo.

'What? Oh God, not now Mo, I'm just getting started.'

'I want toy-toy Mommy.'

'Can't you hold on?'

'Toy-toy – '

'Ella – could you take her to the toilet?'

'*Me?*'

'Mommy I'm going to do wee-wee in my pants.'

'Mo you hold on, Ella's gonna take you to the toy-toy. Eenie, you go too.'

'I don't wanna go.'

'Eenie, you go just in case – if I don't unpack now the steward'll be back for the bags and we'll never get done – and if I don't get my feet up they'll drop off – Ella *please* – now!'

So I jump down and take each child by a hot, sticky hand. They pull me out into the corridor and seem to have a magnetic sense of direction, dragging me straight to the bogs. Eenie runs into the first cubicle straight away. Mo however hangs back, rocking from side to side and chewing at her finger.

'Well go on then,' I say.

The child just looks up at me and pulls a strand of hair into her mouth along with the finger. 'Go *on* – use it then – the bog,' I say again.

'What?' she whispers.

'The – you know – the toy-toy,' I say, wondering if the word will choke me. 'You were making all that fuss – *use* it.'

The child turns her head into my skirt and whispers something.

'What?' I say.

'I already did it.'

'What – oh no . . .'

She holds up her own skirt. A saggy pair of knickers hangs damply from her crotch.

I squat down so I'm at child level, eye to eye. Tears are welling in hers, and my irritation fades.

'It doesn't matter,' I whisper back.

'Mommy will be so mad at me.'

'No she won't – you couldn't help it.'

'Mo!' shouts Eenie from behind the closed door of her stall. 'You finished yet?'

Mo's face flashes with panic.

'No,' I shout back, and push Mo into another cubicle, putting my finger to my lips. 'Shhhh . . .'

Relief. The tears are blinked away.

'Give me those,' I whisper, and Mo kicks herself out of the damp knickers. There's a loud flushing from Eenie's stall as I turn to rinse them quickly under the tap. Now flushing comes from Mo's stall too, and both girls emerge at the same time, all panic fled. I keep the scrunched pants behind me in the basin, feeling a slight saintly glow in having saved the situation. Mo holds up a hand to take mine again.

'You just run ahead – I'll be right with you,' I say, now stuck with the damp bundle.

'Mommy won't like that,' says Eenie solemnly. 'Mommy doesn't like us to go anywhere alone. We could get lost. We could fall overboard.'

'You just go straight back the way you came – it was you who brought me, remember?' I say and usher them out.

I have a look at myself in the mirror. The wind up on deck has wrecked my Tom Jones again and I haven't got a comb. I pull out the elastic band and shake my hair free. I'll just have to lug round an emergency repair kit everywhere on this ship if I'm going to keep up any semblance of chic, darn it. And how am I going to get dressed and made-up in that cabin, over the bodies of the Keropoulos family? I give Mo's pants an extra hard wringing out in the basin, walk out into the corridor, wondering vaguely where I'm going to be able to put them to dry and walk slap bang into the Beatle boy. He looks more cadaverous and gorgeous than ever in the artificial light.

'Hello – again,' I say.

'Oh you're down here with the plebs then are you?'

'Of course.'

'Well – with that toffee-nosed voice I thought you were just slumming it.'

Toffee-nosed? *Me*? 'No – ' I try to laugh – better squash his mistake on the head fast – 'No, I'm down here.' Then, recalling Mrs Keropoulos's phrase, I add, 'Practically in the *hold*.' I have a stab at Mrs Keropoulos's voice too – a touch of *Guys and Dolls*. The boy, who'd looked as if he was already moving on, has paused and I go for a light giggle – flirty? Shall I tell him I'd spotted him at lunch – clearly he hadn't noticed me.

'I'm Paul by the way,' he holds out his hand. 'Paul McGovern.'

Paul . . . McGovern . . . how much more Beatley could he be – not so very far from that other Paul, whose angel face hangs on my bedroom wall. Behind my back I transfer the bundle of Mo's knickers to my left hand, lightly wipe the fingers of my right hand across my skirt and extend it to shake his.

'Ella Feast,' I say.

'Are you first or second sitting for dinner?'

'Second.'

'Me too – see you later then maybe . . .'

'Yes . . .' I murmur, and maybe my luck's changing after all.

Back outside D9, I realize my right hand is still damp. I hope he didn't notice, otherwise he might think I was sweaty with – well what? Nerves? Hope? Not *desire*? Gosh, how embarrassing. Worse if he knew the real reason why – and come to think of it, now I'm stuck with these blasted wet knickers. Chic or what? – and what am I going to do with them? Owning up to Mrs Keropoulos is the simplest solution, out of earshot of the scornful older sister.

Inside D9, the chaos is unabated. Eenie and Mo now have a huge cloth bag up on the top bunk, labelled in scarlet lettering 'PLAYSACK'. It seems to be stuffed with toys and they're scavenging through it, producing handsome dolls and quantities of miniature clothes. As I try to squeeze in, Mo stops hunting for whatever she was after and turns full anxious eyes towards me. No – somehow any admission I make to Mrs K. would be too much of a betrayal. I scramble up the ladder to my bunk and drape the knickers along the inside of the curtain rail where they can't be seen from below. The rest of the bunk is now laden with the clothes I'd hung in the wardrobe.

'Ella – hi.'

'Hello Mrs Keropoulos.' I peer down cautiously, wary now of what she'll land me with next.

'Thanks for doing that – we would have had an accident and we could do without one of those on top of the day I've had.'

'Glad to help Mrs Keropoulos – only – ' I'm about to start claiming wardrobe rights, but she runs straight on.

'But I just want to say something serious Ella – '

'Yes?'

'Letting the girls come back on their own – '

'Yes?'

'You can't do that on a ship – God only knows – '

'Yes?'

'They could get lost – you know the size of this thing.'

'They seem to know their way better than I do Mrs Keropoulos.'

'They could fall overboard – anything – '

'We're an awfully long way away from anywhere any of us could fall overboard – unfortunately,' I say.

'You shouldn't tempt fate young lady.' Mrs K. is crossing herself, down on the floor.

'I only meant – oh look, it doesn't matter. I'm sorry I let them come back alone Mrs Keropoulos.'

'God forbid anything should happen to them.'

'You're right Mrs Keropoulos – only I'm just wondering . . .'

'Yes?'

'Do I get a bit of wardrobe?'

'Bide your time young lady – bide your time.'

Eventually Mrs K. grants me storage rights as follows: four inches of hanging rail in one of the wardrobes, plus the top of both of them, up to the ceiling – only as this is also where the lifebelts go, it doesn't leave much room over. She is clearly thrilled with her generosity, and happily leaves me crushing all my lovely new clothes into this minuscule space while she hauls the children off to the first sitting for dinner. They all go roaring down the corridor with Mrs K. shouting at Mo and telling Eenie to catch up. And then they've gone. The silence. The bliss. Except the cabin looks as if it's been hit by a small tornado – stuff everywhere, spilling out of drawers, and bits from the girls' dolls – miniature shoes and combs and stuff – scattered on the only bit of floor we've got, and stabbing my bare feet. I shove everything I can back up on Eenie's bunk, and then have the luxury of changing for dinner. Yes – get that – *Me* – Changing for Dinner – sounds pretty good doesn't it? You don't actually *have* to change in Tourist Class, no dinner jackets for the men or anything, which is a bit of a shame – anything for an excuse to dress up – it's not as if I've ever had the chance before now is it? I choose the narrow pink shift with the Empire neckline. I think I'll keep the Mary Quant stripy number for later on, when I want to shock. And I stick my hair back into a Tom Jones, only this time I add my fake Chanel white camellia and a black velvet bow.

So then I'm all ready, but it's still too early for second sitting and I don't know quite where to go. I take the lift again and go up to the Promenade Deck to the Observation Bar in the bows, but once I get there I lose my nerve. It's packed. I stand in the doorway for a few moments, trying to look as if I've got a real appointment with somebody and am just quickly checking out whether they've turned up. I don't want to look like someone who doesn't belong – and I don't want to look as if I've been stood up either. I scan around for a glimpse of my very own Beatle, only I can't see him. Then I try to spot the Wagenburgs, but I can't see them either. I begin to feel silly. Talk about 'all dressed up and nowhere to go' – so I flee, back down the stairs, hunting for anywhere I can just sit and look unobtrusive.

There's this place called the Winter Garden, also in the bows, immediately below the Observation Bar. It's got a bar too, as well as tables and chairs and some banquette things along the walls, and circular portholes quite high up looking out over the sea. It's nearly empty so I creep in and stand staring out at the view and wishing I'd brought a book. Then this steward/barman comes over and asks me what I'd like to order and I haven't a clue. I think of cider, but then I wonder if that's quite the thing. So he says would I like a cocktail, and I say why not, and he says how's about a screwdriver, which doesn't sound very nice, so I just say the only thing I can think of, which is what Dad used to make me when we all still lived together, a Shirley Temple. Only once I've said it, I remember that the whole point was it was for children of course, with no booze in it, but I want to cover my gaffe up a bit so I add really quickly, 'With gin' – and the barman says, 'Let me get this straight – you want me to make you a Shirley Temple with *gin*?' I can see he's laughing at me, and I really wish I'd just stuck to cider like I thought at first, and he says, 'If you like gin, why don't I make you a Tom Collins – not too heavy on the liquor?' So I just laugh then and say, 'Yes, why don't you?'

It's really nice this cocktail. Delicious. It has a plastic swizzle stick with a little *Queen Elizabeth* ship on the end, and I sit stirring it and feeling really professional. I'd like another one actually but I don't want to look greedy.

Anyway, the Winter Garden's so empty that the barman seems at a bit of a loose end, so he comes over and starts talking. All the usual questions – is it my first trip, am I travelling alone? – same old stuff. When I tell him I am, he says it can get really lonely, that this is only his third crossing, and that *he* finds it quite lonely. He's from Hastings. He says he's worked in a hotel since he left school, but that this job is going to help him see the world. Then he asks for 2/6 for the drink! – If this goes on, I'll be broke by Saturday. And then he asks for my cabin number, because it gets so lonely he says – and I can see his game of course, and think he'll be lucky – me, him and the whole Keropoulos clan

– not exactly a setting for Romance?! But at last it's time for dinner so I can scoot.

The Wagenburgs and Sydney Maxton-Bligh are already seated at Table 54, and Sydney M-B gets up to greet me like an old friend and sort of half-bows, waving his napkin about as if it's a sword or something ceremonial, and shouts, 'Miss Eleanor is gracing us with her presence' – talk about embarrassing, and I really hope that no one else sees him do it. I have a quick look over to Paul's table. He's there all right, but he has his back in my direction and is deep in conversation. So at least he doesn't see me being bowed to by this daft old man, except I can't seem to catch his attention at all – maddening.

Then the waiter comes up with a bottle which he shows to Sydney M-B, and Sydney says, 'Mateus Rosé – that's the ticket' – and the waiter goes all through the taking out the cork business and pouring out a little of it, and Sydney's smacking his lips and saying, 'Just the ticket – pour it all round.' So here I am with this glass of pink wine on top of the Tom Collins – which is nearly as much as I'd drink on Christmas Day, I should think – though maybe not. I don't like the wine all that much, but I tell Sydney M-B that I do, because he looks so pleased and I don't like to disappoint. Of course I know it's 'rosé' – I'm not *that* ignorant for goodness sake – only I don't think I've ever had it before. M. always buys 'Entre Deux Mers' at Christmas, and that's white.

Anyway, the wine is what turns out to be Sydney M-B's 'treat' – the one he'd promised us earlier. He says a good dinner without a good wine is like a good woman without a good man, and then he does something funny – he strokes my hand and says, 'Good girl, good girl.' Then he says he's told his boss the Commander all about me – and that the Commander's really interested to meet me as he has daughters of his own. Also that he gives a cocktail party in his cabin every night at 6.30. He invites all the best people – I mean like the Captain and the Purser and the First

Officer or whatever they're called, plus any celebrities. There's a rumour that Sir Laurence Olivier is on board, and if so, Sydney M-B says he'll be sure to go to the Commander's party – so would I like to go tomorrow night? So of course I say yes – because honestly who wouldn't for Sir Laurence, and anyway, now I know what cocktail to ask for. I could drink Tom Collins till the cows come home.

We're all just starting to wade through the huge menu again – this one has a picture of a Beefeater on it – when a woman comes to join our table. Her name is Madge Drinkwater and she came on board at Cherbourg. She's American, from New York, very glamorous. She says she's a model, been working in Paris. She certainly looks like a model, though quite an old one: very tall and thin – super thin like a pipe cleaner – and very elegantly dressed. *She* clearly doesn't think puff petticoats are the thing. She's in this tight silk suit – shantung I should think – navy blue with a sheen like oil in a puddle.

Sydney M-B and Ken Wagenburg are reading the menu out loud between them, as if we women are illiterate or something, and smacking their lips and making a terrific fuss – but Madge Drinkwater just orders jellied consommé, followed by asparagus, followed by lemon sorbet. No wonder she's so thin. Quel chic. I feel a real lump wading through Seafood Cocktail Creole, Supreme of Chicken Stanley and Exotic Gateau with a compôte of peaches. And whipped cream. And Gorgonzola and crackers. But – well honestly, it's all here and it's all paid for, and if I didn't take advantage what a waste. Only the Gorgonzola is a big mistake because I'm just starting in on it, when Paul finally leaves his table and comes right past us and waves hello. Except I have this mouthful of cheese and cracker, so even though I want to say something, I can't swallow fast enough, and I'd only choke and there'd be cracker crumbs everywhere, so I just have to wave back and then pretend to be really busy with the Wagenburgs.

Madge Drinkwater starts smoking from her lemon sorbet

onwards, using a long jade green cigarette holder. Quel chic again. I'm always going to use a holder when I smoke. Well, if I smoke. I expect I will – everybody does. Except for M. She says it's really bad for you and it's common as well – especially in the street. Ladies should never smoke in the street. Anyway, Madge Drinkwater has just lit up yet another cigarette and is pulling really hard on the holder which she has clamped between her teeth, so she has to talk through the corner of her mouth. And she says, 'Cute – huh?' About Paul. Then she says, 'A boyfriend?' Just like that. I mean, the embarrassment. So of course I have to say no – just an acquaintance – recent, for obvious reasons. And she says, 'But you'd like him to be?' And I could die. *Honestly.*

So by now we're all getting to the end of dinner and I'm wondering what I'll do next – yet again – I mean where I'll go, because it's still only about 9.30 so I can't go to bed. Then Madge Drinkwater says, 'Are you going to the Teenage Lounge?' Which is the first I've heard of such a thing. So I say, 'No – are you?' And she bursts out laughing and says, 'Honey, the last time I'd have qualified you'd have been a little glimmer in your Daddy's eye – and then some.' Then she says, 'I'm going to take in a movie – anybody want to join me . . .?' Sydney M-B says he has to see the Commander, but the Wagenburgs say they'll come along. And so do I.

And that's what I do this evening: sit in the cinema between Madge Drinkwater and Ken Wagenburg, watching Margaret Rutherford as Miss Marple. All over this huge ship people must have been having parties, whereas I might just as well be back in the Brixton ABC.

When I return to my cabin, the light is out, so I creep around trying to be as quiet as possible in the dark. I keep the door open a bit so I can see by the corridor light, and I can feel bits of jigsaw puzzle under my toes. I try to find the ventilator valve things in the wall, the ones that let in some fresh air, but Mrs K. says suddenly, really loudly in the darkness, 'Could you keep it down there Ella? Some of us are trying to sleep.' So I just climb up on to my bunk in my slip, and stretch out. I'd like to read for a bit, but I can't find the switch for the little bunk light – not in the dark.

I lie still, on top of the blankets. It's hot and I can hear the sound of the children breathing – not snoring exactly, just rhythmic noises, quite sweet really. I'm tired. It's been a long day – a long time since the taxi didn't come and we missed the boat train.

Tomorrow the first thing I'm going to do is buy a torch.

Friday

8a.m. – *RMS* Queen Elizabeth

It's a tossing around sort of night. For me that is. The Keropoulos family seem to sleep well enough. But it gets even hotter – stuffy – and there's that smell around I caught before. Part oil, part I don't know what – singed gym shoe? In the dark – pitch black in there, it's so dark, not a crack of light squeezing through the door seal – my senses sharpen in a weird way so I'm totally, constantly aware of the sea and of the ship moving through it. Nothing rocky – no rolling or pitching, but a feeling of all that water, hundreds of fathoms of it, swelling below me. It should be comforting – safe in crisp white sheets in my little bed. That's how I've always imagined situations like this – romantic like a gypsy caravan – but instead I feel claustrophobic. Maybe Mrs K. put the idea in my head. Every time I drop off into a doze, I get a feeling I'm being shut up in a box. So when I do eventually fall properly asleep, the morning seems to come round far too quickly. If it is morning yet. The way the inside of my head feels, it's probably still only 2a.m., except there are these sounds wound up in my dreams – squeaks like mice – only they're not mice, and I'm not asleep. Not any more.

A tiny voice is doing this sing-song 'Bouncy, bouncy little horsy', and I can feel light pats along the side of my bunk. When I open one eye, I see Mo half-way up the ladder, using my legs as a showjump for her rubber pony.

Unfortunately she sees my one open eye and takes it as an invitation.

'Hi Ella,' she whispers, very loudly.

'Hello Mo,' I whisper back. Bad mistake – should have kept my mouth shut.

'This is Trigger,' she says, holding the horse right up to my eye. 'Say hi to Ella, Trigger – "Hi Ella".' She's imitating a horse. If a horse talked. '"Hi Ella – it's real kind of you to let me ride across your ranch . . ."' My what? '"We're going to get up into the hills 'cos this is Injun country . . . with *bears* . . ."' Mo leans down to my feet and gallops the horse up as far as my chin, at which point she gives a very good imitation of a whinny.

'Cut it out Mo,' comes the voice of Mrs K. from below. I roll my head over to the side of the pillow to look down and it's then I realize the lights are fully on. Well of course they are. There's no daylight in the cabin, so how else would I be able to capture the vision below – Mrs K's lumpy body still stretched out on her bunk, and Eenie kneeling in the middle of an entire Toy Town built out of the contents of the Playsack, which now takes up the whole middle of the floor.

Somewhere around now there's a knock on the door.

'Good morning ladies.' Vera, beaming, steps over the lip of the cabin threshold, bright in her uniform, and carrying a tray. She looks down at the toy construction, and seems just the tiniest bit put out for one second, but no longer. 'My we have been busy,' she says and sidles in to pass the tray up to me, at the same time guiding Mo firmly back down the ladder with her other hand.

'Tea dear,' she says to me, 'as ordered. Plus the passenger list, today's programme and your copy of the *Ocean Times*. Would you like your own reading lamp on dear – and your curtain drawn? Give you time to come round nicely.' She winks as she closes me in – except I have to make a dive for Mo's knickers which are still hanging inside the rail. Suddenly it feels pretty good up here in my bunk, alone behind the curtain, sipping tea, while, unseen by me, I can hear Vera sorting out the Keropoulos clan with coffee for Mrs K. and orange juice for the girls. 'And shall we clear away our toys dearies, so Mrs Mop can do her stuff with the Hoover?' she adds brightly.

I prop myself up, as far as I can with the cabin ceiling feeling so close to the crown of my head, and examine the *Ocean Times*. It's a proper four-page newspaper with today's date – then 'RMS *Queen Elizabeth*', and then 'North Atlantic Edition' printed across the top. I like that – reminds me of the *Evening Standard*'s 'West End Extra' – as if there's a South Atlantic edition too. And another for the Pacific. Maybe there is.

Today's headlines are a mixture of the UN in Cyprus (Mr Christo will be interested in that), the Aswan Dam, and President Johnson saying he's convinced America must keep sending aid to South Vietnam. Where *is* South Vietnam exactly? There aren't any news pictures. Not of President Johnson and his big ears. Would people ever have voted for him as President with ears like that? President Kennedy was so handsome – with those teeth – American teeth again and, come to think of it, American hair too – seem to go together. And now he's dead – teeth and hair rotting away in Arlington Cemetery. So sad – doesn't bear thinking about. I wonder if people will vote for President Johnson anyway, despite the ears. They shouldn't matter, but then they say President Kennedy only won in the first place because Mr Nixon always looked as if he needed a shave. It's depressing if looks matter so much.

The rest of the *Ocean Times* is mostly stuff about the stock exchange and racing results and lots of advertisements for things like Scotch whisky, Camel cigarettes and Canada Dry. There's also an article on the New York World's Fair and a whole lot of stuff about hotels and restaurants in New York. I now know I can stay somewhere called the Hotel Astor for 'from $10 per night with t.v. and full air conditioning'. Also there's an article on pieces of jewellery made in the shape of the Unisphere at the World's Fair. They come in '14-karat gold' and you can wear them as a pendant or put them on your charm bracelet. One of them lights

65

up – could you believe it? It's fitted with a tiny bulb and a battery – but how? How could you get a battery that small – amazing what they'll invent. And sort of so American too – typical. I mean, in a way why would you bother – except I suppose it's all 'progress'? I hope I get to see the real Unisphere though. *Vogue* did a big feature about the World's Fair – it sounds fabulous. I wonder if Dad will be taking me some time this summer – and that makes me think of Dad, and I get this great lurching feeling, as if I'm going to be sick, and I wonder what he's really like. Only four days to go now. What does he sound like? I can't remember his voice at all. I've tried, and even closing my eyes and thinking myself back to being four years old I still can't quite get it. It keeps slipping away. Once M. spoke to him on the telephone. It was Christmas maybe four or five years ago, but I didn't get a chance to join in. She'd had to book the call days in advance and it was diabolically expensive – something like £5 I think. She had to do it from the headmaster's office – it was when she was a matron at Immingham School and we didn't have a telephone then either because we were 'staff'. She hasn't tried since. I can't imagine talking across the Atlantic from the GPO phone box on the corner of Bissett Street. 'Press Button A' and all that – as if one could – as if you could even get £5-worth of coins into the box in pennies – you'd be at it for ever! So I've just had to imagine his voice – except in only four days' time I'll know what it's like for real.

The other things Vera brought are today's programme and the Tourist Class passenger list. The first thing I check is my own name, just confirming I belong – 'Feast. Miss Eleanor (D9)'. Then I look up Paul – 'McGovern. Mr Paul (D26)'. Then I check Keropoulos and see how to spell it – Mrs Vasilios and Miss Eleni and Miss Magdalena. I'd sort of assumed 'Eenie' and 'Mo' were nicknames, but when I ask Mrs K. she says Mr K. always assumed they'd have sons but when Eleni was born he said never mind she was just Eenie and they'd have Meenie, Miney and Mo to produce a boy – only when Magdalena arrived Mrs K. called her Mo and said that was it – 'Finito Vasilios, I told him – you think I'm gonna have any more kids you got a screw loose.'

The 'Programme of Events' is printed up on another thing like a birthday card and I start reading it, feeling full of anticipation which soon wears off. There are two Keep Fit sessions in the gymnasium – one for Gentlemen and a later one for Ladies. There's something called A Coketail Party for the Under-12s in the Winter Garden at 11.45 – dig the pun, but not exactly my age range. Then there's something between 11 and 12 called Dancing Can Be Fun! – CHA-CHA-CHA – informal instruction by Manger and Pierce – come and join the fun (but who on earth dances the Cha-cha now?). At 2.30 there's a concert of recorded music in the Smoke Room – *Swan Lake*; and at 3.30 there's a table tennis tournament ('competitors to meet at tables' – which sounds just like school on a wet day). At 6.00 there's the BBC News Broadcast in the Main Lounge and at 8.45 something called the 'Voice of America News Broadcast' in the Smoke Room, followed by Bingo. The only thing that sounds promising, if I can get my nerve up, is described as 'For Teens and Twenties – a Get-Together in the Teenage Lounge' at 9.30. And the film for tonight is a new Alfred Hitchcock called *Marnie* which might be fun – more exciting than Miss Marple anyway. There's also a General Knowledge competition, plus tournaments for Shuffleboard and Deck Tennis – oh, and Scrabble, Chess, Canasta and Draughts are all available in Public Rooms 'on request', and somebody called the 'Social Directress' will 'effect introductions for those passengers wishing to make up fours for Whist, Bridge etc.' Then at the bottom it says: **Clocks will be advanced 20 minutes at 5.00p.m., 11.00p.m. and 2.00a.m.**

I have to admit that none of it leaves me exactly breathless with excitement. Still, I passed the Gymnasium yesterday when I was exploring, and it's got lots of those machines they tell you about in *Vogue* which might be fun.

I'm still only just thinking about going, when I'm forced into a snap decision. I'm in the middle of trying to get dressed up on my bunk – because now they've finished their juice, the K. family have immediately taken all the floor space again, and there's nowhere else for me to wriggle into my undies – when Mrs K. calls up to me, 'Ella – sweetheart . . .' I look down and see Mo hanging on to Mrs K.'s hand, with her legs crossed, and suddenly I just know for sure another 'toy-toy' accident is heading in my direction. So I jump straight down – 'Sorry Mrs K., got to dash – late for the gym' – and I skedaddle for the nearest bathroom and shut myself in until I hear them going past the door on their way to breakfast.

10a.m. – London

Kitty is late for work. She uses the tube as an excuse; a pretend delay between the Embankment and Charing Cross. In fact she'd slept badly and then missed the alarm. The flat felt strange without Ella; but not uniquely so. Ella's been away occasionally before – overnight with friends, the odd school trip. No, it's not the lack of Ella which disturbs, not yet anyway: it's the invisible presence of Gilbert Denby. Gilbert. Still a shame about his name, the only disappointing thing about him so far. If it were 'Gavin' now, or even 'Guy' . . . but Gilbert . . . not a lot you can do about a 'Gilbert'. Maybe he has a middle name though, something she can use when she knows him better. If she ever knows him better.

She's nearly an hour late for the gallery in Museum Street, even having run all the way from Tottenham Court Road. Mrs Croxton oozes irritation. She's going to be late for her osteopath in Wimpole Street – really, if *only* Mrs Feast had let her know. But

how could I from the Embankment tube tunnel? thinks
Kitty, already believing her own lie and prepared to feel indig-
nant.

'Never mind for now,' says Mrs Croxton, rustling papers,
carbons and notes in Kitty's direction. 'Mrs Henley will be in for
her stag bronze in half-an-hour. Can you make sure it's packed
and ready – but don't let it out of your hands if she doesn't settle
up. We don't do art on tick.' She's already half-way out of the
door, when something else occurs: 'Oh and there was a message
for you.'

'Yes?'

'Someone called Denby – Gilbert Denby – telephoned. He said
he'll ring back later.'

'Right.'

'That wouldn't be about the Cooper etchings would it?'

'No.'

'No . . .' Mrs Croxton pauses in her flight from the shop, and
steps back in over the mat. 'You know how I feel about private
telephone calls Mrs Feast . . .'

'Yes Mrs Croxton – I know,' says Kitty.

'Just as well to re-establish our lines of demarcation don't you
think?' and she lets the door close, slowly, with a sigh.

9a.m. – RMS Queen Elizabeth

It's only 9 and according to the programme, the Keep Fit class
doesn't start until 10. I'd quite like some breakfast too, but I
suppose going hungry is quite chic in a *Vogue* kind of way – and
then if I don't hurry up and make a quick get-away from here,
Mrs K. will be back and landing me with stuff again. I can tell
she's getting all set to treat me as a convenient resident nanny. I

change into the most suitable things I've got, my hipsters from Richards and my school white Aertex shirt, and set off for the gym, weaving my way upwards through the ship. Only today something's a bit different. Various ropes and chain barriers have been put up, and gates put across corridors with either 'Cabin Class' or 'First Class' written on them – but they're not locked. I assume there must be some other way up to the gym, but I don't know it, so I go through anyhow. No one stops me or says anything, so I reckon it must be all right.

When I get up there, the door is open and I can see that the class for women has already started, much earlier than it said on the programme, but then I realize I haven't put my watch forward as advised, so I assume I've got the time wrong, and I slip in at the back. Now I look around I see that most of the women in the class are in proper black leotards and tights. There are about ten of them and they've all got their backs to the door, though the instructor, who's a man, sees me and smiles, and just waves me into the back row – so that's all right. We start doing all these exercises – stretches – 'To the right, right, right . . . and over we go ladies . . . to the left, left, left . . . relax those shoulders and swing-swing-swing' – and we're touching our toes, and walking our buttocks across the floor, and it's really good.

Then we're allowed to use the machines. There are stationary bikes with big dials at the top to show you how many miles you've gone; rowing machines with handles like proper wooden oars; and those bottom-busting vibrator belts. I'd like to use one of these but there are only two and they're both taken, one by an old woman with grey hair and half-moon glasses, who's surely too old to need her bottom busted, and one by a tall thin girl with Hiltone blonde hair who seems to know everybody and calls the instructor 'Tommy' – as in 'I can't seem to adjust this properly Tommy – can you come and give it a hitch?' So I end up having to use the Bucking Bronco because no one else seems to want to – only as it happens, *I* could do with some of Tommy's help too, because once it starts it's hard to control. It's made of slippery leather and bucks like anything, so before I know it I'm sliding off and landing on the floor. There's a mat underneath so I don't hurt my head all that much.

The instructor looks concerned – in fact everyone looks concerned which is embarrassing, because instead of melting into the background I find I'm the centre of attention, and for all the wrong reasons. And then it gets worse because towards the end the instructor goes round the room asking for everybody's names and their 'stateroom numbers', and I begin to think that something might be wrong because the names are things like 'Lady Biggles' and 'Mrs Fitzgerald-Farley-Fart-Bags' and that sort of thing. Then it's my turn and I say my name and 'D9' and there's an awkward kind of pause. Eventually the instructor clears his throat and says, 'But Miss Feast – this is the First Class Gymnasium – *your* gymnasium is on B Deck,' and his nose scrunches up as if he's just caught a very bad pong. There's a horrible silence for a moment. Well – talk about embarrassed. My face is about to catch fire it's so hot. I can't get out of that gym fast enough, and from the passageway outside I run straight out of the nearest door on to the deck and stand in a freezing blast of air, cooling down.

Everywhere I look there's just sea – a deep dark blue like a rippled carpet all the way to the horizon – and I'm feeling very stupid, very lonely and wondering how the heck I'm going to crawl through the next four days.

'Quel buggeroonie – you poor lamb. Want a ciggie?' I turn round to see who's saying this peculiar sentence and who it's being said to, and it's the tall girl from the vibrator belt. She's blocking the door I've just escaped through and is holding out a packet of Consulate in *my* direction. *Me* – being offered a cig! Only I don't. Not yet. Though I will, once I've got the knack. I'd like to say yes right now, but I reckon I've just made enough of a fool of myself, and trying to smoke in front of this girl, when I don't know how, will only make things worse, so I shake my head.

'Don't worry about Tommy,' she says. 'He won't say anything – and anyway what does it matter – who *cares* if you shouldn't have been there?' She's older than me – perhaps seventeen, or eighteen even? She's got one of those ballet-wrap cardigans over her leotard now, and she looks very sophisticated. Her voice is loud and swoops from high to low inside a single word – practically inside a single syllable.

'I didn't know there was another gym,' I say. 'When I saw the class on the programme I just assumed it would be up here – it's the only one I've seen . . .'

'I think there are three – one for Cabin Class too – silly really but I suppose they feel they have to justify the *staggering* expense of a First Class ticket somehow, so exclusivity is the name of the game – too absurd.' She's flicking at a silver cigarette lighter now, sucking hard on the Consulate, blowing a stream of smoke into the wind which is chucking it back at us and making me cough. 'Sorry,' she says. 'I'm Henrietta Thring by the way – commonly known as Hen. *Very* commonly.' I start to mumble my name, but she interrupts, 'Yes – I heard in the gym. It's so nice to see someone up here who doesn't date from before the ark. Are you travelling alone?'

'Yes.'

'Me too – I actually *begged* Daddy not to send me First this time – it's *too* ridiculous to be all alone at my age and expected to change for dinner every night, but he's such a funny old stick, wouldn't change the habits of a lifetime. And you're in Tourist?'

'Yes,' I mumble, then, rubbing my own nose in it, I add, 'D deck.'

'Lucky you – you get all the dishy students down there – whereas last night I had to dine with two oily old captains of industry and a very randy Frenchman with the breath of Satan, who says he's in reservoirs, and spent the entire pudding course trying to undo my suspenders while he lectured me on the Aswan Dam – the *piggery* of it . . .'

So I tell her it's not all that much better in Tourist because *I've* got an American in Volkswagens and a fat Englishman from Basingstoke who keeps saying words like 'perambulate'.

'God – poor us – when you think of the talent on this ship it's *so* unfair. I think they sort these tables out specially to keep the young apart don't you – to spite us – just because they're past it themselves – ' and thinking of the yawning gap between me and Paul McGovern's table I thoroughly agree.

'I don't know about you,' she says, 'but all that exercise has given me the most cracking thirst – want to join me for a drink?'

I'm assuming she means juice or even coffee, but she rushes me into somewhere called the Midships Bar and orders two Bloody Marys – and of course I haven't even had breakfast yet. Still, once they arrive they look harmless enough and very decorative, with fronds of celery sticking out of the top. In fact I'm so hungry by now that I grab the celery and start munching like a rabbit. I know about Bloody Marys of course, but I've never actually had one. They look just like tomato juice, except there's something fiery in them too which makes the back of my throat smart and my stomach feel warm. I sip mine, but Hen knocks hers back fast, and calls out to the barman to order another. Instead of getting it for her, he shakes his head and says, 'Now Miss Thring – we're very young and it's pretty early in the day for over-indulgence' – and Hen goes a bit pink and hisses at me, 'See what I mean – talk about not being independent. Daddy's got his spies *everywhere*. He's afraid I'm a chip off the old block – meaning Mummy's block, not his. The Thrings are all born Puritans, whereas Mummy's people are Cavaliers through and through. What about you?'

'What about me?' I say, because I've never met anyone who talks like her and I'm losing the thread.

'Roundhead or Cavalier?'

A picture flashes in my mind – Puritan steel versus Cavalier ostrich feathers, like the costumes in that play we did at the convent a couple of years ago, *Children of the New Forest*. I'd longed to wear those feathers, but I'd been cast as a peasant trooper, so I wasn't even allowed a helmet.

'I suppose I'm an unwilling Roundhead with secret yearnings to be a Cavalier,' I say now, relieved to have come up with an answer so quickly, because it's not the sort of question I'm used to.

'Always the most dangerous mixture.'

'*Really*?' I say. 'Why?'

'Converts – always far more enthusiastic than those born to it. Where do you live?'

'London.'

'Same here – where?'

'Kennington.' I mumble, because I'm used to mumbling it.

'*No*. Same *here*,' she shrieks. 'Talk about a small world. Whereabouts exactly?' If she's surprised, so am I. According to M.'s lore, no one in the whole world would live in Kennington unless they had to.

'Bissett Street,' I say.

'Bissett Street – oh – can't say it's ringing familiar bells. Whereabouts, in relation to the Albert Hall?'

'What?' I say, stupid.

'Or Church Street – just trying to picture where you are somehow. I'm in Queens Gate . . .' So then I realize she thought I'd said 'Kensington' – and I'm stuck. Do I admit the truth or leave her in ignorance and pretend Bissett Street's hidden behind the Cromwell Road? It's a toss up – and for two pins I'd lie because I'm already pretty embarrassed by the business in the gym – but then, really *because* of that business, I decide honesty's the best policy, so I say, 'No – *Kennington*' – really firmly – and decide she can just flounce off if she wants to. Only she says, '*Oh* – I know what you mean – it's on the black line on the tube map isn't it?'

'Yes, the Northern Line,' I say.

'Yes – I always try and avoid it, being a Circle Line sort of girl if you see what I mean – kind of near the surface. The Northern Line always seems so *deep* doesn't it – and dark. And it's got that place at the end which always sounds as if it's come out of *Lord of the Rings* – they write it up on the front carriage and you see it as the train comes into the station. "Mordor" . . . terribly sinister.'

'Mor*den*,' I say.

'That's the one. So you live on the way to Mordor?'

'Morden. Yes.'

'How *wonderful*,' she says, though I can't see what's so wonderful. 'House or flat?'

'Flat,' I say, but I don't add what sort of flat. She needn't know it's over Mr Christo's shop, need she?

'*Same* here. At least it's not really mine – it's my Aunt Eve's. I live on and off with her for part of the holidays and exeat Sundays and that sort of thing – boarding school of course. Daddy's on secondment you see and Mummy's gone along for the ride.'

'Oh,' I say, wondering what 'secondment' is.

'It was only supposed to be for a year – with the UN in New York – really he's in the oil business, so we've moved all over the place, only then of course they got all worried about my education – inevitably. I don't know why people get into such a hoo-ha about it do you? It's been such a waste of time where I'm concerned. I begged Daddy to let me be finished instead of staying on at Crichton Hall – it would have been far more useful – whereas now I've got to do a course at Lucy Clayton once I've got back from New York. They never taught one how to walk at Crichton, just made you slog through A-levels and let you slouch – *such* a mistake – what about you?'

'School or exams?' I say, already green. I'd sacrifice more or less anything I've got available to be sent to Lucy Clayton – everyone knows it's the only place for models. Jean Shrimpton went there – and Celia Hammond. I wonder if Hen's going to be a model – she's tall enough, and thin enough. In fact, now I come to look, she doesn't in the least need her bottom busted.

'Both,' she says.

'O-levels next year,' I say.

'God darling, you're a babe in arms.'

'I've done three early – waiting for results.'

'Aren't we all – Daddy's going to disinherit me when he gets mine. Where are you at school?'

'The Convent of the Holy Sepulchre.'

'God – that does sound solemn. Where is it?'

I'm feeling pretty dazzled by all this outpouring from Hen by now, and wish I had something half as glamorous to offer back, so I toy, just for a moment, with lying – but once again I opt for the boring old truth. 'Tooting,' I'm forced to say. Perhaps I needn't have worried though, because from her reaction I might just as well have said 'Timbuktu'.

'*Tooting* – ' she screeches. '*Too* blissful – so you're a *day* girl – you don't know what I'd have given to be a day girl. I tried to bribe Aunt Eve to say she'd look after me so I could go to school in London – I'd have loved to have a bash at Holland Park Comprehensive – but of course Daddy wouldn't hear of it, and in any case Aunt Eve made it perfectly clear I'd queer her pitch if you know what I mean – she's terribly racy. She's Mummy's sister – that's the problem I told you about – Cavaliers, every one of them.'

'Tell me about your father,' I say. I'm always interested in people's fathers.

'Hmm?' but she's looking at her watch now, and suddenly leaps up. 'God is that the time? It *can't* be – I'm in the process of missing a hair appointment – must dash – super to see you like this – ' and she's already disappearing through the door. The barman is watching her progress with a grin on his face, and when he looks back at me he says, 'What a girl!' And I know he means Hen and not me of course. Nobody ever means me.

I make my own way back down to the boon docks – i.e. Tourist Class (what *were* 'boon docks' I wonder?). Since being caught out in the gym I feel more like an alien interloper, worse now that I know for sure I shouldn't be here, so it's a relief to get back where I belong. Only by now I'm also feeling a bit peculiar, what with not having had any breakfast and the Bloody Mary and all. My feet don't seem to be making total contact with the floor – something is giving way beneath them. Rather than heading all the way back down to D9, I decide to go up to the Sports Deck until lunch.

We're truly out at sea now, with absolutely no sensation that there's any land hiding just beyond the horizon. Beyond *this* horizon you just know there's only yet more sea. The sun's out, the light is clear and sharp, the wind's blowing. The rippled blue carpet I'd noticed an hour ago has changed to blue and white, each wave now tipped with foam. I hang over the rails, watching the occasional clever seagull slanting overhead or hitching a ride. I envy their freedom – and their not having to bother. They're just there, themselves, and they don't have to wake up in the morning wondering if they're going to get it right.

12 *noon – London*

Gilbert Denby rings back just before lunch. Kitty is dealing with a customer and Mrs Croxton hasn't yet returned from Wimpole Street, so it has to be a truncated conversation.

'I'm so glad I've managed to reach you,' he says. 'That other woman this morning sounded none too welcoming.'

'My boss,' says Kitty, forced to keep one eye on the customer, who's holding aloft an *animalier maquette* to search for a signature underneath. It's of an English setter with a dead partridge in its mouth. Croxton Fine Art specializes in wildlife subjects, though, like its customers, it seems to prefer them dead.

'Well, I've got you now,' he says, and she feels a shiver in her neck. 'I enjoyed yesterday – tremendously . . .' he continues, leaving a pause which she immediately fills as silently requested, with 'I did too . . .'

'I wonder if you'd like to repeat the experiment – I think we could stretch to dinner this time don't you?'

'That would be lovely,' she says, trying not to sound too eager.

'Actually, I wondered about tonight – could you make it?'

'Well . . .' She allows a pride-salving pause to hang around a few seconds. The customer has put the setter down and is now examining a pile of bronze trout – dead of course, with hooks hanging out of their mouths. 'Yes – tonight sounds fine,' she says.

'Well, as it happens I've got tickets – I mean *a* ticket for the Wigmore Hall – a guitar duo.'

'Yes – oh, well, don't cancel on my account,' she says, disappointed.

'No – I mean I've already taken the liberty of checking – I can get another ticket – they've a few available – if you'd like that – then we could have dinner afterwards.'

'That would be lovely,' she says, '*really* lovely . . .' hoping she doesn't sound too keen.

'Right – it starts at 7.30. Shall I pick you up – you can't be that far?' Well of course the MUSeum telephone number will have revealed her whereabouts. But she's wary and ever private. Why give Mrs Croxton's nosy inclinations any food for thought?

'No, I'll see you there,' she says.

'All right. Let's say 6.30 in the foyer – then we'll have time for a drink.'

When she puts the phone down, she's not seeing the customer any more, even though he's got the bronze trout upended, in danger of parting company from their green agate baseplate. In her mind she's already scooting along New Oxford Street to

Bourne and Hollingsworth or maybe Peter Robinson – she'll just have time in her lunch hour. She'll go mad for once – buy something in silk or Moygashel. Something stunning – just for once.

1.30p.m. – RMS Queen Elizabeth

'I've got a little surprise for you Miss Eleanor,' says Sydney Maxton-Bligh at lunch. 'I've spoken to the Commander, – told him all about you, and you're *in*.'

'In?'

'With the set. I've told him *all* about you and he's quite intrigued, what with you being American and all, but with the English accent. I told you he's got daughters of his own didn't I? You're invited for drinks, 6.30, in his suite, First Class and all – you'll get to see how the other half lives.'

'You wouldn't know from the First Class passenger list if Sir Laurence Olivier is on board?' says Madge Drinkwater. She's eating jellied consommé again, with a fork – quel chic. 'Only there's a rumour going around . . .'

'I'm not really at liberty to divulge,' says Sydney, tapping his left nostril, 'but if you're getting my meaning I think you might be on the right track – though we're talking pseudonyms here because in certain cases Privacy is a must.' He says this like an American – 'Pryvacy'.

'In other words you don't actually know?' says Madge.

'In other words Madam, word to the wise – keep stumm – discretion is often the name of the game.'

'But that's amazing,' says Laura Wagenburg. 'I mean if he *is* actually on board, do you think *she* is too, Lady Olivier? I just loved her as Scarlett O'Hara. I must have seen *Gone with the Wind*

79

six times – every time it came back to town I'd get to the movie theatre somehow.'

'He's not married to her any more,' says Madge.

'To Vivien Leigh – but of course he is!'

'Unh-unh – someone else – another actress.'

'Joan Plowright,' I say. I've read it in *Vogue*.

'That's the one – she was in *The Entertainer* – that was with Olivier,' says Madge.

'I never saw it,' says Laura.

'Black and white,' says Madge, 'in Cockney accents. I didn't understand half of it – kind of interesting though.'

'Still, *Ella*,' says Laura, 'if Sir Laurence is on board maybe you'll get to meet him, can you *imagine* – maybe Sydney could wangle us all an invitation?'

But Sydney doesn't answer her, just leans in to me and says, 'That'll be all right then Miss Eleanor? I'll RSVP for you then shall I, before the Commander settles down for his nap – and I'll meet you outside the Purser's Office at 6.20 – take you up there. He's a stickler for punctuality, but otherwise I think you'll find he's a very stimulating man.'

8.30a.m. – Point Harbor

By the time Lynn wakes up, Jack has already left – for the factory, she hopes. A scribbled note is Scotch-taped on to the breakfast bar, to make certain she can't miss it: 'Honey – could you call Flower Fayre – order up a corsage for Monday – something I can take down to New York for when I meet Ella – probably won't have time once I hit the city. An orchid maybe – something pretty anyway – XX Jack.'

So now it's to be orchids for the cuckoo. Lynn stifles the stab of irritation she feels, but then perhaps she's only mistaking the very physical movement happening inside her right this very moment. Junior's full of him/herself this morning. Kicking up a storm.

She goes out of the kitchen on to the wide stone terrace, and eases herself back on to a chair. The air is still, the sun already strong, the scent of pine resin heady. She lets her cotton robe fall open, and tracks the shape of Junior's antics across her naked belly's tight drum. She fancies him/her tumbling and turning. Makes no difference what the doctors tell you, what the books or baby magazines have to say. Makes no difference, this is a tale as old as time. For Lynn right now this is the deepest mystery – the unborn child she and Jack have made. Him or Her? Everybody asks, all the time: what do you want, a boy or a girl? – and she always comes back with the expected 'as long as it's healthy – ten tiny fingers and ten tiny toes'. But Jack wants a boy and says so. The new company is his baby of course, but ever since he's known there's a *real* baby on the way, his imagination seems fired up by the idea of children and dynasty, and, as ever, he sweeps her along in the wake of his latest enthusiasm. She's always known him as a dreamer – a fantasist even. From the time she'd met him – only a couple of years ago – he was building castles in the air for her benefit; sketching out a life he didn't yet own, though blurring the edges so she was never quite sure.

But now he says that things have changed: the air castles have transformed themselves into stone and bricks, though he still doesn't let her in beyond the glowing surface he describes. She's not to peer too hard into the workings of the new business – that's strictly his territory. She's pregnant for crying out loud, he says – she should relax and concentrate on producing a beautiful son for them both, shouldn't she? She's to pick out drapes and orchids for the cuckoo at his request – but not to plan anything too concrete (or expensive?) for the future. At the very least she'd like to be fixing up Junior's room, but Jack has his own mysterious

81

schedule she can only guess at. He's already saying that can wait – give it another month, they've got the time – but what's there to wait for? she's asked, and Jack's laughed and said, 'Timing is everything in life. We shall see what we shall see . . .'

Below the terrace, she can hear the sound of the stream's shallow waterfalls, burbling over stones. The water is clear and sharply cold on even the hottest day, revealing trailing weed and the cases of caddis flies. She heaves herself upright, tying the robe back around her extended waist, intending to go down, sit on the bank and cool her toes. But the orchid instruction niggles her still, and instead she goes inside to call him, to stake a claim on his attention span for herself and the unborn Junior.

When she tries his direct line she's put through to Bernice, his newly acquired secretary.

'Hi Mrs Feast – no I'm sorry – he's not in yet.'

'Did he give you any idea when to expect him?' asks Lynn.

'What time did he leave home?' Bernice is a cool customer, already defending her boss's line. So what is Lynn to say now? Admit she doesn't know when he left, that she was asleep, that he wasn't around for dinner last night either: or stay silent? What I'd like to do is stamp my foot and holler, she thinks, but that would get me nowhere. So out loud she says, 'That's all right,' swallowing her surge of anger, 'only when he comes in, just get him to give me a call.'

At 9.30, Sadie Dorling arrives in her big beaten up old Dodge, chugging along the driveway, steering with one hand. Her other hand grips her grandson Leroy by the seat of his pants. He is six years old, cram-stuffed with vitality, dangling out of the far open window, waving his arms and cranking up the air.

'Mornin' Miz Feast – how're ya doin'?'

'Morning Sadie.' Lynn has already risen from her terrace seat, shy of being caught in her robe, except if so shy, why do it? Since trying to call Jack, she's had time enough to shower and dress, but instead has sat in a trance looking out over the trees down towards the bay. Something's happened to her energy – drained clean away. But if she's going to give in to this lethargy, sit transfixed watching the sea while within her the baby grows, why not do it without guilt?

Guilt, however, already hangs around in abundance. Sadie Dorling is officially 'the maid' – here to do the 'heavy work', though not averse to ironing or polishing up the odd piece of silver either. Lynn wasn't brought up with maids, and back in Buckling, Montana was mostly a maid herself. She doesn't want a maid now, feeling awkward and ignorant of the relationship – thinks even the idea of it is faintly ridiculous. But Jack has insisted: the other households of Point Harbor have maids, so they must have one too.

She doesn't want a maid, but she sure could use a friend. It's a relief to have the silence broken, to be forced back into the world, and she almost breaks into a run to greet little Leroy, whose skin has a damson's polished bloom, but whose teeth are blackened stumps to match.

'Hi there Leroy – how're ya doin' Buster?' she calls. In the kitchen, just to add to the tooth damage, she's got some Hershey's chocolate kisses for him, bought specially in case Sadie brings him along. Sadie minds Leroy for her daughter Darlene who works a night shift in Detroit. Nights pay better than days and Darlene's husband blew out of their lives when Leroy was barely one. Every other month she comes home by Greyhound bus over a weekend, and hands over a lump of her paycheque for Sadie to guard. One day she'll have enough for a down payment, one day she'll find a job that pays as well in Point Harbor – or one day another man will come along and kiss it all better. Meanwhile Leroy's baby teeth have to go on the back burner, though when his adult ones come through she'll get him to a dentist somehow.

Leroy, released from the oven of the car and evidently impervious to the steam bath atmosphere of the back yard, races down to the stream where he can go scare the ducks and build a dam.

'You mind the poison ivy, you hear?' calls Sadie, her regular warning, though the patch of poison ivy is on the far bank, across to the neighbouring property.

She swings a big pile of ironed laundry out of the trunk. Lynn reaches to help, but Sadie's ready to fend her off with an elbow – 'Just you go minding your baby there Miz Feast – you'll do yourself some damage' – though Sadie and Sadie's daughter and all the Sadies have to manage well enough, pregnant *and* working. Guilt in abundance. 'Call me Lynn, why don't you?' Lynn had asked when Sadie'd first arrived. All this 'Miz Feast' stuff increased the awkwardness, made her feel more alone. But Sadie hasn't ever obliged – as a matter of fact hasn't even seemed to hear. Just stuck to 'Miz Feast', maintaining her distance.

'And so I should hope,' said the snooty WASP woman at the end of the road who'd asked Lynn in, ostensibly for coffee, though in fact she was after a donation to Teddy Kennedy's Senate campaign for the upcoming election. '*Dear* Teddy,' said the woman (whose own name was Caroline too, just like the dead president's daughter). Amazingly she spoke as if she knew the ex-First Family well – 'The things those darling people have suffered. How we've *wept* for Rose and Joe' – which left Lynn feeling dazzled and then dazed.

However, this use of first names does not, it seems, extend between the Sadies and their employers. 'You don't want to go upsetting things,' said Caroline. 'Start messing around with too much familiarity and no one knows where they are.' She'd eyed Lynn quite sharply, and hasn't asked her in again; though maybe that's more because Jack hasn't after all sanctioned a Kennedy contribution, having himself an eye on the Republicans this time around, and a sneaking admiration for Barry Goldwater too.

'What you got for me today Miz Feast?' says Sadie.

'Well – we've got Jack's – Mr Feast's – daughter coming you know? She's on her way now.'

'Is that so?'

'Left yesterday – she'll be in New York Tuesday. Jack's driving down to fetch her. So there's her room – the painters have finished and you know they said they'd clean – '

'Like they'd know *how* to clean,' Sadie laughs.

'Yeah – well, it's what you might call an approximation of a clean, but it could do with going over – and then I've got the new drapes to hang . . .'

'She's goin' to feel like a little princess.'

'Not so little. She's fifteen.'

'From what Mr Feast said, I've seen her kind of younger than that.'

'Yes I know what you mean.'

It's true. Jack's in some kind of dreamland with this daughter, as if she's frozen in time. Not that he'd want a four-year-old again – God forbid – but neither does he seem to glimpse the vision she can catch so clearly, of a lumpen acned adolescent, oozing hormones and discontent. What are they going to *do* with her this whole long summer? she thinks, watching Sadie climb the steps to hang the drapes. They're cream glazed cotton, printed in raspberry pink with little pictures of people from the olden days, scattered all over. 'Toile de jouy' the decorator called it, though why they couldn't have perfectly ordinary drapes made from the kind of material she'd have bought back home in Montana had her beat, it really did. Another of Jack's quietly insistent demands, and the bill will be enormous won't it?

'Fancy,' says Sadie, regarding the first swathe of material as she lets it unfold to the floor.

'Fancy-*smancy*,' says Lynn, swerving her western vowels into a Brooklyn put-on. Catching each other's glance, both the women laugh.

Lynn looks out of the window. Sadie's ancient Dodge is pulled up next to her own new Chrysler, gleaming with chrome. Hasn't there been too much financial cart before the horse around here?

Madness. A madness she seems forced into ignoring because – well, why because? Because that's the way Jack likes it, that's why.

He's a magic man – that's how he seemed when he came into Buckling, Montana that Tuesday afternoon in his white foreign car. For Lynn it might as well have been a white charger and Jack all done out in silver armour. She'd been waiting tables at Kim's Chat'n'Chew, the only restaurant next to the only stop light in town. That's how you gave directions in from Route 17. 'You wanna eat? Take the next left and keep goin' till you get to the only stop light in town – Kim does you a real fine pot roast.' Jack wasn't there for pot roast though. Jack was on his quest – truly a knight for the twentieth century – a quest for what he called 'The Great American Original' because he was sure there was one out there – somewhere.

It was only half-an-hour after taking his order for a tuna melt with a side order of onion rings, that Jack had her hooked. What is America, he told her, but a great cooking pot filled with the richest stew in history? And there are foods out there – foods which are the total essence of America. Find yourself a special one of these, one with a truly unique twist, and you've got yourself a Great American Original. Refine it, sleek it down, process it, and you've got the beginnings of a business. Do all of the above, produce it and sell it for a year or so and the monster corporations will be banging your door down because word gets around. That was his dream, his personal version of the American One: get himself a Great Original, and sell it off to Birds Eye, Nabisco or Kelloggs with a handsome royalty attached. And then what have you got? Roses that's what you've got. Roses all the way, or even the pot of gold at the end of the rainbow.

He'd come into Buckling on the track of a chili corn dog he'd heard about, a special one with *internal* mustard. It was the idea of the portable mustard that really intrigued him. Although she couldn't see it herself, because four years as a waitress had taught her plenty of people didn't even like mustard. Plenty of people liked ketch-up instead. Plenty of people liked plain. And in any case, as it turned out, he'd got the wrong Buckling. It was Buckling, Wyoming he needed – he was a couple of hundred miles too far north, and he departed straight after the tuna melt, leaving her a handsome tip and a real yearning for what might have been.

Only he came back; that was what was so amazing. Came back the following week, booked into the motel, drove her into Butte for a steak dinner. Took her to the movies to see *The Music Man*, told her the chili corn dog wasn't going to make it on to his development list, but that maybe the readi-stuffed English muffin he'd found on the way would. And the next day they took off. easy as that – heading south, eventually holing up in Las Vegas where they got married in the Silver Bells Wedding Chapel – no nonsense hanging about for licences. And boy was it something, racketing around America with a magic man, chasing the illusive product, after her life at Kim's Chat'n'Chew. How it was funded was always something of a mystery, because surely he couldn't be keeping them on the road just via the winnings from poker and crap games, could he? A magic man with the cutest crooked smile, and a lick of auburn hair that kept flicking on to his brow. Except they couldn't keep wandering for ever, and every few months they had to make what Jack called 'development time' to test the newest product ideas. That's when they'd head back to his brother and sister-in-law in upstate New York and the fireworks started.

Five minutes were sufficient to have him erupt. He couldn't seem to stand them, though for the life of her Lynn couldn't see why. They were kind enough, and God only knows they were patient enough, allowing him space in their factory to work up his latest project. It was on the first of these visits that she learned she didn't even share a last name with them. 'Feast' was the one on her marriage certificate. Only his brother Salvatore – always known as 'Sally' for short – was called 'Festini' and had taken over the family business in bottled spaghetti sauce.

It must have been a good business, because it bought a nice piece of property with its own pool and tennis court, plus membership of the local country club. But instead of relaxing and enjoying any of it, the source of these riches seemed to drive Jack crazy as they unpacked in the guest suite (guest suite – as if she'd ever expected to find herself in such a place – and as a guest!). He told her he'd spent half his life trying to escape. Hadn't he changed his name years ago – from little old Giacomo Festini – before he even went overseas for Uncle Sam? He'd had a whole childhood of spaghetti sauce wars – napolitana versus amatriciana. His old dad could practically write a sonnet on the subject of goddam linguine with clam sauce – he'd taste their product and go into ecstasies. 'You know you can get a clam sauce that's kind of clammy,' he'd say, without a ghost of a smile as to non-intentional puns, 'but ours is smooth, light, it just floats over the linguine like a dream – taste it, you see what I mean – ' and this to his school friends whose fathers were maybe doctors or lawyers, amazed at him having a dad who stood in the kitchen in a goddam apron twizzling linguine and forcing it on total strangers.

So he was crazy to escape – of course he was – who wouldn't be? he argued. Except, maddeningly, there turned out to be money in spaghetti sauce – only not until he'd already bailed out with his new name and his wife from England and cut the family ties. Lynn doesn't know a lot about the life with the English wife – it's a subject which remains taboo. Only that it didn't turn out too well – that maybe it's hard to pluck someone from the other side of the world and expect her to grow in foreign soil. And then there was the daughter – the one whose birthdays had to be remembered, but always by Lynn – who got a nice cheque in her Christmas card and who sent back smudgy black and white photos of herself and even smudgier letters about her life. Jack used to examine these photos and then explode, 'Goddam Limeys, you'd think Kodachrome was never invented!'

A girl from Europe. A girl who lives in London. Lynn has never been to Europe, never been outside the US – not even to Canada. Doesn't possess a passport. Will the cuckoo lord it over her, snootily parading her cosmopolitan life and exposing Lynn's naïveté? Only to think that Lynn's become that creature out of a fairy tale – a stepmother. Thinking of the word, she sees only one vision – of the wicked one from Disney's *Snow White*. 'Mirror, Mirror on the Wall . . .' And who will be the fairest in Jack's eyes – his new discovery of a daughter with her European gloss, or his newish youngish wife carrying, so wearily, her extra breeding load of forty pounds?

Sadie has finished hooking up the drapes and makes her way back down the steps.

'What do you think?' asks Lynn.

'Mighty pretty – that's one lucky girl, that daughter,' says Sadie.

'She surely is,' says Lynn.

3p.m. – RMS Queen Elizabeth

Madge Drinkwater and I go up to the Sports Deck after lunch and stretch out on our steamer chairs. It's a battle against the wind up here, but not so bad now we're sitting because we're sheltered in the space between the two funnels. It's too windy for people to be playing deck tennis or quoits, and if you stand up at the wrong angle it's like the blast of some giant cold fan and you feel as if you might just get tossed over the side. The stewards come along with rugs and tuck us in again. It's very comforting. I've got my hair tied back and Madge has hers covered in a headscarf which goes around her neck like Brigitte Bardot, and she's wearing sunglasses even though it's not that bright.

As soon as we're settled she lights up another ciggie using the pulled-up rug as a shelter for the flame, and I get out my book. I've decided *Middlemarch* isn't quite right for the ship – not at all with-it, and heavy too. Holding it up was giving me wrist-ache. So instead I've decided to read one of next year's French set texts instead – *La Peste* – in public anyway. It's all about a plague in North Africa – but the trouble is, I could really do with a French dictionary as well and I don't want to cart one of those around. Still, it looks pretty professional I think, and I skim through a few pages getting a general idea, though I'll have to look up heaps of words later.

Madge pulls her sunglasses down her nose and peers at me for a moment. 'Camus huh?' she says, and she sounds quite impressed.

A little later she's grabbing my arm. 'There's something that might interest you – or rather *someone*.' I glance up, trying to make it look as if I'd been deeply absorbed in *La Peste*, though in all honesty I'm having a bit of a problem with it. She's nodding at Paul McGovern who's coming this way from the direction of the stairs. His thick black fringe is being blown totally sideways by the wind and he has a whole bundle of books under his arm. She calls out, 'Hi there – we meet again!' She's shameless. I look up but try to seem suitably uninterested, though actually I'm feeling pretty hot under that rug already.

'Hello,' he says – only it's a real northern ''ellooo', which comes up at the end like a question – *faaa*bulous. 'What're you reading then?' he asks, because by now I've lowered the book. I hold it up for him and he says, 'Oh *The Plague*,' just like that, in English.

'You've read it?' I ask.

'Oh yeah – and *The Outsider* – that's pretty good.' He flings himself on to the next chair which, thank heaven, just happens to be empty. As soon as he's down at our level, his fringe stops blowing and he combs his fingers through it and stretches out his legs. They seem to go on forever.

'Only "pretty good"?' asks Madge. She's peering over her sunglasses again and her eyes look as if they're smiling, though her mouth isn't.

'Well,' says Paul, 'personally I don't subscribe to his post-Freudian hypothesis – if we're truly in this nihilistic lacuna we've only ourselves to blame and knowledge of totality should have pre-warned us of any such likely outcome.' Well, actually, I'm making all that up because he says *something* like that, only I don't understand a single word of it. Madge Drinkwater doesn't look particularly fazed though, just flicks her ash into the wind.

'You're into all that then are you?' Paul seems to be ignoring Madge and is leaning directly towards me.

'Into . . .?' I ask.

'Yeah – "into" – as in "interested" – existentialism – cosmic meaninglessness – '

'Well – actually it's a set text,' I say. I have to really. It's the truth.

'Oh right – what are you reading?'

'Well . . .' Is he stupid or something? '*This* . . .' I say, waggling the book in front of him again, and he laughs.

'No, I mean what are you reading at university – what degree?' and then as I obviously still look blank, 'What are you *studying*?'

And then I feel so stupid – well you can imagine – and then a bit flattered at the same time because he thinks I look old enough to be at university. *Me*! And presumably clever enough too – even though he's hardly ever spoken to me. But then I have to spoil it by being honest and telling him I've only just done French O-level – though at least it's a year early – and as I'm explaining I can see I'm getting younger and younger in front of his eyes, so that by the end I might as well be in plaits and ankle socks again. I look at his long legs stretched out on the steamer chair, and I see *he* isn't wearing any socks – just slip-on shoes with curly black hair peeping out from the bottom of his trousers which aren't grey flannels, but blue jeans – and on his top he's in a black polo neck sweater, and I feel the strangest feeling in my insides – and it isn't like anything I've ever felt before. Not at *all*.

Thank goodness Madge is there because she keeps the conversation going while I would probably still be wasting it all on feeling so peculiar and not thinking of the right thing to say. But now I'm finding out that he's at Sussex University 'reading' (I'll never forget that one will I?) – '*reading*' Anthropology – and I don't even know exactly what *that* is either, though I'd be willing to have a guess, only Madge saves me by butting in with, 'Clever huh? And is Sussex in Oxford?' Paul says, 'No – Sussex is in Sussex.'

'Would that be close to Oxford?'

'No,' says Paul, 'why the hell would it be?' Very rude of him, but he goes on anyway, 'Who wants to be near bloody Oxford? Who wants their life dried out by a load of pompous old gits before they've even got started? At Sussex we're all young – we've got real blood running in our veins, not port wine and desiccated coconut – '

'Coconut?' I say, but give up.

'So this "Sussex" is a new college?' asks Madge. *She* doesn't give up.

'One of the newest – right outside Brighton – smashing campus and tutors with their fingers on the pulse. In Oxford they'd be lucky even to *have* a pulse – '

'I'm not surprised, on top of all that coconut,' says Madge – very dry. 'And why are you on the way to America, Mr Paul McGovern, with your anthropology and finger on the pulse?'

'Summer camp,' he says. 'Mine's called Camp Weehaupak. The Yanks have all these summer camps – and they send their kids to them for weeks at a time – get rid of them for the holidays – well, being a Yank yourself I suppose you know all that . . .'

'You could say it's a phenomenon I'm pretty well acquainted with,' says Madge, looking now as if she's trying not to laugh, though Paul doesn't seem to notice. 'So you are going to be a camp counsellor for the summer? Surely not in anthropology?'

'No – rambling.'

'Excuse me?'

'You know, walking and climbing rocks and stuff – I'm from Liverpool but I spent most of my holidays when I was little in the Yorkshire Dales with me auntie and uncle.'

'Oh you mean *hiking*,' says Madge, while I'm just chewing on the information that my very own Beatle isn't just from 'up North' but is a real live Liverpudlian. And then I have to go and ask the inevitable.

'Have you been to the Cavern?'

And he says, 'Which one – Mossdale or Alum Pot?'

And I say, 'No I meant the Club. The Cavern Club – the Beatles and all that.'

He laughs and says, 'Yeah – I was afraid that's what you meant.' I feel such a fool again, and I get up to go to the bog to cover my confusion. While I'm in there I retie my hair which has gone all blowsy, and powder my nose which has gone all red. How *do* models keep it up?

But I'm glad I've come away from the chairs because, on my way back past the top of the stairs, I see Hen Thring coming up. She's in a dress I recognize from Mary Quant – grey flannel with a key-hole neck – and her hair is also in a Tom Jones now, only hers is a proper one with a bouffant back which looks fab. I wonder what on earth she's doing here in Tourist, and just for a split second I want to dive behind something and hide myself. I don't know why. It's just this reaction I always feel – only then I get over it and I'm really pleased to see whoever it is, which is what happens now, once I've said hello. But she's completely the opposite. The second she spots me she shrieks, '*Ella*,' as if she's known me forever, and not just since one Bloody Mary this morning. 'I was *hoping* to find you – I thought I'd be wandering around for *hours* . . .'

I lead her along to my steamer chair, only Paul's in it now, right next to Madge, and they seem to be well into conversation. He doesn't jump up or move or anything, so I introduce Hen to both of them and we have to perch on what was his chair.

'I've come up here to find what Cunard in their wisdom seem to have dubbed the Teenage Lounge,' she says. She puts on a funny voice when she says 'lounge' – *lee-ouunge*. 'It's rather fun up here isn't it,' she adds. 'All the times I've sailed on the *Queen Elizabeth* and I've never once come up to the bit between the two funnels – isn't that odd?'

'And why would that be so bloody odd?' says Paul. He's incredibly rude.

But Hen doesn't seem the slightest bit put out. 'Because you'd think it would be the choicest bit wouldn't you, on the whole ship? You'd think everyone would come up here automatically. Think of the *Queen Elizabeth* versus the *Queen Mary* and what's the first difference you'd actually notice? The funnels of course – it's *always* the funnels – the *Queen Mary* with her three and the *Elizabeth* with two. It's what I notice anyway – so this *is* the choicest bit really. I mean, if you saw it on a postcard or something you'd always be able to pick out this bit and say, "There I was – 'X' marks the spot."'

'There *are* more important differences,' says Paul. 'I mean, do you know why the *Elizabeth*'s only got the two funnels?'

'Haven't a clue darling.'

'She's a much newer design – the *Mary* has twenty-four boilers, the *Lizzie*'s only got twelve, even though she's bigger. And she's just as fast – she had to be – that was the whole idea of building the two giant ships in the first place.'

'Fascinating,' says Hen, but she doesn't mean it. You can tell she's being sarky, which makes Paul clam up. I wish she wouldn't. I could listen to Paul for hours.

'Go on,' I say.

'No – don't want to bore you with it.'

'You won't,' I say. 'He won't,' I add to Hen and Madge. 'Paul's made quite a study of liners – it's your thing isn't it Paul?'

'Fancy that,' says Hen, sounding sarky again; 'if you have to have a thing, what a fascinating thing to have. Boats. Do you make models of them too – in matchsticks perhaps?'

'Transatlantic shipping has real significance in British socio-logical and economic history as it happens,' says Paul, 'but I expect you knew that.' He sounds sarky now.

'Who doesn't darling,' says Hen. 'As I said – *fascinating.*'

'Tell us,' I say, wishing she'd shut up. 'Do tell us why they built them.'

'Well it was all to do with the postal service really. They're called RMS remember – not HMS like in the Navy – stands for Royal Mail Ship.'

'I never knew that,' says Madge. 'What's HMS then?'

'Stands for Her Majesty's Ship. His Majesty when we've got a king, of course.'

'You see what you miss out on when you go republican?' says Madge. 'We're just stuck with the SS *United States* aren't we – it's enough to make you want to turn back the Revolution,' – but she's only joking. 'So go on then,' she adds, 'why did they build the two giant ships?'

'Well, back in the twenties Cunard used to run three ships to keep the weekly mail service going – much smaller ones – like the *Aquitania* and the *Mauretania* – but they were all getting past it, so the head man at Cunard got this idea for maintaining the service, but with just two new ships. That meant they had to be bigger and faster than anything that'd ever gone before – that was the original plan anyway. It took years to get the whole thing in operation. My granddad was a riveter on the *Queen Mary* – got laid off in the Depression. They had to stop work on her for three years so her maiden voyage got delayed, didn't happen until 1936 – and then the *Lizzie*'s got mucked up by the war.'

'But I'd always understood they were both used as troop carriers in the war,' says Madge.

'They were – Churchill reckoned they took two years off the duration – but when the war broke out, the *Lizzie* was stuck up at John Brown's on the Clyde after her launch, waiting to be finished. She was taking up a berth they desperately needed for war ships. She was like a bloody great sitting duck, with the Germans just waiting to pick her off if they got sight or sound of her. It would have been a huge propaganda coup if they'd managed it.'

'So what did they do?' I ask.

'Painted her grey all over – then leaked it that she was on her way to be dry docked in Southampton. It was totally convincing – they hired all the workers and crew, sent all the new furniture and supplies down there, and the Luftwaffe were totally fooled. Their bombers were even spotted looking out for her over the Solent. Only in fact once she was actually under way, the Captain had sealed orders to head straight for New York as fast as possible. Her engines had never even been tested don't forget, and she was unarmed, with no escort, but she made it – she was like this ghost ship appearing out of nowhere at the entrance to New York harbour. People went mad for her – the first anybody really knew of the whole adventure was when she arrived. The *Mary* was already over there, so that was the first time the sister ships were ever together.'

'Ah *sweet*,' says Hen, terribly sarky again. 'And aren't you the Brain of Britain darling "Ask me another" – does Franklin Engelmann know?'

'You what?' says Paul.

'None of this font of knowledge actually gets one anything useful like a reservation in the Verandah Grill does it?'

'What's the Verandah Grill?' I ask.

'It's a restaurant,' says Madge, 'very special – for First Class only of course and even swankier than their main dining room – as if that isn't swanky enough.' She turns to Hen, 'And are you dining in the Verandah Grill?' I catch an edge to her voice.

'If only – it'd be heaps more interesting if I were – with the right man. No, Daddy draws the line somewhere – and I'd have had to reserve months ago. I only knew I was sailing last week. Up until then I thought I was flying – BOAC on a 707. I'm not sure I don't prefer flying these days – it's less than nine hours now you know – but Daddy wanted half his library shipped over this time, so it's coming for free along with me, packed in trunks in the hold – masquerading as my clothes.'

'So we've got a *Daddy* then have we?' says Paul, sounding really sneery now.

'Yes of course,' says Hen. 'Haven't we all, unless we've been sadly bereaved?'

'Well no, as it 'appens. Lots of us 'ave a *Dad* – and he's suddenly dropping all his aitches in a row, which I don't think he was, up until now – 'a dad who's nearly split 'is 'eart in two, working in British bloody shipping. He's gone deaf and his spine's bent bloody double, and what does he get now by way of a reward but airplanes crossing the bloody Atlantic in nine bloody hours – talk about hammering nails into coffins.'

'Gosh,' says Hen, 'touché darling with brass knobs on. Is that a chip on your shoulder or just a portable baked potato?'

'You what?'

'I mean I'm very sorry about your poor papa's physical deformities but really, what an onslaught – what did I do to deserve it?'

'You've no idea 'ave you – people like you – none at all – as long as your own immediate needs are gratified, that's all that counts. Never mind you're bleeding the country dry – never mind British ship-building's going to the dogs. We soon won't have a shipping industry at all at this rate – and what's that going to do to the country? What's it doing to Liverpool already? Those docks were the whole centre of the universe for people up there, and now what 'ave we got to take its place – the Beatles and bloody Gerry and the Pacemakers. Mention Liverpool now and kids like 'er – ' and he's pointing at me (so I've suddenly become an ''er', and I'm reduced to feeling twelve again) – 'kids like 'er think our fantastic great city with all its history is just a load of twanging guitars. You can't base a whole economic society on bloody guitars. People 'ave all gone mad – a load of bloody sheep, just following with the latest trend. It makes me sick – nobody thinks for themselves any more. I mean, look at you two – why 'ave you both got your hair done in that stupid way? Why can't you just be natural? Because some journalist has told you it's the thing to do.'

'It's called a Tom Jones,' I say. 'After the film with Albert Finney. It's the *fashion*.'

'You've just proved my point – exactly.'

'But like Ella says, it's the fashion,' says Hen, 'and it's supposed to be fun – or aren't we allowed any fun on your own personal agenda? Has it all been drowned in a sea of envious northern bile – or would that be tripe and onions or whatever it is you eat "up there"?' She says the 'up there' in a pretty accurate Liverpudlian imitation.

'You stuck-up narrow minded little cunt,' he says, slowly. Well – talk about a conversation stopper. Madge Drinkwater clears her throat and shifts her sunglasses back up her nose, and I look at the gigantic funnel in front of us and long for the siren to sound and drown us all in noise. And Hen laughs. Then there's a bit of a silence. Imagine actually coming out with that in front of Madge Drinkwater?! I could die. *Honestly.* M. always says it's one of the rudest words in the English language and a lady would never *ever* use it. Madge Drinkwater starts flicking at her lighter and making little gasping noises, turning her head away. I think she's going to choke, but later Hen says she was laughing. Paul is leaning back, looking completely relaxed, not in the least angry – quite smug really – and picking up my copy of *La Peste*. Hen just ignores him and kind of gathers me up and force-marches me off to the stairs, though once we're out of earshot she mutters, 'I think he's a bit *prole* your Mister I'm From Up North don't you?'

———

Hen takes me back to her stateroom. It's far too grand to be called a mere 'cabin'. It's on 'A' Deck and smart as all get-out. Two portholes with full sea view, twin *proper* beds with quilted spreads, a thick cream carpet and a whole private bathroom just for her. I mean, the *luxury*. It also has a cream telephone and Hen's own portable Bush record player stacked with a pile of EPs, mostly French. Thankfully Rosie Hapgood and I practically know all the words of Françoise Hardy backwards because we're real fans. We think *Tous les garçons et les filles de mon âge* is all about us because it's just so true. Everyone is out there in couples walking hand in hand and looking into each other's eyes – except us. We never get a look-in – and sometimes we wonder if we ever will. I mean, we don't exactly meet anyone at the Convent of the Holy Sepulchre – unless you count the boys on the bus, and I don't. Though at least I've had the advantage of having Rosie as a friend because of her brother Joe, whereas I've got no one to offer back which is tough on her. I suppose Joe could count as a boyfriend because he seems really keen, and there was all that kissing we did on Rosie's birthday. We were dancing the Mashed Potato and he pulled me out into the hall and started sticking his tongue between my teeth. Why do they always do that – boys? In films people seem to kiss each other quite gently to start with – it looks soft and sort of cushiony. It's only later they start really pressing into each other – but even so it's always with lips closed. I've studied these things and I know. But boys just open their mouths wide and want to start poking their tongues round your fillings almost before you've said hello. I might have told Hen about this, but thank goodness I didn't because, as we're talking, I realize she's even more heaps ahead of me than I already thought she was.

She has this pile of magazines, American and French, including *Vogue* from both countries – bliss. At first we just flick through comparing fashions – the French *Vogue* is full of people in black, while the American one is full of people in pink and purple Pucci pants. Then Hen finds this article on the Rolling Stones and she flings it across to me and says, 'Get a load of that . . .' It's a photo of Brian Jones peering out from under his blond mop and looking all moody. 'What do you think?' she asks and I say, 'Gorgeous . . .' which is what Rosie and I always say – and Hen says what she wouldn't do with Brian Jones is nobody's business – that he's got cheekbones 'like razor blades and buttocks to match'. Honestly, that's what she says. She's talking about his *buttocks*. Rosie and I never get past eyes, height and quantity of spots. Actually that's the problem with her brother Joe – his face is more or less one great pustule which means I *really* have to close my eyes tight when he's kissing me or else I get a close-up view. I know they're not supposed to be catching, but sometimes you do wonder.

Anyway, Hen takes the magazine back and starts kissing the photo – real smooching so she makes the page wet. A bit disgusting. Then she says she's actually met him at a club in London and that she's been out with a friend of his. Well, what she actually says is she's 'had a bit of a fling with a friend of his' – and as she's telling me, I see she doesn't just mean she's been out to the flicks, she means she's actually done it. *Really* done it. And with a friend of Brian Jones?! So I can see that a few sessions of snogging below the stairs in the Hapgoods' front hall doesn't exactly measure up in the Romance stakes. I'm longing to ask her what it's really like, because no one ever tells you, and in books they always seem to stop at the kissing stage – but at the same time I realize the more I ask her, the more she'll see what a total novice I am, and

I'd rather not give the game away. I mean, so far, considering she's older than me and much more glamorous and everything, she hasn't been at all stuck up. In fact, she seems to be seeking my friendship, which is very flattering. Because obviously she's got all these things in her life, like living in Kensington with her racy Aunt Eve and loads of connections, while I don't even have *one*.

Only the problem here is that I think I let more of this out than I really intended. I thought I was keeping my end up all right – sounding really casual and not asking too many questions, only Hen starts to get very nosy. She keeps saying, 'Go on, spill the beans – I promise not to tell,' but I haven't any beans to spill. I'd spill them if I could. I mean, I do tell her about Joe and anyone else I can think of – well, there was William Allbright last summer, when M. and I were in the caravan at St Austell and I suppose that could just about count and . . . well, that's the problem – and Hen gets the message all right, 'You poor darling,' she shrieks, 'you're utterly sex-starved – we can't have that,' – which may be the truth but isn't what I'd expect to be yelled out loud, especially as there's a knock on the door immediately afterwards and a stewardess pokes her head round, asking if Hen needs anything ironed before dinner this evening. Hen just waves airily (she's *so* in her element here – she obviously knows what to do about everything) and says, 'Not a thing, Meggie darling.'

'Meggie-darling' has a good hard old look at me, and Hen says, 'This is my friend Ella,' and I can see uncomfortable questions about cabin numbers are about to be asked again, only Hen says, 'We're absolutely fine – you should toddle off and get yourself some tea,' and 'Meggie-darling' withdraws.

'God – another of Daddy's spies. He's got them everywhere. He does the trip so often they treat him like an old friend, and I just know he gets them to report back. Anyway, now she's gone, how's about a snifter?' and she starts rummaging in her chest of drawers and brings out a bottle. 'Only advocaat I'm afraid – it's all I could filch from Aunt Eve that I was sure she wouldn't notice, and the off-licence on High Street Ken has got so sniffy about serving people under age. Just you wait until I'm eighteen – only four more months to go and they won't see me for dust.' She starts pouring out great dollops of advocaat into tooth mugs and says, 'Chin chin' – then 'God – simply disgusting,' and she downs it with her eyes closed.

Actually, I rather like it. It reminds me of Gran and Christmas. And her sideboard. When she was still alive, we used to trail back to Norfolk from wherever we were living, and Gran would always make us walk along the dyke through the carrot fields on Boxing Day and the wind sliced through us, so she'd give us tiny glasses of advocaat when we got back – even me when I was little. It never tasted like booze – always like pudding with an extra warm heart. I quite liked those Christmases, except M. was always on edge and couldn't wait to leave. She'd start looking a bit blue the moment we got to Liverpool Street, and she'd stay that way until we got back on the train heading south again. She always said Norfolk was waiting there like one of those pits they use to catch elephants – just ready to trip her up and swallow her whole. I'm not quite sure what she's got against Norfolk though. Apart from it's empty and flat and a bit lonely. But otherwise it always seemed all right – and at least she must have belonged there mustn't she – once? I wouldn't have minded growing up in Norfolk, but there you are. I got London instead – and Cardiff and Cheltenham and Torquay.

Hen picks up the picture of Brian Jones again and starts sending it kisses, only this time at arm's length.

'Do you know any of the other Rolling Stones?' I ask her.

'Only Mick and Bill,' she says. *Only?!* But then she adds, 'I suppose that might be stretching it a bit far. I've sort of been introduced – I don't know they'd remember me – not exactly.'

'Wow,' I say, just for something *to* say, and because I can't think of anything else appropriate which isn't going to show me up even more. Then I go and add 'Gorgeous,' which turns out to be a mistake.

'Do stop saying "gorgeous",' she says.

'Why?'

'It simply isn't a word one uses.'

'Why?'

'I don't know why – does there have to be a reason? It simply won't do that's why. You can say someone's sexy – you can say you fancy them – even "a bit of all right" is better than "gorgeous".'

'Oh.' I didn't know this. I have a go. 'Paul's a bit of all right isn't he?' I ask.

'Actually, in your case I'd stick to "sexy",' she says. '"A bit of all right" sounds wrong somehow. And in Paul's case – no, I don't think he's sexy. Not in the least. I think he's a self-opinionated bore.'

'Oh,' I say, a bit deflated. 'But he is . . .' I'm at a bit of a loss here without 'gorgeous', so I flail around. 'I mean, he's awfully good-looking don't you think? So like a Beatle . . .'

'Really?'

'You must have noticed – half-way between George and Paul – with his hair and his clothes and everything.'

'If I were you, I'd steer well clear of Mr Up North – there are some very sexy Yanks on board – I think it's time we broadened your horizons.'

I can tell that Hen is what M. calls 'a bad influence', but considering I'd quite like my horizons broadened I leave it at that.

I start getting myself ready for the Commander's party at five. The Keropoulos clan must be at early children's supper, so I have the cabin all to myself and even get the chance to try on a few things to check for suitability. It's really exciting, but also a bit strange, not to be able to discuss it all with M. She'll be so amazed when I tell her – me going to my very first grown-up cocktail party and her not even knowing about it. What if Sir Laurence really is there with Joan Plowright and everything? M.'ll never believe it when I write and tell her. I have a good look at my clothes and try to think what she might suggest, because I quite trust her opinion. In the end I go for the Empire shift from Richards – the one with pink cabbage roses on it – and I leave my hair loose because of what Paul said about my Tom Jones, and I wear the papier mâché rose drop earrings because they nearly match.

Although I'm bang on time to meet Sydney Maxton-Bligh outside the Purser's Office, he's acting as if I'm late. He's bouncing around from foot to foot and doing half-knee bends ready to sprint. He hasn't changed for the party – no black tie, not even a blazer. He's still in his lunch-time hairy tweeds so I already feel overdressed. He gives me the once over: 'Very nice, you look very nice my dear – except whatever have you done to your hair? The Commander does like things *neat*,' – which is a cheek, though I tuck it behind my ears anyway. There's no pleasing some people. And now he's bustling me along to the lift and checking his watch.

We get out at the Promenade Deck, and march straight past the 'First Class Only' signs towards the stern, until we reach the Main Hall. It looks much more glamorous now – full of people wandering around in evening dress, just like the Cunard advertisements, and the stories M.'s always told me. Sydney's nudging me in the back and saying, 'What did I tell you – how's this for style. Top class eh?' I don't tell him what Hen said to me this afternoon – that it looks like Harrods Banking Hall on a wet Wednesday to her – because actually I think it looks quite impressive too.

Then we double back down the stairs to Main Deck and along a swish corridor and Sydney's knocking at a door. I'm thinking, 'This is it,' – and a man's voice says, 'Come!' and we go in – only there's nobody there. It's not a bedroom like Hen's stateroom. It's a sitting room with a big off-white sofa and walls decorated like a Chinese cabinet painted with birds and trees. I assume we're too early – and all that rushing too – and I know it's really unsophisticated to be too early for anything, except someone's got to be first haven't they? Only Sydney doesn't look at all put out that we're the first, and the disembodied man's voice, which is deep and American, says, 'Is that you Bligh?'

'Certainly is sir,' says Sydney.

'I'm on a call to New York – fix yourselves some drinks.'

There's a tray of bottles and glasses and an ice bucket laid out on a side table – but nothing else. No food. At the very least I'd expected some things on sticks at my first ever cocktail party, but there isn't even a peanut. Sydney says, 'What's your poison?' and because I'm hesitating for a moment he adds rather slowly, 'What would you like to drink?' as if I'm thick. Only in fact I'm having a think about what to ask for – should I have either a Tom Collins or a Bloody Mary, because they're my only two ever cocktails so far, or are they too complicated in the circumstances given that there's no barman to do the honours? So I say, 'Something with gin in it please,' and he looks a bit surprised and says 'Pink or tonic?' and I say 'Pink' because that's what they drink in Agatha Christies and it's always sounded so nice and it'll go with my dress. Only actually it's bitter and very strong and makes me want to sneeze.

So we're just sitting there, facing each other with nothing to say, and the voice keeps coming through from next door, only we're trying not to listen, though I keep hearing 'Goddammit Harry!' – and then a lot of mumbling. Sydney is whistling quietly and looking up at the ceiling, and when I try to work out the tune it's 'Daisy, Daisy, give me your answer do'. Suddenly he stops and whispers, 'What did I tell you? Nice isn't it?' and I whisper back, 'When's the party?' Only I don't get an answer because the talking stops and the man comes in. Sydney leaps to his feet and salutes.

'As you were, Bligh – and what have we got *here*?' The man comes straight towards me with his hand held out.

'This is Miss Eleanor Feast, sir – the one I told you about – Eleanor, the Commander.'

'Miss Feast?' He shakes my hand and all the time he's staring at me very directly as if he's looking for clues. I want to ask about the rest of the party, and especially about Sir Laurence, but I'm already wondering if I've got the wrong end of the stick again – and anyway, how can it be a proper party with no food? Also, the Commander isn't dressed for a party either. He's in a sort of silk coat – dark blue with swirly patterns like a very smart short dressing gown, and trousers to match – and velvet pumps with gold embroidery. He's much pinker and plumper than you'd expect a Commander to be. Not like an old salt of the sea at all – and he's wearing big black-framed glasses like Alan Whicker on television. He asks Sydney to 'fix' him a scotch and soda 'on the rocks', and once he's got it he says, 'That'll be all, Bligh, I'll see you later.' And Sydney practically backs out of the door like the Lord Chancellor leaving the Queen. Which leaves me alone with the Commander who all the while never takes his eyes off me. It's jolly uncomfortable.

'And how are you enjoying the voyage so far Miss Feast?' he asks, once Sydney's left.

The same old question. Take a voyage and all everyone seems to talk about is taking a voyage it seems to me. 'Fine,' I say, 'it's lovely,' because what else am I going to tell him? I'm hardly going to reveal gate-crashing the First Class gym or life with Mo Keropoulos and the toy-toy.

'You're travelling Tourist, I understand?' he continues.

'That's right,' I say.

'Perfectly adequate for someone of your age – one shouldn't pamper the young. It spoils them for later. And you're English?'

'Half. My father's American.'

'You don't sound at all American – that's what Bligh told me. He said you were quintessentially English.'

News to me. I've never felt quintessentially anything.

'Well, it is where I've lived most of my life,' I tell him, 'so I suppose it's not surprising – ' but he interrupts and speaks right through me.

'I'm very fond of England. I spend a great deal of time there. I've been thinking of buying a house – something in the country. Where would you suggest?'

'*Me*?' Is he taking the mickey?

'Let's call it a parlour game – like analogies – have you ever played that?'

'No.'

'A lot of fun – choices can be very revealing – so where would you choose?'

'I don't know much about the country – apart from in books. We've always lived in towns or cities – quite a lot of them. We live in London now. My grandparents lived in Norfolk, but my mother was always trying to escape it – she says it gives her the willies.'

'The "willies" – what an enchanting turn of phrase. What would the "willies" be exactly or shall I guess?'

'The creeps?'

'Ah the "creeps" – yes, I think we understand each other. Bligh was right – you're just my cup of tea. Or shall we say "char" amongst us anglophiles? A little English rose. Dressed as a rose too. Charming.'

The telephone starts ringing from two directions. There's a big white one jangling on the side table and another bell is sounding through the open door to what I suppose is his bedroom.

'Would you excuse me – I'll take this through here,' he says, and disappears.

I sit down on the sofa, feeling spare and having to sip the horrible drink because it's all I've got. Some party. And I'd been imagining scintillating conversation and famous faces. I'm almost wishing I was back with the Wagenburgs and Madge and I'm wondering what they're up to. I can't hear much of the phone conversation because the Commander has pushed the door to, though the odd shout comes through and it sounds as if poor Harry is having his ear chewed off again. There's a copy of *Tatler* on the table, so I start looking through it and judging all the social occasions and what people are wearing. It seems to me that nobody who goes to Ascot seems to have realized this is the year of the shift.

The telephone conversation has been going on for quite some time, except it must mostly be coming from the other end because everything's gone quiet next door. Amazing that you can talk to people from the middle of the ocean like this. I think of poor Harry whoever he is, in New York, and how he'd like to be left alone and how he must curse the inventor of this ship-to-shore miracle, and then the door swings open again and the Commander's coming back across the thick cream carpet – on bare feet and with bare legs, so that the silk coat looks even more like a dressing gown. There has to be some mistake.

'Let me freshen your drink,' he says.

'No thanks,' I say and the *Tatler* goes and slips off my lap, and I have to grovel to pick it up.

'Oh come on – the party's hardly started . . .'

What party? is what I'm thinking, only now I'm sliding back up on to the sofa, and the Commander's sitting down directly opposite me.

'Isn't this nice?' he says. 'Real cosy,' and he crosses his legs. The silk jacket has ridden up – it's really far too short.

'Cigarette?' he says.

'No thanks, I don't,' I say, not knowing where to look. If I keep my eyes up and level with his, I get the full blast of his stare which seems to bore right through me, and if I look down I get a view of his whitish pinkish legs sprinkled with sparse hair.

'Sensible girl. You're not related to the Park Avenue Feassts are you?'

'I shouldn't think so,' I say, staring hard at the copy of *Tatler* on my lap.

'No – I thought not. Theirs is with a double "S" I think – we can check in the Social Register later. I never travel without it.'

Now I didn't know there were any other Feasts out there – I think Dad thought he'd invented it when he changed it from Festini. So I tell the Commander this, thinking it's a way to fill the gap in the conversation, only he shifts in his chair, re-crosses his legs and says, 'Ohhh' – as if he's disappointed – '*Italian* huh?' – only it comes out as '*Eyetalian*' and I say, 'Yes – originally from somewhere near Naples I think,' – and it's then I realize he hasn't got anything on under the silk coat. I mean he's got his top on all right – a white shirt with a red bow tie – but down below there are these purplish bits squashed between his thighs and looking about to burst. Something makes me think of Tunnocks stuffed pork roll, which is what I had for lunch last Saturday, and I want to laugh, so I do, but it's only nerves.

The Commander laughs too. 'Can we share the joke?'

And what am I going to say? 'No – it's nothing – nothing at all . . .' and I go and laugh again which doesn't help.

'I surely wish you would share – it sounds a lot of fun whatever it is. Do you like fun Miss Eleanor Feast who sounds English but turns out to be Eyetalian? Do you like a little fun?' His voice has changed – it's gone all smoothy silk. Up until now I've been hoping he's just being absent minded or eccentric, but perhaps after all he knows exactly what he's doing and I ought to get out of here. Except, apart from his dangly bits on show, everything else in this room is perfectly normal. He's sitting here quite calmly sipping his drink, not looking the least put out, so again I wonder if it's me being naïve. I always want to be grown-up and sophisticated and here's a chance to be just that, only I don't know what to do. And if he doesn't realize what he's doing and doesn't mean anything by it, then I'll look so childish and silly if I make a fuss. I mean he's a Naval *Commander* for goodness sake – people like that don't deliberately expose themselves do they? In the newspapers it's just men in the park – mostly in the dark.

'Well – yes – of course I love fun,' I say, 'who doesn't?' and I try to sound very light and airy.

'That's my girl – an English rose despite the Eyetalian connection. You've got the skin of an English rose – did anyone ever tell you that?' He sits forward, which improves the view, but I just know he's going to touch me and suddenly it's not in the least funny any more. It's strange and nasty and I know I want to get out of here, even if I do look like a silly child again. And I'm just about to mention I'll be late for dinner, which is the only excuse that comes to mind, when he kind of leaps across the gap between us and lands on the sofa next to me. I jump up and the copy of *Tatler* goes one way and knocks his specs off, while the remains of the pink gin go the other, and I make a beeline for the door. When I look back I get a full view of his bare backside as he hunts around on the floor for his glasses – not a very improving sight.

7p.m. – London

Kitty is late. Again. Late for the Wigmore Hall.

Mrs Croxton had kept her hanging around until the last possible moment at the gallery. As Kitty had feared, curiosity was at full throttle the moment Mrs C. spotted the carrier bag from Peter Robinson. Kitty doesn't make a habit of extravagant lunch-time shopping. In fact this particular instance might well constitute a first, and Mrs Croxton's nose for information was all aquiver. Perhaps if Kitty offered more regular food for speculation, Mrs C. might keep her nosiness to herself. But according to Mrs Croxton,

Kitty could drive a person insane with her obsessive need for privacy. Discretion in *business* is another matter though – a quality Mrs Croxton values most highly, which is why they rub along, Mrs C. and Mrs F., and why perhaps one day – *one* day, she may pass on the baton of Croxton Fine Art to her protégée. Thus, with such a carrot kept permanently dangling in front of her, is Kitty kept in poorly paid thrall.

Tonight Kitty has offered to lock up, which would leave her private time to get herself changed, but Mrs Croxton susses her ruse out instantly and, far from leaving early to drive back to Finchley, hangs around discussing the commission in bronze for 'Barn Owl with Pipistrelle bat (dead)' which came in the afternoon post. In the end Kitty is forced to excuse herself and go and change anyway, in the tiny WC down in the basement, leaving Mrs C. to guess. But it's made her late, squashed into a rush-hour Central Line tube, jumping out at Bond Street and running up St Christopher's Place.

She spots him immediately, standing on the front steps, holding programmes, looking distracted.

'I'm so sorry – work . . .' she says.

'It's all right – don't worry,' he says, but sounds annoyed. 'I wonder if we've still time for a drink – I'd have ordered here if I'd known . . .'

'It doesn't matter.'

'Of course it does – let's get over to the pub, the bar here's a zoo.'

They make a dash for the pub along Wigmore Street – the saloon bar, also a zoo at this time of the evening. It's awkward standing here in a pub, wearing her beautiful new suit in pale lemon silk. It's a suit meant for banquettes at Fortnum's, the vision which fed her imagination when she'd gone mad at lunch time and bought it. It isn't meant for this smoke-hazed, soggy-beer-mat atmosphere. She's never had a penchant for pubs. Pubs – three of them – were the only social outlet back in her prewar Norfolk village adolescence and they've always represented something cheerless to her, especially to a woman alone. This particular West End version doesn't seem that much of an improvement, as he pushes his way through to the bar to try and give his order. He returns empty handed.

'I think we'd better give this up as a bad job,' he says. 'There's only one chap there and he doesn't know whether he's coming or going. They won't let us into the concert if we're late. I'll order drinks for the interval if we have time, all right?'

'Fine,' she says and pulls on her white gloves again, almost relieved not to have to sully them with the schooner of sherry she'd ordered.

Their seats are in the stalls. He guides her along, with his hand lightly on her back. Innocuous enough perhaps, but she's acutely aware of that hand – fire in her spine. It's a programme for two guitars with chamber orchestra. The guitarists are young men from Czechoslovakia, personable, though gleaming sweatily in their tail coats and white ties on a warm summer night. She wishes she knew more – in fact anything – about music, but the first half sounds quite familiar, pieces she must have picked up from the wireless, though she's not a regular listener to the Third Programme. Still, there's something she's sure she recognizes which turns out to be Vivaldi – adapted for two guitars from a lute concerto. When she looks up from reading the programme in the auditorium gloom, she allows herself a sideways glance at his face. It's a strong nose, a full mouth, sketchily highlighted by the dim glow of Exit signs. She'd found all day that she couldn't truly remember it from yesterday, a signal for her that he's already taking on a special significance. Most faces ink themselves indelibly in her mind – she'd be a good police witness. Only those for whom she has strong feelings tend to fade. If she was forced to recall the planes of Jack's face right this moment she'd be lost. Even Ella, out of sight, loses a certain definition in her mind.

In the interval he's amused by the concert choice – the Vivaldi was pretty commonplace, and the 'Concierto de Aranjuez' coming up in the second half is well nigh a cliché – still, the two guitars instead of the customary one should add some spice. She doesn't know the piece and can't pursue his line, nor summon up any words to indicate sophisticated scorn. She'd liked the Vivaldi – liked its faint edge of familiarity. Sipping the long awaited sherry she looks at her watch – 8.45p.m. and out at sea it would be what?

It's the perfect conversational ploy. Already he's working it out: the *Queen Elizabeth* is some thirty-six hours out at sea – four, no maybe five lots of twenty minutes – so it would be something like 7.25p.m. on board.

'I wonder what they're all doing,' she says.

'Just getting to the end of the cocktail hour,' he says. 'Almost time for dinner.'

7.30p.m. – RMS Queen Elizabeth

I feel sick. I feel like crying. I feel furious with myself for being so wet. I've run out of the Commander's stateroom and back up to the Main Hall. People are going in to dinner in their smart clothes. They don't look so elegant now. They look middle-aged and boring and faded. I don't want to be one of them. I want to be me. I want to be safe, and secure, and sure. For two pins I'd go back to my cabin, get up into my bunk, pull the blanket over my head and stay there – for the next four days. I don't want to face dinner or Sydney Maxton-Bligh. Did he know what he was doing when he left me there with the Commander? Surely not? But surely yes – who am I kidding – of course he did. But then again, I'm split. You hear these stories – all the time you do. Dirty old men. Rosie Hapgood had a near miss with that bloke on Clapham Common, slipping out of the shrubbery just past the café when

113

she was taking a short cut. That you'd expect – if you happen to be unlucky. Or take stupid risks. Dirty old Commanders who are supposed to be entertaining Sir Laurence are another thing altogether – but then maybe I've got it wrong. Again. Maybe he didn't mean anything by it. I feel such a twit. Other girls my age surely know what's what.

I'm not hungry. I decide to skip dinner – that way I won't have to face Sydney just yet. I couldn't. I'd feel embarrassed and ashamed. Something I've done, something I've said, must have made him think I'm that sort of girl. But what? How does it all work? The mere thought of that horrible old man with his thing bulging out and those sickly white legs makes me want to puke. And I don't know where to go. The cabin will be full of Eenie and Mo and their toys, and getting ready for bed, and everywhere else on the ship I'll risk bumping into Sydney, or Madge and the Wagenburgs, and having to explain.

I head all the way up to the Sports Deck – surely it's too late now for anyone much to be out there. I take the stairs knowing that Sydney M-B prefers lifts, the great lump. It's a good choice – deserted, everyone must be at dinner. But it's cold. Most of the steamer chairs have been folded up and stacked to one side, but I pull one out, and a blanket, and lie there all wrapped up, looking out at the sea as it gets darker.

Eventually I can't see the horizon any more, or the sea – just hear the hum of the ship and the constant background rush of the waves and the wind. And I'm miserable. Full bloody stop. What else is there to say?

I must have fallen asleep, although I don't particularly remember waking up. Just that there's light shining across the deck and the sound of pop music. I get up, really stiff and cold in spite of the blanket. I intend to go into the bog and do something with myself because my hair's all over the place, but first I follow the lights and the music. A door is open and the sound of 'How Do You Do What You Do To Me?' is blaring out, so I presume this is the Teenage Lounge – the place Hen Thring was looking for earlier. I poke my head in, meaning just to have the quickest look. It isn't a large room, and most people are standing round a juke box. One of them is Hen, talking to a blond boy with a tanned face and a crew cut. I'm just about to dart away again when Hen spots me. No escape.

'There you are . . .' she yells. She doesn't seem to have a soft pedal in her repertoire. 'I've been looking for you everywhere!' and I'm caught. What is she doing up here? Why isn't she with all the rich toffs on Main Deck, tucking into champagne and caviar? She weaves across to me.

'I'd decided you were lost for the rest of the evening – I've been telling Chip all about you and your Commander – we were just betting that you'd get taken on to dinner, maybe the Verandah Grill? Was he there then, Olivier, under an alias?'

I want to shut her up. I want her to stop drawing attention to me. I mumble 'No' – but it isn't enough, she wants more. I tell her sketchily – just the bare bones. She shrieks with laughter and there's no escape, again.

'Poor Ella,' she shouts, wheeling me round towards the juke box – and Chip. 'Her cocktail party turned out to be mostly cock – with a bit of tail thrown in on the side . . .' Well *honestly* I could *die*.

10p.m. – London

Cliché or not, Kitty is stirred by the 'Concierto de Aranjuez' with its swelling refrain. So all right, she knows nothing, *nothing* – but the music speaks to her of pride, heroism, and desperate loss. Already she's planning to buy the LP. While Ella's away she can take command of the Dansette portable gramophone and play it whenever she wants. She lets this slip out over dinner, and sees immediately she's painted herself into a corner. It's a picture of a very mere little life isn't it? One where the absence of a daughter allows her access to a gramophone. Revealing. There's not an ounce of expansiveness in that little vignette.

'I'm glad you enjoyed it so much,' he says, 'and why don't you let me buy it for you? I'd like the excuse, I could live in the Oxford Street HMV.' Earlier he'd been discussing tonal variations, but now he's reining back – to her level? – making himself sound enthusiastic about shopping.

He's taken her to the Trattoria Terraza in Soho, a restaurant she's read about. Very with-it – often mentioned in the *Evening Standard*. Theatrical. 'Oh yes,' he says when she murmurs some such thing, 'post-show time it'll probably be awash with actors and actresses. I'll bring you here again some time, a bit later – if you like that kind of thing. Star-struck are you?'

'Well – perhaps a little. Not that I've had – ' and now she shuts herself up. Stop the 'little me' – right now – and hadn't he just said he'd bring her here again, planting the delicious idea that there will be an 'again'? She changes her tone. 'In America we'd go to shows – on Broadway. I saw the second night of *South Pacific* with Ezio Pinza and Mary Martin. It was fantastic.'

'With Ezio Pinza – in the flesh, that must have been extraordinary – "Some Enchanted Evening" – marvellous song, marvellous voice he had. So you lived in Manhattan?'

'Oh no – if only. Not even in the city. I *thought* that's where we were going to live – when I met Jack. He always said he came from New York – and he wasn't lying, not exactly. He just had a way of being elastic with the truth – he could make it fit more or less any situation he chose. What he meant was he came from New York *State* – and I didn't realize then that there are nearly 50,000 square miles of it. His family lived way up north – place called Sproughton, quite near the Canadian border. The winters were frigid – the summers hot – ' but here she curtails the story.

Why reveal the world of Mama and Papa Festini – the rows and tempests, the intricacies of spaghetti sauce dramas. 'We moved around a lot, didn't ever settle for long – but we did get into Manhattan sometimes, my husband and I, on business.' The truth is that this was Festini Food business. At times of financial crisis, Jack would unwillingly return to the family fold and get landed with flogging cases of Bolognese round the delis of Little Italy: but need she reveal her truths yet? And if not now, for how long should she hold out – when is the time to drop your guard and let the truth out into the air? Never, according to Jack – as she understood him. Keep your front up for ever and a day. His own personal philosophy.

During pudding – zabaglione with amaretti – they get on to the subject of divorce. He describes his as 'a typically grimy little business', a cliché, even down to using a Brighton hotel as the location for the damning evidence. They'd had to go for adultery, he says. The truth – that they simply didn't love each other any more – didn't of course constitute legal grounds. Naturally he'd offered himself up as the guilty party – for the children's sake: well, one of them had to take on the burden. So it fell to him to go through the charade with the room service waiter swearing in court as to the presence of an unknown woman rumpling the bed sheets. Kitty has to admit to an equal cliché, for her divorce was of the speedy Nevada variety, claiming that other legal charade, 'Mental Cruelty', as grounds – though as it happens, life with Jack Feast had been disjointed and strange enough perhaps to merit the description.

After dinner (and he pays the bill, again so subtly she doesn't even realize it's happening – rare joy), they stroll through Soho, down Lower Regent Street, along the Mall. A warm summer's night. There are lots of other couples: men with their ties loosened, women with jackets slung lightly round their shoulders. Couples. How mysterious the state of being a couple has seemed to her in recent years. Yet it turns out to be so simple. You meet someone: you can, after all, meet someone. It needn't, after all, be an issue – something which must be tied to family or friends or work or even making much of an effort. You can meet someone on a train and abracadabra, twenty-four hours later, you're a couple too, strolling towards St James's Park under a darkening cobalt sky.

He's been holding her hand since they came down the steps from Waterloo Place, and in Birdcage Walk under a plane tree he pulls her to a halt and kisses her. And then again, further along beneath another tree – and then each tree – so that they create a rhythm of walking, stopping, kissing and kissing, kissing, kissing. And she doesn't want him to stop and she doesn't want it to change and she doesn't want to grow up.

As they move back towards Buckingham Gate and out towards Victoria however, they're suddenly overtaken with self-consciousness. She's straightening her skirt and he seems to be looking around warily. There are no more trees to act as protective stations for their embraces – only doorways which seem, in contrast, tatty – even sordid.

'I live just round the corner,' he says, 'over there . . .' He's pointing out a mansion block in one of the side roads off Victoria Street. It's an area of London she's never liked that much – too red brick, too strong a sense of transience edging out from the station. But tonight it's magic. Tonight all London is under a spell for her.

'Would you like to come in?' he asks.

Tonight. 'Now?' she says, stupidly. Of course *now*.

'Well yes. For a drink – or coffee.'

Yes. Yes, I'd love to come in. Only not now – now is too soon, too soon after the first holding of hands, and the kissing under the plane trees. And why do I feel fourteen again and lost and confused – and why don't I simply say yes. But no, not yet. Now is too soon. Too fast. Fast. You can't just do it – like that. It won't do – will it? Could it? Years of fear akin to indoctrination hammer in: so then, leave it for now.

'I really ought to be getting home.' Yes, that's what she says. What she'd expect herself to say – though usually she has a ready-made excuse in Ella. No such excuse tonight.

'Must you?'

'Well yes – early start – and . . . Well you know . . .'

'I'm very disappointed – you know that.'

'Are you? I'm sorry – it's just – well . . .'

'You do know that – *very* disappointed – ' and he takes her hand again.

'I'm sorry – it's just – well, with no warning – perhaps another night?' Making it clear that she knows, as he knows, that a mere drink is not what this is about.

'I'd certainly hope so . . .' he says, but leaves it hanging, without making any alternative suggestion – drops her hand and leaves it, so that she's cornered into saying something herself.

'Perhaps over the weekend?'

They've turned away from his block of flats and are walking more purposefully now towards the station. The time of dreamy wandering is so rapidly cut short and already she's missing it.

'Not possible – not this weekend,' he says. 'I've got to go down to the country.'

'Oh – of course – no, I didn't necessarily mean this weekend . . .' Except she did. Of course she did. And now she's regretting her caution. Why not just throw it to the winds – why *not*?

'But when I get back,' he continues, 'why not Monday?'

Saved. She's saved by a Monday. Two days is exactly what she needs . . . Time to reflect, time to organize, before releasing the cords of her discretion.

'Monday then . . .' she says, and this time rapidly flags down her own taxi as it slows to make the turn on to Vauxhall Bridge Road. So swiftly is it all done that she's closing the door before there's even a chance for a last kiss. It wouldn't have amounted to much anyway would it – a simple peck now they're standing beneath the glare of neon outside the Victoria Palace Theatre, away from the magic shadow of the trees. When she looks back through the smoked glass of the cab's rear window, he's already turned away.

11p.m. – *RMS* Queen Elizabeth

We don't stay long in the Teenage Lounge. Hen says, 'It's not happening, you dig?' and Chip agrees. Though actually I quite like it. The juke box has some good records and you don't have to pay to use it. There's 'Glad All Over' by the Dave Clark Five so we could Stomp. Only nobody does. And Little Eva so we could do the Loco-motion, only nobody does. And I can't get the ball rolling. Not if nobody asks me. And nobody does. Honestly, it's better at Rosie's house without a proper juke box.

Chip is American and Hen met him in the Cabin Class swimming pool. She says she was 'slumming' and Chip pretends to punch her. We Tourists don't have a swimming pool. Chip's been living in Europe all year, doing a liberal arts course in Madrid. He keeps saying things like 'muchas gracias' and 'hasta la vista' and making eyes at Hen. I think he really fancies her. He doesn't take much notice of me.

There are drinks on offer and when Chip goes off to get us some, Hen pokes me in the side and says, 'What do you think? You should see him with his shirt off – he's got a chest like Bronco's – muscles like a Greek statue – yummy.' He's on the way back with three bottles of Coca-Cola. He is quite short and solid and his hair in its stubbly crew cut is as yellow-blond as Hen's – the exact opposite of my very own Beatle.

'Umm,' I say.

'Don't go sounding doubtful on me darling,' says Hen. 'He's right up your street, I've got a feeling for these things.'

'Hey you guys – this is all they've got,' he says, waggling the Cokes. 'Let's split and get ourselves a real drink.' Only, I'd quite have enjoyed a Coke. Still, there you go. And there we go. Except first there's a debate as to *where* we can go.

'To a bar of course,' says Chip. 'This goddam boat is a floating booze palace and we guys get stuck with Coke – I mean come *on* – Cuba Libre babies – I could do with a slug of rum.'

Hen says we can't go to any of the First Class bars because everybody knows her, and knows she's under age and she's really got the wind up about her father's spies. Chip says maybe we could go to the Westward Ho in Cabin Class – except that only I am dressed properly for it, because of course I'm still in my glad rags from the Commander's party. Hen says, 'How's about the Tourists' Observation Bar – Ella can slip us in.'

I don't see that I can – after all I'm under age too – except when we get there it's crammed and no one seems to notice us. Chip, who actually is nineteen, goes to get us some drinks. This time I ask for tonic water because it sounds more professional than lemonade, which is what I'd really like, and after my session with the Commander I don't care if I never drink anything with gin in it again, for the rest of my life. And I mean never *ever*.

We stick ourselves as far away from the bar as we can, over by the windows, so as not to attract any attention – only it's all a bit pointless really because Hen can't seem to help herself. She's squawking and laughing and making a heck of a row, so we get noticed anyway.

In the middle of all this I see Paul, and he comes straight over to us, only at the last moment I see he's actually making a beeline for Hen, and he says, 'Wotcher bitch – ' and she says, 'Hi – bastard' and they both laugh. *Honestly.* I don't understand it at all. I mean he was so rude to her this afternoon and 'bitch' isn't exactly a very nice thing to call anybody is it – neither is 'bastard', come to think of it.

Then, to make it worse, he turns round to me and says, 'Wotcher squirt.' *Squirt*?! I *mean*. He bends down and sniffs my drink – 'On the booze already?' Only Hen interrupts with, 'Ella's playing Goody Two Shoes – teetotal.'

'Oh yeah?' he says and I don't have a chance to explain about the pink gins, because Hen rushes on with 'Ella's started before us you see – she's been to a *cock*tail party in First Class – '

'So I've already had enough,' I say, jumping in, trying to stop Hen's cocktail joke coming out again, 'enough booze for one night.'

'What's enough?' says Paul, and that starts them comparing booze experiences. Chip gives us a detailed description of how he got what he calls 'wasted' on something called 'Fundador' in Barcelona, and then Paul starts listing the quality of stouts in the Sussex Student Union, and Hen's talking about a beer festival in Munich she went to on an exchange visit – and they're all comparing how much they could get down before passing out under the table, which sort of excludes me, and I feel silly standing there laughing when I haven't anything to laugh about.

But then I get saved by Laura Wagenburg of all people. She and Ken emerge from the far side of the big horseshoe-shaped bar. They're on their way out, but she spots me and comes rushing over.

'Ella, hi – glad to see you're all right. I was worried about you – missing dinner and all. We wondered if you'd gotten sick,' she says.

'No,' I tell her, 'I'm fine – just busy.'

'Well, so I *see*,' she says a bit meaningfully, raising her eyebrows. I suppose she means the bar and being too young and everything.

Ken's in the doorway calling 'Honey . . .'

'Coming sweetheart,' she answers, and then she turns back to us and says they're just off to the 'movies' – 'It's an Alfred Hitchcock with Sean *Connery* . . .'

'Yummy!' says Hen. *Honestly.*

But Laura's nodding – 'Isn't he just the *cutest*?'

Once she's gone Hen says we should all go to the flicks too – which is what we do.

By the time we get to the Tourist Cinema the lights are already going down and we have to squeeze our way along a row in the dark, stepping on people's toes. Hen hisses that the seats are mingy, and that the ones in First have proper tip-up seats with velvet covers and that she'll smuggle me in some time – but everyone's shushing us because the film's starting, and we have to sit down in a hurry. I couldn't care less about the quality of our seats, but I could care a bundle about the order in which Hen's somehow got us seated. This is the way the row's arranged: me first against the wall, then Chip, Hen, Paul. A problem. This is the way I'd have liked the row to be: Paul first, me, Chip, Hen. But there you go.

So then the film starts and it's an 'X' I think, which of course I couldn't get into on dry land – except Rosie and I did last year for *The Chapman Report*, though we had to put our hair up and wear a lot of makeup to get away with it. Anyway, this film is all about this blonde woman who can't help stealing and Sean Connery plays an American businessman who falls in love with her, marries her and takes her home to this incredibly luxurious country house which reminds me a bit of Aunt Bea and Uncle Sally's – only this woman can't stand him to touch her – I mean can't *stand* it – which doesn't make sense because he's absolutely gorgeous – and he sounds exactly the same as when he's James Bond too. There's this bit on a ship which looks like the *Queen Elizabeth*, only smaller of course – and they're on their honeymoon, so of course he wants to do it – I mean he's married her and everything so of course he does – only she won't let him. And there's this bit where he sort of accidentally on purpose tears her nightie off and you can see her bare legs, so it doesn't leave much to the imagination – and then there's the sea crashing about beyond the portholes and I think I can hear Hen sniggering, though *I* can't see anything to laugh about. I sit forward a bit, and in the flickering light from the screen I can see that Chip has his hand on Hen's knee, but she's got her head turned towards Paul and I can't see beyond. Chip's other hand, the one nearest me, is resting on his own thigh. So that's a relief. Sort of.

Anyway, by the end of the film, Sean Connery's psychoanalysed the blonde woman and uncovered her gruesome past, which was all about her mother being a prostitute. Which makes me quite relieved at having a mother like M. really. For which many blessings, thank you and amen. The End. Though as if this woman wouldn't have fallen for Sean Connery. I mean *honestly.* Alfred Hitchcock should have made it with someone else to be believable really. Rod Steiger or Fred MacMurray – then it would have made more sense – but then maybe we wouldn't have been so keen to watch it.

So then the lights go up, and I look along the row. Paul's slumped back in his seat looking bored and Hen's talking to Chip. For a moment I think it's all right, but then I think I see a metallic gleam on Paul's upper lip where his moustache would be if he had one. But then again, maybe it's a trick of the light. Only, Hen's wearing pearly lipstick – something like Revlon's 'Barely Peach' – and most of it's worn off. But surely I'm wrong because you can tell that Hen's just not his type, or she his. Chip's her type. I hope.

I'm noticing all this in a flash of course – that's how long it takes, but it's long enough to start feeling disappointed, especially as Chip doesn't even seem to know I'm there and is moving on ahead of me, keeping up with Hen, so that I'm alone and mixed up with the other people in the aisle. Only suddenly I feel a hand on my shoulder and 'Hi there you made it . . .' and I look round and see Laura and Ken Wagenburg. 'I mean truly is Sean Connery a dreamboat or not?' says Laura, right there in front of Ken, only I don't bother to answer because right behind Ken is Sydney Maxton-Bligh. I can feel myself starting to go red, but I look straight at him and think maybe he'll apologize or something.

What he does is amazing. He waggles his fingers at me and says, 'Hello-a-lo – I wouldn't have expected to see you here. Didn't the Commander take you to dinner then?'

'No,' I manage to get out. I'm so choked my tongue's almost sticking to the roof of my mouth.

'A bit of all right – posh – what?' he says. And that sort of shakes me. I mean could he be so barefaced if he'd really set a trap for me? The trouble is, I get so many things wrong don't I? Paul and Hen for example. They seem to loathe each other – yet they don't do they? So suddenly I'm not sure about the whole Commander business any more. Maybe I've been thinking the worst. Perhaps, after all, I've exaggerated the whole thing.

Saturday

3a.m. – London

In the flat above Mr Christo's shop in Bissett Street, Kitty lies awake, wrestling with the spectres of love, lust and her own fertility: though she's not so crazed she doesn't see she may be jumping the gun a bit. One high tea, one dinner and one London night-trail of magic may well constitute the beginnings of a love affair – but *love*? Yet self-knowledge doesn't somehow douse this glow she's feeling. She hasn't felt it in a long, long time, has forgotten its madness, how it twists and twines into the mind and smothers everything else.

There have been too few men since the divorce, far too few – and those who have appeared have always been found wanting. She doesn't think she's fussy – not particularly – but just 'any old man' has never seemed to fit the bill for her. She's not that desperate, she tells herself. She's not that alone. Why waste herself? There was the handyman when she was a matron at Immingham School, but she'd thought he was mentally two penn'orth short of a shilling, as her mother would have said. And the Art master, oozing an attractive bohemianism, who'd begged her to pose in the buff, tried to woo her with brandy – and who turned out to be queer – what a disappointment. Other occasional assorted types had always been found lacking in some essential. The attractive men, the ones she might dream of loving, had almost always proved to be already married – very married indeed. She's never happened just to bump into a fellow divorcé. They're pretty thin on the ground and other women – more predatory women – always seem to have got there first. But now there's

Gilbert who so far seems perfect in every detail, and the mere thought of him pierces her with the dart of desire – delicious, but dangerous, for lust and its possible consequences are the other looming spectres.

If there was anyone to whom she could voice these fears, right now in this 3a.m. wide-awake sleepless state, then 'nightmare' is the word she might use, once she'd quelled the surge of excitement. Too strong? Yet a nightmare is what the dire consequence would be – will be – if her body betrays her. The possibility of pregnancy has tainted every attempt at a relationship since her divorce. It hangs around now, threatening spoilage of this magic. The smell of him – and the taste. The sheer physical strength of a man's arms around her, holding her. In the years of manlessness she'd forgotten that feeling. Ella hugs her of course, but daughter to mother, they are both narrow and bird-boned, compared to that breadth of muscle and musk she'd felt this evening.

And there's the trouble, for this evening was only the overture, just a taster of the main production which he clearly expects and wants. And she's almost surprised to realize that she wants it too. Maybe she's been cursed with too vivid an imagination coupled with too cautious a nature? Or maybe the first has cursed her into developing the second? 'An unwanted pregnancy' – a chilly little phrase representing several lifetime's agonies. An unwanted bundle of cells with the power to disrupt and destroy – and because she has imagination's curse, the thoughts are followed through. Already she's seeing herself in a month's time – with that other curse overdue, and the sickening sense of fear. What would such an event do to Ella? A baby, an illegitimate baby, would shatter the fragile world Kitty has so carefully constructed around them.

If not a baby, then what – an abortion? But how? She's known of women, of course she has – of bundles of five-pound notes stuffed into foolscap envelopes in places like Kensal Rise and Tufnell Park – but how would she find such a person? And then the risks – the infections. Already she's dying of septicaemia and Ella is an orphan and has to spend the rest of her growing-up in the dubious American care of Jack and his invisible new wife. Imagination's curse.

Other people manage though. Other women have lovers and seem to manage, to get off scot-free. But how? And who is there to share these fears and divulge their secrets? Her friends – what friends? There's been no time, no opportunity to develop such friendships. There's been work of course – but the idea of sharing the merest wisp of these thoughts with Mrs Croxton is laughable. In any case, Mrs Croxton's own fertility must be long dried up. There are women Kitty knows through Ella – mothers of Ella's school friends – but all without exception are married; not one other divorcée in the entire school it seems – a widow or two perhaps, but none she knows. Ella's best friend Rosie, the one who lives in the big raggle-taggle house on the edge of Clapham Common, has a mother called Phil. Phil is big – tall and plump with it – representing everything that Kitty is not, that Kitty *has* not. She wears large floaty garments and sweeps Ella into her huge embrace, for she has a large, warm heart to match. Phil would probably know what one does these days – all these married women with their clearly limited quantities of children must surely know. But there's the difference – they're married. How could you go into your GP – how could *she* – into stern Dr Perkins who saw her through Ella's bad case of mumps and who knows her marital status all too well? Feme Sole – that's how she was categorized in one of the lawyers' papers she'd had to sign a few years ago – the one which tried to prise alimony payments out of Jack from across the Atlantic. Feme Sole, lone woman – sometimes it felt like a label of damnation. But now there's Gilbert and for one whole evening she was no longer 'sole'. Now too, there's an ongoing prospect of change, of being one half of a couple. Except – except the fertility spectre snaps its jaws again.

So other women manage – but how? It's not as if she doesn't

know herself to be particularly fertile. It was always a struggle with Jack. Ella herself was the result of a slip-up in their arrangements, for children were not on Jack's original agenda for self-improvement, involving as it did the escape from his family's grasp, the endless reaching for the American Dream which had them chasing through all forty-nine states. (Be thankful Hawaii wasn't yet in the union or he'd have hauled them there too.) Contraception then had involved a Dutch cap of course – huge and rubbery – and a vast rubber douche bag – uggh – too much rubber, swamping passion, wrecking spontaneity. Of course now there's all this business of a contraceptive pill. She's read about it in the newspapers – but how does it, could it, work? Could she trust it? Could she even find it? Did 'they' give it out to the guilty ones like her – Feme Sole every one of them?

8a.m. finds her up and dressed, standing in the phone box on the corner of Bissett Street, riffling through the pages of the telephone directory F to N section. 'Family Planning'; there's an address in the Elephant and Castle, but when she rings the number there's no answer. Saturday of course, nothing will be open. So what do people do? Trust to French letters? She'd done that with Jack – rarely, nervously, in the war – and suffered agonies awaiting her fate. So again – what *do* people do?

Another name occurs while she's still standing there in the phone box – Marie Stopes – a name her mother Florence muttered just before her marriage to Jack. She'd gone home to Norfolk for the wedding – a post-war utility do in the parish church. She hadn't given her mother much of a warning and Florence would have proclaimed her disappointment to the Heavens if she'd thought they'd bother to listen. Instead she had had to make do with silence and the wide grey sky over the flat sepia land. *What* a disappointment. If she'd had more notice, even a month or two, they could have saved some coupons, hoarded their sugar ration, got hold of some sultanas – somehow they'd have done it.

The marriage of an only daughter is an event – *should* be a real event. And only to think of sending her off without even a proper wedding cake to her name. Had to make do with a Genoa sponge – managed to use real eggs courtesy of their own hens, and the cherries – cherries again, always her downfall – the cherries were a bit sparse, being a bag of the glacé variety which had been hanging round the larder since the summer of 1939 for just such a contingency. And speaking of cherries – there's this other business – you know, sex business – said Florence. One of those things men need – and she'd shoved a copy of Marie Stopes's *Married Love* into Kitty's hands the night before the ceremony. Dog-eared it was – well thumbed. Impossible to act blasé though: if Florence had known what Kitty and Jack had dared to get up to in the back of his Jeep with the aid of Uncle Sam's rubber johnnies, the shock might have killed her. So – Marie Stopes is the name she now recalls – and she turns to the S to Z volume of the directory. It's only half there, hanging out of its metal protective hinge with many pages missing – vandalized – but the Ss are still intact, and here, miraculously, the name of Marie Stopes is listed. The Marie Stopes Clinic, Whitfield Street. That would be just off Tottenham Court Road wouldn't it? Kitty inserts four pennies, dials the number and prepares to press Button A.

8a.m. – RMS Queen Elizabeth

Printed on the front of this morning's *Ocean Times*: 'President Makarios sues for peace' – Mr Christo will say, 'What I told you – I told you so, is what I told you.'

Printed on the back of this morning's *Ocean Times*:

Passengers are kindly requested to remain in the accommodation allotted to the class in which they are travelling.

A message to me. It's obvious isn't it? Expressly to me. I've been watched. Every move I've made, from gate-crashing the First Class gym to being with the Commander must have been observed somehow. Even coming on the wrong boat train. I bet you. Big Brother is watching me – it's all very futuristic and 1984. A bit creepy. The feeling almost spoils my early morning tray of tea and the comfort of lying in my one little piece of private space. I must be blushing all over.

I suppose it's funny to feel comfort squashed up like this, because I'm practically under siege from the Keropoulos possessions, which now seem to have taken up every nook of D9. It's just as hot and stuffy in here – probably more so, but there's something quite endearing about hearing Mo and Eenie playing from the early hours. They seem to be making some sort of effort to keep quiet – if they don't, Mrs K. rolls over and groans, 'Cut that out,' in her sleep – but even so their voices keep up a permanent running tinkle of sound. Innocent. It's all so simple next to being nearly grown-up and having to worry what people think of you – and love – and being loved, and having periods and hairy armpits, and your bra not fitting. And being jumped on by Commanders. Being nearly an adult is so complicated.

Anyway, I take the message on the back of the *Ocean Times* as being meant for me, and decide I won't venture out of Tourist for the whole day. Not even for the whole rest of the voyage probably. Look where my gallivanting got me – cornered by a pervert with his thing hanging out, that's where.

It's funny I should have thought about periods, because it turns out that's exactly what Mrs K.'s got – only she calls it her 'monthlies' and they're giving her 'one helluva beating' so would I mind taking the children to breakfast – and by the way, do I have any Tampax – which I do of course, only mine are Regular and it turns out she needs Super Duper Double Maxi-Strength, or something like that, which doesn't really bear thinking about.

So I mean, what can I say? She's still in her bunk, all creased up with the stomach ache, and the children are looking expectant and hungry. So I give in. Well of course I do. Only I try to keep some discipline going. I make them pick up most of their toys, so we can at least get to the washbasin without stabbing our feet – though I let them keep the jigsaw out, because Mo's nearly finished it and otherwise it'll make her feel she's done all that work for nothing and things like that can warp a girl for life.

Breakfasts don't seem to be as well attended as the other meals, which means there are lots of gaps and people sometimes move from table to table. There are gaps on ours this morning, so there's no problem about the children sitting with me. Madge isn't there which isn't surprising – I expect all she has by way of breakfast is a quick suck on half a lemon slice. Neither are the Wagenburgs – but, says Sydney Maxton-Bligh with one of his finger-to-nose-taps, that's 'only what you'd expect of honeymooners' wink, wink – because of course *he's* there, wouldn't you just know it, tucking into the full fry-up. In a way it's a relief I did see him last night because I already know he's going to bluff it out – the business with the Commander, I mean. He's not going to admit to anything, so unless I'm going to make some sort of scene, I suppose I'm not going to either. I don't feel up to a scene – especially as I'm not absolutely certain of my ground – and I'm feeling less certain of it as the time moves on.

Having Mo and Eenie to look after turns out to be useful because I can bury all my attention in them. I feel very adult, very mature, organizing these tiny tots. I'd quite like it if Paul could see me now – being calm and responsible, motherly too, the ideal mother that's me. But he's not at his table. The girls want pancakes and maple syrup which aren't on the menu, but the waiter says he'll organize them anyway. Sydney goes into raptures about that – how helpful the staff are and how the chefs will do anything for you. Then he starts talking to the children who are having bowls of Rice Krispies to start with, and messing about with all that snap, crackle and pop.

Sydney tells them the very first Cunard ship that went to America was back in 1840 and it had a cow on board to give fresh milk – and he moos, and they moo too. Then he asks them do they know how much breakfast cereal is on board the *Queen Elizabeth*? And they look up at him with great big eyes and of course say no – and he tells them 'one thousand five hundred pounds' – and Mo asks what's a pound and holds her hands out six inches apart and Sydney says, 'Bigger than that' – and then Eenie joins in and they both start holding out their hands wider and wider so they end up with their arms right out on either side of the table, and Sydney's still saying 'Bigger than that', and giving them all these facts and figures about the food on board. He calls it the biggest larder in the world. Once they're on to toast he makes them guess the amount of butter on board (5,900 pounds); then the amount of jam and marmalade – only they don't know what he means so I have to translate it into 'jelly' for them – and that turns out to be 1,500 pounds 'give or take the odd jar of Chivers Old English'.

Then he starts playing Round and Round the Garden with Eenie – moving his finger around the palm of her hand and leaping across the table when he gets to 'tickley under there'. Then of course Mo wants a go too and he plays it again and again, so they're both nearly having hysterics they're laughing so much. It's not a very peaceful breakfast.

And not once does Sydney mention last night – except at the very end when he gets up and says he must go and get his orders for the day and have I written my bread and butter letter yet, because if so he'll deliver it for me. I say, 'What?' and he says, 'Your thank you to the Commander – for last night,' and I say, 'No,' really sharply, but he doesn't ask me why or anything – so I don't know, perhaps he didn't know what he was leading me into last night. Otherwise could he really have such bare-faced cheek?

After breakfast Eenie and Mo want to go to the shop 'to see the toys'. Which reminds me I still haven't bought a torch yet, so I can read in my bunk at night. The shop is up on A Deck. It looks a bit like those Findlay Tobacco places you see round London, really more of a large kiosk with extra windows curving round on either side so you can see more of the stock. It's not a patch on the shops I saw yesterday in First Class which you can actually walk right into, with real counters. Still, the windows are just about at Eenie and Mo's eye-height, so they wander slowly backwards and forwards, leaving sticky syrup runs wherever they go. There's lots of stuff with the ship on it – spoons and mugs and bookmarks and little chrome notebook holders embossed with enamelled *Queen Elizabeths*. Then there are the dolls – Beefeaters, guardsmen in bearskins, King Henry VIII, and one that's supposed to look like our Queen in her Coronation robes – except it's got blonde hair and long painted-on lashes. Mo is mesmerized by this. She stares and stares at it with her tiny little syrupy nose pressed right into the glass.

'I wish we had pwincesses in Nerica,' she says. 'I'd be a pwincess and always wear my crown. Are you a pwincess Ella?'

'No.'

'But you're from Ningland?' she asks. Yes – I'm from Ningland and I'm from Nerica too – but that still doesn't make me a princess.

'Will you buy it for me?'

It's got a £7 price tag so of course I won't. 'You'll have to ask your mummy,' I say, but as I'm feeling generous and very motherly, I do treat them to propelling pencils with a little model of the *Queen Elizabeth* floating in water at the top: 5/– each, and as an afterthought I buy one for myself as well, and a *Queen Elizabeth* torch with a picture on the handle. So in all I spend £1 5s. 6d. I'd better watch it.

'I really *love* you Ella,' says Mo and she takes my hand. Hers is so tiny and her legs are so slender they look as if they could snap. And she's got that thin shiny hair little children have, breaking over her ears, so that they poke through. And she looks up so adoringly. I mean it's really nice – even though it's a pain. I haven't had all that much to do with small children – I've never had the chance – but I can see they're a really good idea. It'll be nice to have some of my own – one day. Except Eenie's scowling and saying she wants her 'Mommy' even though she's standing there waving her new five-bob propelling pencil in the air – but she's six, whereas Mo's only four, so you can see that somewhere along the line the rot sets in.

Because I'm quite enjoying this new maternal glow, I decide to wear the children out a bit before depositing them back with Mrs K. I take them up to the Sports Deck, and make them take the stairs. They're not easily tired though. They dash ahead of me and once we're up there, they start playing hopscotch using the marks painted on the deck for shuffleboard as their numbers. It's a good place for that, with the wind blowing and the great line of the dark blue sea as a backdrop. They're little Jumping Jacks with their skinny legs leaping and their hair whirling. I watch them from the railings and carry on with my motherhood dream – Mrs Darling in *Peter Pan* perhaps. Yes, it'll be all right I reckon.

And then Hen turns up.

'I've been looking for you *every*where,' she says, 'only then I remembered you practically live on this deck – '

'You shouldn't be here,' I say. 'Haven't you read the *Ocean Times*?'

'Of course not.'

'They're after us,' I say, and quote the 'Passengers are kindly requested' message – 'It must mean you as much as me,' I add. 'They probably don't like the classes mixing – it upsets their arrangements.'

'Bugger that for a lark,' she says. 'Have a ciggie – ' and she dives into her bag for her smoker's clobber. She's wearing what looks like a Foale and Tuffin shift in red crêpe and her bag's in quilted leather to match, with long chain handles – and she's got little red leather slingbacks as well, probably Kurt Geiger or something very grand like that. I've certainly not seen anything like them in Dolcis. And her hair's all loose and floaty, like Christine Keeler – and all in all she looks so fab. She isn't like anyone I've ever known. She's leaning over the railings, blowing Consulate smoke out of her nostrils, and – well here's the problem – I mean it's all very well knowing she's a bad influence, but maybe a bad influence is what you need to get yourself kick started in life. Up till now I've never had one – and maybe that's what's been missing. So I have a ciggie too. The smoke's like Vick inhalers and I blow it out as fast as I can through my mouth – can't see how you can do the nostril trick. Nevertheless I feel *really* professional. I mean it is pretty with-it isn't it? I'm leaning on the railings of the *Queen Elizabeth* with a girl who's done it with a friend of Brian Jones and we're blowing smoke over the North Atlantic together. Fab.

Then I remember all that funny business with Paul last night. Not so fab. I'm about to broach the subject – as soon as I've finished the ciggie – but Hen starts before me.

'Chip really fancies you.'

'What?' Talk about knocking a girl off her course.

'Something rotten.'

'*No.*'

'Says you've got curves in all the right places.' It's that wretched bra from British Home Stores. I warned M. it wasn't right – it doesn't do what it oughta – talk about June-is-busting-out-all-over. Substitute Ella for June and you've got the picture.

'But he hardly said a word to me all evening,' I protest, though not all that vigorously.

'That's just his way – man of action – doesn't need the gift of the gab – and anyway he's *American*.'

'And he had his hand on *your* knee all through the film.'

'That's just *my* way – no seriously, he didn't know you were available or anything, he needed to talk to me after he'd met you – get the lie of the land. You don't have to worry darling, I didn't go into any details – he doesn't know you've come from a sexual desert – and anyway, why look a gift-horse? He's terribly sweet and his muscles are from heaven. He's got a rich daddy too – always useful if it comes to anything.'

'But what about Paul?'

'What about Paul? I told you about him – he's not for you. I warned you – I told you he's a bit *prole* – and he's got that terrible chip on his shoulder. All he can talk about is his dad's redundancy and Lévi-Strauss.'

'What's Lévi-Strauss?' I ask.

'It's "who" darling. An anthropologist. Paul thinks the sun shines out of Lévi-Strauss's fundament – get him on the *sujet* and he never shuts up.'

Well, I can see I'm out of my depth again already. Anthropology. I *mean*.

'Also, he says he wouldn't touch a virgin with a barge pole.'

'*What*?' I yell – but it's straight into the wind so I don't think the general populace can hear.

'Well, you know . . .' says Hen, looking very innocent.

'You didn't tell him I'm a virgin did you?' Talk about embarrassing.

'Don't be daft darling – I didn't need to. You've got virgin written all over you – it might as well be tattooed across your forehead.'

'Oh God,' I say.

'It's nothing to be ashamed of. I mean we all were once.'

'It's just being discussed like that – I mean oh *God* – '

'We weren't – I mean not you particularly – it's just in general, that's all he meant. In general he obviously goes for experience. Well, of course he does. I mean, he agrees with me that just snogging doesn't do it for him any more.'

Just snogging. The phrase gives me the glums. I feel about six. Yet again. Which reminds me of Eenie and Mo, and I turn round to check on my darling little charges – only they've gone. Oh *God. Really* this time.

We dash round the Sports Deck shouting and looking. Into where they keep the rugs and chairs. Into the bar. Round the side to the Teenage Lounge. Closed. Back to the bogs – no one in the Ladies. God this is really awful – have they run off and slipped overboard? Eenie's gloomy forecast come to reality? Are they dead – already? Watery graves and all that? Am I going to be arrested and then rolled into a pulp by Mrs K.? Then suddenly I hear that same background tinkling stream of conversation that fills the cabin all night. They're in the Gents. I dash in, and there is Mo, sitting in a stall with the door open and her knickers round her ankles, while Eenie is holding one of her feet under the jet of water in one of the urinals – and I realize I've never actually seen one before, not in the actual porcelain.

'What are you *doing*?' I shout – stupidly I admit, considering it's perfectly obvious.

'Wanted toy-toy,' says Mo from the stall.

'You should have *told* me,' I shriek. 'I thought you'd *drowned* – ' And she starts to cry.

Eenie takes one foot out from the water and is just going to stick her other one under the jet when I yank her back.

'I think it's time we got these little angels off your hands,' says Hen.

She insists on coming with me and grips each child firmly by the wrist.

'It was incredibly stupid of you to run off like that without telling Aunt Ella. *Incredibly*,' she opines, as we storm down to D Deck in the lift.

'Increbily,' says Mo. She's staring up at Hen, awestruck. 'Are *you* from Ningland?'

'Where else?' says Hen.

'Are you a pwincess?'

'No,' says Hen, 'I'm a witch.'

We arrive at D9. The comparison with Hen's stateroom couldn't be greater. I'm acutely aware of the contrast. So evidently is Hen. 'It's just like a hobbit hole,' she whispers, '*fascinating*.' The main light is off and just the reading lamp by Mrs K.'s bunk is on. Her back is towards us and in the gloom her bulk rises under the covers like a miniature killer whale. She doesn't roll over to greet us.

'Is that you Ella?' she whispers.

'Yes Mrs Keropoulos – I've brought the children back.'

'Already?' she groans.

'Actually I've been keeping them quite busy since breakfast.' I'm keen to get credit where it's due. 'I thought you needed the rest.'

'I still do,' she says.

'Mommy,' says Eenie, 'Mommy we were just *increbily* stupid . . .'

'*Increbily*,' echoes Mo.

'What's that sweetheart?' Mrs K. slowly rolls over.

'No, they've been fine,' I say loudly, 'absolute darlings – '

'*We* ran away,' says Eenie slowly.

'You did what?' Mrs K. heaves herself up on one elbow and sees Hen. 'Who is this?'

'A friend of mine – Henrietta.'

'Excuse me Ella,' says Mrs K., 'but this is neither the time nor the place for introductions – I'm sick, I'm not dressed and altogether I'm a little upset, you understand me? What's all this about the girls running away?'

'Normal high spirits Mrs Keropoulos,' says Hen, who can't be kept down, despite the lack of an introduction.

'You're telling me my daughters were *unsupervised* – '

'Hardly,' says Hen.

'Excuse me miss, but I'm talking to Ella here – *Ella*?'

My daydream of responsible motherhood (me in an apron as Mrs 1970 in the gas advertisements) is fast fading.

'Mo needed the – well, the *toy-toy*.' I hate having to say it in front of Hen.

'I thought I could trust you . . .'

'You can Mrs Keropoulos – you could – '

'No you can't,' interrupts Hen. 'Ella isn't here as your unpaid nanny – you'd better organize your own.' She is *so* rude. But it sort of works. Mrs K. sits further up and looks more alert, and as she does, Eenie flicks at the main light switch and we're suddenly all fully illuminated. Mrs K. blinks, looking as if she's shaking off a trance.

'Could you possibly take the girls up to the nursery for me – say I'll collect them just before lunch?'

Which is what we do. Trail back up to B Deck, by the stairs this time, and hand them over, though not before Hen's had a good look at the facilities. Big mistake as she reckons they don't come up to scratch.

'In Cabin Class,' she tells the girls, 'there's Snow White's house – a proper little house with a red-tiled roof and its own front door, and a pretend ship's bridge, with a real ship's wheel, so you can play at being the captain.'

'I want one,' says Eenie.

'I want one too,' says Mo.

'I dare say you do,' says Hen, and laughs. Perhaps she *is* a witch.

Once we've safely got rid of the children, we find ourselves a corner of the Promenade Deck. Stewards are serving bowls of bouillon and crackers from a trolley. Cunard is hell-bent on preserving us from mid-Atlantic starvation. It must be at least one whole hour since anybody here last finished stuffing their faces, and good golly Miss Molly it's another whole hour and a half before we're due to start in again at lunch. Makes you wonder what they're feeding us *for* – would peckish voyagers tend towards mutiny or something? I may scoff but I accept a bowl of broth anyway. Hen refuses, but lights up another cig. She's wearing sunglasses now – big tortoiseshell ones like Audrey Hepburn in *Charade* – leaning back in a steamer chair we hope won't be claimed by anybody else. I'm not even sure what ship's class I'm in any more, my resolution of remaining where I belong having already broken. Weak – that's me. I'm already regretting accepting the broth though. It feels old womanish next to Hen's streams of exhaled smoke and the way I can't see her eyes through the dark specs; much more mysterious than sipping soup.

'I've got a thought,' says Hen. 'Actually I've had it all morning – it's what I came to find you for.'

'Oh yes?' I say, wary now. Her thoughts haven't been that helpful so far.

'What's on your programme for tonight?'

'Apart from the cinema? Recorded music followed by bingo,' I say. 'What's on yours?'

'Not much more exciting – orchestral selections in the Main Lounge followed by the horseracing game and bingo. There's dancing later, of course, in the Verandah Grill – if you've booked – but I happen to know that Cabin's got something special going. It's the night for their gala dinner and then after that the fancy headdress competition and their ball. Full band – the works.'

'So?' I say.

'Obvious darling. Let's go. Chip's already asked us.'

'But it's in Cabin Class.'

'So what?'

'"Passengers are kindly requested to remain in the accommodation allotted to the class in which they are travelling", that's what.'

'Honestly Ella, I can't decide if you're a wet or a Nazi – '

'A *Nazi*?'

'It's this terrible tendency you have for obeying orders. Who cares what passengers are requested to do? It's hardly a hanging offence. We won't arrive till after the gala dinner, so we won't even be nicking their food. We'll simply be joining in the fun. They ought to be grateful to have us – we'll lend them some style.'

'Don't they have this sort of thing in First then?'

'Well yes, of course they do, but everyone's so *old* – I told you. I'm stuck up there on my ownsome. It's no fun dancing with all those old captains of industry, stinking of cigars and Brylcreem. I want to have some *fun*. And I thought we could ask Paul to join us.'

Oh. Not good. 'He won't want to,' I say quickly.

'How do you know?'

'Not his sort of thing at all – balls and stuff. You must be joking.'

'I think we can get him to unbend a little – and you would like him to come wouldn't you?'

'Me? Well yes, of course, but I don't think Paul . . .'

'Leave that bit to me,' says Hen.

'And anyway, what about the fancy dress?' I object. 'How can we manage that in the time?'

'It's only fancy *head*dress,' says Hen. 'Leave that bit to me too.'

11a.m. – Point Harbor

Despite her pregnant bulk, Lynn is tackling the garden. She's left Jack upstairs, still asleep. He didn't get in until the small hours again, and once more she doesn't know why. Maybe she'll ask him once he's up – or just as likely, maybe she won't. If she does, she knows already that he'll only wink and murmur soothing words. 'Business' is the usual, said with a twinkle, or a wink and a finger lightly held to his lips. Though what is the business that keeps such regularly irregular hours? What the eye doesn't see the heart doesn't grieve over – that's what she suspects. The thought gives her the briefest sinking sense of nausea. Better by far to concentrate on the moment – on now – on the garden.

The back of the property extends down to the shallow clear brook which little Leroy has had such a fine old time damming with stones and wood. There's a dense cluster of trees here and an old stone wall, now breached in places, sprouting leaves and fronds whose names she doesn't know. She doesn't know that much about gardening either, to tell the truth. She never had much of a chance back in Buckling, Montana. The winters there were so fierce they blasted every fancy plant to blackened shreds. The front yard of Jack's dream house is, thus far, a rough swathe of grass extending out to the road which leads eventually down to the bay. It's a salt-licked kind of an area, echoing the shoreline, and instinctively she feels that flowerbeds here will surely look out of place. She wants to wait a bit – or at least until she's learned more of this way of living, and found out what other people do.

The back though, with its slabbed stone terrace built out over the sloping lawn, already feels like a garden. There are old shrubs dotted about, part of some long-lost planting scheme. And rose bushes, and low dense green foliage which the snooty WASP woman, who'd had her in for coffee and Teddy Kennedy contributions, called 'pachysandra'. There's lots of that, and scattered all over, tucked below walls, peeping from under bushes, are brilliant orange bell-shaped flowers. 'Tiger lilies' Jack called them – and she'd called them that too, to the woman with the pachysandra. She'd felt quite proud and relieved to have a flower name like that, right on the tip of her tongue and all ready to go. 'Don't you mean day lilies?' the woman said. (Caroline her name is.

Time, Lynn tells herself, to start thinking of her as 'Caroline', okay?) 'Don't you mean day lilies? Hemerocallis? They're wild – *everywhere*,' she said in that hoity toity Brookline oh-so-WASP drawl. Lynn allowed herself a little 'awshucks' kind of a laugh – real light, to hide any sense of put-down – and said, 'Day lilies – *exactly.*'

So now she's digging them up – all those clumps of wonderful orange colour hidden in the rough scrub beyond the old wall, hauling them up the hill in a bucket and transplanting them amongst the roses where she can see them. She's read about them too by now and knows the bell-flowers only last the single day, though another bud is usually ready to burst on the morrow. Already she's growing to love them; likes the fragility of the idea of them – and with a scarcely conscious sense of fellow feeling, links their fate with her own.

It's hot work out here, hot and very peaceful: just the rushing crescendo of cricket song again, followed by bands of silence, and sometimes, in the distance, the puttering of motor boats out in the bay. She works steadily, surprised at her own energy. She's had so little energy lately, but suddenly she wants it all to be right, all to be perfect for this new child. On Monday perhaps she'll start decorating the baby's room, whatever Jack says. In fact she won't tell him. He'll only veto the plan, huff that no wife of his should have to wield a paint brush (or be seen to do so) – that if she'll only be a little more patient it'll all happen in plenty of time: the best of decorators will be called. Has he ever let her down yet? That's how he'd commandeered the room for the cuckoo – all ready now, all prepared. Still, Lynn thinks, with this new-found throb of energy, she'll do it without him. Something very primitive is urging her to stake out her baby's space – make a start, *now.*

Some time after noon Jack emerges. Not in his robe as she would have expected, but fully dressed in light weekend clothes – Madras shorts, white T-shirt, sneakers – and flapping a big book at her from up on the terrace. Then he's running towards her as she hauls yet another bucket of lilies up the slope. He doesn't stop to notice her garden – arrives breathless and brings her to a halt.

'The ships will cross,' he says. 'The two *Queens*. I had this feeling maybe they would. I just called Cunard in New York and they could confirm it – any time now – and probably close enough to see each other, just about here – the fiftieth parallel – *here*.' He's got his finger in the book and flips it open. It's a world atlas and the double-page spread he opens is of the Atlantic with a slice of the North American coast rimming the lefthand side and the outer edge of Ireland on the right. A big pool of pale blue in the middle represents the ocean. '*Here* . . .' he's stabbing at the page. 'You know that's virtually the only way the *Queen Mary* and the *Queen Elizabeth* ever get in sight of each other now – two great ships charging across the ocean in opposite directions, every week – really something huh?'

And he hasn't noticed my garden. What I've achieved. All the dancing day lilies, scattered round the terrace. He hasn't noticed at all.

'So what?' is what she says. Why does she say it? Watching his excitement deflate in front of her, she instantly regrets the words.

'So what?' he says. 'So it's amazing is what. There's a history here – something that matters. So *what*? Doesn't it rouse anything – your sense of curiosity, for crying out loud, your sense of *romance*?'

What would rouse my sense of romance is you, she thinks – your attention, Jack Feast. Your attention on me and our child. On our day lilies dancing. So *what*? But already he's clawing it back with 'Hey – hey – I'm sorry, but this is important to me. It's bringing it all back you know?'

Bringing what back?

The war – bringing that back. That vivid time, long before *her* time, with memories she can neither grasp nor share.

145

He's taking the bucket from her, and pulling her down on to the grass, flinging the book to one side.

'It was the *Queen Mary* I took – you know that – I told you that.'

But no he hadn't – not really. His war has blurred in her mind into a shapeless tale she hasn't wanted to absorb. Another world excluding her. Europe, adventure – the biggest adventure of the century – and the other wife. It's all too threatening.

'We were crammed in.' He's flung himself back on the grass and is looking straight up at the sky with his arm resting on his forehead. 'They took upwards of fifteen, sixteen thousand of us at a shot, and the ship was only made for two thousand passengers. We had these bunks fitted all over the place – metal, like kind of racks on their side, three berths to each stand. In the daytime you could fold them up. Everywhere they put them: saloons, lounges, companionways, even the empty swimming pools – wherever. You got three days to sleep indoors and two on deck – you had to keep moving. They could only serve two meals a day – two thousand of us at each sitting. As you left the dining room they'd give you a pack of sandwiches to last through to the next meal. And they had a traffic system – kept us going in the same direction round the ship – you couldn't have people going every which way, we'd have had a total log jam – and then if we'd all tried to move in the same direction at the same time we might have destabilized the ship – can you imagine? That's how many we were. Once you got going after breakfast, you just kept going all the way port to starboard – and eventually you made it back for dinner. There were guys whose entire war was spent making those sandwiches, can you believe it? Back and forth across the Atlantic making goddam sandwiches – and it wasn't as if they weren't in danger the whole time because they were. The Atlantic was full of U-boats just waiting, full of torpedoes, just waiting to take a pot shot – and the *Queens* were too fast for a regular convoy so they did it all alone – zigzagging, running and hiding – back and forth. Hitler put a price on them – a hundred thousand dollars – but no one ever claimed it. Uncle Sam took them over from the Limeys – Churchill offered them to Roosevelt rent-free. Well, what else were they going to do with them? Over a million of us on the *Queens* – pretty good huh? Somewhere on one of those decks I carved my name – Jack Feast was here – and someday I swore I'd go back and find it, find my name and drink a toast to myself that I'm *still* here – because then you know, we *didn't* know. Who only knew what we were headed into? For most of us it was our first time overseas – and a hell of a lot of those guys never made it back. So there – that's so *what* – you understand?'

'Have you written Ella about that?' Lynn asks.

'About what?'

'Your name – carved on the deck – she could have looked for it.'

'It was a different ship, I told you – you didn't get that? – it was the *Queen Mary*. The one I was on was the *Mary* – so was Kitty when she first came over, after the war – that was the *Mary* too, with all the other new brides. The *Elizabeth* is what she took when she left for that last time. They're sisters these ships – they *both* did it – didn't you get that?'

Yes she got that, but she's uncomfortable. All this talk of shared times past, before her time – it shuts her out.

But 'Yes' she says. 'Unbelievable.' She, the soother of egos; so that's what she says for now, in the heat of this Saturday afternoon, when there's only peace and the crickets and the day lilies dancing.

2p.m. – RMS Queen Elizabeth

It's towards the end of lunch that the buzz gets around. The *Queen Mary*'s on the horizon. We're going to pass each other – and even better than that, *see* each other passing each other – not all that common an event, according to Sydney Maxton-Bligh, because even though the *Queens* mostly run a regular service, going east and west each week, they're often too far apart in mid-Atlantic for this – the curve of the earth hides them from each other.

The Wagenburgs are thrilled – they didn't get to see the *Queen Mary* on their trip over – and I'm pretty interested too, so we abandon our puddings. Madge of course doesn't have a pudding to abandon, only what she calls a 'demi-tasse' of black coffee, but she comes with us too. We leave Sydney M-B to his jam roly-poly and custard and make a dash for the bows, starboard side.

The *Queen Mary* is already well in sight – not a distant speck on the horizon, but moving towards us briskly. 'Something like seventy miles per hour joint speed,' says Ken, and suddenly I have a sense of how fast we're going. It's happening all the time, only you don't actually feel it all that much when you've only got the passing sea to judge it by. She's such a familiar sight, with her three red and black funnels, that you'd almost think she was a model of the real thing, like all those toys down in the shop – except then you do a double take, and see all these little people on board, waving and jigging about, and you realize that's what you look like too, to them. So we all start waving back like crazy, and everyone's taking photographs or staring through binoculars.

Amazingly quickly we're abreast of each other and probably a few hundred yards apart, maybe less – and then behind her is this wake – a great wide pathway of white foam extending all the way back towards the horizon. It's like a gift she's left us, and I find that comforting. She's just come from New York and she's left us this marker line, right across the ocean, leading straight back to our destination – and we must've done the same thing for her, only up till now I've never hung around the stern of the *Queen Elizabeth*, so I haven't noticed our wake. It's good to have this sense of a contact being made because otherwise the ocean is so strange. It's so open it could be going anywhere – I mean we could – except, of course, we all take it on trust that we're heading where we ought to. I say this to Madge and she says, 'Honey, you'd just better believe it – some things in life you have a right to leave to the experts.'

The other odd thing though, is that the Queen Mary doesn't look that huge – not with all the great expanse of sea around her – and again I realize that that means we don't look that huge either. It brings it home – just how vast the ocean is and how utterly insignificant we are in comparison. Maybe that's why they need to keep us so well fed – to stop us thinking about things. Because it could get to you, this realization of being all alone in the great sea, even if you are on 83,000 tons of steel. How did the early settlers do it – how did Christopher Columbus? Were they brave – or foolhardy? In those tiny little boats they must have bounced around like little rubber balls, and at the beginning they didn't even know what they'd find at the other end. And at the very beginning some of them must have thought they were going to fall off the edge.

I leave the Wagenburgs and Madge, and start to run back towards the stern, so that I can see the Queen Mary disappearing. And now she's following our wake – all the way back to the Ocean Terminal at Southampton, two whole days away.

I run right the way along the Promenade Deck, ignoring any First and Cabin Class signs, hopping over any locked gates, not caring any more. It's not that I don't think I might get caught – I just think we've all got a right to see what's going on, and if it means breaking out of our ranks, well, too bad. Anyway, maybe Hen's right and my sense of obedience is far too developed. Time to kick over some traces, or whatever you do.

There's open deck at the very end, and right away I spot Paul – so someone else is class-jumping too. He's got a pair of binoculars trained on the Queen Mary. The whole thing has happened so fast that in the time it's taken me to get here, along the whole length of the Queen Elizabeth, the Queen Mary already looks like a blob in the distance – but there, sure enough, is our wake, frothed up like beer foam and stretching back into mist on the horizon.

I sidle up beside Paul but don't think I'd better interrupt him. Eventually he brings the binoculars down and that's when he notices me.

'Hello there Ella . . .' He sounds surprised, but he also sounds pleased. Even in three words you can tell. 'Did you see her then – the *Mary*?' he asks.

'Yes.'

'Something special about that don't you think,' he says, 'when you remember their history, when you think of everything they saw together all through the war – fantastic – and now here they are, travelling to and fro, carrying all us lot: boring old passengers – spoilt, overfed – don't know our arses from our elbows.'

'Tell me more about the history,' I say, wanting him to go on talking in his true Liverpudlian Beatle voice which makes my knee joints feel wobbly. 'You started to tell me – that Cunard wanted to run just the two ships instead of three . . .'

'Yeah – that's how it started – with the *Mary*. To do it, they had to have bigger ships than anything there'd ever been before.'

'What about the *Titanic*?'

'Much bigger than the *Titanic* – she was maybe a hundred feet shorter and about half the weight. These new ships had to be really gigantic if they were going to keep up with the need for mail, passengers, cargo, the lot – a complete transatlantic ferry service – there'd always be a ship leaving at either end each week. I think I told you they started to build the *Mary* back in the twenties, but then the Depression began and they couldn't finish her and she became this symbol hanging over Glasgow – this terrible feeling that there'd never be any work again. That's what my granddad said it was like. Isn't that a thought – my very own granddad was responsible for stitching bits of that ship together – the one that's just passed me by, right in the middle of the bloody Atlantic. I bet he never thought his own grandson would be making this journey, did he? No wonder it's got to me. It really has . . .' He sniffs and rubs the corner of his eye with the edge of the binoculars. 'The wind's making me teary,' he says, but I don't think it's that. 'Anyway,' he goes on, looking back at the wake again and sounding much brisker, 'eventually they finished her – and then there's a funny story – but they reckon it's true. That Cunard wanted to call her the "Queen Victoria" because their ships almost always ended their names with an "a" – like if you think of it, there was the *Mauretania*, *Lusitania*, *Berengaria* and so on. So Sir Something or Other Cunard, some Bigwig anyway, goes to Buckingham Palace to see King George – the Fifth, that is – and says, "Sire we'd be honoured if we could call the new ship after England's greatest Queen." Only King George says something like, "Excellent idea, I'll go and ask her now." So he rushes off to tell Queen Mary – his wife – and that's how they got saddled with it – the name. Funny i'n't it?'

'So what about the *Queen Elizabeth*?' I ask.

'Well, they started her shortly after they launched the *Queen Mary* – 1936 maybe? – well before there was any inkling of a war. The *Mary* was the biggest ship in the world up till then, but they decided to make the next one even bigger – longer. She's longer by about twelve feet.'

'And they didn't get to call her Queen Victoria either.'

'What? No – they named her after the present Queen Mum. She and King George the Sixth were fantastically popular after there was all that business with Edward the Eighth and the Abdication – but like you know all that.'

'Not really,' I say.

'I've got a book on them – on the ships – it's in my cabin. I'll lend it to you if you like.'

'Thanks,' I say, glowing. I must be making strides I reckon if he's going to start lending me his books.

'Do you want to come and get it now?' he says.

He's *asking* me to his cabin. I have to steady myself not to

151

sound too keen – except then I remember I was supposed to be with Hen half an hour ago, only all this *Queen Mary* spotting has thrown my timetable out.

'Could I come a bit later?' I say. 'Only I've got to see Hen – we're making hats for the fancy dress tonight.'

'So you're doing that too are you? She's roped me in. Dragged me in more like.' Ah. Good old Hen. I try not to look in the least pleased.

'Yeah?' I say, sounding really offhand. 'Great,' I add, but I don't put a lot of effort into it. It's a limp sort of 'great' – as limp as I can make it.

'What are you going as?' he asks. He's grinning now.

'Don't know – that's what I've got to work out with Hen. What about you?' – because to tell the truth I'm really staggered that he's going at all.

'I'm leaving all that up to *Henrietta*.' That's how he says it, in a slightly sneery kind of way, as if he's taking the mickey out of her. Not out of me, I notice. Which is pleasing.

'I wouldn't have thought it was your sort of thing,' I say, because suddenly I'm feeling we're on the same side of the fence – and Hen's on the other, on her own.

'It's not,' he says. 'Not one bloody bit – but she's twisted me arm, promised me non-stop booze – and all free.'

'Right,' I say. So that's how it's done.

'I'm going as the Queen of Hearts,' says Hen. 'I usually do. I've already got one of the stewards in Main Lounge to bag me some jam tarts this afternoon – strawberry probably – got to be red. Obviously.'

'What are you going to do with them?' I ask.

'Stick them round the brim of course – mostly UHU and trusting to gravity. As long as you don't shake your head around too much it works fine. And what are we going to do for you? With you? Who do you want to be?'

I, of course, have no idea. It's not the sort of thing I've ever gone in for. Charades and dressing up things don't happen in my life all that much. We're in Hen's stateroom kneeling in front of her trunk. It's a real cabin trunk, lined with grey silky material. To open it you stand it up on end. On one side is a hanging rail which slides in and out, now empty, because most of her suits and dresses are in the proper wardrobe, but the other is fitted with wooden drawers, all lined in the same grey silk and crammed with wonderful bits and pieces. One drawer is just for scarves and gloves, another for jewellery. There's a pink ostrich feather boa from Fenwicks, and a Jean Varon bolero made entirely of white silk daisies. I remember it from *Vogue* in the spring. I'd loved the photograph of it – I think it was Jean Shrimpton floating around Versailles. Beautiful. And now here I am holding the real, actual thing. Not even a copy from Richards. Amazing. I'd love to wear it – just once.

'Well – what do you reckon?' says Hen.

'Does it have to be nursery rhymes?' I ask.

'Of course not. Better not really. I only do the Queen of Hearts because it's easy and I like wearing red. You can do anything, it just has to be familiar – song titles are quite good. Mummy usually does "Around the World in Eighty Days" because she can stick a map on to an inflatable beach ball and it packs flat – though it gets terribly tatty from voyage to voyage so she has to revamp it each time.'

I sit back on my heels still holding the daisy bolero, trying to think of a title which could provide an excuse for me to wear it, even for one evening.

'How's about "Daisy, Daisy"?' I say, suddenly inspired.

'What?'

'"Give me your answer do" – that Daisy. Then I could wear this?'

Hen takes the bolero out of my hands, instantly proprietorial.

'It's not fancy dress you realize. It's fancy *head*dress. I don't see how this could help you – '

'If I made a daisy bonnet – I could use paper for the petals, stick them on some ribbon and make it go right round my face like – ' I'm casting about for additional inspiration, 'like the rays on a sun, the way a child would draw it – except I suppose it really needs a yellow middle – and that's where my face would be. I don't want to paint my face yellow . . .'

'You can have a yellow paper mask,' says Hen. 'I was going to suggest masks anyway. That way they won't know who we are, in case anyone gets tricky about us being in the wrong classes again.'

'I thought you said we'd be Chip's guests?'

'We are – we will be – it's just sort of stretching it a bit.'

'Stretching what?'

'Don't nit-pick Ella. It'll just make things much easier if we aren't instantly identifiable – and don't start getting Nazi on me again – if you don't want to come, then don't. I'll have all the fun to myself.'

'No,' I say, 'I just like to get things clear.'

'Exactly. Nazi.' Hen slips the bolero on over her red crêpe. 'I got this for the end of term ball – we always share it with the boys from Henham College. It's got a floaty voile dress that goes with it – pale peach, Empire line, but I left it at home.'

'I could wear it over my green linen . . .' I say. The green linen is my only full length dress, a sale bargain from Trotters of Tooting.

'Green?'

'Perfect,' I say, now truly inspired and running with it. 'Like a stem – the stem of the daisy with my daisy face-hat on top.'

'I don't know you're exactly the shape of a stem Ella – *particularly* on top . . .' and she's looking hard at my June-is-busting-out-all-over bosoms again.

'That's where the bolero would help,' I say, and that seems to clinch it. She slips it off and hands it over.

'A Daisy,' she says. 'I suppose it'll just about do, though you have to think how you'll look with Chip – I don't know what he's going as yet.'

'Chip?'

'As your partner.'

'I didn't know he was going to be my actual partner. I thought we were just going as a group.' I did too. I've been nurturing the idea of Paul again since our talk.

'No,' says Hen, 'you'll be with Chip. He's invited you after all – it's his idea.'

'But Paul thinks – ' I start, only Hen jumps in sounding impatient.

'The point is, Ella, that Paul's tall. That's the point. And I'm tall too. You do see don't you?' Impatient and sharp. 'It's so much easier for you – being short. You've no idea what a bore it is being tall. There's nothing more depressing than dancing the night away with someone who comes up to your waist.'

'Right,' I say. It's called seeing the writing on the wall isn't it? She's making the position perfectly clear and I don't like it. Not that I have anything against Chip. But *I* found Paul first. Bagsie. That's what I want to say – childish, I know, so I don't.

'Anyway,' Hen goes on, clearly thinking it's all settled, 'what shall we organize for Paul? He hasn't got a dinner jacket, so whatever we do will have to work with a black polo neck and black jeans.'

'What's he said?'

'Nothing – not much – he did suggest "The House of the Rising Sun" but I don't want to spend the night dancing with a man with a cardboard brothel on his head.'

'What about "My Old Man's a Dustman"?' I say and hit home.

'Inaccurate,' says Hen briskly. 'He's a docker, I think – something like that anyway – or was. Anyway, I was thinking more on the lines of Elvis. You can do a lot with Elvis titles.'

' " Jailhouse Rock?"' I say.

'"Wooden Heart" – that'd be easy – but with me as the Queen, perhaps too many hearts? What do you think?'

'"Devil in Disguise"?' I suggest, intending to be flip.

'Perfect,' says Hen. 'Spot on Ella. We'll do it all in black – mask, horns, we'll even do a tail. I can stuff a stocking.'

'What's the disguise?'

'*He'll* be – that's the beauty – he'll be in disguise and no one will know – the Tourist Transplant – '

'No one will get it then – the judges – no prizes – are there prizes Hen?'

'God Ella, grow up. This is a *night* – a night for us. The point's *not* prizes.'

And of course she's right – it's not. Only what the point actually *is* makes me feel odd, and something inside me registers that peculiar sort of tweak again. Very peculiar – and quite exciting.

7p.m. – London

Kitty alone. Lies stretched out on the unfolded put-u-up – her bed. She hadn't bothered to return it to its sofa-shape this morning. There hadn't seemed much point. Already, with Ella gone, she's letting her standards slip. That didn't take long. Normally she's a bit of a stickler – feels she has to be. Living in such a severely limited space – the two of them – she's always felt she had to maintain order for Ella's sake: even attempt somehow to infuse their lives with a certain sense of style. Have a stab at it anyway. Hence the books, the Braque reproductions, the bits of old pottery gleaned from junk shops, the bedspreads of handwoven linen –

things to add colour and texture, to lift their spirits from the plastic norm. Nothing from Croxton Fine Art though – nothing wildlife nor dead.

Usually she'd have folded up the bed before breakfast, and tucked one of the handwoven spreads around it, to cover the unpleasant maroon fabric underneath. Tossed some cushions on top for added colour and comfort. The whole thing would have metamorphosed into that altogether more salubrious item – the studio couch. Much better.

This morning though, she'd come back inside after phoning the Marie Stopes Clinic, stripped off to her underwear, and then spent much of the day just lying here by the open window. It's a raw hot day for London. Almost feels Saharan she thinks – or rather, as she'd imagine Saharan to be. Not like the dense humidity of New England heat. This is dry, dusty – she can almost feel grit on her teeth. Outside, the view across the back is of the tiny yards and gardens of Bissett Street, bounded by a row of corrugated iron garages. The sounds are of traffic, trains, the squeal of children – someone's got a hose pipe out there, a paddling pool maybe – dogs bark. Not much of a place perhaps. How Jack would scorn it if he knew – how he'd mock her modest attempts. She can hear the acid in his voice coming at her through the years. Aspirations? Call this dump an *aspiration* – is she out of her mind? Well, too bad Jack – you forfeited the right to an opinion didn't you? – and modest though this is, at least it *is* here in its solid rent-paid bricks and mortar, and not floating on some fluffy cloud of dreams.

Only, maybe things have changed now? Could they have, truly, in reality, rather than in Jack's heavily coloured imagination? This new address sounds real enough – the one that first came to them with last year's Christmas card: 'Bay Lane, Point Harbor, Mass.' – not even a street number, just PO Box 770.

'Settled at last!!!' was the first part of the message after the printed 'Happy Holidays' – the exclamation marks added in festive red ink, and not in Jack's handwriting. Though it was definitely his at the bottom, a scribbled note in ballpoint: 'This place is beautiful – Ella, you'll love it and you'll love Lynn too – how about you think of coming to spend the summer with us? Keep your fingers crossed and we shall see what we shall see . . . love Dad.' Well that much hadn't changed – an offer made, but always, in almost the same breath, half withdrawn and hedged about with provisos. All the more extraordinary that this time it's come off, with Ella right now on her way, somewhere in the middle of the ocean – and doing what? Tasting the flavour of a whole new life, probably changing already? It doesn't take long at that age, when minds are susceptible, pliant as new putty. It's something which has niggled at Kitty ever since Jack at last finalized the plans, and his long-promised mythical Cunard ticket became a reality when it arrived in the post. Ever since she'd known the trip was on for sure, a sneaking fear had started – that Ella will be changed irrevocably by this summer, that she'll come back in September and find everything wanting – their lives together dwindled, diminished.

Except, supposing it's a whole new life for her too? Stupid fool to let the imagination rip like this – but hard then not to be a stupid fool. That taste of coupledom last night, however brief, has taken hold and already she's weaving herself a fairy tale. And why not? – alone here, stretched out, near naked, her skin slightly damp with sweat, one hand flung back, covering her eyes against the light, the other resting on her breast bone. Her skin's not bad is it? She tries an exploratory stroke, silky surely, or silky enough. She'll pass muster won't she? – when she has to – when they – if they – come together. She and Gilbert Denby in the flat near Victoria.

The woman on the phone at the Marie Stopes Clinic had been efficient – sounded matter of fact, quite kind. They could fit her in on Monday morning, 9.15 – with luck she'll only be a little late for work and Mrs Croxton's curiosity will not be too aroused.

There's rapping on the door. But no one ever calls. She sits up, embarrassed. Early evening and here she is in her underwear.

'Who is it?' she calls.

'Mrs Feast – it's me.' Mr Christo.

'Just a sec.' She rolls off the bed, scrabbling to pull her dress over her head, poking her feet into sandals. No time to fold up the bed – hurriedly she smooths out the spread, then opens the door on to the landing with caution to hide the mess behind.

Mr Christo is smiling, half-laughing, looking as embarrassed as she feels. They don't usually invade each other's territory, an unspoken rule of living in such proximity.

'Mrs Feast I come with invitation – Mrs Christo say you come to supper – I tell you yes? She make her kleftiko – she make her souvlaki too. You come?'

'When?'

'Tomorrow night.'

'Oh – well . . . ' Instantly she's searching around for a way out, but no excuse comes fast enough to her aid.

'You cannot?' He looks deflated. 'You going out?' But no she's not going out, and she doesn't want to have to pretend to go out either, to bang down the stairs past the Christos' flat, heading to some imaginary assignation. And anyway, why not accept?

'It's very kind of you – ' she says, and instantly his smile glows again, 'if you're sure it's not too much trouble . . .'

'You'll like,' he says, kissing at his fingers, 'real Greek food – ambrosia for the Gods – you'll like.'

5p.m. – RMS Queen Elizabeth

I go back to D9 to make my hat. I wasn't going to at first. I started it in Hen's stateroom. She gave me a length of white silk ribbon and I was cutting long oval petals out of the *Queen Elizabeth* envelopes on her writing desk. Only they were too floppy. And all the time I was trying to do it, and concentrate on my effort, she was calling me over to come and admire hers. Most of it she had ready-made in her luggage – bit of a cheat I think. She's got a heart shape covered in red silk which goes round her face like a frame, and then across it is a red silk mask – just enough to cover her eyes and the top of her cheeks – 'a domino' she calls it. Then on top of that is a crown covered in gold foil with a ledge running right the way round where the fur would usually go, and that's where she's stuck all these real jam tarts she's got from the steward. She's going to look great.

She finished hers in no time – what with having most of it done anyway – and then she got started on Paul's. I'd have liked to do Paul's too, but I couldn't really – not with not having done my own yet. So that's when I decided to go back to D9 – partly because I was getting sick of her going on about Paul and what she was up to, as if she owned him or something, and partly because I could see the paper petals weren't going to work – and then I remembered Mo and Eenie's Playsack, which is full of useful things like paints and glue. Perhaps they have some cardboard too.

When I get there, I find Mrs K. back in her bunk, nursing her stomach cramps again. The girls have built another toytown across the floor and up on to Mo's bunk. Mo beams at me as I stick my head round the door. I try not to let my own smile slip too far as I realize I'm going to have to retreat back up to my bunk again if I'm to get anything done.

'Hi Ella – we're playing Snow White and the Seven Dwarves.'

'Are you? Who's the Wicked Stepmother?'

'Your lady,' says Eenie.

'My lady?' I'm puzzled.

'The witch lady.' Ah, Hen again. She's haunting all of us.

'Could you let me borrow your paints maybe?' I ask. 'Just for a little while? Only I'm going to a very special party and I've got to make a very special hat.'

'We're going to a party too,' says Eenie. 'We're going to the children's party tomorrow – '

'Where we get the special pins like a boat,' says Mo.

'Well, isn't that wonderful,' I say, buttering up like mad. 'So you wouldn't mind if I used some of your paint for my party would you?'

Mrs K. has been lying on her bunk facing the wall up until now, and we've all been communicating in loud whispers. Now she slowly turns over and eyes me.

'Are you going to be here for a bit Ella?'

'A *little* bit,' I say, warily.

'Only I could maybe get an appointment at the beauty parlour – get myself a wash and set.'

'Well . . .' I want to demur, but she's already ahead of me, and swinging her legs off the bunk.

'If you want to be using our paints and stuff . . .' she says.

So of course I see the way of it. Babysitting for services rendered.

'You wouldn't have any cardboard would you?' I ask – worth a try.

'No – we got paper though,' she says, already putting on her lipstick and reaching for the door. Only, once she's gone, I see the empty Kotex box in the rubbish bin. It's made of stiff card; not exactly what you'd call the height of millinery chic, but needs must and all that. At least with Mrs K. out of the way, I can sit on her bunk. I open up both of the ventilators and get as much air circulating as possible, while I cut out petals from the Kotex box and paint them all white.

'Are you going to be a pwincess?' asks Mo.

'No – a daisy,' I say.

'Whassa daisy?' asks Mo.

'You know a daisy,' says Eenie. 'A daisy's a *daisy*.'

'Whassa daisy?'

'Mo doesn't know whassa daisy . . .' Eenie sing-songs with satisfaction. Sometimes I'm really pleased I'm an only child.

'A daisy's a type of flower,' I tell Mo.

'How can you be a flower, Ella?' asks Mo, her eyes getting bigger by the second.

'You should be a pwincess,' says Eenie. 'Pwincesses get *all* the pwetty clothes.'

'I've got pretty clothes too,' I say, and show them the silk bolero while my petals are drying.

Later, when they've returned from first sitting dinner, along with a crisply washed and set Mrs K., I model the completed outfit for them just before they get ready for bed. It's not bad, though I say so myself. I've got the green linen long dress which is dead straight, then the daisy bolero on top, then the yellow paper mask I've made from Eenie and Mo's drawing paper, with the shoelaces from my plimsolls tying it on at the back and hidden in my hair. And then the daisy circle of petals all round my face, down to my chin.

Mo and Eenie look gratifyingly awestruck by this vision and I'm just about to glow when Mrs K. says, 'With that thing on your head you could double for the Statue of Liberty – you should paint it all green and hold yourself a flashlight in one hand . . .'

'It's supposed to be a daisy,' I say.

'Whassa daisy?' says Mo, staring up at me from her bunk, as I try to twirl amongst the pieces of scattered toytown on the floor.

'*I'm* a daisy,' I say firmly.

'Nah,' says Mrs K. 'Paint it green – Statue of Liberty – no contest.'

6p.m. – Point Harbor

Martini time at the yacht club and the locals are a-gathering. Yacht Club? A fancy way to describe this bunch of clapboard shacks grouped along a wooden dock on stilts. Pushing it a tad,

Lynn thinks. Still, that's what they call it – these locals whose families have been vacationing round here for generations. The *real* locals – the full-time residents who've hunkered down day in, day out through winters without number – are known to think it all pretty funny. The 'Yacht Club' huh! The fishermen are particularly sharp – la-di-bloody-da, they laugh. These city guys with their motor cruisers and squeaky-clean sail boats decked out in shiny brass, not to mention those peaked caps some of the men favour, with PHYC thickly embroidered in gold thread – just who do these incomers think they are?

Sadie Dorling keeps Lynn informed – passes on the gossip from the downtown Five & Ten and Pinker's Hardware, where they really know how to dish the dirt. It's a conspiracy of information which cheers Lynn up no end. Nice to know, when you're feeling a little put down by the Carolines with their Kennedy connections and goddam pachysandra, that the true inheritors of Point Harbor have a secret snigger at their expense. The only awkward thing is, she can't share this information with Jack – or not in a way which would put them in comforting league with each other against the rest of this new world, because Jack seems bent on throwing himself right into it and taking her along with him. No room for mockery then, however gently done.

The man who carried her away from Montana seemed a maverick: a wizard with his own separate path of a life – not clearly laid out, but spontaneous, even erratic. Someone who teased her out of her conformity and set her senses flying in new directions. Why else would she have jumped in his car that day, without even packing an overnight bag? She didn't even call her mom until they were already married by the Perry-Como-look-alike minister in the Silver Bells Wedding Chapel. Even then she didn't call right away. She left it a full couple of days because they'd gone directly from the chapel to the bridal suite and made love practically non-stop in that heart-shaped satin bed. They'd had so much sex she couldn't even walk straight for the rest of the week. Try telling that to your mother long distance, when only ten days ago you'd been taking orders for tuna melts and scrubbing out the men's room.

But it wasn't sex that Jack had snared her with – she didn't even sleep with him until they'd hit the road. The process of enchantment – because that's how it feels to her now, little more than a couple of years later, enchantment like what happens in old time fairy stories – that all started with his eyes and his attitude: the way he laughed at the whole rest of the world; the way he seemed so totally free of all the usual constraints of expected behaviour. Those first months had a crazy energy like nothing she'd ever experienced before. Her life until then had always had a steady sense of itself – steady and deadly dull. Every morning you could pretty well guess the outcome of the day. Whereas life with Jack was an ongoing whirl. A new town, a new hotel (rapidly down-grading to a new *mo*tel) – the endless open roads – mountains and deserts – the fun of his quest for the Great American Original.

But somewhere along the line the Quest died. It was a subtle process, so subtle she doesn't think either of them truly noticed until it was too late. A sell-out really. It started on a trip back to the guest suite at Salvatore and Bea's house. Maybe the contrast was too much to take; that steady enclosing of luxury, compared to their life on the road. Not that she'd ever complained, why would she – she liked it. But something wriggled its way into Jack's soul so that on that very last trip he was ready to be corrupted by Sally's offer.

Festini Foods, the family business Jack had been fleeing since childhood, had a new project – ice cream. Not just any old ice cream – Italian ice cream. If you're Italian you should exploit it, reasoned Sally, and they'd only *half*-exploited it with spaghetti sauce. Ice cream was a gap just waiting to be filled – and this was going to be special ice cream too – real fruit. They'd even got the ad campaign roughed out – 'Festini's Fruits – Flavoriciously

Good'. Not that Sally had thought it through all that carefully – if he had, maybe he would never have dropped it so opportunely into little brother Giacomo's lap.

It was getting the factory that got the ball rolling, and that arrived as an unforeseen bonus, courtesy of a near-bankrupt customer, as payment in kind. Here was a lease, albeit a short one, on a shabby little outfit on the New Hampshire / Massachusetts border. It was ready-fitted with plant – not exactly the most up-to-date, but serviceable for immediate needs – for mixing, freezing and packing. There was even an ongoing arrangement with two farmers' co-ops for milk. What they didn't have was any sort of overseer for the project – not yet. Sally was about to start hiring. What kind of madness allowed him to offer this new baby to his brother? But then maybe it wasn't exactly offered – surely Sally would've been too certain of rejection from all the previous years of sibling irritation to allow himself to make any sort of offer? Maybe Jack proposed himself – that's what Lynn's beginning to think, though he's never admitted it to her. Maybe his disillusionment with the Quest had already set in, because suddenly he was talking about the Great American Ice Cream instead. Americans love ice cream. Americans *are* ice cream, is what he said. It needn't be Italian ice cream – that's just Sally's idea and he's got it wrong. Jack'll make him see sense, given time, for the real clue is the all-*Americanness* of ice cream. These are details he can fix later, once he's gotten things moving.

There must have been an uncomfortable few days when he felt the prison gates of family closing in, but a look at the map was pretty reassuring. The new factory was sufficiently far from Festini Foods' main base near Sproughton, NY to allow him his independence, and there was beautiful country round there with the ocean close by. They could settle – at last they could settle – wouldn't that be wonderful? And then Sally made it all seem like a done deal by offering the irresistible prize of the family mortgage, interest-free (for the moment) – enough to allow the purchase of a house somewhere near the factory. Though surely Sally can't have meant a house as elaborate as the one at Point Harbor, could he? Surely he'd meant a regular kind of house – a split-ranch maybe on some quiet development near Methuen. Well, if he did he should have known better. No way was Jack going to sacrifice the Quest for anything less than at least a portion of his dream – and Point Harbor Yacht Club already seems to fit the bill.

It's dry Martinis all round. Jack's nearly finished his third, Lynn's just toying with her first. Full-blown liquor hasn't agreed with her since she's gotten pregnant, but it seems kind of wet-blankety not to have at least one. She sucks on her olive though, and sits perched on a bar stool while Jack holds court. That's a funny thing about Jack – they've only been here just under a year, and already he seems to be King of the Castle. The women love him – he's flattering, considerate, funny – but then the men seem to go for him too. He's too insubstantial to pose a threat perhaps – you can't hate a leprechaun can you, it'd be bad luck. Not that he's Irish, they puzzle – seems to be maybe Anglo-Scottish with a name like that. And then he's so sweet with his pregnant wife – and she's just a girl really, real hick from out west, doesn't know anything from anything. And isn't there something a little intriguing about this new couple – she so young, he not so young, seen service overseas, hint of World War II hero maybe? He's regaling them all now, over a fourth Martini, with this story of his daughter coming over from England on the *Queen Elizabeth*, and hasn't everyone here taken one of those ships at some time? For those graduation trips to Europe, or honeymoons or business? There's a real sense of fellow feeling here – the guy's one of us even though he's a stranger. With this pretty young wife, and an ex-wife from England. Plays the coolest hand of poker too; frozen eyeballs at the table, spices things up around here. Everybody have a ball – the old time bluffers bluffed.

'We'll be having a party some time soon,' he's saying now, 'for

Ella – my daughter – something outdoors maybe – big barbecue – *big*.'

This is news to Lynn. So it's a party for the cuckoo now – and yet thus far they haven't even managed to get a few people round for drinks. The house isn't ready, Jack's insisted – wait until it's just right.

'Your boys'll all be invited,' Jack's saying, expansively, his gestures enlarged by booze, 'so's I can have my first turn at playing the heavy father – it'll be kind of a novelty won't it? You guys who've seen your kids grow up – you don't know how I envy you – '

'With teenagers? Today? You've got to be kidding,' says Blake Mulherne, the man who owns the beachfront property, a Point Harbor summer regular and rich with it. 'She's cute – this daughter?'

'Ella? Cute as hell,' says Jack, from the hazy uncertainty of those few smudged photos.

'Then they'll be there,' laughs Blake. 'Try keeping them away.'

10p.m. – *RMS* Queen Elizabeth

We dress for the party in Hen's stateroom. Her idea. Chip is to join us later after his Gala Dinner. Hen says it'll look suspicious if we try wandering round the ship from class to class in fancy dress. 'Can't be caught in full fig' is how she puts it. I lead Paul up to her bit of A Deck, feeling like an old hand, slightly superior that I know how to wriggle my way into First Class, striding past all the stewards and taking no notice. That's the only way to do it, Hen says. Just look as if you belong and everyone will think you do. That's what I tell Paul too. I also tell him it's 'stateroom', not 'cabin', and he says, 'I don't give a monkey's arse,' which makes me feel a twit.

I've got the whole of my outfit in a carrier bag, but Paul's already wearing the black jeans and polo neck bits of his, which is what nearly gets us into trouble because every other man in sight is in a dinner jacket. A couple of stewards do stop us en route, in mid-stride, and ask suspiciously if 'sir' needs any help, but Paul answers in his best Liverpudlian, 'We're all right thanks mate,' – and you can see they're just flabbergasted. You can tell they're thinking about stopping him, but then they're trying to work out who he is – if not a Beatle, then someone special – and by that time we've moved on.

Hen's put together the whole of Paul's headdress 'sight unseen' as she calls it. It's all made out of her black gym tights.

'Washed, I hope,' says Paul, and he's laughing. To be honest, this makes me feel a bit funny, as in supposing they're *un*washed – it's a bit peculiar isn't it – the thought – disgusting but also a bit animal? There's a sort of Balaclava helmet thing which he pulls over his head, and it's got two black curvy horns sticking up. She's made them out of one of the legs of her tights and stuffed them with cotton wool. Then there's the tail she's made out of the other leg, stuffed with ordinary nylons – 'American Tan,' she says, '*fully*-fashioned', which makes Paul laugh even more. She tucks it into the back of his jeans and curves it up so the end, which has a black cardboard arrow sewn on to it, hangs around his neck. I feel a bit torn. The truth is, if I'm going to be honest here, that it's really good. Very good. She's made a mask too – another one of those 'dominoes', out of double thickness black tights material, tied across his eyes. She forgets it at first, so he has to pull the helmet off – and when he does he sort of mouths a kiss at her. She's got a bottle of vodka on her desk and they're taking swigs. I have a swig too but it's horrible. No real taste, just hot.

Once he's got the full outfit on, Paul starts modelling. 'Get me!' he says, mincing round the beds on his toes. He's much more uninhibited than I'd have thought – maybe the vodka has something to do with it. He's swinging the tail round his head but then it comes unstuck from his jeans and Hen has to tuck it in again. She seems to spend an awfully long time round the back of him, poking and prodding around, and Paul's rolling his eyes all the while and making a growling noise. He says it's devil-talk, but I tell him it sounds like a cat to me. 'Yeah,' he says, 'the cat that got the cream – wwrrrr.'

We leave Paul with the vodka and both try to get changed in the bathroom, but it's such a squash with the two of us in there that Hen says she'll leave me to it, and goes out to be with Paul, shutting the door very crisply so I'm definitely being excluded. I wiggle into the Trotters of Tooting green linen, a snip at one guinea reduced from ten). It's a bit tight. Then I get the rest of it on – the bolero, the petal hat, the yellow mask. It's the first time I can get a really good look at myself, because the mirrors in Tourist are all a bit small, and the effect's not bad. All right I'm a short sort of daisy – but then, daisies are pretty short. It's not as if I'm trying to be a lily or a sunflower. The silk bolero is beautiful and, where it doesn't join across my middle, you can see a bit of my bosoms in the green linen underneath. I have a last look at myself, then open the door and shuffle through. Paul's over by the porthole staring out, but Hen's right there ready to scrutinize. She glares down my cleavage. 'Ummm, get you,' she says, 'it's the Valley of Ella.' Well all right, so it's very unfashionable to have bosoms, but there's nothing I can do about them.

'The jacket's lovely,' I say. 'Thanks for lending it.'

'You won't go and split it will you?' says Hen – she's turning me round and feeling under my armpits – 'It's very tight.' Well, not so very tight, Henrietta Thring, thank you very much, showing me up right behind Paul's back.

'It's fine,' I say.

'Just you make sure that's all, I don't want it ruined,' says Hen, disappearing into the bathroom for her own quick change.

Paul turns round and sees me. I'm ready to quail.

'Nice,' he says and comes over. 'You're a right little flower,' and if my petals were real they'd be turning pink all over.

'How's about my tail then,' says Paul, 'big enough for you?'

'Terrific,' I say, but he's being a bit odd. He might be getting drunk – his eyes are starey and very black.

'Long enough for you is it – my *tail* – little flowery Ella girl.' I can see of course he's trying to get at me – embarrass me, or flirt with me? If I knew for sure it was flirting I could do it back, but I'm not sure. I'm never sure. How do people tell? So what I do is try to sound a bit mysterious – 'The Devil Incarnate,' I say, though I'm only using it for show.

Paul breaks into song – 'Devil in Disguise' in a mock Elvis voice. Then he sticks the end of his tail in his teeth, as he brushes close by me and growls down my neck. So it looks as if I hit just the right tone, even if it was by accident. I have a go at growling back, pretty flirty, and he stops and turns round to me, only then the door goes and opens (wouldn't it just?) and Hen comes out. Paul says, 'Bloody 'ell,' and the tail drops out of his mouth and hits the floor.

She's wearing a tight sheath dress in scarlet silk, strapless and ruched around her bosom, not that she has much of a bosom – no Valley of Hen – but that doesn't seem to matter to Paul. He's gaping. There's an awful lot of flesh showing – quite freckly, spotty flesh if you were being really critical – but still a lot of it. Even more so because she's stuck her hair up under the heart hat/crown, exposing extra bare shoulder below. She's added some extra bits to the brim since this afternoon – playing cards are now stuck in between the jam tarts all the way round. It's not going to be hard to guess what she's meant to be. Anyone could get it. She drapes herself against the bathroom door jamb.

'What do you think?' she says. Her voice has gone all husky.

'You look like a red-hot bloody poker,' says Paul.

Officially, according to the programme, we fancy-dressers are meant to gather in the Cabin Class Smoke Room. But underneath this instruction is printed 'to be registered' – and we don't want any of that, according to Hen. 'We don't want to get noticed and chucked out before we've even started.' I thought the whole point was we wouldn't get chucked out because we're Chip's guests. I protest about this, but Hen says, 'You're at it again Ella – Nazi – *stop* obeying orders.' It turns out she's already arranged for us to meet up with Chip in the cinema because it's shared between First and Cabin and is thus perfectly legit. There are two entrances and we walk through the cinema to get to the Cabin Class one and stand waiting for him. We've taken off our hats and masks so we don't draw too much attention to ourselves – but even so we look peculiar, what with Paul's jeans and our long gowns. Eventually Chip arrives. He's wearing a dinner jacket with a shoe-lace tie instead of a proper bow, and a black cowboy hat on his head with silver coins stuck round the band.

'What are you?' says Hen.

'Hopalong Cassidy,' says Chip.

'But you're supposed to be an illustration of something – a rhyme or a song . . .'

'I am – I'm Hopalong Cassidy.'

'I don't think you've quite grasped the gist,' says Hen. 'It's not supposed to be quite so literal – it's supposed to have a touch of metaphor about it – '

'Jeezus,' says Chip. 'I'll do it with a limp – is that metaphorical enough for you? Anyway, what's so non-literal about you – you've got goddam pastries on your head.'

'They're symbolic,' says Hen. There's a bit of tension between those two.

The actual ball is down one deck in the Cabin Main Lounge and from where we're standing we can see various fancy-dressers going into the Smoke Room, but Hen starts worrying we'll get spotted and roped in too early. She doesn't want us to be unmasked as impostors when we haven't even worn our real masks yet, so we slip back into the cinema to hide. Only by now the film's started – something with Frank Sinatra. We didn't realize that until we got in and we're being a bit giggly I suppose. It seems to me the whole audience hears us come in, because there's a collective swish of faces turning our way and we can't see any vacant seats, so we squat down on the floor behind the back seats to get out of the way. I can hear Frank Sinatra bursting into song and I'd have loved to watch, but I can't see anything from down there – though I can hear giggling further along. I imagine it's Hen doing something unmentionable with Paul's tail. Then Chip whispers in my ear that we're to put our hats and masks on – not easy in the dark, and it's making us more and more giggly and people are shushing us. I could do with a mirror, my petals feel lopsided, and I can see Hen creeping to the door and peering out to see what's up by the Smoke Room, and that's the signal. We all follow her practically on all fours so we don't get in the way of the screen.

We're just getting ourselves upright and making sure our headdresses are all okay when this woman comes running out of the Smoke Room. She's in a uniform and she's got a clipboard pressed to her breast.

'Oh no,' she cries out, '*latecomers* – come along you people, everyone else is already down there, we did say 10.30 sharp – I thought I'd done you all – come along – come on down – you don't want to miss the boat . . .' and I bet she's said that a few times in her career.

It's no use trying to wriggle out of it. I can see Hen's trying, but the woman's got us all categorized whether we like it or not, and she's pushing us ahead of her as if she's a cowherd.

'There's no time to get you on the list,' she gasps, ' – just tell the compère who you're supposed to be before you go up on the platform. Who are you by the way?'

'The Blores,' Hen mumbles – or something like that – might have been 'Bores' or 'Broars' and the woman's looking puzzled at her clipboard, but Hen walks through the doorway, and straightaway from this angle I can see her caught in a spotlight. She says something to the man on her left, and over the loudspeaker we hear, 'And now ladies and gentlemen, we have "The Queen of Hearts".' There's a little burst of applause, then I'm poked in the back and feel myself being propelled forward – 'And another latecomer – we have "Daisy, Daisy, Give Me Your Answer Do"' and I'm tottering up on to the platform in dazzling light to a clash of cymbals. 'And a little touch of wickedness – we've got "The Devil in Disguise"' – more cymbals. 'And last but not least – your very own HOPALONG CASSIDY.' If I look straight ahead, I'm almost blinded by the light streaming on to us, but to the right I can see Chip in the corner of my eye, climbing up the steps with an exaggerated limp – a roll of drums and the audience seems to be laughing. It's all going wrong – we weren't supposed to be in the actual competition, we were meant to miss it all and join in afterwards – but there's no escape now. We're being asked to twirl slowly round. I can see Paul's mouth in a set line below his devil's mask – 'I'll kill that fucking cow for getting us into this.' My daisy smile feels glued to my face along with my paper petals – and now Hen's been called to the front – the judges are giving her a second examination.

'What happens if she wins?' I hiss at Paul.

'The game'll fucking well be up won't it.' Even though he's gorgeous, he uses the most horrible words.

But then two other people are called up – a man ('The Biggest Aspidistra in the World') and a woman who's 'How much is that

Doggie in the Window?' She's got an entire small shopfront on her head and an Amanda Jane doll being the customer pointing at a felt dachshund.

'Ladies and Gentlemen – our three finalists – let's have a big hand for them!'

And Hen's grinning and acknowledging the applause – and then she goes and nods her head too hard and the jam tarts start sliding off in all directions.

'Lummy,' says Hen – and she's trying to get down on the floor to pick them up, only her skirt's too tight and she sticks half-way down. Then she can't seem to straighten up again. It's a mixture of the skirt and the weight of the hat I think, because she's using both hands now to hang on to it, and the Biggest Aspidistra catches her round the waist just before she topples over. So much for being unobtrusive.

'How much is that Doggie?' is the winner, Aspidistra is second and Queen of Hearts gets an Honourable Mention – 'for bravery in the face of flying tarts' says the compère. There's another drum roll and at last we can file off the platform and the dancing begins.

'Quel buggeroonie,' says Hen. 'Can I ponce a fag?'

'Sometimes,' says Chip, 'I need a dictionary to talk with you – American/English with detailed definitions.'

'Don't be a fart,' says Hen.

'*That* I understand,' says Chip.

The band is playing 'Blame it on the Bossa Nova' and everyone's starting to get with the rhythm. Hen's still sagging against the wall, pulling on the ciggie she's 'ponced' from Paul. But we should have got whirling because the woman with the clipboard is heading our way, and class exposure is surely about to occur.

'Miss Blore – is it?'

'What?' says Hen baldly.

'It is Miss Blore? Only . . .' she's waving her clipboard, you can see a question about names and passenger lists is coming up any second, 'Only we've got you down as Mrs on the passenger list – I do apologize.'

'It is Mrs,' says Hen, not an eyelid batted. 'And this is Mr,' she adds, pulling on Paul's tail, which promptly comes apart from his jeans again. 'Mr and Mrs Paul Blore.'

'How peculiar – I've only got you down as Mrs – C26, that *is* you isn't it? It's for your prize. We'll pop it down to your cabin.'

'Is it booze?'

'Pardon?'

'The prize.'

'A miniature *Queen Elizabeth* lifebelt – a charming souvenir.'

'Then deliver away to Mrs Blore in C26 – she'll have quite a thrill – *I* will I mean – thrilling – too thrilling – what a hoot it's all been – ' and Hen winks through the eye of her mask at Madame Clipboard and glides off into the dance, dragging Paul with her. Which leaves me with Chip, feeling foolish – a Daisy and a Hopalong Cassidy all alone and expected to take to the floor.

It's not as if I'm not willing – I'm perfectly game to have a go with Chip – I just wish he seemed a little more enthusiastic. But he's looking after Hen as she disappears into the crowd, like a sad bloodhound who's lost the scent – so I'm left standing there in no doubt that I'm definitely marked down as second best. And the fun of being in fancy dress has already faded. It's like those paper hats you get in crackers. They're supposed to make you feel festive, but the moment you put them on you know it's a lost cause, any attempt at glamour straight down the drain. That's how I feel now in my daisy hat, but I don't trust myself to snatch it off without the benefit of a mirror, because I know it'll leave me with my hair standing on end: it'll have to do for the moment. Everyone else in a mad hat is dancing, so that's it – off we go – bossa-novaing like anything. 'Blame it on the Bossa Nova' – one Daisy and one Cowboy; a picture of me at my first ever proper ball. *Honestly.*

Gradually things improve a bit because everyone gets more and more tipsy, and it's funny how you stop caring really. It's not as if it isn't all just as embarrassing when you look back on it, sober, the next day, but at the time it doesn't seem so bad. Maybe that's why people get drunk – to stop it all feeling so bad. Because that's what happens to us. Chip's bought several bottles of wine, waiting for us at his table, and every time a number ends, we meet Hen and Paul there and have another swig. Paul doesn't ask me to dance, though I thought he would. I stand there really close to him but he takes no notice. He and Hen are getting louder each time we meet. Hen's crown is tipping over her left eyebrow and one of Paul's horns has gone wonky.

The band's good – very adaptable. We don't get stuck on the bossa nova or the cha-cha – which is just as well because neither Chip nor I know how to do them properly, we just wiggle about a bit. But then they do a Chubby Checker number: 'Let's Twist Again' and then into 'Twistin' the Night Away' and 'Twist and Shout'. I'd love to Twist and Shout with Paul, but he is way over the other side with Hen, shakin' all over. At least twisting means Chip and I don't have to hang on to each other, which is just as well because I have this awful creeping feeling that he doesn't want to hang on to me – not a bit. I've tried various ways of talking to him over the racket from the band, but I'm only getting one word answers, and he doesn't ask me anything back, which proves he's not interested, doesn't it? Not that I'm interested either – except maybe I would be if he was.

In the middle of 'Sweets for My Sweet' he yells in my ear that he's got to 'go to the john' and he disappears. I'm left alone on the floor with everyone gyrating around me, so I go to the 'john' too. The mirror in the Ladies reveals the full collapse of my daisy delight – my mascara's running in big black rings behind the yellow mask, my petals are all bent. I whip off the whole hat and turn myself back into me – only it's a better me in a beautiful silk Jean Varon bolero I'd never normally get the chance to wear.

When I get back to our table, the lights have dimmed and the band's playing 'Little Children'. Couples are hanging round each other's necks, some of them smooching. I have a big gulp of white wine. I concentrate hard on the bottle, then on the glass, trying not to catch anyone's eye. In a minute I'm going to slip out of here and get myself back to D9. This has all been a mistake. I'm a total failure.

'Where were you – I've been looking all over.'

It's Chip. He's taken off the Hopalong Cassidy hat and his dinner jacket. He looks much more approachable – quite good really. 'C'mon . . .' He holds out his hand and there we are, doing the slow dance too. It would have felt awkward, except he's just circled me in his arms and has his chin tucked into my hair, right at the top of my cheek. He feels warm and solid. It's so different to feel someone like this – in real life, not your fantasy. And the lights are dimmer, the band's playing 'A World without Love' and he's tipping my chin up to him – because even if he's shorter than Paul, he's still taller than me – and then we're doing the smooch too. I close my eyes and go with it. I suppose we're dancing, but I'm not thinking where I'm putting my feet for once. It doesn't seem to matter. I'm floating. I'm loving it.

Somewhere in the middle of the band's version of 'True Love Ways' I feel a different sensation – my stomach's kind of lurching, swerving sideways, and I click my eyes open. That's better – better to be able to see, focus on something. Over Chip's shoulder I stare at the spotlights, at the drummer, at anything. I wonder if I'm drunk – maybe all that wine wasn't such a great idea. It's suddenly very hot in here.

'I think I need some fresh air,' I say.

'Sure – sure – me too,' says Chip, and he's guiding me backwards, still supposedly doing the smooch, straight out of a door and on to the deck. We're directly at the stern. Below, I can see where Paul and I stood this afternoon to watch the *Queen Mary* disappear. Back then I was still full of excited hope, thinking Paul and I were on the same side of the fence, against Hen. Wrong.

I lean out over the railings, taking in great gulps of cool air and trying to settle the lurching sensation. The sky has clouded over now, not as one solid mass but separately, like vast layered meringues piled one against another and each picked out by the thinnest slice of moonlight. The moon itself is hidden by cloud, but shafts of light are escaping from below, striking the sea and catching the edges of the wake so that the pathway to the horizon has changed to silver. On either side, the smooth sea of this afternoon is now broken up into sharp curving triangles, moving, dipping, each tipped with silver.

'It's so beautiful,' I say.

'Umm,' says Chip. I can feel his tongue on my earlobe.

'But isn't it? Have you ever seen anything more beautiful?' I say. His tongue is working its way up – it's wriggling into my ear.

'Umm,' says Chip. 'Mmm – *beeootiful* . . .'

I can see the glories of the seascape aren't exactly enthusing him, but at least the chance to focus on the distance and feel the cool air is working. I suppose I *must* be drunk and I'm not at all sure I like it. I turn back from the railings towards him and try to concentrate on the business in hand. We're not exactly alone – there are a few other couples scattered along the railings and a lot of snogging's going on.

Snog. Concentrate. At least I've got his attention now – that's something. As we're face to face, he has to give up on my ear and we're at it mouth to mouth. Lips – soft, squashy, warm. Tongue – in it comes, yes, doing its exploration. Here we go – round the molars – tongue to tongue – a substitute form of conversation to make up for the verbal ones we haven't had. It's so peculiar. Chip's a near-total stranger. We don't even know we like each other – we probably don't. Yet here's his tongue sliding towards the back of my throat. Isn't this the strangest thing, this love business? It's not like normal social behaviour at all. I slide my tongue into his mouth. It seems only polite to reciprocate. I run it along his teeth – I try to feel what maybe he's feeling – but all I get back is the sharp edge of his incisors. And now here's his hand – sliding round from my shoulders, pushing aside the silk bolero and making its way into the Valley of Ella. And all the time, I'm *thinking*, not feeling. I try to drown out the thoughts, let my senses respond. That's what they seem to do in films. Respond. But all the time I'm trying, I have this picture in my mind of the both of us – it's as if part of me has stepped away and is watching. And the other me is asking what I think I'm doing on the stern of the *Queen Elizabeth* in the middle of the Atlantic Ocean letting a total stranger do that curious thing to my left nipple.

So now Chip's twisting me round. He's got one hand in the Valley of Ella and the other one is fiddling round the back of the Trotters of Tooting green linen, trying to find the pull-thing on the zip I suppose – only I keep seeing the woman at Trotters, the one who sold us the dress. It was on the sale rail. It had already been reduced twice – the one guinea price tag was what she called its 'last gasp'. She kept holding it out from the rail and shaking it at us. 'Green,' she kept saying. 'Always acceptable. You can do a lot with green – not like pink or purple which limits your range.' And I feel the zip start to give and I know that June really will be busting out all over the aft deck if I don't watch it. As he twists me around I open my eyes, trying to quell the feeling giddy, and past the edge of his cheek I see through one eye that I'm facing the wake again. Suddenly he's opened his eyes too, and I'm caught. We're looking at each other – iris to iris, pupil to pupil. He stops pulling at the zip and lets me go.

'Want to come to my cabin?' he asks. He sounds completely matter-of-fact. Bored even.

'Well . . .' I don't want to turn him down, not exactly. I want him to want me to go to his cabin – that's what it is – but I'm not sure either.

'You're not really up for this are you?' he says.

'What? No – really – go on – '

'S'fine,' he says, 's'fine by me – you can make your own way back can't you?'

'Umm – yes,' I say. 'Sure – fine,' I add, trying to sound as detached as possible with one bosom half-exposed. It's all ending faster than I'd intended.

'Ciao baby – hasta la vista . . .' and he disappears back into the dance.

I stand alone by the railings, not sure what to do, pushing the Valley of Ella back down where it belongs and pulling the bolero as tightly round me as it will go. It's cold out here – the wind is getting up. The snogging couples are still at it. There are some stairs to the open bit of A Deck below, at the very furthest stern of the ship. Instinct wants me to hurtle down them and hide in the deep shadows, but I've left my bag at the table – with my cabin key in it. I walk back to the doorway and look to see if there's any way of slipping in unnoticed. The dance has thinned – people are leaving. I look for Hen and Paul's distinctive heads poking up over the remaining crowd but they're not here. Neither is Chip. When I reach the table I see his jacket and cowboy hat have gone too. I gather up my bag and the crumpled remains of the daisy petals and scuttle away.

It's a long trail back down to D deck. The treads on those seventeen flights of stairs are shifting, rising up to meet my feet, then giving way again. My stomach's going with them and I have to cling on to the banister to keep from falling. So this is being drunk. I don't like it. I creep into D9 in the dark, stumble over assorted toys, and climb up on to my bunk, still in the green linen dress. It's stifling in here, hotter than ever, but maybe that's just being drunk too. I lie on top of the covers, trying to get cool, trying to stop my head from whirling. For a while I make myself think back to the evening, anything to get my mind off whatever my body's feeling, but the memory doesn't comfort. Everything hurts.

Sunday

Kitty is buoyed up on a float of adrenaline which doesn't allow her much in the way of sleep. Far from feeling tired, the sense of anticipation is keeping her alert. It's not always been easy to feel so alive these last years, and too much of her energy has been won vicariously through Ella. A child brings its own needs, life, vibrancy, and Kitty's fed on Ella's almost greedily. It's something she's aware of, and of its dangers too. With the child gone the source will dry up: and the child's almost grown now, will be gone in the winking of an eye – and what will she have left? It's not to be thought of too closely – the prospect too sad and dry. So far from being drained by lack of sleep, she's excited by the possibility of change.

Then there's the unaccustomed heat of the city. On the wireless, the Meteorological Office claims records. It's too hot even for sheets. When she looks out of the window a dulled yellow sky at dawn is changing rapidly to clear, strong turquoise. If it weren't Kennington it might almost feel exotic. Sunday morning and a day alone without Ella. No shops open, apart from the newsagent on the corner until noon, for papers, cigs and ice cream. Normally she'd slip out for the *Observer* or the *Sunday Times*, sometimes both – vicarious living again through journalists' eyes. This morning however, she has no taste for anybody's life but her own.

She doesn't think through any sort of plan for the day – just lets her instincts flow. Dresses quite carefully though, as if expecting to meet somebody, because perhaps, who knows, she might? A light summer frock – apricot and waisted – Ella wouldn't approve, but then she's not here to object. As an afterthought takes the straw hat, even though she'd sworn never to wear it again – sees it now as a talisman of introduction perhaps, though ostensibly it's to protect her from the glare. Sets off towards The Oval, heading for Vauxhall Bridge. The river is high, steely blue. She doesn't think she's ever seen it blue before. It's always gunmetal grey or manure green, flecked with rubbish and floating pieces of wood. But today it's blue: herring gulls are bobbing and an early pleasure boat chugs upstream.

On Millbank she thinks of walking down to the Tate, but it won't be open yet, and in any case she hasn't walked this far today to look at pictures. She's drawn by an invisible magnet, pulling her towards Victoria. But she'd forgotten what a long walk it is along Vauxhall Bridge Road, through the heart of Pimlico, with the buses tearing past, throwing up a haze of dust from the gutters.

There's a café half-way along and, miraculously for a Sunday morning, it's open, a Gaggia machine spluttering on the counter. Italian-owned presumably, adding a welcome puff of Catholic civilization to this Protestant land. God bless them, she thinks, sipping her frothy coffee in its glass cup – wouldn't we otherwise shrivel up in our tight-lipped world – and isn't an Anglo-Saxon Sunday a sad space for lonely people? Except I'm not lonely any more. Two nights ago I was one half of a couple and I shall be again – tomorrow. Not long to wait she thinks, as she looks around the café, with its bamboo paper and Chianti-bottle candleholders. What was it with Jack and his Italian inheritance? She'd never understood. Would it have been so terrible to have embraced it, and thus allowed the three of them into the protective fold of his family? She herself had always got along pretty well with his mother, on the rare occasions Jack allowed them to meet. Rosa Festini was not the pasta butterball Jack had always painted her. She was solidly built it's true, but shrewd, Kitty was sure, in contrast to her boisterous husband with his huge smile and enveloping hug. Jack seemed allergic to both. The father's open earthiness made him shudder, the mother's self-containment made him freeze. It was a topic forbidden for debate between them.

When, in the midst of their gypsy wanderings from state to state, with the infant Ella in tow, Kitty had demanded outright to be taken back to Sproughton, at least for the winter, to give them some semblance of stability, he'd become quite nasty. 'Goddam it,' he'd say, 'you don't know what you're talking about. For Christ's sake you're not even American, you never took citizenship, you don't know what it means. You're all stuck up with that inheritance thing – that everything comes with all that garbage, all that stuff to glue you down – like my parents going on and on about the good old days in Salerno, the old country, all that nostalgia crap. You know what? They want the good old days, they can go back there – pronto – I don't want to be stuck with all that shit – I want clean, I want new. What's all that gotten us anyway – all that hankering after the past – two World Wars. Our ancestors didn't come here for that – making that journey, running those risks, just to gum themselves up with that old world – the future is free, free of the past . . .'

Even when she was living in the middle of it she could see the gaping holes in his logic, but argument exhausted her and upset the child. Even when she'd finally decided to leave she hadn't argued. That constant feeling of living on the edge of a precipice, desperate for the roots he wouldn't allow, began to fester inside her – drawing with it the totally unexpected phenomenon of homesickness for England. Who would ever have thought it possible: the place she couldn't leave fast enough back in 1946?

When she'd first arrived in America, she'd been totally over-whelmed. The abundance of it – the colour of it – the speed of it – the *wholeness* of it. In the England she'd left behind, smashed and torn by war, nothing seemed whole any more, everything seemed partial, broken, waiting for a renewal of energy to mend it again. After the initial shock, the atmosphere of relaxed American plenty had been all too easy to get used to. She fell into it gratefully, abandoning years of ration-book psychology. But life with Jack had gradually drained the gratitude – now you see it, now you don't.

She resumes her walk and once she reaches Victoria Street, crosses over, looking for the place where she and Gilbert had stopped, after the magical time in St James's Park: when he'd pointed out his block of flats; when he'd asked her to stay. Except he hadn't – not in so many words – but that's what he'd meant, and why hadn't she just said yes there and then? Why put herself through this agony of waiting and indecision – and excitement? Why didn't I simply let myself go with it, she thinks, cursing caution, and with her next breath, allowing it back again.

She reckons she's picked out the right building, though there are several tall Edwardian mansion blocks, and maybe his is further down. They're quite handsome places, though a bit gloomy in all their red-brick solidity, facing up to each other across narrow streets – Thirleby Road, Ashley Gardens – it must have been one of these, but which? She wanders, trying to pinpoint it more clearly, and already her imagination's taken off. What would it be like living in such a building – solid, in the solid heart of London? A pretty good sort of a life, though, in Gilbert's case, lonely surely? What a waste of a man and his building, though by now of course she's already envisaged herself filling that sad vacuum.

At the entrance to one of the blocks, a family is emerging – smartly dressed, for church perhaps or Sunday lunch with granny: two small girls in hats and white gloves, heading straight for a large Wolsey saloon parked at the kerb. It's only when the man in the group seems to pause before getting into the driver's seat, and looks at Kitty for a full few seconds, that she snaps herself out of it. How odd she must look, standing staring. She whips herself out of her daydream. What was she thinking of, coming spying like this? It would look like spying wouldn't it – to Gilbert – if he suddenly saw her here? Though he's away in the country; that's what he said. Unless he was fobbing her off – she's no way of knowing. He could be here still – or have returned early. He could come out at any moment, and she'd have no excuse, nothing to say.

The thought sends her scurrying up a side street which brings her out, unexpectedly, at Westminster Cathedral. The vision of that presumably church-bound family she'd just observed prompts her to slip inside. A service is on and she lingers, standing at the back, almost blinded after the strength of sunlight, keeping out of the way. Can't join in of course, doesn't belong – uncomfortable in the rich atmosphere of incense and holy water, genuflection and body-crossing: too exotic for a girl brought up Ebenezer Chapel in the gaunt Norfolk landscape. But this faith is Ella's birthright, and she still could embrace it. Jack had specifically forbidden a Catholic baptism, or any baptism as it turned out. 'I won't let you mess with her mind,' he'd said, though when they got back to England, Ella herself had chosen C of E, unsurprisingly, considering she was at the local church primary school and had been picked to play Mary in the Nativity Play. Anything to blend in – for already she felt her oddity as an alien interloper with her funny accent and absent father. Chameleon-like she automatically changed her surface to fit what she perceived was the norm. It was partially in deference to this ignored Catholic inheritance that Kitty had sent her to the convent school at eleven, though along with the deference came a sharper reality, that the education it offered was good by repute, and the fees were cheaper than most. Still, this rich-scented, ancient faith could still be Ella's – as of right. In her mind she sees Ella as a small child in the first confirmation dress she'd never worn – and Ella now, veiled perhaps, as part of this summer Sunday congregation. When she goes back out into the street, she spots a pale moon, insubstantial as a communion wafer, left hanging in the fierce blue sky.

8a.m. – RMS Queen Elizabeth

I must have slept. Because I remember waking up to the painful blaze of the overhead light and a terrific mess and muddle of sounds from down below. The whole cabin still feels as if it's moving. I screw my eyes tight to keep out the light and wait for the sensation to stop. It doesn't. I've got a pain extending through both eyeballs too. And to think people get drunk all the time for the love of it. The hell of it. They must be bonko. I'm thirsty. I'd do anything for some water, but it's down there in the white flask, mixed up with all that noise, and I'm all the way up here. I don't see how the two of us can meet – that flask and me. The distance seems insurmountable. I open my eyes and stare up at the ceiling. It looks closer than ever – surely it's moving in on me? I roll over to the edge of the bunk to see if I can attract attention. Mrs K. is at the washbasin with Eenie, who seems to be in the process of being sick. Mo is sitting on the edge of Mrs K.'s bunk, grey-faced, her eyes staring, watching events.

'Okay sweetheart – that's it honey – let it all out – ' Mrs K. is keeping Eenie's hair out of the way as an arc of green bile hits the porcelain. The sight of the vomit immediately makes my own compromised stomach clench and I roll back again, shutting my eyes, wishing to shut my ears as well. In my hungover, sleepy state I don't yet grasp what's happening: the girls can't be drunk too.

Eenie's stopped throwing up. She's gasping – little smothered sounds – 'uh – uh – uh'.

'Okay my angel . . .' says Mrs K. 'You're gonna be okay – naughty ocean – it's a naughty, naughty ocean.'

'Mommy . . .' I hear Mo, her voice a whisper.

'Give me a moment here Mo – '

'Mommy, I wanna throw up.'

'Hang on a minute baby . . .'

'I wanna throw up *now* – '

'Oh my sweet Jesus – okay honey – '

I can sense a toy-toy moment being thrust upon me so I keep absolutely still, as a corpse, whilst unable to block out the sounds of Mo vomiting too. Then I hear Eenie joining her for the next attack. A chorus of retching, the smell rising. Comparisons with hell.

'Ella – Ella are you awake?' The inevitable call from Mrs K. I lie rigid. 'You can't be asleep through all this – hang on Eenie – okay sweetheart – *Ella* – '

I make myself rise slowly on to one elbow, as if still lost in sleep, though in reality I'm growing more conscious by the second.

'Thank God,' says Mrs K. 'I thought you were dead or something. Can you give me a hand – the kids are seasick . . .'

So that's what it is. Not drunk like me. I hear myself groan as I flop back on the pillow.

'Me too,' I say. Because maybe it's the truth, though I didn't think seasickness stuck daggers through your eyeballs. And now I notice that the cabin really is moving – or rather we all are – rhythmically, steadily, heaving forward and back.

'That's all we need . . .' says Mrs K., in the midst of vomit mayhem. 'Ring for the stewardess for God's sake Ella, I've got my hands full down here . . .'

I'm saved from having to lift even a bell finger by a rap on the door. It's Vera with tea and *Ocean Times* – only even she looks as if she's hanging at an angle, gripping on to the doorknob with one hand, and swinging the tray wildly in with the other.

'Good morning ladies – oh my – we are in a bad way.'

I heave down the ladder to rescue the tray. I get a swift glimpse of myself in the mirror over poor Mo's head and remember I'm still in the green linen, with my makeup on from last night – panda eyes, stiff and dishevelled. Eenie rescues me from comment or explanation as she explodes with another fit of retching.

'Poor dearie,' says Vera. 'We've hit a bit of a storm – probably won't last that long – blow itself out.'

'I thought we were stabilized,' I say, because I did.

'We are dearie – and they're out – the stabilizers – the Commodore ordered them a couple of hours ago, though they'll slow us down so it's not ideal.'

'So what's happening?' I say.

'Head wind dearie – pitching. The stabilizers only deal with rolling. See – feel it, we're not going from side to side.'

She's right, we're not. Just heaving up and down.

'Oh God . . .' says Mrs K. as Mo lurches for the basin again.

'I'll get you some pills from the surgery dearie – make you right as rain – poor little lambkins.'

'Didn't I know this?' says Mrs K. 'Couldn't I feel it? Every time I do this trip we hit a goddam storm. Mr Keropoulos travels, does he hit a storm, does he heck. Not even in hurricane season does he hit a storm. October even – the ocean's smooth as glass for him – but I get it every time, and every time I'm near enough stuck in the goddam hold, and we all know it's worse down here – '

'Hardly the *hold* Mrs Keropoulos.' Vera looks quite shocked, though whether it's the 'goddams' or the notion of D Deck being in the hold is not clear.

'And all the time you know that damn sea's there,' Mrs K. continues, her voice rising, ' – right through that itty-bitty little piece of wall. That's all we've got between us and the bottom of the Atlantic – this is just what I need . . .'

'You're on the *Queen Elizabeth* Mrs Keropoulos dear,' says Vera, quite firmly, 'and there's nothing itty-bitty about her. Just have to hold on to your hats for the next couple of hours while we ride this one out. I'll fetch those pills.'

I make a quick getaway, dressing in the bogs and doing my best with my washed-out face – anything to escape the horror of the cabin washbasin. Mrs K. is suddenly a touching sight. Essential motherhood, with her weary arms stretched out to comfort both little girls. I harden my heart – rather her than me. Already I can feel yesterday's maternal yearning slipping away as I head off up to R Deck in search of some sort of sustenance for my wobbling tum.

The dining room is virtually deserted. There are more waiters than breakfasters and they stand around, looking spare. But – shouldn't I just have known it – our table is already occupied by Sydney Maxton-Bligh, sitting in lone state eating porridge with gusto, his napkin tucked into his collar.

'Miss Eleanor,' he says, grinning, then wiping off his moustache, 'welcome, welcome. You've not succumbed I see – well done, that's the ticket – always sorts the men from the boys, the old *mal de mer*.'

I sit down a bit gingerly at the far end of the table. Even the faintest whiff of the porridge is unpleasantly stirring to the gut. I order tea and toast.

'You look a little on the peaky side, if I may say so – not *quite* got your sealegs then?' he asks.

'Hungover I think,' I say. My voice sounds a bit cracked and weak.

'*Are* we now,' he says in quite an approving tone. 'Been burning the candle? We do know *how* to burn it then, do we?' I guess that might be a reference to my running away from the Commander, but this is not the moment to rise to any bait. I keep it simple.

'Last night,' I say. 'Bad timing. Of course I didn't know we were going to hit a storm.'

'Oh you can't call this a real storm, Miss Eleanor – this is more what I'd term a bit of a blow.'

The waiter is approaching with my order, zigzagging across the carpet to compensate for the motion. Like Vera earlier, his body seems to be pitched at an angle to the floor – something like 45 degrees. He makes it safely to my side and deposits the tray, but already the idea of tea and toast doesn't seem quite such a good one. On the serving table the salt and pepper pots are gently sliding. So are the packets of cereal.

'Maybe I am seasick,' I say, 'only I never have been before. Not on cross-channel ferries. We went on a school trip to see the Bayeux tapestry and I was the only one from my class who didn't have her head hanging over the railings. And I like roller coasters and Ferris wheels.' I nibble a bit of the dry toast. It's comforting.

'Then I don't suppose you are,' says Sydney. 'The real McCoy makes you want to die – apparently. I've never been a victim myself, but of course I've seen it over the years, countless times. My shampoo heiress – the one I told you about – she actually told me she'd prefer death to seasickness. She always said the worst bit of getting it was knowing that it *wouldn't* in fact kill you, because at the time death seems the preferred option.'

'How horrible,' I say, suddenly feeling much sorrier for the Keropoulos clan I've abandoned down in D9.

'But all that was before Dramamine and stabilizers. These days most people pull themselves together – eventually. I've been in some real Atlantic howlers – not like this little bit of business today. I remember one December trip, a few years back, when it blew a non-stop gale for three and a half days – hurricane force. They had to stop all dancing because of injury, and put out the guide ropes all over the public rooms – threaded them everywhere, so you had something to hang on to, otherwise you couldn't get across on two legs. We weren't even allowed out on the Boat

Deck – they had to seal up all the portholes because some of them up on A deck got smashed in by the sea – and that's about forty feet above the waterline, so that was waves for you – *real* waves – held us up a bit, we were nearly a day late. So this little bit of business is nothing much – amazing how people will make a fuss about nothing these days.'

The waiter shimmies back sideways with Sydney's next course. Kippers. The smell precedes them. Sydney greets their arrival with glee. 'Nothing like a pair of Lowestofts to line the stomach,' he says. 'We may have oysters on at lunch too – there won't be much call up in First Class on a day like this, so they'll pass them on to us. Waste not want not. I *love* a heavy sea.'

'The stabilizers are out,' I say. 'The stewardess told me – so it can't be such a little storm.'

'Oh they just do that to cheer people up a bit – nothing like the word "stabilizer" to calm a dodgy tummy. Going to the morning service are you?'

'What?' I say.

'In the main lounge – divine worship?'

'Oh. I didn't realize.'

'It's on today's programme.'

'I haven't looked at it – not yet,' I mumble. The future of today hasn't so far looked bright enough to warrant anything as hopeful as a programme.

'I won't be going,' says Sydney, expertly removing a tiny bone from his teeth. 'Can't be doing with it. I'll be in the Smoke Room with a crossword and a pipe – *observing*. Mark Twain said it was one of life's pleasures you know.'

'What was?'

'Seeing people being seasick "when we ourselves are not".' He laughs.

'He can't have,' I object, 'he wouldn't be so cruel.'

'Only human nature.'

'He must have been joking.'

'You've got a lot to learn, Miss Eleanor. Human beings like a bit of cruelty – adds a touch of spice – as long as there's no *actual* harm. We all need to toughen up a bit if you ask me. Namby pamby – that's what we've become. No war you see. You can say what you like about Hitler and the Nips, but we didn't half have some backbone stuffed into us – like it or not.'

As far as I can see from my speedy, lurching circuit of the public rooms, there aren't going to be all that many victims for Sydney to gloat over. The ship looks deserted. The passageways are sprinkled with a few members of staff who all seem to be running around with trays. In the entrance hall, near the shop, a steward is busy mopping up, though whether it's water or something more sinister, I don't allow myself to inspect.

In the Winter Garden I find Madge Drinkwater. She's looking very pale, with her head buried in a copy of *Life* magazine. There's a Bloody Mary on the table next to her, though maybe it's only tomato juice; it looks untouched. When I say hello, she raises very weary eyes and says, 'Shh Ella – not now huh? Don't speak – all things will pass . . .' So I back out very quietly, leaving her to her misery, and head up to the Promenade Deck.

Outside it's become a world of grey and wet. The glass screen windows are cascades of spray. The horizon has disappeared. Yesterday's strong banding of blues has melted into a single mass of heaving sullen liquid lead.

I head for A Deck and Hen – it's instinct, like a homing pigeon. The truth is I can't think of anywhere else to go. All the gates to First Class are open, and there seem to be more people around up here, though they're mostly hanging on to the grab rails to make their way along the corridors. There's the odd burst of laughter as somebody makes a dash for the other side: you can tell it's all taking on the texture of a challenge for those with iron stomachs – a bit of a lark. The higher up the ship I go, the better I feel. The air is cooler, the pitching not quite so pronounced, so maybe Mrs K. was being quite accurate on the sinister implications of being 'down in the hold'.

I knock on Hen's door. The answer is a wordless groan, and I go in.

Hen's bed is a mountain of tossed sheets and blankets. Somewhere out of the bottom of it, she pokes her head. Her face is a delicate shade – palest eau de Nil.

'Oh Gaaad . . .' she says. 'It's you.' Not exactly welcoming.

'Are you seasick?' I ask.

'Oh Gaaad – no – yes – I don't know. No. I'm never seasick. I'm just *sick*. Still *pissed* I think.'

Pissed? That's a new one on me. It sounds really revolting. I have to stamp on my instantaneous need to ask for a translation.

'What about you?' she asks. 'You don't look too clever – pissed too?'

I nod and click my tongue. 'Yeah,' I say. 'Pissed.' Perhaps she'll let out in a moment what it is. I hope it's not what it sounds like – an adult version of one of Mo's toy-toy moments. It's got to be something sophisticated hasn't it – maybe it's drugs?

'What happened to you last night?' she asks. 'The last I saw of you, you were in a deep smooch with Chip.'

'Yes?' I say.

'Come up to expectations did he?'

'Well – ' The cabin floor suddenly seems to swell up beneath me and I stagger sideways, toppling on to the other bed.

'God I wish it would stop doing that,' says Hen shakily. 'Pass me my cigs will you?'

I reach for them on the bedside table, then settle back, propping myself up on my elbow, watching her flicking at her lighter and failing to get a flame. 'God – I can't believe this – triple buggeroonie – ' She catches me watching her, and her look of irritation intensifies. 'Don't start getting cosy,' she says. 'I'm not up to visitors yet. Have you brought my jacket back?'

'What? No,' I say. What with one thing and another, I'd forgotten all about it. Presumably it's still back on my bunk where I'd tossed it last night. I hope it's well out of the Keropoulos vomit-firing line.

'If anything happens to it, I'll never forgive you,' she says, plucking my thoughts. She really *is* a witch.

'It's fine,' I say. 'I just forgot – what with the storm and everything.' At last she's got the lighter to work. Her hand is shaking as she tries to light the cig. She's in a bad way.

'So how was it – with Chip – from *your* perspective?'

'What do you mean, "from *my* perspective"?' I ask, suddenly suspicious.

'Well, I already know from his – he crawled in to see me a while ago. Terribly hung over. He says he got pissed as a newt last night – had to – you'd got him all worked up and then you blew cold. You shouldn't do that you know Ella. It's not good for men – does terrible things to their bits.'

'Does it?' (Does what? I'm getting a bit confused here. And 'pissed' again – it's got to be either booze or drugs – which? And if drugs, what sort? And is the being pissed part of what I've done to Chip's 'bits'?)

'You don't want to get a reputation as a cock-tease do you?' she says.

'What? No.' I'm truly out of my depth now. Me – a 'cock-tease' *and* 'pissed'? I try to swing the conversation around to more familiar ground.

'He was fine. I mean, we just don't have much in common or anything – but it was fun.'

'*Fun?*' She makes it sound like Dame Edith Evans saying 'a haaandbaaag' – about six syllables.

'Well – yes,' I flounder, ' – quite – only you know – I didn't know him or anything – and he didn't seem to want to know me – '

She's crawled out of the blanket mountain by now, on all fours, the cigarette stuck to her bottom lip, and she's totally nude. I don't know where to look. We're not allowed to be nude at school. Reverend Mother says it fosters impure thoughts: we even have to change for gym under cover of our skirts. I mean, it's not as if I'm a prude or anything, but even so . . . I stare up at the portholes and watch the water streaming down them as she wiggles around just out of my sight line.

'What's with all this "knowing" business?' she says. 'What's that got to do with anything?'

'Well . . . you *know*,' I say, because I should have thought it was perfectly obvious. Now I look back at her, she's wrapped in a towel.

'No I don't, Ella, or I wouldn't have asked – you'll have to fill me in.'

Now that's it, there you have it – *she* can ask *me* outright what I mean and make it sound perfectly all right. Whereas I can't ask her something perfectly simple, like what does 'pissed' mean, in case I look a fool. It's like having a special talent or knowing a code – she does, I don't. I have a bash at explaining.

'It's people, isn't it?' I say. 'If you're going to get – you know – involved with people – you want to know them, as *people* . . .' She doesn't respond, so I add, 'don't you?'

'I can't imagine what you're banging on about,' she says, through a haze of smoke, and starts coughing. 'God I feel terrible.'

'Because,' I add, warming to my topic, 'the whole point is that I did think I knew Paul – a bit anyway. I mean, we'd started to have things in common and – well, you know, we'd talked – and I really liked him – it was, you know – *romantic*.'

'Ye Gods Ella – is that what this is all about – *romance*? What's that got to do with anything? We were talking good old fashioned sex here Ella – remember?'

Infuriatingly, I can feel myself flushing. I'll look like a boiled prawn in two seconds flat, so I rush to my own defence, 'Only I never got a chance with Paul did I, because you stole him and left me with Chip – and I expect Chip's all right – he's probably very nice but – '

'He says you're frigid,' Hen interrupts.

'He says I'm what?'

'Oh for God's sake Ella – *frigid* – you do know what that is, don't you?'

Well, as a matter of fact, possibly I do, but I'm on wobbly territory again. That X film Rosie and I got into last year, *The Chapman Report*, was all about this sex survey, and Jane Fonda was in it in a big white hat, and her husband accused her of being frigid. She looked shattered when he told her. She slid down the wall in their front hall, into a small weeping heap on the floor, saying, 'I'm not – I'm not frigid . . .' as if it was just about the worst accusation on the entire marital agenda. Rosie and I talked about it afterwards because by the end of the film Jane had gone off with the sex doctor, so presumably she wasn't frigid any more. But we couldn't see that anything all that much had changed – and why would it matter anyway – because they could still *do* it, couldn't they? Whereas if the man was frigid, it couldn't work could it – his 'bits' wouldn't actually function, would they?

But meanwhile I've got to come up with an answer for Hen, and fast, because she's looking awfully confrontational, standing wrapped up in her bath towel, pumping smoke like a dragon.

'It wasn't me,' I say.

'What wasn't?' says Hen.

'Who was frigid,' I say, thinking of last night. Because it wasn't. I'd even let him stick his hand down the Valley of Ella for goodness sake – how much more inviting does a girl have to be? 'It was him.'

'What?'

'You *know* – it was him who was frigid.'

'Men don't get frigid Ella – it's a woman thing. Men get impotent.'

'Oh – well, there you are – same thing.'

'Hardly – don't they teach you anything in that convent in Tooting?'

'Not a lot,' I have to admit.

'Not books – *Lady Chatterley* even?'

'Certainly not *Lady Chatterley*,' I say. Sister Marie-Francis thinks *Lady Chatterley* is the direct work of Satan.

'Or manuals? What about sex education classes?'

I shake my head.

'This can't go on Ella. I think you need taking in hand – here borrow . . .' She grabs a book off her bedside table and shoves it at me.

It's in a yellow paper cover with no picture on the front, but I don't have time to examine it, because there's the sound of a bog flushing. As I look up, the door to her bathroom swings open and Paul is standing there, totally naked. I move my eyes instantly from the vision of his crotch up to his face. He looks as white as a lump of lard and his hair is all stringy and wet. He must see me, but he doesn't seem to register recognition at first. He totters into the room, wiping his bare chest with a tiny hand towel.

'That's it,' he says, 'I don't reckon I've any more insides left to chuck up. Once I reach land I'm never getting on a fuckin' boat again. I've 'ad it.' He sees me. 'Oh, 'ello Ella – ' He says this quite socially, as if we've just met by chance in Oxford Street.

'Hello Paul,' I say, forcing back an unexpected prickling sensation in my eyes.

'You all right?' he says, faintly.

'Yes.'

'Good for you. I'm not. I'm on my last fuckin' legs . . .' and he crashes on to the spare bed like a skinny silver birch tree – felled.

'He's been vomiting since dawn,' says Hen with a shrug. 'Honestly Ella – talk about "Can't Buy me Love" – *hopeless*.' She laughs. I try to have a stab at laughing too, but it comes out wrong. It sounds more like a smothered sob and I have to leap for the door, scrabbling at the handle – can't get out of there fast enough.

I run up the main staircase, slap bang into a small swaying crowd being herded into the Main Lounge. I recognize one of the herders, the Assistant Lady Purser from Tourist, and unfortunately she recognizes me too, as I try to cut past the shops towards the nearest open deck.

'You're going the wrong way Miss,' she calls. 'Morning service is through here.'

I'm about to protest that Matins is not my current destination, when I see I'm cornered. What other excuse have I got for being in Forbidden Class Territory again? So that's why all the gates were open – to allow all us plebs access to our Maker, and I'd put it down to some freedom offered by the storm. I can't see I have any alternative but to join in – try to think higher thoughts, though the timing couldn't be worse, my thinking about Hen and Paul being particularly base at this moment.

Several rows of chairs have been lined up and I'm directed to the second of these, too close to the front for comfort, too exposed. I examine the printed order of service. Sister Marie-Francis would be disappointed; not a Hail Mary in sight. It looks basically C of E with space for a couple of hymns. 'For those in peril on the sea'? I look around – people are still coming in. I examine the room – the wooden panelling, the lofty ceiling with its Odeon concealed lighting. I notice the pain in my eyeballs has gone: it must have faded a while back. Now there's just a dull ache in my temple.

No one seems to be kneeling for private prayer. We're all still heaving and swaying along with the ship's motion as we sit on our chairs. I try to think holy thoughts, but a mixture of what I saw in Hen's cabin, plus the slightly weightless sensation in my guts, keeps driving them away. The sound of the wind penetrates, even in here. I've still got the book Hen gave me, and now I have a look at it. It's a copy of *Fanny Hill* – that book there was all the fuss about back in the spring – banned by the magistrates. I flick through it. It doesn't look at all as if it deserves to be banned. It has a picture of a woman in eighteenth-century costume as a frontispiece, and the printing is very old fashioned, tiny and uneven, like the print you find in old Bibles. It looks pretty heavy going too. 'Madam,' it starts, 'I sit down to give you an undeniable proof of my considering your desires as indispensable orders; ungracious then as the task may be, I shall recall to view those scandalous stages of my life, out of which I emerged . . .' It's a bit like Jane Austen – not what I'd expected. I'd thought Hen was giving me some sort of sex manual full of diagrams – something from the 'Look at Life' series perhaps. This book looks more like an Eng. Lit. A-level set text. I stick it on the empty seat beside me, and try to concentrate on my higher thinking.

While I've been reading, the congregation's filled out a bit, plumped up by members of staff in their various uniforms, including some waiters I recognize and the nice steward from the Winter Garden who winks at me when I accidentally catch his eye. But then, just behind him, I see someone else coming in – Sydney's Commander. I whip my head round and stare straight ahead, willing myself into invisibility, or, failing that, willing the Commander into temporary blindness. Someone starts playing the organ – an electric one, at the far end beyond the make-shift altar – suitably solemn, churchy music. I keep rigid in my seat.

'Excuse me – would this be yours?' I turn towards the seat on my left. Sydney's Commander is holding out the copy of Hen's book to me. How fast does a brain work? Must be pretty amazingly fast, because here's an example. There's no possibility we don't recognize each other – not for the tiniest split-atom of a second. Yet he doesn't give even a whisper of a hint. He looks straight through me, and it's fast enough for me to realize that that's what I'll do too, just look straight back through him, apart from the fact that I'm still in the process of retrieving the book.

'Thank you,' I say, trying to take it from him. But he's not releasing it – not immediately. He's turned it on its side and is reading the spine. His head's at an angle and his forehead is all rucked up.

'Are you *sure*?' he says.

'Quite,' I say, and pull it out of his grasp. It's at this moment that a line of uniformed officers troop in and settle along the front row, and the service begins.

The Commodore of the ship takes it – terribly grand. He starts by apologizing for the weather. He calls it a 'freak summer squall', says that we'll soon be out of it, but in view of the ship's motion we're welcome to remain seated throughout the service. The officers all stand though, so I notice we all do too, hanging on to the seats in front of us, and moving in unison with the pitching, like a very ill-matched chorus line. We start with a hymn – 'Blessed are the pure in heart'. Talk about irony. 'Blessed are the pure in heart, For they shall see our God; The secret of the Lord is theirs, Their soul is Christ's abode.' Sydney's Commander has a loud fruity voice which does its own thing round the familiar chords, bursting with sincerity. I stare down at the hymn sheet, even though I know the words backwards – trying to disassociate myself from him, even though our elbows are practically touching – seeing, instead of the words, the image of him on Friday night, leaning towards me with that purple thing bulging between his legs. When we get to the prayers for the Royal Family, the Commodore adds 'and the President of the United States' and Sydney's Commander says, 'Amen, Amen,' under his breath. Any stab I might have made at communicating with the Almighty is being foiled by my planning a swift getaway at the end of the service, so we don't have to eyeball each other again.

During 'Praise My Soul the King of Heaven' they pass a

collection plate. Sydney's Commander puts a *five*-pound note on to it (!), and passes it on to me. I don't have anything – I'd only come to First Class to see Hen, so I don't even have my handbag, not even sixpence in a pocket. I pass the plate on quickly to my right. Then we have a blessing and the electric organ launches into the 'Toccata and Fugue' as people start to file out.

The row to my right is blocked by some people talking to the Commodore, so I have to turn back to the left. Sydney's Commander has already squeezed along the row, and I hang back waiting for him to go, but he doesn't move. He's barring the end of the row, watching me.

'Miss Feast – I think that was your name?' Was my name, is my name. 'It *is* Miss Feast?'

'Yes.'

'Are you *sure* that's your book?'

'Quite sure,' I say.

'Strange child,' he says, and turning abruptly away from me, he walks out.

Noon – Point Harbor

It was an impromptu invitation. Vanessa Mulherne called early – sorry if she was waking them on a Sunday, only Blake had decided on the spur of the moment to have a floating brunch. Last night's forecast had promised a southerly storm, but it hadn't materialized – the prevailing winds had veered into westerlies and blown it back out to sea. So why waste a Sunday – it's beautiful out there – would the Feasts care to join them? Nothing fancy – come as you are, and meet at the tender to *Marietta* down at the dock by 10.30.

Jack's face says it all – he's thrilled by the prospect, glows like a child at Christmas. The Mulhernes are one of the oldest summer families round here – on the mother's side they could easily go back to the *Mayflower*, something like that – had probably come over with the Winthrops even. It's quite something to be asked to join them. It really shows they're being accepted. Lynn would prefer to settle here for the day, grab the chance of Jack's rare presence maybe to work on the baby's room on this last weekend they can be alone, before the invasion of the cuckoo. Instead of which, she now has to squeeze herself into those pedal-pushers with the elasticated waist, rather than a comfortable smock. The smock would be too undignified when scrambling on to the Mulhernes' boat.

Now Jack's snooping round the kitchen – says they must take something, but what? Lynn asks why, when it's all supposed to be so spur of the moment and all. Champagne – it'll have to be that, says Jack. It's just one of those things you have to do – you have to get it right. But the only bottle they can rustle up in the basement is domestic. Unh, unh, that won't do, got to be French – and suddenly he's panicking – they've got to get it right, it *matters*.

But *how* could it, Lynn wonders – if these people really want to see them, as new friends, why would they care? Inspiration strikes – we could take cookies, she says. Are there any cookies in the house, Jack asks – home-made ones? Not home-made, she says, only Pepperidge Farm. Wrong again – and he's making her feel wanting – as if she should have been making a tray of brownies daily on the off chance, when he leaves her here all alone day after day. Brownies to fulfil some empty destiny, a symbol of wifeliness with an all-American slant. Then she does think of something they could take: the big box of Panettone that's sitting in the pantry – the Italian bready cake thing that nobody eats, sent by Bea last Christmas – a fancy box, imported too. And for answer, he gives her one of his hard disconcerting looks.

Altogether they're quite fussed, and she quite mussed, by the time they get down to the water. Jack's got himself one of the PHYC caps, has it set at a jaunty angle, with a sharp crease ironed down his chinos and a cable-knit sweater slung round his neck, despite the heat – the very picture of a modern yachtsman, straight out of the pages of *Esquire* magazine. Totally inappropriate – Lynn sees it at once. The others – the Mulhernes and a couple called Brady with two silent sulky kids in tow – are in blue jeans and sneakers, with a heap of brilliant yellow slickers just in case the weather turns on them. In the end Jack decided on bringing another bottle, not the Californian 'champagne', but one of Pimm's No. 2. He hands it over to Blake who passes it on to Vanessa with scarcely a glance. Jack feels the need to explain. 'It's English,' he says. 'Something they enjoy in summer.'

'Of course,' says Vanessa, 'they drink it with soda don't they?' Lynn can see her looking down at the big strapped up wicker picnic basket and gesturing vaguely with the bottle which doesn't belong in her organization. 'We've just brought along beers, and coffee,' she adds, 'but this is . . . sweet of you. So kind.' But she leaves the bottle on the dock along with some rubber boots and an empty gas canister.

They go out to the yacht in two trips. Lynn goes on the second, along with Blake at the rudder, the Bradys and the basket. They putter out into the centre of the bay where the bigger boats are moored.

'Done much sailing Lynn?' Blake asks.

'Almost none. I'm a girl from out west – horses are more my thing.' She hadn't even seen an ocean till she met Jack.

'For me sailing's in the blood I guess. I can't imagine not being able to get my toes in the water – figuratively speaking of course,' says Blake.

'Me too,' says Marian Brady, 'just love the wind in my hair – the lady is a tramp – ' her voice breaks into a girlish giggle. She's too elegant and sleek for giggles, Lynn thinks.

'No tramp, but definitely a lady.' Blake has one hand on the tiller, but Lynn, sitting close to the stern, sees the other brush along Marian's thigh.

'Why, Mr Mulherne, I didn't know you cared . . .' says Marian as a mock-southern belle.

Karl Brady is watching this open flirtation. He looks glum. Lynn shifts towards him, trying to ease her aching back. She'd like to distract him, but it's not easy when she's feeling she's such an unattractive lump. Marian's legs are long under the denim, the hair she's drawn attention to is thick and strawberry blonde.

'You know, I'd never even seen an ocean till I met Jack,' Lynn says, and sure enough Karl's attention shifts from his wife.

'You're kidding me,' he says.

'Nope – plenty of mountains and desert – and Lake Michigan, so I thought I knew what an ocean was – but it turned out I didn't.' If Jack were here he'd be shushing her, trying to cover up her ignorance, but she doesn't care all that much. It's the truth and why should she feel she's got to sidle around it. With the baby dancing a jig inside her belly, she's not in the mood to utter anything but the truth.

'I should say not,' says Karl. 'That's amazing. I can't imagine not having seen the ocean in childhood. What did you think of it, when you first saw it?'

'Mighty. I thought it was just *mighty.*'

'Which one was it?'

'The Pacific – near Seattle. These huge breakers were crashing in, but the thing that really got to me was knowing it was clear water all the way to Russia. You didn't get that feeling on the shore of Lake Michigan – you just knew it was more of America the other side. In the middle there you get a sense that America's *mighty* too, of course, but the ocean's something else . . .'

'So you've never been overseas?'

'Never.'

'I envy you.'

'Why?'

'You've got all that discovery to make. Most of us have had the excitement drained out of us – our kids didn't raise an eyebrow when we took them to Europe last summer.'

'What's that?' says Marian. She's turned her attention away from Blake, now she sees Karl has momentarily detached his from her.

'It was different for us wasn't it Blake?' says Karl.

'Huh?'

'Going overseas – that first time – England first, then dropped in by parachute – straight out of a C47 into Normandy with a hundred-and-seventy-pound pack on your back. Didn't allow you much time to bother about *Baedeker* . . .'

'Yeah – Normandy was something else,' says Blake, 'after all that time we'd been hanging around in England – and that crazy voyage over from New York – '

'Did you travel in one of the *Queens*?' Lynn asks.

'Sure did – the *Elizabeth*.'

'But that's the ship my husband's daughter is on right now – ' Lynn swallows the urge to substitute 'cuckoo' for daughter. 'Quite a coincidence . . .'

'Not really – when you remember those two ships took over a million of us to Europe in the war, it was pretty likely to be one of them wasn't it? I came back on the *Mary* in '46.'

'Jack was on the *Queen Mary* too – when he went over. He was telling me about the guy who made all those sandwiches – '

'*Sandwiches*?' Blake sounds surprised.

'Oh . . .' says Lynn, wondering if she's already made a gaffe, 'well, that's just one of Jack's things – he always notices anything to do with food – '

'Really,' says Blake. He still sounds surprised.

They've reached the *Marietta*. She's a sailing yacht, painted dark navy blue, with lots of shining butterscotch wood. There's a metal ladder to climb – detachable. Lynn hopes it doesn't detach now. This is not the easiest thing to be doing when you're this pregnant, even when you've had the foresight to wear elastic-waisted pedal-pushers. Blake is keeping the tender steady against the hull, and it's Karl who comes to her aid, climbing behind her, and giving her a strategic push on the backside at the right moment. She could have wished for a more elegant arrival, but she doesn't care that much. She has no real need to appear attractive to anyone else but Jack, does she? If Karl Brady sees her as a sexless lump, so much the better. And Jack isn't down here at the stern, watching for her arrival. He's up at the bow with Vanessa. The PHYC cap has been shoved in his pocket, the sweater abandoned. With sleeves and trouser legs rolled up he's already taken on an approximation of the Mulherne look and is helping her set out the picnic, rugs, cushions. The leprechaun is dancing attendance, and already Lynn can see that Vanessa is charmed.

They're to eat before they get under way. The adults range themselves round the cushions – Karl is solicitous of Lynn, now he's felt the weight of her behind she thinks, and takes special care to prop her back.

The food couldn't be simpler, after all that fuss Jack made; it's only cold cuts, coleslaw – Kim's Chat'n'Chew fare. The Brady kids fill their plates and go and eat on their own with their legs dangling over the water. Lois Brady is fifteen – the cuckoo's age. Lynn watches her for clues. She has a well-developed figure and her mother's long legs, but nothing's quite filled out yet; she's still the promise of a woman rather than the real thing. She may be going to be a beauty, but these things can take a funny turn can't they – the too-deep set of the eye, the lengthening of a nose. Lois's mouth is currently bent in a frown, which looks as if it might just settle in there for life if she's not careful. What could have disappointed her thus far, Lynn wonders, to have sketched that sulky line so deeply?

The cuckoo must have had an up and down sort of life – will her face reveal it yet? From those few photos, it's been hard to get much of an idea of her. Her letters haven't sounded sulky, it's true, especially since plans for the trip were finalized. To start with, her response had sounded guarded. She wrote her usual stuff about school and friends – she never writes anything about her house or her mother – but she didn't seem to leap at Jack's summer invitation, there was no bursting of excitement. At first Lynn resented this – spoilt kid, what *she* wouldn't have felt to make such a journey at her age. But gradually Lynn has come to understand that this is simply the latest of many such invitations and promises Jack has made. Occasionally he'd let things slip out – how he'd almost had Ella over that summer she was ten, when he'd nearly bought a house in Albuquerque – but it fell through, he didn't say why, and the plan was shelved for another year. So the cuckoo was probably right to keep a tight hold of her enthusiasm until the ticket arrived in the mail. Now Lynn knows him better, she too has learned to keep a tight hold of enthusiasm. The leprechaun seems to mean well, but doesn't always deliver.

'*Beautiful* boat,' he says now to Blake. 'Classic lines,' he adds, though until they moved to Point Harbor the nearest he'd been to sailing was a row boat on Sproughton Lake. They're stretched out on the deck, drinking coffee, eating brownies – for Vanessa clearly bakes from scratch, though on second thoughts they were probably made by her live-in housekeeper.

'Beats bunking down on the deck of the *Queens* doesn't it?' says Blake. 'Lynn says you did it too.'

'Yeah – '43 over, '46 back.'

'Camp Kilmer!' says Karl.

'Camp Kilmer – I'd forgotten the name,' says Blake.

'Wasn't that place the weirdest – and weren't they ever smart, those guys?' says Karl.

'Come on gentlemen, you're leaving us ladies in the dark – what is Camp Kilmer?' says Vanessa.

'Would any of this still be classified?' says Blake.

'After twenty years – amongst friends?' Karl shrugs, turns to

Vanessa. 'It was this place over in New Jersey where we practised boarding the ship. They had these two life-size mock-ups made of wood – one for each of the *Queens* – enormous. Then they'd get us to practise. We'd be given our gangway number, whatever we'd been allocated on the real ship, and then we'd "go below" – because they'd built pretend wooden decks as well – to the exact quarters we'd be having on the real ship – and they'd film it all and show us afterwards where we'd messed up, and we'd practise until we got it right.'

'Why?' Lynn asks. 'Why not do it for real?'

'Security – and time,' says Blake. 'It was a crazy situation when you think of it – they had the two largest liners in the world parked right there in the middle of Manhattan, where any enemy spy could spot them without even needing a permit, just standing out on Twelfth Avenue. And then they were sending them out, filled to bursting with US military and no escort, into an Atlantic bristling with U-boats, fifteen thousand of us at a time. If we'd embarked in full view we might as well have sent a direct signal to Admiral Doenitz – "Hi guys, we're here – come and get us!" But this way we were never seen in Manhattan. They ferried us in from Hoboken, landed us directly on to the pier at the stern and, because we'd practised, we knew exactly where we were going. We had to get straight below and keep our heads down until we were out at sea – but that was the beauty of it, we were crammed like sardines in a can, but at least we knew exactly which bit of the can we belonged to, and where to stow our equipment. It took, I don't know, how long, Karl – to get us embarked?'

'Twelve hours or so – the whole ship?' says Karl.

'And of course we never knew in advance when we'd be sailing – ' says Jack.

'You remember Kilmer too?'

'Sure – '

'And Lynn said something about "sandwiches" – ' says Blake.

'Did she?' Jack looks at her sharply.

'Come to think of it, I do remember those packs of sandwiches – and those boiled eggs cooked in big garbage cans – thirty thousand of them every breakfast. I haven't thought much about those journeys for years – what happened in between wiped it all out. You see things in war that . . . well, you guys know what I mean . . . don't let's spoil a beautiful Sunday. Let's get sailing.'

4p.m. – RMS Queen Elizabeth

This book of Hen's is absolutely filthy and I'm glued.

I spend the whole afternoon tucked up in a deck chair on the Promenade Deck, reading it. I'm glued – he's glued:

My beauteous youth was now glued to me in all the folds and twists that we could make our bodies meet in; when, no longer able to rein in the fierceness of refreshed desires, he gives his steed the head and gently insinuating his thighs between mine, stopping my mouth with kisses of humid fire, makes a fresh irruption, and renewing his thrusts, pierces, tears, and forces his way up the torn tender folds that yielded him admission with a smart little less severe than when the breach was first made. I stifled, however, my cries, and bore him with the passive fortitude of a heroine; soon his thrusts, more and more furious, cheeks flushed with a deeper scarlet, his eyes turned up in the fervent fit, some dying sighs, and an agonizing shudder, announced the approaches of that ecstatic pleasure I was yet in too much pain to come in for my share of . . .

Well, I *mean. Honestly.* I can feel myself tingling all over. I wish Rosie was here reading it with me – she'd shriek. And Sister Marie-Francis would just *die*, wouldn't she?

'Hi Ella – you're surviving the weather okay?'

I've been so immersed in the deflowering of F. Hill and her subsequent adventures that it takes a second or two to come back down, if not to earth, then at least to deck – a deck which is still moving around too much for some people's comfort. Laura Wagenburg is standing in front of me. She's dressed for outdoors, in a coat with a headscarf tied tightly under her chin. She looks very wan. 'Mind if I join you?' she asks.

She lowers herself quite delicately on to the next-door chair and pulls a rug over her knees. 'This isn't yours?' she asks. 'You haven't moved down from the Sports Deck have you?'

'No,' I say, examining its label. 'It's Mr G. Fosket's chair – but he doesn't seem to need it just for now – and the Sports Deck's so windy I was about to take off.'

'Yes, I went up there to get some fresh air – fresh air! I was really hoping it would have all calmed down by now,' she says faintly.

'Have you been seasick?'

'Not exactly,' she says. I wait to hear how unexactly you can in fact be seasick. 'It's Ken – he's flat on his back. He can't even keep the Dramamine down. The doctor's given him a shot, so maybe . . . We didn't have this going over . . . I mean, if we had he might have made us fly home after all . . . so I'm kind of glad we didn't, because it can't last that long can it? – and really I'd have been fine to join you at lunch, but Ken didn't want me to – '

'Why not?'

Laura sighs and re-ties her headscarf. 'Needed someone to hold his hand I guess . . .'

Couldn't he have held his own hand, I wonder?

'I mean,' she continues, 'he's never been too terrific when he's gotten sick. If he gets a cold in the head, we all have to know about it. His mom always made a big fuss of him and – well, old habits I guess. Sometimes you kind of wonder if the looking-after is ever going to stop . . .'

'What?' I ask.

'It's not as if we even have kids yet, but Ken's like one great big kid all of his own – and I was always looking out for my dad after my mom died. I was about your age I guess – how old are you again?'

'Fifteen – and a bit.'

'Yeah – well, I was fourteen when Mom died. Cancer. After that I had a whole lot of looking-after to do because someone had to keep house and cook and everything . . .'

'It's hard with only one parent,' I say.

'Well, yes it is – of course you'd know wouldn't you?'

'No – I've never had to look after my mother, she's the looking-after kind herself.'

'You're lucky.'

'Yes. I suppose I am.'

'Anyway, Ken lifted me away from all that – only, I can see it's hard once you've been a looker-after – you get in a rut I guess – and it's hard to break free . . .' She's looking so sad and soulful that I have an urge to jolly her out of it.

'It's only one bout of seasickness,' I tell her, 'can't go on for ever.'

'But it's awfully symbolic – he says he wants to *die.*'

'Sydney says that's normal.'

'It can't be – '

'Perfectly. Happens all the time, apparently.'

'Mighty inconsiderate when a person's only just taken their wedding vows – what price eternity?' She sounds pretty much in a huff and flings herself back in the chair, closing her eyes. I sneak the book back out from under the blanket, and open it up at where I'd got my finger stuck on a page.

'What are you reading?'

'What? Me – oh – just a book.'

'Looks pretty absorbing.'

'A friend lent it to me.' I let it slip back under the blanket again. Something's telling me not to reveal its identity, and in any case,

I'm embarrassed. I look at Laura in a different light now – she and Ken have been doing what Fanny and her Charles have been doing in the book. All over the ship people have been doing it. All over the world since time began. They can't all have been having all these transports of delight though, can they? Wouldn't more of the delight rub off on the rest of us – and less of the worry and pain?

7p.m. – London

'Sit – eat – drink,' says Mr Christo. In the front room Mrs Christo is perched on a chair arm, surveying proudly the mosaic of small dishes laid out on the coffee table. This is the first time in the three years of living here that Kitty has penetrated so far into their domain. The ceilings are much higher than in her flat upstairs, but the place is crammed with enormous pieces of dark brown furniture and feels enclosed as a cave. A huge mahogany dresser has command of the whole back wall, and looms over them, laden with knick-knacks and photographs standing on doilies and little embroidered cloths. The sash windows are wide open to the sounds of Bissett Street, but the curtains hang limp. No stirring of the hot evening air. Kitty is sweating already.

'Mezzé,' says Mrs Christo of her culinary creations, wafting her hand over the spread of dishes, smiling shyly.

'Kaskavalli – cheese,' says Mr Christo, 'octopus in its ink, peppers, aubergine in oil, olives, tahini – you try – you try.'

Kitty can feel Mrs Christo watching her closely as she tastes, and propels herself into appreciative noises, exploring the unfamiliar flavours. The vegetables are delicious, though the cubes of octopus, which sound so exotic, taste of salted rubber. Mr Christo is pouring glasses of red wine. It's festive and cheeringly un-

English. Mr Christo seems to think so too. He's laughing about the weather, his forehead damp.

'Is strange – yes – this heat for London?' he says.

'Yes – though not for you I'd imagine,' says Kitty.

'In Cyprus is different – we live outside – is not so easy in London – feels not quite right you know?' He laughs again.

'Never I remember it hot like this in London,' says Mrs Christo.

'How long have you been here?'

'We come 1956 – winter.'

'Somehow I thought it had been longer – you seem very well settled. Did you have family in London?'

Mr Christo shakes his head. 'We came alone. Later her brother and his wife come too. There was, you know, bad trouble – we had to get away.'

Of course there was trouble, an ongoing saga of disruption and violence that seeped into Kitty's consciousness through wireless bulletins on a daily basis. The Greeks and the Turks each claiming the island as their own, each certain of their historic rights: the uneasy transition from crown colony to Commonwealth – terrorism, schism. And now, this year, once again the name of Archbishop Makarios has been stealing the headlines, his dignified almost Christ-like face with its curtain of a black beard commanding the front pages, but dragging with it renewed dark phantoms. Uncertain of the Christos' allegiances, and hazy as to facts, Kitty nods and keeps her question neutral. 'Do you think it'll work – this UN peacekeeping business?' she asks.

'For a while, perhaps, but no – it's not natural – too much pressure. The whole thing will burst, they'll never agree. We are better to be here.'

'You must miss it – stupid of me – I'm sorry – of course you do.'

'In my heart yes, in my head no. We had EOKA bombings in our town. People were killed, my father's business was burnt to the ground.'

'By EOKA?'

'Who knows? After all we are Greeks – Greeks should not be killed by other Greeks, no? But we had Turkish landlord, so who knows?'

'That first winter here – was it a terrible shock – the differences – the cold?'

'No. We have cold in Cyprus too – the mountains – but the grey though – and the fog – the first real "pea-souper", yes? We learn what to call it pretty damn quick – pea-souper. That was surprise – not to see your feet on the road or your hand in front of your face.'

'I remember my first pea-souper too, back in the war. Yes, it was a shock. My first posting was to London – we didn't have pea-soupers in the country where I grew up. We had fog of course – lots of it – but I suppose we didn't have the smoke, so it was thinner.'

'You were in the army?'

'The WAF – but working in an office.'

'In London – all through?'

'No – that's what I wanted, but they sent me back to my roots – the country again, unfortunately. I'd have put up with the pea-soupers – and the bombing – anything, to stay in London.'

'Me, I was in the army – voluntary force with the British. I nearly lose my leg in Macedonia – with the partisans.'

'He did,' says Mrs Christo. 'Show her – roll up your trouser.'

'No . . .' Mr Christo looks embarrassed.

'He have cut from down here . . .' Mrs Christo rises from her perch and marks the spot on her own lower calf, then traces a line up to the pocket of her apron, 'to right up here – and it go bad – *green* . . .'

'*Gangrene*?' says Kitty.

'No – just *green*,' says Mrs Christo, but she's interrupted by a flood of Greek from her husband, and sinks back down, looking abashed.

'You don't want to hear these things,' says Mr Christo. 'This was not a good time, not for any of us.'

Kitty knows she's expected to agree, and tries to get away with a non-committal grunt. Because the guilty truth is that her own personal war was really not so bad. Not for her the agony of close family loss. There were the two dead aunts of course, her mother's sisters, Maev and Prue, but Kitty hardly knew them. Florence had let the contact dry up over the years. In Kitty's early childhood, they'd occasionally meet and always the same old family tales would emerge: Florence refusing to collect the eggs for Mam; Florence running away to Mr Sawyer's Seaside Saucies; Florence and that cheat of a cherry ice – how everyone giggled at that one – you should have seen her face when she finally told us, they'd say, talk about *riled*. Florence's view was that they were envious; had never forgiven her for, literally, fleeing the coop; had always resented her verve and flair – and husband. Maev and Prue had never married – a shortage of men after the war – and had settled as spinster sisters in Sevenoaks, where they were picked off in 1942 by a stray bomb, whilst sleeping in the supposed safety of their Anderson shelter behind the compost heap. Florence seemed more affected by the irony of this event than by its consequences. Typical of life, she said with a huge sniff but no tears – always ready to catch you out.

So Kitty's own personal war brought only benefits, offering her an escape route by joining the WAF. Both she and Florence saw that first London posting as a blessing, though Percy fought to keep his daughter on the land, working for him, reserved occupation and all – surely safer than facing the terror of the blitz.

It was a heavy blow to be sent back to Norfolk, after only four months, even if this time round Kitty was trim in her WAF uniform – but that was the way of it. East Anglia was suitably flat and the right side of the country for aerodromes. The fact that RAF Watton threw her straight back into the middle of carrot and potato country was just another of life's little jokes – one which Florence always suspected her husband of engineering, though how Percy Combs was supposed to have nobbled Bomber Command was surely a conspiracy too far for even her imagination.

'We should forget the war,' says Mr Christo now, 'we should only look to the future.'

His words break across Kitty's thoughts, dispelling the flat fenland vision, and replacing it with another unknown land. 'You went straight back to Cyprus, after the war?' she asks.

'Of course, it was my home – Famagusta. We had business – family business – a grocery bar.'

'That sounds an unlikely combination.'

'Is what we have in Cyprus – a little bit shop and a little bit bar – café – I'd like to do it here you know. The Cypriots miss home – they would like it too – but with your licensing laws it's not possible. I have to be the vegetable seller instead – the green-grocer.'

'*Green*,' adds Mrs Christo, laughing. 'Is funny – the grocer who is green . . .'

They relax through the dinner. Mrs Christo's kleftiko turns out to be an unctuous dish of lamb with buttery rice, and there are more things in oil and herbs and a sharp fresh salad. With coffee, Kitty and Mr Christo eat little nut pastries and Turkish delight. Mrs Christo eats nothing after the main course, but brings out a bundle of white crochet and starts busily clicking with the hook against her thumbnail. I must learn more of this food, Kitty thinks in the warm embrace of the wine. I must travel to find it. With Gilbert. Gilbert will be a travelling man. Gilbert will know all about kleftiko and octopus cubes, and the land they come from. We'll explore it together.

'Do you have any photographs?' she asks. 'Of Cyprus – of your home?'

Mr Christo holds an expansive hand out towards the dresser.

Kitty gets up, aware she's slightly tipsy and swaying. There are pictures of houses, a raw concrete villa in the middle of an orchard, a woman in black, a group of laughing men sitting in a square, a child in a white headdress like a wedding veil, made from the same material as the doily the photograph stands on – the same crochet Mrs Christo is clicking away at now.

'Our daughter, Constantina,' says Mr Christo.

'I'd no idea – you've never mentioned . . .' Kitty goes to pick it up, but some blessed instinct stops her, and instead she leans closer in to examine the face. 'She's beautiful,' she says automatically, though it's a solemn little face, of a child maybe eight or nine.

'She's dead,' says Mr Christo.

'Oh – Mr Christo, I'm so sorry – I didn't mean . . .' Kitty steps back. Now she reassesses the dresser, sees it's more an altar than a mere receptacle for knick-knacks and doilies. 'Oh I'm so *sorry* . . . I . . .' she says, and sees that Mrs Christo's hands have stilled, the piece of crochet suspended, dangling over her lap. 'How . . .?'

'The burning of my father's shop.'

'How terrible for you – what a great sadness.'

'Yes, truly terrible – so Mrs Feast – you know what I say – forget the war – forget all the wars. *That* to the wars . . .' He draws his fingers to his mouth, then blows them sharply away in a spasm of disgust. 'We look to the future – our children are the future . . .'

Kitty looks back at Mrs Christo. Her hands have restarted their methodical clicking of the crochet, but tears have swelled along the rims of her eyes.

'And you have your Ella. You are lucky woman Mrs Feast – she is your future.'

'Yes.'

'Very precious – a daughter is very precious.'

'I think so too.'

'We drink to your Ella – a little raki – we toast her on her way, yes?'

218

'All right Mr Christo – thank you – yes – we toast her on her way.'

10p.m. – RMS Queen Elizabeth

The sea has calmed right down. People begin to emerge quite quickly round about teatime. They aren't as boisterous as usual I notice: everyone is tip-toeing around, as if they're not quite sure they can stand upright, as if they're expecting the ship to start plunging around again. I'm a bit like that too. After this morning it's a hard feeling to shake off. It still seems safer to sit down as much as possible.

Dinner is fairly quiet, though Laura, Sydney, Madge and I all tuck in pretty well. There's no sign of Paul at his table, nor of Ken at ours. He's stayed in bed. Laura says he's still only well enough for chicken soup, and she orders him a special kosher kind with matzo balls which she says will remind him of his mother . . . and then she pulls a funny face and giggles. The evening's programme is a choice of bingo in the Lounge or a Peter Sellers film. Madge is off to the cinema, dragging Laura with her, even though she'd said she ought to go back and check on Ken. Madge says, 'Oh come on kid – live dangerously,' – and Laura says, 'Okay – but I'd better just go take a peek at him,' – but Madge's expression changes her mind and she adds, 'Okay then – not even a peek.' They ask me to join them. Only I'm dying to get back to *Fanny Hill*, so I say no. When they ask why, I just mumble, 'Busy,' and Madge looks pointedly over at Paul's table, and Sydney says, 'Don't enquire Madam – she's a lady of mystery, aren't you, Miss Eleanor? They seek her here, they seek her there – eh? No telling what the young get up to, eh?' But he leaves it hanging in the air, staring at me, and I can see they're all expecting some sort of answer, so I just say, 'Busy – that's all,' and I abandon my coffee and petits fours, rather regretfully, because I can see if I don't get away quickly they'll be hard to shake off.

The book is in my handbag, squashed in there, and I feel as if it's radiating heat, about to burn a hole right through the side. I don't know when I've ever read a book so quickly. I'm nearly half-way through, and I'd be even further if I could find somewhere private to get on with it. I still can't face my cabin. Even though the Keropoulos children have stopped throwing up, the memory lingers on. Vera's been an absolute whiz with the bleach and carbolic, but the atmosphere is still like a sick room. Mrs K. has turned into a ministering angel. Vera's found her an armchair which takes up nearly the whole of the floor, and she's been sitting there all day, reading a Walt Disney version of *Cinderella*, and feeding them arrowroot biscuits. So it's not the most obvious place for me to continue my sexual education according to Mistress Fanny Hill.

The lounges, bars and Smoke Room aren't any good either, all too busy with people, bingo or booze, so the Sports Deck yet again seems my best refuge. The wind has dropped, the sky is thickly clouded and I can't see much of what's happening down on the sea, except for the little flicks of light reflected from the ship's portholes, but it's not cold and, best of all, there's no one else up here. I pick one of the steamer chairs in the shelter at the back and get myself a cushion and rug. It's quite cosy; I'm all tucked up and there's just enough light from the lamps behind to be able to read.

I'm totally absorbed in no time. The things this woman gets up to – Rosie's never going to believe it when I tell her.

The high-wrought agitation, the sweet urgency of this to-and-fro friction, raised the titillation on me to its height; so that finding myself on the point of going [going *where* I wonder?], and loath to leave the tender partner of my joys behind me, I employed all the forwarding motions and arts my experience suggested to me to promote his keeping me company to our journey's end. I not only tightened the pleasure-girth round my restless inmate by a secret spring of suction and compression that obeys the will in those parts, but stole my hand softly to that store-bag of nature's prime sweets, which is so pleasingly attached to its conduit pipe from which we receive them; there feeling, and most gently indeed, squeezing those tender globular reservoirs; the magic touch took instant effect, quickened, and brought on upon the spur the symptoms of that sweet agony, the melting, moment of dissolution, when pleasure dies by pleasure, and the mysterious engine of it over-comes the titillation it has raised in those parts, by plying them with the stream of a warm liquid that is itself the highest of all titillations, and which they thirstily express and draw in like the hot-natured leech . . .

'I thought I might find you here . . .'

I look round. Sydney is standing near the entrance to the stairs and he's blocking out the main source of light. I've been so involved in Fanny's adventures that I don't snap to attention quite fast enough.

'Interesting is it?' he says, and walks over.

'Yes,' I say.

'You looked in another world.'

'Did I?' My voice doesn't come out quite right. I'm breathing rather fast.

'Are you all right my dear?'

'Fine,' I gulp.

'Good – that's the ticket. Mind if I join you?'

'Well . . .'

He drags the nearest chair over to me and sits down.

'You're nice and cosy – under that rug.'

'Yes,' I say, trying to hide Fanny beneath said rug, but managing to ruck it up with my heels at the same time. Sydney reaches over and straightens it back over my legs, smoothing it down.

'Nice,' he says. 'Nice and cosy.'

'Yes,' I say.

'Funny night to be out like this though – bingo didn't tempt you then?'

'Not my thing.'

'Nor mine, nor mine. I don't mind a flutter on the ship's auction, but bingo's a bit tame for an old goer like me.'

'Yes?'

'And for you too – you're a young goer aren't you then, Miss Eleanor?'

'Oh I wouldn't say that.'

'Wouldn't you then – but I would. Good is it – that book?'

'All right.'

'Looked a bit better than all right my dear – from where I was standing – looked a lot better than all right.'

'It's interesting.'

'Got it from the ship's library?'

'No. A friend.'

'So we've got *those* sort of friends on board have we?'

'I beg your pardon?'

'Friends with dirty books.'

'I don't – '

'The Commander told me he'd seen something at the service this morning. He said he couldn't believe his eyes – but I told him he must have been mistaken. She's not that sort of girl I said – seems I was wrong.'

'He can talk,' I say.

'Well, there you're right my dear. He *can* talk. He very probably will – a girl of your age, wandering round the ship with dirty books . . .'

'It's not a dirty book. It's historical.'

'Let's have a look then.'

'No.'

'You see, that's what I like about you, Miss Eleanor. You've got spirit – despite appearances.'

222

'What do you mean, despite appearances?'

'Butter wouldn't melt in your mouth. That's what the Commander said. She's sly that one, he said. Makes out she's all innocent, but she knows more than she cracks on, that's what he told me.'

'He's a dirty old man.'

'Don't say that dear, you don't know what you're talking about. He's not had it easy you know. He's had trauma in his life. You shouldn't go chucking accusations about.'

'He was exposing himself.'

'Now that's just wicked.'

'Yes – it was.'

'You shouldn't jump to conclusions.' He takes my hand. 'You're a good girl, Miss Eleanor – don't go spoiling things. You don't know what it's like, thank God – you're too young. Things don't always work out the way you'd hope – and it's not so easy once you're old. It does no harm to be kind – you could be kind, Miss Eleanor, it wouldn't take anything from you and it could do a service.' He's got my hand layered between both of his now, flat like a sandwich, and he's sliding it between his palms.

'I don't want to do the Commander a service,' I say as firmly as I can and try to pull my hand back.

'You're a good girl, Eleanor,' he says again, 'and it's not the Commander I'm thinking of. Be kind. You've got your whole life ahead of you – it wouldn't hurt to be kind . . .' He pulls my hand towards him, he's pressing it against the whiskery tweed of his waistcoat.

'Please,' I say, trying to get my hand back, and as I lean over, I'm blocking the light so I can't see what he's doing, only the hairiness of the tweed has changed, it's softer, and then it's warm and smooth and fleshy. Sydney makes a funny noise, a bit as if he's straining to pull out a cork and a bit as if he's smothering a sneeze, and he suddenly goes very rigid, then sighs.

'There's a good girl,' he says, and gets up. 'Just the ticket.'

When he's gone I realize my hand is all wet and sticky. When I hold it up to the light, I see it's smeared with what looks like a dollop of wallpaper paste. Honestly. I *mean*.

Monday

'If you could just keep your legs up like that Mrs Feast we'll have another go – you probably need the next size – don't want any of the little beasties getting through do we? I'll just see if we've got one across the hall. Shan't be a sec . . .' The doctor closes the door behind her. Merciful relief – at least the doctor is female and at least she closes doors, for otherwise this is not a high point in the life of Mrs Katherine Feast (née Combs).

Kitty is lying on a high examination couch. From neck to navel she's fully clothed, quite prettily (you could almost say prissily), in a silk blouse printed all over with butterflies. Her skirt is pushed up, gathered in a lumpy tyre round her waist, but from there down she is naked and exposed to the ruthless light of an Anglepoise lamp pointing directly up what Florence would have called, in a coarser moment, her 'jacksie'. The thought of Florence, flitting through her mind like this, uncalled for, makes her laugh – a brief honk of a laugh – out loud. And what should draw this sound from her but the memory of Florence pushing that copy of Dr Marie Stopes's *Married Love* into her hands, the night before her wedding to Jack, for now here lies Kitty in the very temple of 'married love', the Marie Stopes Clinic.

The doctor returns. She's a robust-looking woman with salt and pepper hair, flat Clarks sandals and a blue cotton dress peeping out from under a white coat. She looks like someone whose sexual life has been vigorous and uncomplicated – as if you could tell (!), thinks Kitty. She's asked a few searching questions of her patient, has been perfectly happy to explain the various methods of contraception, and is completely uninterested in Kitty's marital status or lack of it. No unspoken disapproval of a 'feme sole' here, although the permanence or otherwise of any sexual relationship her patient might have does of course have some bearing on the recommended method. Yes, they do have the new pill available. It seems to be extremely effective – not without side effects of course, what isn't? However, it can be prescribed, if Kitty's blood pressure is normal, though she'll have to wait until her next period before she can even start taking it, and it won't be effective for some weeks. In the meantime, will she be needing additional protection? Kitty says she might, then changes the verb to 'will' – otherwise why waste the doctor's time? From here on, the alternatives are too familiar and pretty disappointing. Things really haven't moved on much since all that rubber ten years ago. There's the coil of course – painful to fit, with a variety of potential risks, and unnecessary if the pill is to be her final choice. Apart from that it seems to be back to rubber again in various guises, with accompanying tubes of gooey spermicide or jelly pessaries. So, rubber it is then – so much for scientific advance.

The doctor produces the other, larger Dutch cap, the one she'd gone to find, removes it from a neat plastic box like a fat powder compact, and proceeds to fit it with vigour. Kitty stares at the ceiling, and talks about the weather to disguise the squelchy noises coming from below.

'Yes,' says the doctor. 'It's been boiling hasn't it – though not if you've worked in Calcutta, which I have. Now, that seems a better fit – let me just try – yes . . .' Most of her fingers seem to disappear within and pull the cap out again. She holds it up on the end of her thumb like a conjuror with one of those plate-balancing acts, her expression triumphant. 'I think we've done it – now you have a go.'

Is this worth it? thinks Kitty, squatting down on the floor and attempting to obey instructions. Could this possibly be worth it?

'Now you need to be sure your cervix is covered,' says the doctor. 'You should be able to feel it through the rubber – got it? – yes?'

'I think so,' says Kitty.

'Got to be better than "thinking so", Mrs Feast – got to be *certain*. Have a rootle about – you should be able to feel the edge of the cap – yes? – now move in and try again . . .'

Then there's the comedy of retrieval, for the last thing you want is the blasted thing lost in there for ever.

'Hook your finger over the edge – got it? – now pull – but hang on – it's slippery . . .'

Kitty pulls gingerly, trying not to turn her vision of the cap bouncing off and away across the floor into grimly humorous reality.

'Well done. Now have another go.'

Finally it's over. Kitty steps out into the hot bright sunlight of Whitfield Street with a brown paper bag of supplies, her head full of provisos and prohibitions. For the sake of sexual spontaneity, the doctor urges, it's always best to be prepared in advance – though any longer than a couple of hours and she'll need to add an extra boost of spermicide.

Spontaneity – don't make me laugh, thinks Kitty. How spontaneous can you be, rolling around London with your tubes and packets? Can she really arrive at Gilbert Denby's mansion flat in Victoria, ready primed, as it were, for action? How awkward it all is – and yet, and yet – other women seem to manage, other women do.

'You're late Mrs Feast – *again* – '

'Sorry Mrs Croxton.'

'What was it this time – the tube – *again* – your alarm clock not gone off?'

'The tube . . .' Kitty mumbles.

'You seem to be out of luck with the tube at the moment –

perhaps you'd better switch to buses – and if you know you're going to be late perhaps you wouldn't stop for shopping.' Mrs Croxton is beadily eyeing the brown paper bag.

'Just my lunch Mrs Croxton,' says Kitty, foolishly hoisting herself on her own petard. 'I thought I'd stay in today – get some extra work done . . .' now condemning herself to lunchlessness, then unable to hide a rueful smile at the thought of trying to glean nourishment from the bag's contents. If Mrs Croxton did but know, eh?

'Good, good . . .' Mrs Croxton says now, suspicious of the smile; Kitty can see her mind turning over the possibility of secrets. 'Better get on then. There's a letter from the foundry – we need to confirm the Slater edition. I thought we might push the boat out and go for fifteen? Yes?'

'If you think so Mrs Croxton.'

'Well, yes, I do – oh, and there was a telephone call for you first thing.'

'Yes?' says Kitty – too fast, too urgent.

'But of course you weren't here.'

'No.'

'I think it was that chap who rang the other day – Denby, would that be the name?'

'Yes?'

'Said he'll ring later. He's not the man who was interested in the pair of frogs is he?'

'No.'

'No – you said. Yes – well . . .' Mrs Croxton hangs around at the door, though really she should be on her way: hair appointment in Berkeley Square. 'How are you getting on without your daughter?'

'Fine.'

'Lonely for you, I should have thought – weekends are funny things . . .'

'Better get on with work now then, hadn't I?' says Kitty and sits down decisively behind the desk.

9a.m. – RMS Queen Elizabeth

I think I've gone off Fanny Hill, what with one thing and another.

I stay in bed. The thought of breakfast with Sydney Maxton-Bligh on the other side of the toast rack is too unappetizing. I make do with Vera's usual tray of morning tea and read the *Ocean Times*. There were race riots in Harlem the day before yesterday and Dr Martin Luther King went on television in America and asked everyone to 'close the springs of racial poison'. Too right. Why so much poison? Why is it so hard to be generous? Sydney made that business last night sound as if *I* wouldn't be generous – but the way it's left me, is . . . well I suppose 'poisoned' wouldn't be a bad way of putting it. You can kill plants off if you give them the wrong fertilizer can't you? And I'm feeling like a wilted flower: subconsciously I'm probably still identifying with daisies.

Eenie and Mo are the opposite of poisoned this morning. Now the sea is calm, it's as if they've been reborn; their faces have gone back to being pink and shiny. Mrs K. has also reverted to type: she spent half-an-hour telling the kids to 'shuddup', and sticking her head in the pillow, but she's got herself going now. The children's party was cancelled yesterday because of the storm, but it's on again for today, and Eenie and Mo are already clamouring for their glad rags. They go off to breakfast fully kitted out in blue organza with smocked bodices, and Mrs K. telling them she'll have their guts for garters if they get them dirty.

Once they've gone, I climb down from my bunk and take a look at myself in the mirror. I've got dark circles under my eyes and I may even be getting bags. Already. Can you believe it? I hold my hand up – the one Sydney did his thing over last night. It's just the same old hand but it feels dirty. I feel dirty too. I head for the bath. I run the salt water taps and use the special salt water soap to get up a lather. The salt surely makes it cleaner somehow. I scrub and scrub, but the feeling of dirt won't go away.

Back in the cabin I stick some rollers in my hair while I get dressed and start to do something with my face. There's a knock on the door. I assume it's Vera and shout, 'Come in.' It's Paul. He still looks very pale.

'Oh – hello . . .' I automatically start pulling the rollers out. I mean why do these things happen to me?

'I just thought I'd . . .' he starts but doesn't finish.

'Yes?' I say, whipping out the last roller and frisking up my hair with my fingers.

'Didn't mean to interrupt . . .' he says.

'You're not,' I say, trying to sound airy, sophisticated. 'Pull up a pew.' It's a daft thing to add because of course there isn't anything that's even an approximation of a pew. Or anything to pull up for that matter. The armchair Vera brought yesterday has been taken away. He sits on the edge of Mrs K.'s bunk.

'Are you all right?' I say.

'Yeah . . .'

'You don't look all that all right.'

'Yeah – well I meant it, what I said – once we dock in New York I'm never going on a sodding ship again, as long as I live.'

'How will you get home?'

'Have to fly.'

'Isn't it more expensive?'

'I'll have to earn the extra – pay me mam back or something – I'll walk on the bloody water back to England rather than sail again – I'll turn myself into Jesus Christ.'

'Don't,' I say. 'It's blasphemous.' Sister Marie-Francis would *faint*.

'It's bloody ironic i'n't it – a true son of Liverpool that's me –
I've probably got fifty per cent seawater running in my veins, and
it turns out I can't stand the sea. I don't understand it. I'm never
like this on the Birkenhead ferry.'

'But it's calm now. The storm's over – everyone feels fine.'

'Except me – the inside of my head's still going up and down
like a bloody yo-yo. Are you all right then?'

'Me? Yes – I'm fine. Never been finer.'

'Are you? – good – only I looked out for you at breakfast and
you weren't there, so I wondered.'

'Wasn't hungry.'

'No. Me neither . . .' He's staring glumly down at his feet. I
use the pause to turn back to the mirror and start whacking on
mascara as fast as I can.

'Have you seen Henrietta this morning?' he says. I keep my back
turned away from him, but I can see his reflection in the glass.

'No.'

'Oh,' he says. 'Only I have, you see . . .'

'Oh?' I say.

'Yeah – and she weren't alone.'

'No?'

'No – she had that Chip with her. "Chip" – what a name. Why
have Americans got so many names that are really nouns – have
you noticed that? Chuck McKinley playing at Wimbledon. *Chuck*
– I ask you . . .'

'That's a verb,' I object.

'Not if it's a steak it's not.'

'No.'

'Anyway, the thing is – the thing about Henrietta is, she was
with that Chip – and I think someone should tell her . . .'

'What? Tell her what?'

'Well, it's sick i'n't it – she's sick. She's just throwing herself
round the ship like she's a bloody tart. She slept with a steward
on the first night.'

'No – how do you know?' I'm fascinated.

'Because she told me. She was bloody boasting about it. Then there was me – now that Chip bloke – it's not right. She's sick in the 'ead – someone ought to tell 'er . . .'

'Why? Why is it sick?' I ask.

'Oh come on Ella – you know why.'

'Would it be sick if it were you?'

'What?'

'You who'd slept with three different girls on three different nights?'

'Oh come on, that's different.'

'Why?'

'You know why.'

'No I don't – '

'Because I'm a bloke that's why.'

'I thought that's what you might have meant.'

'Well, why ask me? It stands to reason, it's different for a bloke. Anyway, what I mean is that somebody should give that lass a bloody good talking to, before it's too bloody late. That's what I mean.'

'Well – yes – I expect you're right,' I say, though he must be bonko if he thinks I'm the right bod for the job.

10a.m. – Point Harbor

The delivery boy from Flower Fayre brings the orchid early. It's packed in a cellophane box, arranged with wisps of fern and a blue satin ribbon.

'Did you order blue?' says Jack.

'I didn't say any colour,' says Lynn. 'I just said an orchid.'

'I don't like the blue – supposing it doesn't go with whatever Ella's wearing?'

'You can take the ribbon off.'

'But won't the whole thing fall apart?'

Lynn peers through the cellophane. The cuckoo's orchid is large and fleshy, with lobes of dark maroon and a lolling greenish tongue. It's really very ugly. 'I don't think so. It's tied up with wire underneath.'

'It's supposed to be a corsage – don't you need some sort of a ribbon on a corsage – and do you think it'll last? Does it have water in there?'

'Stick it in the motel icebox when you get there – isn't that what they do?' says Lynn, knowing she doesn't give a hoot or a hang for the cuckoo's orchid.

Jack leaves at nine. He's stopping off in Boston – says he has a meeting – then he'll take Route 95 south via Providence. He'll be in New York by evening. The *Queen Elizabeth* is due into Pier 90 at 10a.m. tomorrow, and Jack intends to be there in good time. Lynn kisses him goodbye, then follows the car down the driveway to the slip road, waving him on his way. He's been so excited. He even seems to have dressed with extra care. As well as the orchid, he's taking four shirts – all new. He looks like a guilty little boy when he realizes she's watching him pack.

'It's just in case,' he says; 'the heat – don't want to be all sweaty.'

'Of course not,' she says, and wishes the thrill of the cuckoo's arrival could rub off on her a little more. Instead she wonders when he last made this kind of effort for her, and can't truly remember.

At the driveway's entrance, she collects the mail from the box and today's *Boston Globe*, then stands looking back up at the house. With its stone walls and white shutters it looks more fairy tale than real to her – so clearly outlined against the backdrop of pine trees and brilliant blue sky that it could almost be a movie set. She has a sudden sense of catching it out unawares, so that if she could transport herself instantly back up the hill and peep round the corner, she'd see it was only a wooden flat, a pretence of a stone house, propped up on scaffolding. It's all as insubstantial as a dream.

The apparition is instantly dispersed by the sound of Sadie Dorling's car chug-chugging as it makes the narrow turn round the bend on to the slip-road.

'Hi Sadie – no Leroy today?'

'Hi there Miz Feast – nope, his mom was home for the weekend, and she's stayin' on – taken him to the beach.'

'Good day for it.'

'You want a ride?'

'Sure – lazy huh?' Lynn slides herself awkwardly on to the front seat of the Dodge.

'Might as well make the most of it while you can – Junior's going to change a few things around here,' says Sadie.

'That's what I keep hearing.'

'Personally I don't recall what you might say was a solid night's sleep for the next ten years after my first arrived on the scene.'

'Was that Leroy's mom?'

'No – that was my son Eddy. Boys are worse I guess. Darlene had more what you might call sensitivity to her mom's needs – slept through pretty well from day one. But Eddy never really got the hang of it – not until he had himself shot through the head in Korea.'

'Oh my God – Sadie, you never said – I'd no idea – I'm so sorry . . .'

'Oh he survived it all right. The bullet's still there, though – got itself stuck some place they can't get it out.'

'What's it done to him?'

'Well, not a lot of good, you could say that. He sure sleeps through the nights now, that I can tell you – and most of the days too.'

'How old is he?'

'Just thirty. He was nineteen when it happened. At the time, you know, I thought I'd die with the worry – but you can't keep dying can you? Once you're a parent you open up the door to all that. It ain't easy, all that pain, because suddenly you really care – about everything, I guess. None of it's unimportant any more.'

They've reached the front of the house. Sadie switches off the ignition, but neither of them moves. It's hot and still. The cicadas scratch and sing, the pine warblers flute.

Sadie breaks their moment. 'What you got for me today Miz Feast?'

'Do you know, Sadie – do you know . . . I have no idea.'

'You'd better get yourself an idea or I've come all this way for nothin'. Shall I get going on with the laundry?'

'There isn't any. You did it all Friday – and we were out all day yesterday on a sail boat, new friends of Jack's – so we're spick 'n' span Sadie, there's been no time to mess anything up. We're so spick 'n' span you'd never believe it – apart from Junior's room.'

Lynn lays her hand on her belly – thinks of the little head, the tiny limbs turning; thinks of bullets in Korea, and missiles on Cuba, and riots in Harlem, and the assassinated president, and how suddenly she cares, so much, about the future; how this unborn child is forcing her to an investment she wouldn't have sought for herself. 'Well there is that . . .' she adds.

'What?'

'Junior's room – it all needs doing. I've got the paint – it's called Dawn.'

'Pink or blue?'

'Neither – creamy light – I didn't want to tempt fate either way. I bought it weeks ago, but Jack keeps putting it off – says we've got to have professional decorators in, but then he won't let me call them, says it can wait . . .'

'It's only paint?'

'Only paint.'

'You got brushes and stuff – ?'

'And rollers . . .'

'Well, I'm what you might call Wonder Woman with a roller.' Sadie flexes her right bicep.

'Me too – done enough of it in my time.'

'I guess we could give Mr Feast a nice surprise. When's he gettin' back with his daughter?'

'Tomorrow night. He's booked a table at the Harbor Inn for dinner.'

'*Fancy-smancy* – so you don't even have to cook then . . .'

'Nope.'

'Want to give it a shot?'

'You'd help me – really?'

'There's no way I'd let you do it alone Miz Feast – and you're not to go climbing no ladders, got that?'

'On one condition – you call me Lynn,' says Lynn, feeling a renewed surge of that energy she'd felt on Saturday – oh so welcome – something that has deserted her for what seems like weeks. A real buzzing of electricity, straight from her brain to her bones.

3p.m. – *RMS* Queen Elizabeth

The presence of Sydney Maxton-Bligh won't go away. He's been hanging around in my mind uncomfortably all morning. I feel like a small hibernating animal in my need not to face him, but then again why should I be the one who hides? I've done nothing wrong. I haven't even led anybody on, I'm sure of that.

Everybody's making up for lost time after the storm. The sun is out and the Sports Deck is crammed. On the principle of safety in numbers, I make up a four with Madge and the Wagenburgs for shuffleboard, and we all get fiercely competitive, even though no one really knows the rules, which makes Ken argumentative. Laura says Sydney wasn't at breakfast – no one's seen him. So, has he locked himself in the bathroom, soaking in the seawater? Trying to scrub off his sense of shame? I wish I wasn't joking.

Ken and Laura win the match, and then we troop down to lunch. Ken announces he feels so much better he could eat a horse again, and Madge says the chicken soup must be good voodoo, and Laura says, 'Jewish penicillin – didn't you know that?' and everyone's having a laugh. It's fun, being part of the group, even if they are so old – and suddenly I realize I've shaken off most of the Sydney feeling – for the moment at least.

After everyone felt so queasy yesterday, we all attack the fantastic menu like vultures – apart from Madge, of course, who settles for a few leaves of Caesar salad and a shaving of cold chicken breast. This is what I order, just for the record – because it *is* a sort of record: Crab Flake Cocktail followed by Danish Brook Trout followed by Roast Aylesbury Duckling with Orange Salad. After that I'm so full I can hardly breathe, no room for pudding – except there's something on the menu under the ice creams called 'Cherry Vanilla' and I sort of feel I *have* to order that, just for old times' sake.

Madge starts teasing me – says they'll have to take me off the ship by crane if I eat any more. But I tell her I can't *not* have the cherry ice, in memory of my dear old granny. And then they want to hear the whole story. When I've finished, Ken says, 'What a scam,' and wants to know why Gran didn't 'go get her dad to trash the guy', which sounds so un-Gran it might as well be Double Dutch with a sprinkling of Swahili. By the time the waiter brings this particular cherry ice cream, it's taken on embarrassing significance and everyone stares at it – not much to write home about really, half pink, half white, with a fan wafer sticking out of the top. It tastes a bit dull too, though after everything else I've had, it's probably not a fair trial. I give it up after half a spoonful, on the basis that Madge is right – and if I eat any more I'll burst.

'You know, maybe it's just something to do with cherry ice cream,' she laughs, 'maybe it's not *supposed* to be all that exciting.'

Back in Cabin D9, however, the atmosphere is close to erupting with emotion. With absolutely certain inevitability, Mo has by now mucked up her organza frock with a great streak of cream of tomato soup. Eenie is still in a pristine state and is sitting up on her bunk with her legs dangling over the side, looking very smug, while Mrs K. is on her knees tossing clothes out of the chest of drawers on either side of her, like a cartoon dog digging for a bone. Mo is standing in the middle of this vestment hill, wearing just her knicks. She has grey streaky lines of tears running down her cheeks and every so often a big sob heaves out and shakes her skinny little ribcage.

'Cut it out Mo!' shouts Mrs K. ('Cuddidoud!'). 'What did I ever do to deserve you? One thing I ask – just the one – keep your dress clean. What did I ask? Huh?'

Another sob is all she gets as an answer.

'Mommy,' says Eenie.

'Quiet now Eenie – I got my hands full.'

'Mommy – *I* kept my dress clean.'

'Shut up Eenie. What are we gonna put you in Mo?'

'I wanna be a pwincess.'

'You should be so lucky. You remember the story of Cinderella – what she wore before her fairy godmother came along? Rags, that's what she wore . . .'

'I don' wanna wear rags – I wanna be a pwincess.'

'You'll have to wear your sundress. It's all we've got that's clean.'

'It's not a pwincess dress . . .'

'You wrecked your princess dress. Now you gotta take the

238

consequences, you understand – and your sundress is *pretty* – '

'Can I help?' I interrupt.

'Not unless you keep spare princess dresses under your pillow,' says Mrs K. Just the mere idea sends a wash of hope over Mo and she's staring up at me as if I'm about to tap my fairy wand. I run my mind rapidly through my wardrobe.

'There's my tiered petticoat,' I suggest.

'Your what?' says Mrs K.

'My half-slip – it's made of white tulle – I have to soak it in sugar and water every time I wash it, to keep it stiff – that's a bit princessy.' I yank my pile of clothes from the top of the cupboard, fish it out and slip it over Mo's head. With the elastic pulled up under her armpits it's like a strapless crinoline on her, the hem just reaching the top of her feet. She's wearing silver sandals and has pink varnish on her toenails. She points each foot delicately out from under the slip now, and inspects the effect.

'I'm a pwincess.' she says. She's glowing again.

'It's not a *real* pwincess dress,' growls Eenie.

'It is, isn't it Ella?' says Mo.

'You're gonna wear Ella's slip, Mo? Huh?' says Mrs K.

Mo nods, solemn.

'Whaddya say to Ella then, Mo?'

'Thank you,' she whispers, and I tip her a wink.

Once they've gone off to the party, I start to gather up my clothes again and spot Hen's daisy bolero lurking in amongst my blouses. I'd forgotten all about it since yesterday and the storm. I'll have to get it back to her – and the book too, I suppose. There may not be much more of a chance, once we start the business of arrival, because tomorrow morning we'll be docking in New York. Tomorrow morning I'll be seeing Dad. I dig my nails into my arm to double check. Yup – I'm here all right. It's not one of those meandering dreams where you wake up and find yourself back in bed in Bissett Street. Only to see Dad – actually *see* Dad . . . What'll we do first? Kiss each other? Hug?

239

Will we be shy? Will he recognize me? I'll recognize him all right. I've got his face in my brain for keeps. So I'd better return Hen's stuff now. After that, I don't suppose I'll ever see her again.

The trouble is, I don't want to see her now either. When I get to A Deck I wonder if I can just give the things to a stewardess to deliver, but then I think she's bound to take a peek at old *Fanny Hill*, which might cause uproar, so I don't really have an alternative. Only, when I knock on the door, there's no answer. So what? – she's probably off having a grand old time – probably doing it with Chip again, or the steward, or both. I try the door, in the unlikely event it's not locked, and it isn't. Thinking I may as well leave the things inside, I open it very warily. And what am I expecting to see – a naked Chip laid out on the spare bed like Paul was yesterday – or a naked Chip *plus* a naked Paul? I don't know quite – by now I wouldn't put anything past her – but it's not what I do find, which is Hen asleep in her bed. The covers are pulled right up to her chin, so only her face shows, very pale and thin like one of those women on a medieval tomb. The other bed is tidily made up – no sign of lovers' tussles. I leave the bolero and the book on the coverlet and turn to creep out on tiptoe.

'What do you want?' Hen's voice sounds creaky.

'Oh – hello – I thought you were asleep. I tried knocking.'

'I heard.'

'I thought no one was here.'

'Obviously.'

'Only I wanted to bring your jacket back – '

'Oh that – you shouldn't have bothered – keep it as a memento.'

Well, here's a turn up – not her previous attitude at all. 'But it's part of a matching set,' I say.

'I don't suppose I'll ever wear it again.'

'Why not?'

'I don't suppose I'll ever *do* anything ever again.'

'What's happened?'

'Nothing. That's what's happened.'

'Right,' I say. You mean like normal life for the rest of us, Hen. 'Are you ill?' I ask.

'Yes.'

'Seasick?'

'No.'

'The curse?'

'Yes.'

'Take an Anadin.'

'Oh God, Ella – stuff it. Don't go all bracing on me – and don't look so cheerful. Stop grinning.'

'I'm sorry – I didn't know I was.' I try to recompose my mouth. 'I think that's just what my face does – and the whole ship's very cheerful – it feels a bit like the last day of term. Everyone's excited about arriving.'

'Not everyone. I've had a horrible trip – nothing's happened. Nothing ever happens. I try so hard, but it just blows up in my face . . . it's all so sad and dull . . .'

Well I ask you – of all the unlikely people to bang on about nothing happening – she should try life in Bissett Street for example. How dull is dull I'd have to ask myself?

'And now I've got to deal with Mummy and Daddy and all that crap. You can't begin to imagine . . . I'm dreading arriving. I just want to stay here under the covers for ever. You don't know how lucky you are, just being you and your mother, being so important to her. I'm not important to anybody. Nobody in the family knows what to do with me. I don't belong anywhere. Aunt Eve wants me out of her hair all the time, and the parents just have me as a duty visit. It's going to be a horrible summer. We'll be shut up in that dark air-conditioned apartment with all the windows closed, and Daddy'll be in a foul mood all the time he's home, so he'll stay out till all hours, and Mummy'll be sozzled by 11 every single morning, and I'll have to cover for her. She goes all droopy when she's drunk. She doesn't get violent or anything, just more and more like a lump of lead and one of her eyelids hangs

241

down – like this . . .' Hen has a stab at doing an impersonation – it looks like Charles Laughton as Quasimodo. I can't help it: I laugh – and that makes her crack a bit too.

'Well, all right,' she says, ' – so I'm making a meal of it. But it's no fun – honestly. I don't know anyone in Manhattan, and the only people *they* know are old dried up sticks like them. Nobody really wants to know Mummy because she's such a bore. Drunks are. You don't get to meet your neighbours in apartment blocks and they'll keep such a sharp eye on me – they won't let me go out.'

'What?'

'Not on my own.'

'You can't mean it.'

'I bloody do. They won't have it.'

'But surely . . . in the daytime . . .?'

'In New York? You're joking. They keep me nailed to the bloody floorboards – and even if Mummy's half-cut and half-asleep there's the evil housekeeper. Leona she's called; she's like Rosa Kleb in *Goldfinger* – she reports back if I so much as poke my nose into the front lobby, let alone chat up the doorman. And in any case, I never have any money. You can't get away with much in New York when you're stony broke all the time.'

But it's all sounded so glamorous – Hen's world. Kensington and the father in the UN and Lucy Clayton and holidays in Munich and shoes from Kurt Geiger.

'Perhaps it won't be so bad – not this time,' I say.

'What makes you think that – *hope* that – exactly?'

'Because – I don't know – things do get better – on the whole.'

'That's your experience?'

'Well yes . . . I mean I always *hope*, don't you? I think I always *expect* improvement.'

'No – I don't. Life's a fucking pig. That's what I think. And I haven't got the curse. If only. I'm two weeks late and I'm never late. I've done everything I can think of – I've spent hours on that bloody vibrating belt thing in the gym. You'd think something would shift wouldn't you?'

'You think you might be preg – '

'Don't say it. Don't you dare say it out loud.'

'All right.'

'Oh God. Because – no. I *can't* be.'

'That's all right then.'

'Not in that sense Ella – I *can* be – only I just *can't* be – it'd be too gruesome . . .'

'Yes.'

'Well, why do you say that?'

'I was agreeing with you.'

'Well don't. Would it be so terribly gruesome?'

'Not necessarily,' I say as a careful compromise, though in reality I think it would.

'It's only a baby isn't it? It's not as if it's the plague.'

'No.'

'Only, it might as well be. My parents will be grim – if I'm preggers it'll be total cat among the pigeons time.'

'Do you know who? The father I mean . . .'

'God, yes Ella, I'm not a slapper – not yet.' But that's not what Paul thinks.

'Well who?'

'It's a boy from Henham College – we had each other behind the cricket pavilion after the joint school dance. It was bloody cold and I laddered my fishnets . . . stupid really. I don't actually know his full name – his friends called him Spot. Which was apt, in the circumstances. He was a Clearasil emergency zone. Oh God – what a pain . . .'

'But what about Chip . . . and Paul?'

'What about them?'

'Well, you know – you and them . . . if you have this other boyfriend . . .'

'Who said anything about him being a boyfriend – I thought I'd made that clear – and Paul's different. He seemed to have definite possibilities . . .'

'*I* thought so,' I say.

'Anyway, it's all been a dead loss. They were hopeless – both of them. If it wasn't *mal de mer*, it was brewers' droop. You wouldn't believe it would you? You'd have thought a bit of additional action would get something moving down below, even if the gym failed me. Totally pointless – and now they've all buggered off . . . left me alone . . . *again* . . .'

'Except, if you're pregnant . . .' I say.

'Yes?'

'Then you're not alone are you? There's the baby . . .' Fascinated, I find I'm staring at roughly where her stomach is, shrouded by the blankets.

'Gruesome thought.' Hen sits up slightly and stares at the same bit of blanket. 'Sort of "You're never alone with a Strand" – which reminds me, I'm suddenly dying for a fag. Want one?'

'No thanks.'

She lights up, then flings her head back on the pillow. 'So – it could be me and Spot Minor against the rest of the world you reckon?'

'It's just a reality – whatever else you think of the situation, you wouldn't actually be alone. There'd be someone else to think of.'

'If I didn't get rid of it of course.'

'Oh that. Could you – would you know how to find someone, a doctor?'

'Not in New York I wouldn't. Oh God. What a mess.'

But I'm suddenly thinking of Mo – her tiny wiry little body dancing around in my petticoat. How touching and fragile and strong she is – a woman in miniature, with not an inkling yet of how complicated it's all going to be.

'Having a baby might not be so bad,' I say out loud. 'You'd

be starting your own family, and you'd matter to the baby – you'd never be a sideline any more.'

7p.m. – London

To prime or not to prime? That is Kitty's question. In the end she plumps for being primed, slipping down to the basement WC in Croxton Fine Art and valiantly struggling with all that Marie Stopes rubber and spermicide in a space no bigger than a cardboard box. To be frank, she could have done with being more supple. Considering the contortions she has to attempt, training as a gymnast might not have gone amiss. Such is the practical reality of a responsible woman preparing to kick up her heels and abandon herself to lust.

Mrs Croxton simply refuses to go home early. Her hair has been freshly tortured into a handsome confection by her Berkeley Square coiffeur, and the long-dead Mr Croxton being unavailable for appreciation, she's keen to share the creation with any passing customer, lingering late at the gallery. Thus she's very much around and looming as Kitty comes up the stairs, secretly primed and publicly primped, with a change of jewellery and freshly applied makeup.

'Going somewhere special, Mrs Feast?'

'Not particularly special,' says Kitty, grim and amused all at the same time. For wouldn't Mrs C. like to know of her plans, of how Gilbert telephoned again, suggested they have dinner, but perhaps drinks first at the flat – why doesn't she come over as soon as she's free from work – he'll be there from 6.30? And she knows, and he knows, that drinks are not what he's talking about. And that dinner tonight may either be very late, or not at all.

'But you look very nice Mrs Feast,' says Mrs Croxton, sniffing. 'Thank you Mrs Croxton,' says Kitty, with a broad smile (maddening to Mrs C. – you can catch it blazing in her eyes). 'How kind. I'll leave you to lock up then?' and away she goes, briskly towards Tottenham Court Road.

Gilbert's block of flats in Victoria is indeed the same one she'd stood outside yesterday, when she watched that young family climb into the Wolsey. The main hall matches the Edwardian ponderous splendour of the exterior, with its dark mahogany panelling, its polished brass nameplates and bell-pushes, its intricate tiled floor. The lift is an openwork cage of wrought iron, around which a stone staircase twists from landing to landing. Kitty slides its outer door closed, then tugs at the inner gate and swings it across with a satisfying crash of metal. She presses the button for the fourth floor and feels her nervous stomach lurch as the lift starts a slow and creaking ascent. When it arrives, she stands for a moment, not stepping out, hearing her own pulse throbbing in her ears, breathing shallowly through her mouth – then calming, stilling herself.

The landing presents her with three doors, none of which is open in greeting. She'd hoped perhaps he would have been looking out for her from a window – assuming his flat has a street frontage. That he'd be waiting for her now, ready to take her into his arms and stop her mouth with a kiss. Or something like that. Her imagination's had, after all, a whole weekend to weave a variety of such scenarios. Instead, here are three closed doors, with identical stained glass panels of art deco lilies, and matching brass lily knockers – feminine touches in this otherwise masculine clubby atmosphere. She raps at 4a. There's too long a pause in answering. So he wasn't even ready, waiting for her impatiently – as she knows she would have been for him, if their roles were reversed. There's just enough time to allow a fissure of doubt to crack open in front of her; a self-mocking realization for one instant that she's allowed herself to build an entire emotional edifice out of a few shared hours with him.

Only, suddenly, here he is – the door giving into a long narrow hallway filled with paintings and prints, a flowering daisy in a pot, his hat and jacket hanging from a stand, umbrellas – details she must be registering subconsciously, for she can recall them later. He doesn't take her in his arms. There's an awkward moment.

'I was on the telephone – wouldn't you know it,' he says, 'bad timing – come in – come in – ' but now he is gathering her to him, his arm across her shoulders, and as he clicks the door to, he swings her round and at last they are kissing again, the weekend's mental speculation come to life and setting her body – so carefully primed and primped for this very moment – instantly on fire.

Their progress down the hall echoes their Birdcage Walk, spinning round slowly as they embrace, utterly fulfilling the most fanciful of her imaginings. Vaguely she's aware that the flat is very large – doorways opening off on either side, the hall doglegging to the left at the end, double doors on the right into a spacious sitting room. They break off as he manoeuvres her through these and across towards a sofa. He stands, holding both her hands, looking at her still – searchingly, she imagines, into her eyes – he's smiling now.

'Hello *you*,' he's saying. 'Hello my Mrs Feast. I've been thinking of you all the time . . .'

'Have you?'

'Non-stop. *All* the time. I've been missing you. How can that be? We've only just met, and all weekend I've been missing you . . .'

Oh yes. He's saying all the right things now, and she's letting herself slide into the happy warmth on offer – of being kissed, of being missed, of mutual wanting.

'I'll get us some drinks,' he says. 'What'll it be – something cool? G and T?'

'That'd be lovely.' Only before he goes, there's another

embrace, on the sofa now, their legs and arms beginning to entangle. There's the luxury of time available – all the time in the world.

'Mrs Feast,' he's murmuring into her hair, 'Kitty, Kitty . . .' His hand is stroking her neck . . . then he's up and pouring the drinks, because after all there's no hurry, not now, and the hint of a delay sweetens the anticipation.

'Ice and lemon?' He's plinking ice cubes into glasses – so he had thought ahead a little, been prepared. Then – 'Blast,' he says, 'the tonic's flat.' And she's saying it doesn't matter, because it doesn't – but he's already heading out of the door – 'Won't be a moment – there's bound to be some more in the kitchen . . .' and he's left her alone.

She looks around. It's exactly what she'd dreamed his room would be: floor-length velvet curtains, dark green walls covered in woven grass paper, oil paintings of country landscapes, lamps with pleated silken shades, a hearth displaying a mock-Adam electric fire beneath a heavy marble mantel and surmounted by a large gilt-framed mirror.

She gets to her feet, using the excuse of wanting to check her hair. There's a baby grand piano in the corner. On its closed lid is a display of silver-framed photos: some formal black and white studies from the thirties – a woman with dark painted lips, a man in uniform – his parents perhaps? Then several of small children in various stages from rompers to school uniforms, and laughing holiday snaps – one with palm trees on a beach, another of small girls with almost smaller ponies. She searches them for a likeness to Gilbert – is there something familiar about the eyes? It all looks idyllic. Were these taken before the break-up of their parents' marriage, days of innocence, ignorant of the clouds ahead? Could such times truly exist – for other people?

She moves on to the fireplace. The face which looks back at her now from the mirror is literally radiant, as if lamps are shining out from her eyes and cheeks. It's embarrassing, for how transparent can she be? She lays the back of her hand against her chin in some instinctive cooling gesture, and it's now that she sees the first card, half-hidden behind a vase: a traditional white invitation, its black twirly script announcing 'Mrs Angela Hunter – At Home' and the date 'August 10th 1964' – 'Black Tie – RSVP' – and at the top lefthand corner in handwritten ink – 'Mr and Mrs Gilbert Denby'.

Kitty pulls the card out from behind the vase and re-reads it, trying to soak in its significance. Then she sees another one: another invitation, this time to a Private View for the end of July and also inscribed to 'Mr and Mrs Gilbert Denby'. There are others stacked behind, held at bay by a candlestick. Without needing much else by way of explanation, a chilling sensation is streaking up from her toes, weakening her knee-joints, reversing the effect of gravity and pouring upwards over her.

'Got it . . .' He's back, waggling a bottle of Schweppes. 'Sorry I was so long. I had to hunt all over. You'd have thought it would be in the fridge – instead of which it was hidden under the sink. No logic . . .'

'Perhaps your wife should have left you with a list,' says Kitty.

'I beg your pardon?' The bottle hangs suspended.

'Or perhaps she did – but tonic water wasn't on it.'

'I don't . . .' He slaps the bottle down by the glasses and comes towards her. She has hold of the first card and reads aloud, 'Mrs Angela Hunter – At Home?'

'Oh. That.'

'Yes.' She's expecting, hoping for, the explanation – the one that will make it all come right. Something he can make her believe in again, rapidly – that it's a mistake, that Mrs Angela Hunter, whoever she is, hasn't yet updated her address book? Nor all those other inviters on all those other cards, crammed behind the candlestick. Something as banal as that.

'Well – what can I say?' is what he says. And no, that doesn't do it at all.

'You're still married?' she says.

'Not happily. It's not what it seems.'

'But you *are* still married?'

'For the moment . . . yes.'

'And you do have children – the daughters you told me about?'

'Good Lord, yes – what do you take me for?' But as she doesn't answer him, he runs rapidly on, 'It's all true – the girls and everything . . .'

'And you were seeing them off on the *Queen Elizabeth?*'

'Yes.'

'Why? Why were they travelling?'

'To see her mother . . .' He must be catching now something of the weight of Kitty's utter dismay, for he lets out a whoosh of a sigh and looks down at the floor. 'She takes them over every summer to visit her family – every summer.'

'So the divorce – the tale of Brighton and the room service waiter – just a tale?'

'I see it looks bad. I wish I could make you understand. It's very lonely to be left behind – *every* summer – and you were there – alone too – and, you know, you're really very lovely. There's something about you – a hidden treasure – I thought I was making a great discovery, all of my own . . .'

'But I didn't need discovering,' says Kitty.

'Oh yes you did – sweet Mrs Feast – you did . . .' He reaches out a hand towards her cheek but she steps away.

'And you would have let us go on,' she says, ' – with everything that means – and all the while lying to me?'

'I'd have told you – of course I would, but after all we scarcely knew each other. There'd been no time . . .'

'But it was you who set this thing rolling – and you started it with the lie.'

'But that was just a whim – on that train – feeling so blue. It's the only explanation I can offer. I thought it might be fun – then – for both of us – nothing too involving . . .'

'But based on a lie.'

'Does it matter so much? Now you know – can't we go on from here? There's something happening – it's not just . . . well . . . not just sex is it? Don't you feel it too?'

But he can't begin to imagine her feelings – the dream of an ongoing life which her mind has already constructed for them both. Imagination and foolishness. And how *could* she take this any further, now that she knows – at the expense of another woman's misery and all those children too? Which is what she tries to explain, though cold anger is deserting her now and she's not sure she can keep the choking from her voice.

'Don't get too moral sweet Kitty. What's the point of it? Can't we just enjoy each other – now? She's thousands of miles away – she's in her own world, she's no saint herself, a very self-centred human being. It's not going to last much longer I can tell you that. It's been cracking for a long, long time . . .' but surely he sounds hollow even to himself?

She doesn't wait for the lift, but runs down the twisting stone stairs, out of the building, walking quickly towards Vauxhall Bridge, retracing yesterday's dreamy meandering. Feeling flayed. I'm a foolish woman – caught in the dust and traffic, my handbag crammed with Marie Stopes's brown paper bag, my body pointlessly primed. But I will not feed on another woman's misery for my emotional sustenance. I will not.

5p.m. – Point Harbor

They've done a good job.

Sadie started with the ceiling – you couldn't fault her. Tricky up the ladder with her neck bent back like that and Lord only

251

knows when it was last painted – years ago probably. She'd given it a good old scrub first with washing soda, spackled all the holes, then got moving with the roller. Lynn was confined to woodwork – windows, baseboards, doors – fiddly, but no way was Sadie letting her climb up high.

It's near to broiling upstairs with no air conditioning, but kind of fun and companionable too. In the end they get so hot and sweaty they strip down to their underwear. Lynn's in her cotton maternity slip, supposed to be loose but even so it's stretched across her belly. Sadie's in her big blue panties, with her generous breasts spilling out of a brassiere like a couple of sling-shots. At the sight of the pair of them – the women, not Sadie's breasts particularly – Lynn starts cracking up – and that's it, they're both staggering around with the weight of their laughter, scarcely able to wield a brush with any accuracy. Paint's beginning to find itself where it didn't ought to – like in a big streak across Sadie's nose.

It's near-enough lunch time, when Sadie should normally be heading back into town, but today she says she'll stay – see if they can get the whole job done, why don't they? Lynn goes down to the kitchen to fix them some rough and ready tuna salad sandwiches, then grabs a couple of sodas and calls Sadie to come cool off by the brook. It's deeply shaded down here. They sit on the bank and balance their feet on the cold stony remains of one of Leroy's dams.

'So, when're you expectin' Mr Feast back?'

'I don't know for sure. The boat docks in the morning – then I guess there'll be things like Customs won't there?'

'Don't ask me – I've never been out of the country.'

'Me neither.'

'No kidding?'

'Nope. I'd never been further than Chicago before I met Jack – and that was only the once – so I don't know what they'll have to do.'

'Some of that "anything to declare" stuff you reckon – like in the movies?'

'"Nothing but my accent . . ."' says Lynn, putting it on.

'Hm?'

'She's bound to have an English accent isn't she – his daughter?'

'That'd be kind of nice. I like an English accent.'

'Yeah – I guess so.'

'You sound – well – can I say this – none too excited?'

'I'm not. Oh Sadie I've tried. I really have tried. But I don't think we've got our own lives put together yet – I *know* we haven't – let alone starting in with a whole new person. Jack isn't exactly what you'd call stable, you know what I mean? He's every which way. The latest thing is the best thing for Jack and this child for him *is* the latest thing – but you see she's not really a child is she? Not any more. She's a young woman – and she's his daughter but he doesn't *know* yet how to be a father . . .'

'How old was she when they split up – him and his ex-wife?'

'Only four.'

'Well that ain't so bad – four's a *real* age – can make sense to a man. Not like she was a baby. Carl left me when Darlene was nine months and Eddy barely two. He'll have an instinct for it – you'll see . . .'

'But I don't know I want him using up that instinct on *her* . Shouldn't he be saving it up for *our* baby?' Lynn shifts her legs, realigning her belly, feeling that tumbling presence within.

'You'll probably find he's got plenty to spare. It's not on ration you know.'

'No?'

'The more you need, the more you have – it'll just come. Don't you waste time worrying about it.'

It's now they hear the crunching of wheels on the driveway, coming slowly up the hill.

'You expecting someone?' says Sadie. Both women are regarding each other, in their sweat-streaked, paint-spattered underwear.

'Not a soul,' says Lynn, horrified, giggling.

'A delivery or something?'

'No.'

'Maybe they'll go away.'

They hear a car door slam – a woman's voice calling: 'Lynn – hi there – hi – anyone at home?'

Down here in the gully Lynn sinks her head further. 'It's Vanessa Mulherne,' she whispers. 'That woman we went on the boat with yesterday – lives over at Rockman's Creek.'

Sadie presses her finger to her nose – 'High and *migh . . . ty.* You got yourself some classy friends there.'

'Not mine – Jack's – not his either if he could see straight.'

'Wanna say hello?'

'Like this? You're kidding me. Keep quiet – she'll go.'

But Vanessa and her kind don't give in easily – and in any case, up at the house they'd only closed the screen doors front and back to let any available breeze blow through. It's perfectly clear someone must be at home. Lynn raises her head just far enough to see over the edge of the gully. Vanessa is walking fast across the terrace and heading down this way, still calling, 'Lynn – hi there – *Lynn . . .*'

Exposure seems inevitable. Lynn heaves herself to her feet.

'Oh Vanessa – hello.' She manages to sound pleasantly surprised.

'Oh – there you are. I was just beginning to worry, when I couldn't make anyone hear. I knew Jack was going to be on his way to New York by now, and you in a "delicate condition" as they say . . .' She falters, perhaps she's got the full vision now, of the two women exposed. '*Oh!*' – a very surprised sound.

Lynn's thinking of letting that surprise just lie there unsatisfied; she doesn't owe any explanations – except though – and she sees it instantly – that of course she mustn't leave Sadie exposed to bad-mouthing round town. Sadie's eyes are big and round, peering up at Vanessa, who is looking cool in a navy cotton shirtwaister. Nothing for it but to offer up an explanation then.

'We've been painting the baby's room.'

'*Really*?' She sounds more surprised than ever, but then Vanessa Mulherne can never have wielded a spatula of spackle in her whole entire life. Might have done her a whole pack of good if she had, though. 'Is that something you should be doing in your state – how long is it you've got to go – ?' She sounds quite severe.

'Oh an age – nearly a couple of months.'

'Yes of course – you said yesterday.'

'And Sadie's been helping me – she's done all the brunt of it.'

'So I should hope – and now . . .?'

'We're just cooling off – hot work.'

'I'll bet . . .'

Nobody's moving. Sadie's standing still enough to have had a stroke, and Lynn doesn't want to offer any more visions to Vanessa for the ongoing regaling of the Point Harbor Ladies Circle. No scrambling up the bank by the two half-naked women, one black, one white, both spattered in 'Dawn' eggshell finish.

'Yes . . .' says Vanessa, almost whispering, looking awkward. 'Well, I can see you're . . . busy. I only dropped by with Jack's sweater – he left it on the boat.' His cream cable knit is what she's been screwing up in her hands. Lynn doesn't even want to reach up and take it – the gesture will expose her even more.

'Good – gee that's sweet of you.'

'Yes – well . . .'

'Could you leave it up on the patio wall?'

'On the . . . up on the terrace? . . . Sure . . .'

'Only we're all painty.'

'Yes – I can see. Sure . . .' She backs up the slope a bit, as if she still can't quite believe her eyes, before turning and almost running the rest of the way. They don't relax until they hear the sound of her car retreating to the road.

'That's a tale's gonna run and run in Pinker's Hardware,' says Sadie.

'You think she'll say anything?'

'You betcha – you betcha baby,' says Sadie with a great hoot of laughter you could surely hear down at the bay.

By late afternoon, they've finished the whole of the first coat – walls and ceiling plus all woodwork. It's not what you'd call perfect of course. Streaky in places. The debate as to whether they can get by without another coat doesn't last long. If the job's worth doing etcetera . . . and if it's going to pass muster with Jack it'd better look as near professional as makes no odds – but they'll have to wait for tomorrow says Sadie, firmly. If they don't give the paint a chance to dry thoroughly, they'll end up rolling the first coat off as they apply the second. Also, she's bushed, poor woman: had enough for one day, and Darlene and Leroy will be home already from the beach, expecting dinner. This is a woman who knows all about work – you couldn't fault her.

It's still steamy hot up here under the eaves, but now they're done, they put their clothes back on, soberly, their laughter dried up. It's when they get back outside, just as Sadie is opening her car door, and stirring the hot, thick air with her other hand like a fan, that Lynn catches at it, grabs it, then throws her arms around Sadie's shoulders – and finds she's weeping.

'Hey there – hey now . . .' says Sadie, taking her into the folds of a hug.

'I just . . . I don't know . . . I just want to say thank you, I guess,' says Lynn. 'You mean a lot . . .'

And Sadie, who's had a lifetime of restraint, allows herself to hug back before she turns the key in the ignition.

It's 5p.m. and Lynn goes back upstairs to examine the day's achievement. It'll be perfect. The room is glowing in the early evening light. The baby will love it won't he/she? Earliest memories embedded in the child's mind will be of these walls, these angles of dormer windows reflecting clouds, a fringe of pine trees beyond.

Satisfying – at least it would be if only it were done. Finished. Despite the long day's work, Lynn is still jittery with unaccustomed energy, wants to forge ahead. Nesting – the most primitive of instincts and she can even recognize it in herself. Supposing Jack gets back early with the cuckoo and somehow puts a stop to the endeavour? And he will too, if he's not presented with a done deal.

Sadie's promised to come back tomorrow afternoon, once she's finished work over at the Sanders' property, because of course Tuesday isn't one of her usual days for coming to the Feasts. But supposing Jack's back before then . . . which is how Lynn finds herself opening up the steps again, pouring paint into the tray, squeezing water out of the roller which Sadie has left soaking. Maybe she won't tackle the ceiling – that'd be foolish. But the walls – nothing wrong with that surely?

Later she could never say for sure what happened. Maybe it was nothing to do with feeling dizzy and half falling from the ladder, because, after all, these things can happen anyway – and she had righted herself fast enough, though it wrenched her side. But some time then – when – there was this soft warm flow of clear liquid, as if she'd peed herself – though she hadn't – and she'd stopped, held on to the ladder – told herself it isn't happening. It's just a dream. Stop – think, get a hold. That's it – a dream. Though why would there be blood in a dream of joy? And why am I alone? And who can I call?

11p.m. – RMS Queen Elizabeth

By early evening the atmosphere on board suddenly changes. It's as if the ship had put a spell on us for the whole voyage, or maybe more of an anaesthetic, and suddenly it's wearing off and real life's just over the horizon – literally. So people who have been lounging around, being looked after like dozens of pampered babies waiting for their next treat, are snapping back into their proper adult selves, dashing around, trying to be important, packing, making arrangements, crowding into the Purser's Office for landing cards, sorting out currency and worrying about the US Customs authorities.

Everyone at dinner is very boozy and merry. It's an unofficial gala night with lots of wine all round. Both Ken and Madge order it – something called Liebfraumilch, which is really delicious. Laura arrives with presents for each of us – miniature *Queen Elizabeth* lifebelts with cards attached: 'To remind you of our happy days – fondly, Ken and Laura'. She's brought one for Sydney too, but he doesn't show up. In my own private thoughts, I'm still jokily hoping he's locked in the bathroom, scrubbing off his shame, but Laura thinks he's getting the Commander sorted out for disembarkation.

All our suitcases were returned to our cabins before dinner and by the time I get back to D9, Mrs K. is at the peak of her packing performance, arms whirling, clothes everywhere. Eenie and Mo have brought all kinds of goodies back from the party, including six balloons, and *Queen Elizabeth* brooches now pinned to their pyjamas. Mrs K. has confined them up on Eenie's bunk, where they're all squashed in with the balloons and the Playsack, under strict instructions not to move. Mrs K. hands me back the petticoat.

'Sorry Ella – it got hit by a green Jell-o rabbit, didn't it Mo? It wasn't her fault.'

'There were rough boys,' says Eenie.

Mo hadn't wanted to take the petticoat off when she got back from the party this afternoon. She was still in a dream of being Princess Magdalena. Now I hold it up and envisage trying to wash the long green jelly stains out of it at Dad's house, re-soaking it in sugar solution, to make it stand out again – drip-dry in Point

Harbor, Massachusetts? Having to do any of this, *explain* any of this to Dad and 'Lynn' seems so unlikely somehow. I mean, I suppose she'll want me to call her 'Lynn' won't she – that's what she put on their Christmas card – not anything like 'Mom' – that would be too peculiar. I wonder what she's like. Dad just wrote, 'You'll love her,' – as if it's all automatic. I mean, I'm all *prepared* to love her . . . it's just I can't seem to imagine her or Point Harbor itself, the house, even though it's been hanging around in my mind as a sort of dream for so long . . . I can't smell it or feel it or hear it, and yet this time tomorrow night I suppose I'll be there, won't I, and it'll all be starting to be real? Except, 'real' is exactly what I'm *not* feeling at this very moment. It's almost as if I'm back in that dream, full of apprehension but sort of excited too . . . I'm still holding the petticoat up and I give it a shake. 'How's about Mo keeping it Mrs Keropoulos?' I suggest.

'You mean it?'

'I do – absolutely.' I hand it up to Mo. 'Here you are – from one imaginary princess to another.'

'I do *love* you Ella,' says Mo, and she leans perilously out and gives me a hot, sticky hug which makes me glow. It's a scant price to pay for this amount of gratitude – and anyway, we all know this is the year of the shift. Who needs sugar flounces any more, – unless of course they happen to be princess-bound.

There's no space for me to pack, so I sit outside in the companionway on my suitcase, waiting for the Ks to finish and go to bed. People are having to step around me and it's beginning to feel like a waste of my last evening, so I decide to go back up to the Sports Deck for a last look at the midnight ocean.

I thought it might be busy up here, but it's dead quiet and very cold. The Teenage Lounge is open but no one's in there. I put Dusty Springfield's 'I Just Don't Know What to do With Myself' on the juke box, because it's almost too apt isn't it? – I don't. I'm sliding around in a mock-smooch kind of a dance. Then I start miming along with Dusty. There's an empty Pepsi bottle in the bin – the perfect pretend microphone – only now I might as well sing out loud: 'I just don't know what to do with myself . . . – daa-da-da-daa . . .' There's that bit on *Top of the Pops* where she wrenches her head around – she wears her hair in a bouffant Tom Jones too doesn't she? With a bow. So I'm perfect. And now I'm really getting into it – doing her hand movements – all that wrist twirling she does, as if she's pushing temptation and misery away all at the same time. I'm wearing my false eyelashes anyway, specially for dinner, so we're really alike – it's a great effect. When the record ends I put it on again.

'Well – get you.' Paul is standing in the doorway, wrapped in one of the deck chair blankets like a Sioux chieftain, only with a Beatle fringe.

I stop in mid-Dusty chord. I've got the Pepsi bottle up near my lips, ready to go into my big finale for the second time. This ought to be an excruciating moment of embarrassment – but it isn't. Instead, I amaze myself. I don't say anything to Paul, just go back to the juke box and punch in Dusty's number again. Then I hold my arms out towards him. Afterwards I can see that's what two and a half glasses of Liebfraumilch do to me, but at the time it feels perfectly natural. Paul lets the blanket drop and now here we are – moving slowly round the floor, and it's not a pretend smooch dance any more. I can feel his breathing down my neck, then he's nuzzling the top of my head, then we're kissing and it isn't just an exploration of molars. It's doing something very strange to me, to my legs, and my need for oxygen, and there's a weird and tingling sensation right in the middle of my guts – so maybe *this* is what old Fanny Hill was going on about.

'You're a bit of a little flower, aren't you?' Paul's murmuring in my ear.

'Am I?'

'Oh go on – you know you are.'

'No I don't.' Because I don't. I truly don't.

'Fishing for compliments – bloody birds always at it – '

'I'm not fishing. I don't know.'

'Well you are – I'm telling you – you're a right little flower.' He's standing back now, looking at me. Really looking – as if he's an x-ray machine and he's seeing right through me. For a moment it's not comfortable. It's making me feel awkward, as if I'm stripped naked in front of him – only then he's pulling me towards him again and saying it's too bright in here – and he's right – because what we need is the darkness. It's not dark enough out under the shelter where the chairs are now mostly stacked against the walls, but he pulls me out on to the open deck, dragging one of the open chairs behind.

'I could do with some company,' he says. 'I've been stuck out here all day. I can't seem to face going down below – it does horrible things to me insides . . .' which possibly isn't the most romantic thing that's ever going to be said to me, except somehow it doesn't seem to matter – and here we are, stretched out under his blanket, and it's just Paul and Me in a fizzy haze of each other, legs and tongues and skin . . . and siren. Because somewhere in the middle of this moment, when I'm thinking it can all go hang – let's just *be*, let's just *do* – the siren blasts out from one of the two vast funnels above us. We're both nearly thrown off the steamer chair by its force.

'Shit,' says Paul, ever the gentleman. 'What's happened?' Then there's dead silence, apart from the background throbbing of the ship.

We struggle up from under the blanket and go over to the railings. To say we can see the fog isn't accurate because it's not so much a presence as an absence. In the dark there's nothing to gauge it by, except the feeling of the damp cloud of air around us and the lack of any reflection down on the surface of the ocean. Now I look again, straining to see, there's nothing visible below us at all, only this sensation of dense, wet air. The horn blasts again.

'Jesus – ' yells Paul, 'fucking ships – give you the creeps don't they – '

'It's the fog horn,' I say.

'I know that – you hear them on the Mersey sometimes at night, but I never expected to have to stand right under one of the bloody things in the middle of the bloody Atlantic Ocean.'

'Edge,' I say, 'we're on the edge of the ocean now.'

I look up at the aft funnel. Its outline has been softened, even in the last few minutes, by trailing wispy streaks of mist. Back over the railings there's an invisible wall now, holding us in – the fog must be thickening very rapidly. Another blast of the horn.

'I don't care if we're at the outer bleedin' limits,' he says. '*Fog* – that's all we bloody need.' His voice has gone up an octave. 'Never again – I'm never doing this again.'

'You wouldn't have been much of an explorer, would you?' I say.

'Too right blossom – I'd have had me head screwed on. Stay on dry land, me.'

'Don't you admire them though? Just imagine what it must have been like, being on this ocean in this fog in one of those little ships – caught in a dead calm, no engines, sails flapping, not knowing where land was, the terror of it – icebergs – rocks – don't you think our ancestors were fantastic?'

'I think they were nuts.' He's sliding his hand round my shoulders again, starting to let it creep back to my left breast – except it's different now. It's an absent-minded sort of hand suddenly, searching for comfort for itself, comfort from me – so that whatever exciting thing was happening between us just now has fled. The horn blasts again.

'Shit – I can't think straight with that thing – and it's bloody cold,' he says. 'Let's go down to me cabin. I think me insides can take it – just about. Get cosy shall we?' Now he's rubbing my back – and I know that he's not what I want. My hero? But he's not seeing me any more is he? Whatever he is seeing is totally about *him* and his needs, and, for all this is anything to do with me, I might as well be a hot-water bottle with breasts.

10p.m. – Point Harbor

The hospital has been trying to get hold of Jack all evening. They contacted the Marvel Motel near La Guardia, which is where he'd told Lynn he'd be staying, but the desk clerk said Jack had never turned up – added that as a matter of fact he was pretty darn angry because the room was held on reservation and could have been sold already twice over if he'd known – don't you guys realize they're packed solid around here what with the World's Fair and all?

So Lynn would be facing the emergency Caesarean alone, if it weren't for Sadie Dorling. For who was there to call – when the disaster started? Dr Vale is out of town, and the woman at his answering service says to go straight to the hospital, which is a good twenty miles away, back towards Methuen. And who else could she call – Vanessa Mulherne, Caroline of the Kennedy campaign, her own mother over two thousand miles away in Montana? No one to call then – except for Sadie, who'd just cooked a big fried chicken dinner and is watching a re-run of *I Love Lucy* on TV with Leroy, while Darlene, who's heading back to Detroit on the midnight Greyhound, got herself some shut-eye. And Sadie, who is herself one tired woman, already heaped high with responsibilities, comes straight away, without a moment's hesitation.

She finds Lynn waiting out front, looking smaller already, pinched and wizened with fear for the unborn child, now exposed to who knows what dangers with her waters prematurely broken. They change cars into Lynn's shiny new Chrysler, because Sadie's

Dodge sounds as if it's contemplating a heart attack. Sadie's never driven anything so unblemished in her life, nor ever driven so fast, ignoring the risk of traffic cops and getting them to the Emergency Room by eight.

Lying on a gurney, Lynn holds tight to Sadie's hand while the frightening diagnosis is made – the placenta not functioning as it should, the baby's heartbeat erratic – the jangle and lurch of her own heart as the unreality sinks in. The baby may die, will certainly die if not delivered now, two months early – a tiny scrap scarcely ready to face the world. Sadie tries calling the New York motel once more – Mr Feast should surely have been there hours ago. But no – he hasn't shown up, leaving the empty hole of additional fear – an auto smash, a mangled car somewhere on Route 95 maybe? This they leave unspoken for the moment: there's enough potential tragedy to face here and now, without embroidering the picture.

So it's Lynn who has to take a hold of this reality, sign the consent forms, confirm her medical insurance – no Jack to do it for her and share the responsibility for this decision – not that the medics offer any alternative if the babe is to have any chance of survival. It's not until gone 10p.m. that an obstetric surgeon arrives, confirming the diagnosis, already scrubbing up.

'Who is this?' says a harassed nurse, briskly, dismissively, of Sadie, who's waiting in the doorway while Lynn is prepared for surgery.

'My friend,' says Lynn, nearly shouting. 'She's my best friend – don't let them take her away . . .' and thus it's Sadie Dorling who keeps her close company, right up to the doors of the theatre, and maintains a prayerful vigil outside.

264

Tuesday

The dustmen are due this morning in Bissett Street; Tuesday is their regular call. Mr Christo had already dragged the bins through from the back yard last night, by the time Kitty had returned from Gilbert Denby's flat. It was kind of him to bring hers too. He's not obliged, but then he's that sort of man – thoughtful. They do exist after all.

Kitty had walked all the way back from Victoria, deliberately making a detour along Millbank towards Westminster. Taken an age. Sat on a bench near Lambeth Bridge and silently wept in frustration and self-loathing. To have let herself in for such folly. To have fired up her own idiot imagination to such a pitch – and then to have thrown it all away so instantly; that whole complex construction of emotion she'd built since last Thursday, blown away in a single draught of indignation. Had she been right though, or was she over-fastidious about these things? People stamp all over each other's feelings these days it seems – is she simply oversensitive? Should she 'wise up' now as the current saying goes – harden herself – make a grab for what she wants, however selfishly? It wasn't too late: she could still go back to his flat, offer up her primed body once again, tell him it was all a mistake – that his lying didn't matter. Except that it did. It does.

It's the betrayal that sears – not just of her and the other woman, his wife – but of his children, the same children, presumably, who inhabited the silver-framed photographs on his piano. No pictures of her though – of the invisible Mrs Denby; presumably those he'd remembered to hide away, especially the formal wedding shots which would normally grace such a proud display of dynasty. It was only those invitations, those forgotten clues, which had let him down. He won't forget them next time, will he? When he's tempted the next vulnerable naïf to relieve him of his summer boredom. Because he'll certainly try, won't he – have another go? She can't have been unique? Or could she? Dare she claim that there was something more? Even in that brief time, hadn't they begun to feel something deeper, as he'd hinted – not just the sex?

Further along the river are the Houses of Parliament, where she and Ella have marched in solidarity with hundreds of other Ban-the-Bombers, towards Trafalgar Square. But what's the point of caring about bombs – the greater issues – if, simply for her own self-centred gratification, she deliberately aimed to wreck a family? She couldn't change her nature so instantly, so radically. Even though with his sort – for she seems to feel scathingly that she knows 'his sort' – if he's done it this time, he's probably done it before and is already planning to do it again. Like Jack. Jack-the-Lad – literally – with his crap games, his poker and his trail of women on the side.

It's not something she's allowed herself to dwell on, through these years alone – and of course she's never told Ella either. Why shake any more an already weakened faith in her father? Ella simply knows their lives had been a slip-sliding carnival of hopes and broken promises, and has always seemed to comprehend that, as a form of daily existence, it simply couldn't be borne. It was like trying to build a house on quicksand – that's the way Kitty had explained it. Ella seemed to have understood and had never for one moment been reproachful about the great split her mother had forced into their lives. But Kitty remembers the pain too well, how hard it was to ignore Jack's games and how impossible it had been to change him.

8 a.m. on Tuesday morning and Bissett Street has never seemed drearier. The *Queen Elizabeth* is due to dock in New York at 10a.m.

Eastern Standard Time. Kitty counts the hours back: at this very moment, Ella must be asleep, safely nestled into her bunk, although excited perhaps, so half wakeful? And in a few hours the long wait will be over – the split will be mended, for Ella at least.

Tuesday morning, and the dustmen are due. Upstairs in her flat, Kitty holds the brown paper bag from the Marie Stopes Clinic. Her body has been primed – unnecessarily as it's turned out. I'm a foolish stupid woman, is what she thinks. Why didn't I chuck this bag into the Thames from Lambeth Bridge? Should she go downstairs now and bury it amongst the household rubbish in the rusting bin left out on the pavement? But what if the binmen are careless, miss their mark of the dustcart and the contents are sent spilling across Bissett Street – the paraphernalia of sex laid bare? And then, after all, why waste the experience of yesterday – the earnest, healthy interest of the doctor, the mortification of the Dutch cap fitting, however well meant? Because there could be other men couldn't there? Needn't all be Jacks or Gilbert Denbys need they? There *are* men out there: other women find them, why not she? The future is mystery, but as long as you don't know what it holds, the possibilities remain. So she doesn't dump it – tucking it, instead, behind her chest of drawers, awaiting further developments.

7a.m. – RMS Queen Elizabeth

Paul got the message all right, sounded angry – should never mess with virgins. Broken his own golden rule, they're always the same, all talk and no do. And anyway he'd had it with that bloody fog horn. He has stomped off and left me alone in the foggy night. Stuck.

It's too late to start my own packing now, I'd only disturb the Ks – and if I go back down to D deck I might bump into him again. Salt in wounds. I'm not tired either: I am wide awake, turning it all over, because I think I'd been about to *do* it, with Paul. I'm sure I was. That feeling was . . . was . . . I don't know what it was. Extraordinary – that's what it was. Exciting and warm and scary all at once. And then how quickly the whole thing changed. Now I feel I'd have been a fool if I had. Whatever Hen said about 'good old fashioned sex', shouldn't it be a bit more than that? If the fog horn hadn't started, would I be as deflowered as Fanny H. by now? And here's the odd thing – it's not the being deflowered that's getting at me, it's the thought that I was 'saved by the bell'. For something so important you need to make up your own mind, otherwise it's pathetic. You can't go around having it made up for you by accidents like fog horns, can you?

So what *would* I have done? I'm not sure – that's the trouble. Will I ever know what to do – will I ever get things right? And then, if I had done it, what about sin? It didn't *feel* sinful, but I'm suddenly haunted by the face of Sister Marie-Francis looking shocked, and the face of M. looking sad. Rosie and I always think Sister Marie-Francis can read our minds – she has a nose for sin – and much as I try now to blot it out, I can feel the weight of M.'s trust in me, hanging round my neck. When I was trying to cheer Hen up about her parents and being preggers, it didn't seem so impossible, not when it was her life and not mine – but imagine if it happened to me and I had to tell M.? When it's my life I'm thinking about, nothing seems so simple any more. I can't see I'll ever understand the way these things work.

The siren is still blasting away every minute or so, hurting my ears and making my thoughts even more jumbled, so I take the blanket and head back down, looking for somewhere to hide. The Promenade Deck is more sheltered and the fog horn is muffled by the screen of windows, so I curl up as much as you can on a hard steamer chair, under the blanket, and lie there, feeling the vibration of the ship between the siren calls, and going over it all – the last five days, the people I've met, and the big empty hole marked 'tomorrow'.

I think I'm probably woken by the silence. I sit up. I can see right along the whole length of the Promenade Deck in both directions. It's totally deserted, but its lamps are now dimmed by the pearly light coming from outside. The fog horn has stopped. I rush over to the windows expecting, out of habit, yet more ocean – and seeing instead that the horizon has been taken over by a distant streak of bluish-brown, veiled by a thin mist. *Land*.

I make my way straight down the length of the deck, climbing over any of the chain barriers, aiming forward for the bows. I look at my watch – 7a.m. and we're due to dock at 10. Imagine what it must have felt like in those earliest days – to see land at last – and they'd taken how long to get this far? Weeks, maybe months, instead of our cosseted few days.

I go back to the curved deck right at the bows, the one which hangs over the prow of Main Deck. I'm not alone any more. There are a few other stalwarts, wrapped against the cold, some with binoculars. I lean against the railings, still using the blanket as a cloak, and strain to identify the land mass which shifts into sharper focus even as I watch.

'Hi – another early bird.' Madge Drinkwater is beside me. She's enveloped in a coat and headscarf, cigarette holder in hand.

'I've been out all night,' I say.

'All excited, huh?'

'I'm not sure – excited or scared – it's all mixed up.'

'They have a habit of going together.'

'I wish they didn't. I wish you could have the excitement but feel all right about it – '

'It's only that wicked old adrenaline – pumping around, keeping you on your toes.'

'I don't need that bit though,' I say. 'I think I'm pumped up enough.'

'What have you got to be scared of ?'

'I'm not sure.'

'It'd help if you tried to find out – usually if you identify things, you realize they're not so bad. Is it seeing your father?'

'Yes – no. I don't know. It all seems so complicated . . .' I'm too muddled to want to take the thought any further. 'What's that bit of land do you think?' I ask, changing tack.

'At a guess it'll be Long Island somewhere – Rockaway maybe? We have to cut in across the southern tip before we can make it into the harbour.'

'Will we see quite a lot of Manhattan as we go in – the skyline?'

'Oh sure – the dock's right there slap in the middle of the city. We'll get the whole show from out here.'

'Wonderful.'

'Yeah . . .'

'Are *you* excited?' I ask. She'd sounded as though she was sighing.

'Not really.'

'But to be going home – that's always a good feeling isn't it?'

'Not necessarily. Depends what you've got to go home to, doesn't it? Is that how you feel, Ella – about your home?'

'Yes – of course.'

'Well, I hope you can keep it that way – good to know where you belong.'

'Oh, but I don't – that's not what I meant. It's just it's there, my home, my mother . . . but I do want to get away too – grow up, have adventures – but it's hard. People don't make sense to me. They don't seem to say what they mean – and how are you supposed to know?'

'Well, that's what experience does for you – eventually. You learn by observing I think – and you do make mistakes, you do get hurt along the way. You take the knocks, but you learn to bounce back.'

'You have to, do you – take the knocks?'

'Oh yes, I think so. Life wouldn't be life if it didn't throw problems at you, would it? But there are always compensations out there too. You'll learn who your real friends are – they'll help – and for the rest, well, you also learn what's what.'

'I don't think I will – that's what I mean – *how* do you learn what's what? How did you?'

'Oh no, you don't want to take me as your example – for *anything*. It's not been the perfect life . . .'

'But you're doing things you want – you know about the world. You're glamorous and a model – and you've been off working in Paris and everything.'

'I was a house model at Saks, Ella, once upon a time, not any more – too old, too fat. Even me. Now I'm a *vendeuse* – I sell dresses.'

'But as a model.'

'That was a long time ago. Now what I do is I work in a shop. So I have my dreams too – that's right – and in another life I'd like to be Parisian – and be with someone I know, now, right this second, in Paris. And it isn't going to happen. But it isn't so bad – it's a life, and I just got to visit Paris, didn't I? And maybe one day I'll get to go back there again, for a vacation. So what if it's maybe a bit of a compromise? It's not the sort of romance thing you might have been imagining, because that kind of thing's only a story, and in a story you always get a nice neat ending. Life isn't like that – life's untidier.'

'Does it always have to be?'

'Oh yes – always. Can I give you a piece of advice? You won't take it, but I'll hand it out anyway. You're very young – *very* – you got that? Don't keep setting yourself up for disappointment – let up on yourself. Don't pick away at this growing-up stuff like a scab, and don't waste a second of this precious time on worrying about all of it – because even though you don't see it now, I *promise* you that when you look back, this time will be absolutely precious to you. I know you won't believe me, but I wish you would – because I wish someone had told me when I was fifteen years old, like you. One day, when you look back, you'll see how strong you were, right now – and you'll think, why did I waste that on all those doubts and fears, when I was perfect, just *perfect*, and I didn't know it. So don't, don't waste a second of it. Be yourself, because you're strong, you really are, and you don't need to fit in with what others think and do. I mean it – try and believe me.'

We stay out here for a long time, and gradually the deck fills up with more people. The ship has slowed right down and a small boat has come alongside, way below us, bouncing around in the foam, disgorging Lilliputian men who somehow manage to climb across through an opening down near the water in the *Queen*'s side, which we can't see from this angle. Madge says they'll be Immigration and US Health officers, because they like to clear us all before we dock. It's getting warm now and the mist has thinned enough to reveal a pinkish sky, with up ahead the arch of a beautiful suspension bridge directly in our path, looking as delicate as if it's made out of Meccano.

'The Verrazano,' says Madge. 'It connects Brooklyn with Staten Island. I grew up just over there – on the right. Funny isn't it – when I was a little girl, you know, we'd go into the city sometimes, to Battery Park, and watch the great ships coming up the Hudson. My dad would take us – it was a thrill, I have to tell you – and I dreamed back then I'd sail on them. And here I am – my third round trip – so maybe those dreams do come true – or part of the way – huh? Are you hungry?'

'Why?'

'Because if you are, you'd better go get yourself some breakfast – last chance.'

'Are you?'

'Are you kidding me?'

'Don't you *ever* get hungry?'

'Life's made me a bit of a self-disciplinarian I guess. Anyway, I've got nicotine as a substitute – and *don't* follow my example.'

But I don't want to go below for breakfast, I want to stay here and witness this slow unfolding of the end of the voyage. The air is hot now and the sky has changed again; turned a soft hazy aqua, as backdrop to first the Statue of Liberty and the Staten Island Ferry buzzing so far below us, then to the skyscrapers of Manhattan, with Madge pointing them out: the Woolworth Building, quite close to us and elaborate as a giant church tower, but dwarfed by the sleeker Empire State Building in the middle distance, and far away the silver needle of the Chrysler Building, with in between all the nameless towers, columns and steeples shining in the morning light. The city looks so low in the calm water, it's as if it's floating like a giant raft: pictures from a hundred postcards, and me not sure I can really truly believe I'm here, and that it's not a film or a dream or yet another memory from all that time ago.

Madge and I stay where we are, almost to the very end – watching the whole intricate process of the massive ship making its stately way up the Hudson, which is scattered with dozens of boats looking like tiny abandoned bath toys. Then round in an arc we go, nudged and eased slowly, so slowly into our berth. A hundred feet below is the dock – America. Tiny people rush around – cars, yellow taxis, lorries – but no, this is America so they're 'trucks': and somewhere in amongst them all must be my very own dad – I hope – and me up here, still in yesterday's clothes, not even packed yet, and a voice on the loudspeaker urging us to go to R Deck to clear Immigration.

10.30a.m. – Pier 92, New York

America. At last.

I'm standing in the giant Customs shed under a letter F hanging down from the roof. My baggage is piled up around me, waiting for inspection. The air is hot and damp. Absolutely not English air. The last time I felt this I was four, and I recognize its familiarity at once.

There's a whirlpool of energy whipped up all around us passengers, but we're still looking a bit dazed. We're like animals who've been cooped up in a luxury zoo, set free, but not yet reacclimatized to the world outside. The keepers have been the kind, spoiling Cunard staff, but now they've cut us loose: they've stopped looking after us, and just for a moment we're not sure we wouldn't prefer them to come and lock us up again.

All the letters of the alphabet are hanging along the whole length of the roof. To my left are the Es and further over the Ds. Madge Drinkwater is already having her bags inspected. A man is fishing hats out of one of her boxes and consulting a list. Over to my right, through the crowds of Gs and Js, I can pick out the Keropoulos clan – but only because Mrs K. is wearing a shocking pink two-piece which stands out amongst the grey of all the men's suits. She'd already squeezed herself into it by the time I got back to the cabin, after we'd docked. I didn't have much time by then – had to throw stuff into my suitcase, and myself together, so I'd be all right – look all right – for Dad. The Ks had already cleared Immigration on R Deck, and their bags had been collected. Vera was rushing to round up all us stragglers and collect her tips. I hadn't thought about tips. I didn't know you had to. Mrs Keropoulos was handing out *ten*-dollar notes! I had to make do with a ten-shilling note instead, stuffed in a *Queen Elizabeth* envelope. I hope Vera will forgive. Mrs K. said we were supposed to tip the waiters too. Perhaps they don't expect too much from green girls travelling on their own. I hope not.

Mrs K. looked a completely different shape in her pink suit, but then she told me her girdle was killing her. She'd got a hat on too, a pink shell tipped forward over her forehead with a wisp of spotted veiling across her eyes – not very with-it, but she looked sweet and a bit self-conscious, a great big woman done up like a doll. She said she hadn't seen Mr Keropoulos for two months and blushed absolutely purple. Mo and Eenie were also dressed up, with white gloves and little straw hats, with their *Queen Elizabeth* brooches pinned to their frocks. Mo was holding my petticoat.

'She won't let go of it Ella,' said Mrs K. 'She wanted to wear it, but I hadda put my foot down. Can you imagine what her father woulda said – letting her into Manhattan in someone else's borrowed underwear, begging your pardon? Vasilios woulda given me an earful. She can wear it when she gets home, can't she, and her daddy's not around to raise the roof.'

Now I can see the children and I try waving. Mo's sitting on top of a suitcase, still holding the petticoat, not looking my way, but suddenly she turns and sees me, and she climbs up on the case and starts blowing kisses at me. She's saying something too, but I can't hear it in all the roar and bustle, so I just blow kisses back. As I'm watching, a short thin man in a pale linen suit with a straw hat like Frank Sinatra comes up behind Mrs K. and puts his hands on her shoulders. She spins round and grabs him – and suddenly they're having this huge great snog, right in the middle of the Customs shed, in full view of everybody. She must be at least a head taller than he is and, at a guess, twice the weight – Jack Sprat and all that. The way she's been describing him, I'd imagined this huge ogre of a man that they were all terrified of – and instead the girls are dancing round him, hugging his knees. He doesn't look like a man who raises the roof, and they obviously adore him. I wonder why Mrs K. made him sound so awful – something to spice her life up a bit? Perhaps just adoring Mr K. isn't exciting enough for her – but if so, she's crazy, because they all look thrilled to see each other and be together again. A porter has piled their bags up on a trolley and they're heading out now, out of the shed. They look as if they belong to each other – a family – which suddenly makes me feel very alone. I'm waiting for a family too, I suppose, except my dad's a stranger and there's no sign of him yet. Already I'm wondering if he's got the right day, and whether he'll be able to find me. Only here I am, right under the F for Feast, so it can't be that difficult.

'Hi Ella, I just had to come and say goodbye to you. We missed you at breakfast,' Laura is calling as she weaves through the Hs and Gs towards me. She's carrying one of the miniature *Queen Elizabeth* lifebelts.

I tell her about watching the ship docking.

'Oh, is that it – only Sydney wasn't with us either. Was he watching too? Did you see him?'

'No,' I say.

'Strange – we haven't seen him in twenty-four hours, and he never got his gift.' She holds the lifebelt up with its card dangling: 'To remind you of our happy days – fondly, Ken and Laura'. She looks back towards the bottom end of the shed. 'I can't leave Ken for long – he's getting all set for a real tussle with the Customs. Anything to declare – we've got plenty to declare! He's terrified they're going to make us unpack the whole chandelier, and then we'll never get it put back right – only he really wants to see the Commander's Bentley, once it's unloaded. Sydney always said he could, but as we haven't seen him, we haven't fixed anything yet. I'd like Sydney to have his gift too. I've been looking, but he isn't with the Ms . . .'

'Perhaps he's under B,' I say. 'Maxton-*Bligh* after all . . .' We both look across through the scrum of Es, Ds and Cs. Then I spot him – not in the Bs – he's beyond them with the Commander, whose surname I've never known. He might as well have been C for Commander for all I'd guess, but it has to begin with A because that's where Sydney is now, attending to his boss, who's sitting on a folding chair, a sort of portable throne.

'Isn't that just the fanciest?' says Laura. 'I mean imagine knowing to bring your own chair along like that. Ken would've liked one of those, if he'd known, because I think we may be in for a bit of a marathon. I guess I'd better go see them . . .'

I watch her, skirting round the crowds, arriving at the As,

greeting Sydney, handing him the lifebelt. He's looking at her distractedly, surprised, holding it at arm's length as if it's somehow distasteful, while Laura's talking to him. Then, as she turns away, I see him drop it on the ground.

She comes back towards me. 'He was thrilled with the gift,' she says. 'So touched. But unfortunately they don't think they can show us the car. The Commander doesn't want to be kept waiting. Ken'll be *so* disappointed, but there you go. We couldn't expect someone like the Commander to hang around for us really, could we? They're spending the night at the Pierre before heading off – all the way to Arizona – can you imagine?' She gives a little shrug; her smile has dried up. 'Well, I guess I'd better say goodbye – go and rescue my darling boy from the horrors of Customs. Is your father coming to fetch you?'

'Should be here any time.'

'He's not going to believe his eyes – you take good care you hear?' She gives me a huge hug. It's warm and kind and very human.

When she's headed back towards the Ws, I look through the crowds at Sydney and the Commander. They're in deep conversation now with a Customs inspector. I look back at us Fs. We haven't even been started yet. We're a pretty small group really, only about twenty of us, whereas there's a whole crowd of As and Bs. I think of Laura's kind gesture, of the gift she's shopped for and been concerned about, trodden under foot, and how she thinks they're pleased, but they're not, not behind her back. And Ken wanting to see the Bentley. And disappointment. And of the children like Mo and Eenie – still so innocent, so simple . . . round and round the garden . . . tickle her under there . . . And I think of me.

Why should they be allowed to get away with everything scot-free? How *dare* they.

I leave my bags and head across to the As too.

The Customs inspector is chalking big crosses on the Commander's trunks. There are five of them – very grand, matching, with monograms printed all over – one of them lying open. Sydney is writing in a big leather notebook, leaning in towards the inspector, head to head. The Commander now seems totally detached from them, as if he's far above these little annoyances of ordinary life. Sitting on his chair, he's looking all around him, very lordly, rather bored – and then he sees me – except he doesn't show it. As I approach, his eyes sweep across me and then instantly glaze over, as if I'm invisible.

'Good morning,' I say – airy that's me. I'm a Cavalier after all.

The Commander carries on looking straight through me.

'What – what?' Sydney looks up and wipes the smile off his face. 'Oh. It's you.' He gestures with his hand as if I'm a fly he's about to swat.

'I saw you drop this,' I say, and bend down to retrieve Laura's lifebelt. It's already squashed, with the mark of a big black footprint across it. 'I thought you might miss it.'

I try to hand it back to him.

'Run along, why don't you,' he says, not taking it.

'It'll probably clean up all right,' I say.

'Can't you see we're busy?'

'Because it was so generous of Laura wasn't it – she meant so well. And I *know* how keen you are on generosity. You've told me so.'

'There's a good girl – off you go.' He pushes at me with the notebook.

'*Bligh*?' says the Commander.

'Especially from us girls,' I continue. 'Isn't that right? You *both* like a lot of generosity from us girls . . .'

'I don't know quite who you think you are, young lady,' says the Commander, 'but you're being a thorough-going nuisance. Now, run along . . .'

But I want to make them see, make them care, so I just keep standing there, not certain what to say.

'Did you hear the Commander?' says Sydney. 'You're in the way – run along.'

Still I stand there. The inspector, who has now knelt down by the open trunk, is looking up at me.

'You heard,' says Sydney again. '*Run* along.' But I don't move.

'Your behaviour is disgusting . . .' says the Commander, and that gives me the word I've been searching for.

'But not disgusting enough,' I say loudly.

'*Bligh* . . .' says the Commander, at last getting up from his chair.

'If you don't leave us at once,' says Sydney, 'I shall have you ejected – do you understand?'

'From where?' I say. 'We're not in First Class any more.'

'I shan't tell you again young lady . . .' says Sydney.

'Is there some kind of problem?' says the inspector.

'Yes,' I say, 'they're disgusting.'

In the top of the open trunk I can see the blue silk dressing gown the Commander was wearing at his 'party' – and a row of whisky bottles like felled skittles. I take a step closer, staring at the contents. The inspector stares too.

'They're disgusting, dirty old men,' I say.

Sydney leans in to me, with his back to the inspector, and hisses in my ear, 'If you don't bugger off out of it, this instant, I'll have you arrested – is that clear?'

Perfectly. The inspector asks me again if I have a problem, and looks from me to the bottles and back again, but I just shake my head now and back away.

I've inflicted damage though, for back in the safety of the Fs I stand watching the chaos I've caused. It's like a cartoon from *Punch* – a small crowd has gathered round, another trunk is being opened, another inspector has arrived, and the Commander has sat down again, slumped in his chair. I don't know what they're suddenly looking for – I don't suppose they do either – but the suspicion seems to have been enough to have stirred things. I look round to share my triumph with Madge, but she's already left. Away behind, at the main exit, I can see Paul. He's got a huge rucksack on his back. It dwarfs him. He's lost his swagger. He looks small and uncertain as he walks outside – there's no one to greet him and I wonder how he's going to get himself to Camp Weehaupak. Not so very much my own darling Beatle after all.

The crowds are thinning a bit. From outside come the sounds of the city – the blasts of car horns, the flashes of the yellow taxis – but still no sign of Dad for me. I wonder if Hen's father has come for her yet – I bet he has. The Ts are way at the end of the building. The usual old me would wait here, patiently, for an inspector and Dad. The me I am now is curious. The Fs still haven't even been started yet – and it won't take me long. I head through the thinning crowds, all the time thinking that Hen will have gone long ago, but when I get past the Ss, I see she's still here, standing amongst her bags and a semicircle of trunks – her father's books? Even in her Mary Quant with the key-hole neck, she looks very lonely and forlorn, her shoulders all collapsed.

'Thought I'd come and say goodbye . . .'

'Oh – gosh – thanks . . .' She looks genuinely pleased to see me.

'Nobody come for you yet?'

'No – not a surprise. Daddy'll probably only send his driver anyway – and they'll have to send a truck for this lot.' She kicks at one of the trunks.

'Are you feeling any better?'

'Not so's you'd notice.'

'Nothing happened?'

She shakes her head.

'What'll you do – if you are?'

'Have it I suppose. As I said, it's not the plague is it – worse things happen at sea – ha-ha.'

'Um.'

'I don't suppose you'll get to stay in Manhattan at all, will you?'

'No – back to Massachusetts, I'd imagine, straight away.'

'Pity – we'd have got on.'

'Yes – I expect we would.'

'I'll give you my address, just in case, shall I – and in London?'

'All right.'

'Just in case.'

I look towards the Fs. 'I'd better be getting back,' I say. 'I haven't cleared Customs yet.'

'Right. Well – good luck. I hope he's the father you want him to be.'

'Thanks.' We don't hug or anything. Hen's not that sloppy, and I haven't yet grown so bold as to make the first move. I stick her address in my handbag and run back to the Fs. An inspector has started on us. In the far background I can see Sydney and the Commander, standing beside the five trunks which are now all open – and Customs men everywhere. It looks as if they have actually found something. I'd only done it to put the wind up them, delay them a bit perhaps – I didn't realize they'd have any real actual contraband or whatever. I wonder what they've found – dirty magazines, illicit drugs, gold bars? And the Commander had called *me* strange . . .

'Ella . . . Ella is that you?'

There's a man in front of me. He's not as tall as I remember. He's not wearing a hat either. The last time I saw him he was in a hat. Now he looks a bit hot, a bit wary, holding out a cellophane box towards me with a big fat flower inside it.

'Ella?' he says again.

'Dad?' I ask.

'Sweetheart,' he says.

JULY 1994

To tell you the truth I could have done without it. When I picked up the phone back in June to hear this American woman's voice saying, 'Ella – guess who?' I distinctly felt my heart sink. That's just being honest – because the funny thing is that I did guess who, immediately – even though the last time I'd heard Jackie's voice was thirty years ago, back in that Massachusetts hospital, when she was a tiny premature baby wailing for her next feed.

She'd homed in on that message I'd scribbled on last year's Christmas card, saying I'd be working in New York in July. It didn't occur to me it would have stirred her into action – not with her living way out in Wyoming. So, come to think of it, why had I even bothered to tell her? As some sort of statement I suppose: a little demonstration that I'm not over the hill yet. Still where it's at, that's me. Serves me right really. Seth's always joking I'm a drama queen – always metaphorically sticking my hand up in the air shouting, 'I'm here. I'm here – pick *me*.' You'd think I'd have learned by now.

Anyway, Jackie had come up with this plan – she was full of it. How she'd sold a couple of horses – prize Appaloosas no less – to some fantastically rich couple on Long Island, and how she'd offered herself as chaperone to deliver them by air from Wyoming and see them safely settled. She could arrange it for July, and wasn't that the greatest? For a moment I didn't twig – was still envisaging those flying horses I think – and she was running on with how we could get together at last, wasn't that fantastic? – opportunity just landed in our laps, *meant* to be – that kind of thing. I could hear myself sounding a bit guarded – as in I'd have to see if I could wangle some time off, and then I felt such a negative old cow, so of course I had to say, yes, I was sure I could manage a day or two. And that was it – a couple of days in Manhattan planned, bagged, parcelled up, just like that – come hell or high water, as Jackie added, before she hung up. I couldn't get over the sound of her voice – the maturity of it, quite rich and mellow, very much belonging to a real person rather than the cipher I'd tucked somewhere into the back of my imagination.

I should have felt more curiosity to meet the body which owned that voice I suppose, but as I said, I could have done without it. I had enough on my plate as it was, what with being sole British liaison between Artspec and the Garivelli Gallery. It was a prestigious event for us and a lot of livelihoods were precariously balanced on the outcome. I was going to New York to work – not swan around with long-lost half-sisters. I'd need to concentrate, that's what I told myself. And anyway, did I want to dig all that up – that network of family connection I'd buried for so long?

Whenever I thought about it in the following weeks, I'd realize I was starting to feel more and more peculiar about the meeting. Before she'd rung, I'd been looking forward to my New York adventure. It's not as if Artspec gets me out of the country all that often; usually I'm stuck in the London office while the artists get to do the gallivanting. I reckoned I deserved the chance to break out, needed a bit of a gallivant myself, and although I've travelled to America several times over the years, I hadn't been back to New York since that summer of 1964. Now, suddenly, this delicious, almost illicit, sense of escape I'd been anticipating felt compromised. Lone travel always lets me create a new persona for myself – frees me up a bit – but now I could see the new persona I'd be inhabiting was that of elder half-sister, and it didn't seem a comfortable fit. I felt I'd been trapped.

I tried discussing it with Seth, but I could see he didn't get it. It was a tricky thing to explain really, and I could hardly tell him

I'd been planning anything as weird as turning into a whole new person while I was away. As it was, he was already moaning about being left to cope, but bloody hell – what was there to cope with? All right, I grant you it would be holiday time, but the children were already organized. Dan would be doing work experience at the *Big Issue*, so he wouldn't be around during the day, and Chloe would be well on her way to Thailand, backpack and all. There was only Nat to worry about, and she just needed a bit of TLC until her A-level results came through – and I'd be home by then anyway. But Seth banged on and on about his creative muse and how was he supposed to get any work done, and I just blew up at him. For a start, I said, he could get up in the mornings and make sure he got to the studio at some God-given hour – that would help. Then he had the nerve to start in on they're not his kids and they weren't part of the deal – and I said *what* deal? – oh, the deal where I shell out eighty-five quid a week from my taxable income for your studio you mean? – *that* deal? So we weren't in any kind of mood to discuss such subtleties as me feeling odd about meeting Jackie or stirring up the past.

I did broach it with the kids. After all, Jackie is their half-aunt if you think about it. I started very warily, so I wouldn't get stuck with too many awkward questions, but I was amazed to find they were almost totally lacking in curiosity. You'd have thought they'd be bursting to know more – it's their heritage too – but no, to them it was something totally remote, like a history lesson. In fact, if it had been a proper history lesson they'd have shown more interest. As it was, they just saw it as part of 'Mum's life' I think; as distant and uncool as it's possible to be. The funny thing was that, having been so careful about bringing up the subject in the first place, their very lack of interest started to get at me. Like, *why* weren't they more interested – wasn't my past linked with their present? Why didn't they care? Ironic, I know.

I brought the subject up again one Sunday, just before I left. Chloe was already well on her way to South-east Asia by then, but Dan and Nat still grace the family table when it suits them, and I try to get us all to sit down together at least once a week, maintaining some semblance of being a family. It's funny really. All my childhood I'd fantasized about real family life – other people's families: the way they looked from the outside at least. But once I had one of my own, it seemed to me they're made up of the same separate, disparate entities as the outsiders. Everyone sees themselves as individual; most want to get out from under.

Anyway, we were chewing the cud over lasagne and salad, wondering aloud where Chloe was that very moment and what she'd be eating – the speculation ranged from stewed locusts to a Big Mac – and I started to tell them about the food on the *Queen Elizabeth*. 'Taking a cruise just to New York,' said Nat, '*wicked*.' But it wasn't a cruise, I explained – not at all. It was 'getting there' – that's how we did it, a genuine mode of transport.

'Yeah – but like you could've flown if you wanted to,' said Dan. 'It was like the *QE2* – slow boat over, Concorde home, indulgence for the wrinklies, right?' But no, I explained, that's not how it was, not then, not for a few more years, until the Jumbos started flying and the masses could afford to take to the air. It's true I ended up by flying home that summer of '64, but that was only because I was forced to leave in such a hurry, when things started to get so difficult, and there were no available shipping berths at such short notice.

I was still stirring up remarkably little of their curiosity. We were on the Häagen-Dazs by then, Belgian Chocolate *and* Vanilla Praline – cost me an arm and a leg. Nat was clowning with one of the tubs, pretending to be the girl in the cinema ads who uses it as a come-on – ice cream symbolizing sex – which got Seth on to the subject of semiotics in relation to minimalism, as she pranced round the table, sliding the tub slowly down into her cleavage and panting. Meanwhile, Dan had grabbed the other tub and was cleaning it out with his fingers – another £3.38 gone west

– and I was saying, 'Dan – please – *manners* . . .' but all the time knowing I was on a losing wicket.

Should have put my foot down years ago – trouble with being a single mum; you over-compensate. 'If your gran could see the pair of you, she'd have a fit,' I said, 'and your great-gran would be turning in her grave. She had a bit of thing about ice cream – '

'Yeah, yeah – cherry ice – like we didn't know . . .' said Dan.

'All right,' I said, cutting myself off abruptly from launching into the tale. I felt surprisingly offended. I didn't think I'd told it all *that* often – certainly not enough to become a bore.

'Anyway, waste not, want not,' said Dan, with a loud lick of his thumb. 'Great-Gran would've approved.'

The last week before I left I was working a twelve-hour day at the office, just to make sure I wouldn't come back to a state of total chaos. You'd think I was indispensable or something. Probably my own fault – but, despite my efforts to delegate, it's so hard not to be hands-on when you see things not being done the way they should. And in the middle of all this, when I was beginning to think I really wouldn't make it in time, Hen called me. Haven't talked to her in I don't know how long. She was on the scrounge of course, as ever. She's trying to set up another branch of KidLines, in Croydon this time, and she says it's turning out to be really heavy going – much easier when it was all Tower Hamlets and Southwark, they sounded trendier – but even that's been hit with the recession and the big city firms cutting back on sponsorship. 'Tell me about it!' I said to her – it's not as if Artspec isn't feeling the pinch too – but she said go on, you've got that lovely annual grant. As I told her, nothing's certain – we'll have to re-bid next year, and we have to come up with the goods, can't get complacent. She said – it's goods I'm ringing about – which of course I knew already, because that's always what she wants. Actually, I had to stop myself putting the phone down on her there and then, as her timing couldn't have been worse. I was desperate to get on, I even told her that, and I didn't want to stop and have to think about her problems. But then she is an old friend – practically my oldest – and she's never lost that kind of relentless quality that gets her what she wants.

This time it's a charity auction in the autumn – would Artspec donate some work as a group, so that she could use the name for publicity? And I said *again*? And she said but it's such a good cause and half your artists are spliffed up to their eyeballs, so they ought to think there but for the grace of God etc. I said you don't make great art being stoned, and that most of our artists need to sell their work to *eat* – and she said what about Janetta and Lance, because she'd read about their sales at Christies. So then I had to admit that, all right, some of them are making a real killing, but by no means all – and said that I would ask around, though I don't see why artists are always the first to be expected to give everything for free. You'd think twice before you asked a lawyer or a dentist wouldn't you, and get short shrift as an answer? And Hen said that actually that wasn't a bad idea – a year's free dentistry would make a mega raffle prize.

I did offer her one of Seth's pieces though – one of the box series – and she said, great, thanks a million – but didn't sound that keen – and I was just thinking how a) I could get that green set out of the hall, which would mean we could use the stairs safely again, and how b) it would serve Seth right for being such a wanker about my going away. Then Hen asked after the children and I filled her in – let drop about Nat's Oxford place, assuming her As come up to scratch – and then I asked after Nick, and Hen said he's working for Médecins sans Frontières in Africa – Mozambique I think she said. After I'd hung up I was thinking wasn't that amazing – that out of Hen's sad little secret on the ship, all those years ago, grew this solid-gold citizen saving eyesight in the harshest environments of the world. Then I felt so exercised by that fact, and sort of guilty that I hadn't sounded more helpful, that I spent the rest of the day persuading artists to donate to KidLines after all. She's clever that Hen, knows how to press all my buttons – always did. And of course I hadn't been able to resist having a little boast: 'me, me, me' again – told her about going to New York, just at the end – and she said, 'Rather you than me, ducks. Give my regards to Broadway' – which left me feeling a tit and fifteen all over again.

I'd have been even less keen to meet up with Jackie if I'd had a clue what a nightmare New York would turn out to be. It was the definition of 'Art' which was threatening my downfall. 'Original Work of Art' to be precise – allowed into the US tax and duty free. Fine in theory, but first define your 'original work of art'. The Customs inspector at Kennedy Airport was suspicious from the start. Paint on canvas is art; watercolour on paper, safely clamped into a frame – fine, that's art too; but when he saw the spec for 'The Women's Lunch' by Corporation he blew his top. I kept telling him it was 'mixed media', but he was saying did I take him for some kind of monkey because come on lady, this had a huge dining table made of real wood, with weird chairs to match – weird but *usable*. These were potentially functional pieces of furniture, weren't they? And I was desperately trying to call the people at Garivelli's to back me up, except by then the 'table linen' was being unpacked, and I was trying to explain it was all soft sculpture – but he was saying, who's kidding who here, it's still table napkins isn't it – he wasn't born yesterday – where is the goddam ART? Then, like an idiot, I lost my temper, and the whole consignment was impounded to await arbitration by an expert sent out by MOMA – not the next day of course because that was the fourth of July, Independence Day, no one available – maybe not even the whole rest of the week. And if the work wasn't released in time for the gallery opening, who was to care?

I poured all this out to Jackie when she called me that night, because she had a problem too. Her flight from Wyoming to La

Guardia, complete with horse stalls filled with real live Appaloosas, had been delayed, so that she'd only just got out to East Hampton and wouldn't make it back into Manhattan until the next day – one of our planned precious two days already down the pan. I was about to suggest we jacked it in – feeling relieved that I could wriggle out of it without hurting her feelings – when she said she'd advance booked a Circle Line boat trip for us, the one which orbits Manhattan via the Hudson and East Rivers. Okay, she said, it was corny, couldn't be cornier, but living out west, the city was as much a novelty for her as for me – and this way we'd get to talk and see the sights at the same time. Meet her outside the terminal building, Pier 83, opposite West 43rd Street, 1p.m. – all right? She certainly seemed something of a force of nature, not a smidgen of hesitation on her side, and I could feel myself caving in to her determination. Anyway, I couldn't see what else I could get done by way of work on a public holiday, so I might as well go along with it.

'How will I recognize you?' I asked.

'Oh, we'll know each other all right,' she said.

The gallery had booked me into a small mid-town hotel on the west side, but since I'd arrived I'd seen virtually nothing of New York but the warehouse at Kennedy and a telephone receiver. That evening was my first chance to break free and explore a little. The desk clerk was sweet. When I asked if he could recommend any local restaurants, he got all anxious and warned me against going down to Times Square on my own, and to be careful on the side streets – but then he's not to know you have to be pretty streetwise in Brixton these days. I think he imagines London is still something out of Sherlock Holmes.

I actually had a few goals in mind – wanted to retrace some of the things I did with Dad on those two extraordinary days. I'd got a map and a guide book, though the desk clerk had warned me about displaying either of them in public – an open invitation to getting myself mugged he said, but I didn't worry that much. Even in London I always comfort myself that I don't look like rich pickings. Who's going to be all that interested in a plumpish middle-aged woman in hippie gear?

I found the Algonquin on West 44th where Dad had booked us into a suite – the first of our games. Because, as it turned out, that's what we were doing. Playing games. From meeting me off the *Queen Elizabeth* he'd taken me straight to lunch at the 21 Club – nothing less would do for his daughter. We drank champagne, ate steak tartare and he got me to make a list of all the most New York things I'd like to do. It was mostly all stuff from films, of course, for what else did I know? *The Seven Year Itch* and *An Affair to Remember* – that sort of thing – plus a bit of Dorothy Parker thrown in because I loved her, which is how we ended up at the Algonquin. Then we had this crazy day – up the Empire State Building, out to the Statue of Liberty, Tiffany's, round Central Park in a horse and carriage, all the most clichéd, fun things we could think of. And he'd got tickets for a Broadway show – *Barefoot in the Park*, which starred a lusciously handsome newcomer called Robert Redford.

And all this time Dad never phoned home.

The next day we headed out to the World's Fair. It was enormous. At the time it seemed so important, though who recalls it now? Looking back, we all seemed so innocent and gullible. We still thought technology was going to do everything for us. 'Progress' we called it, ever onwards and upwards. If someone had stopped me that day and asked what life would look like in 1994, I'd have assured him (and I'd have assumed it was a 'him' that was doing the asking) that we'd be wearing boiler suits of silver foil and eating three-course dinners out of tubes – if of course, I'd have added, we hadn't blown ourselves to smithereens by then, which we probably would have – or the Russians would have for us.

And still Dad hadn't phoned home. And I didn't know he

should have. I just went along with it, swept up in the novelty of being looked after. Daddy's girl at last.

Then we did set off north up the highway, driving through the night, and I remember dozing on the seat beside him, and waking up again, amazed at the unreal reality of being back in this place of my earliest memories, and the sight of Dad, very relaxed at the wheel of this huge American car – so instantly changed from dream being to very present physicality. But then, in the early hours, we were stopped by some state troopers. Dad thought he was in for a speeding ticket and joked – called me 'sweetie' and said, 'Hang on to your hat,' as one of them walked slowly over to us. But it wasn't speeding. It turned out they'd been looking out for us; the hospital had asked for a search. And once they'd explained what had happened, he stopped being my dad after all.

I was the first to arrive at the pier, still twitching about what wasn't happening at the gallery, Independence Day or not. I took a cab which snaked under the West Side Highway and dropped me off at the entrance. I stood there looking round for Jackie, but my mind was still all churned up with this work thing. The traffic was streaming by, and I suddenly had this tremendous flash of déjà vu, because I realized this place was only a few blocks down from the big passenger-liner piers where the *Queen Elizabeth* had docked. From where I stood I could only see one quite small grey battleship, but it wasn't hard to imagine the ghost outlines of the two massive *Queens* – their funnels etched against a hazed blue sky, exactly like that steaming hot day when Dad came to fetch me, thirty years ago. In spite of the heat today, I gave this involuntary violent shiver – what do they say, someone walking over your grave?

Jackie was right about recognizing her though. I was standing there, staring into all these strangers' faces in the crowd, and suddenly I saw her, near a cab, the absolute dead spit of Dad – same auburn colouring, same dark button eyes. We had just this moment's awkward hesitation while we made sure – then we threw ourselves into a clumsy sort of embrace.

'But you're so like I've always imagined Dad – from the pictures,' Jackie said.

'You too – it's your eyes,' I said.

'You see why we had to meet,' she said. 'I never met anybody with my eyes before.'

The boat was crammed with fourth of July vacationers and we had to push our way round to find a place to sit, which actually was quite useful as it relieved the initial awkwardness and gave us a chance to weigh each other up a bit. She was short like me, but tanned and muscular, and she was wearing jeans and a tight T-shirt, plus a whole rank of earrings piercing the cartilage of her left ear, and cowboy boots which clattered up the stairs ahead of me. I was in one of my batik smocks, which cover a multitude of sins, with my big Holly Belsher earrings, my big silver rings on my fingers and my big rings of kohl round my eyes. We found a place on the top deck under the awning, close to the stern so we could catch any breath of breeze going, and the boat pulled away from the pier, heading south.

I immediately felt it was up to me to get things started – break the ice – so I told her the last time I'd seen her she was just this tiny little scrap of a thing, and how terrified Lynn and Dad had been for her.

'Both of them – Mom and Dad?' she said.

'Of course,' I said.

'You know, I like to say that out loud – "Mom and Dad" – like they go together. I don't often get the chance – and you know, for a lot of people it's probably the dullest, most regular thing, you know what I'm saying?'

Too right I did. It's not a phrase I've had much call for either. I watched the shoreline slipping past. It was industrial-looking along there – warehouses, gasometers, that kind of thing, with the traffic endlessly roaring by.

'You've never done this before?' she asked.

'No, not unless you count coming in and out on those big voyages,' I said. 'I don't recall much from when I was small, but that time I came on the *Queen Elizabeth* I can really remember what it felt like, being way up there, looking down at all these tiny boats buzzing around. Maybe there was even a Circle Line one – back in whenever it was . . .'

'1964. That would have been that day – the day I was born – '

'Well yes, I suppose it was . . .' And of course I knew perfectly well it was.

'They've become like a real legend in our family, those two missing days,' she said, ' – an absolute no-no. A kind of symbol about what life with Dad was all about, you know – with Mom lying in the hospital and only Sadie to help, and having to go through the Caesarean all alone. I mean, it *was* kind of dramatic – because by then everybody thought he'd had an auto accident. She thought he was dead and that I'd be born dead . . .'

'Yes, it was a terrible thing to do . . .' and even after all this time I felt implicated and ashamed. I *knew* I didn't want this meeting.

'Mom always says I only weighed about as much as two sticks of butter – that was me, and just look at me now . . .' She held out one arm, very well moulded with very three-dimensional triceps. 'That's what a life with horses does to you.'

I shook my own flabby arm in her face and said, 'I wish, I wish – I'm so envious.'

And she said, 'That's what I always felt about you.'

'*Me*? In what way?' I asked.

'So envious of you – that *you* had it all. You were the big sister that Dad actually knew – and I was just the baby – and he couldn't relate to me at all.'

Well, she couldn't be more wrong about that, but how to make her understand? As I started to fill her in about Dad's game playing, I could see she'd heard it all before, but with a different slant. It wouldn't have been difficult to have another point of view either, for what else but scorn could Lynn have felt, alone in the hospital, in pain, her sliced abdomen held together with stitches, her child barely holding on to life in an incubator – and her man running wild in the Algonquin? But as it turned out I only got those two crazy days to feel like a daughter, because once we reached the hospital and it all sank in – what had happened, what was so nearly lost, and still might be lost – well, once that happened, Dad went crazy in a whole new way: crazy in love with his own miniature doppelgänger, his Jacqueline, his *Jack*ie.

'Yes, but my name was just in honour of Jackie Kennedy – that's what Mom's always said.'

'Well she's wrong,' I told her. 'I'm sorry, but that's the truth. It was Dad staking a claim on you. Once he knew you were there, were a reality, he adored you.'

'He *adored* me?'

'The moment he knew about you, let alone saw you, you became this – this most precious treasure. He was terrified for you. He more or less lived at the hospital you know . . .' but no, it seemed she didn't know, and so I filled her in.

How he lived at the hospital and Lynn lived at the hospital and the tiny new life lived at the hospital – while I lived at the house out on Bay Road, Point Harbor, all alone. I'd never been in such a beautiful place. The house to me was perfection. I'd wander from room to room, initially scarcely daring to touch anything. The deep mahogany furniture, heavy chintz curtains, New England coiled rag rugs on slippery, shiny floors; the smell of cedar wood in a kitchen straight out of *House and Garden* to my Bissett Street eyes; the unknown mysteries of built-in ovens, freezer and dishwasher. And outside – the hot summer silence, the big sloping garden, the lazy stream, the blue of the bay beyond the pine trees. For me, an Eden.

He came back sometimes of course – a change of clothes, a snatched shower – and Sadie would come too and fill the 'ice box' as she called it, with Tupperware boxes of fried chicken and tuna fish salad to keep us going. It's not that I couldn't have done the catering myself, just that nobody asked – and I, once more removed from centre stage, didn't have the nerve to offer. Sadie was kind and funny, but busy too. Called me 'Cuckoo' which made me smile. I'd try to talk to her about Dad and Lynn, attempting to reveal anything she might know which could fill in the great gaps in my knowledge, but she was hard to pin down, and either very discreet or nearly as ignorant about them as I was.

After nearly a week of this strange limbo, when I was already tanned from lying out in the sun, reading *Middlemarch* and *La Peste*, I was discovered by Mrs Mulherne, who carried me away in her station wagon, to a life of sea, swimming, sailing, clam bakes, barbecues, picnics – and 'making out', as I quickly learned to call it, on the dunes, with her son Billy. It was like living in a Sandra Dee film – as Technicolor and as innocent. Whatever I might have been about to get up to with Paul on the ship, by the time I reached shore, I'd decided to give Hen's 'good old fashioned sex' a miss, until I felt old enough to cope with it. Madge's advice about being myself, about being strong, must have started to take hold about then. Until I'd gone on board the *Queen Elizabeth* that summer, I'd always thought that adults knew the answers, and that there'd be some abracadabra moment when I'd know them all too. That journey and the crazy two days with Dad showed me a different scenario.

We were passing the towers of the World Trade Center by then, and the commentary over the loudspeaker was pumping out the statistics – the world's second tallest buildings at 1,350 feet; the outdoor observation deck on the 110th floor; the Windows on the World restaurant . . .

'Did you go up there with Dad?'

'It wasn't built then.'

'No kidding – they weren't even here?'

'You heard the man – they weren't even started till 1966.'

'I wasn't listening.'

'No, in my time the Empire State Building was still the bee's knees.'

'The *what*?'

'The . . . well, you know, the epitome – top notch.'

'So,' she said, 'it was a long time ago wasn't it, and all the while that's what you were doing – with Mom and Dad going crazy with worry over me – you were making out with Billy Mulherne?'

'Among other things, yes, that's what I was doing – and living in that beautiful house. I'd have liked it to go on for ever.'

'Only none of it really existed,' said Jackie, and broke my reverie.

'What do you mean?' I asked.

'That's the way Mom tells it. It was all like a dream, because they didn't own any of it. It was just like a house of cards, like your fantasy days of being together in New York – it's what Dad wanted, so he just kind of snapped his fingers and it happened. Only then, *shazam*! Blink your eyes and it's all gone – and he was gone too.'

Only as I remember, it all seemed solid and substantial enough to me when I was there, and I was never offered any sort of satisfactory explanation as the status quo disintegrated around me. It seemed that one day I was out sailing with the Mulhernes, and the next Sadie was helping me pack, and driving me to Boston airport. My return Cunard ticket, booked for mid-September, was exchanged for one from TWA for a Boeing 707, bought in a hurry by Uncle Sally and sent by special delivery to Point Harbor.

Sadie didn't know what it was all about and Dad never came back to the house to tell me. I remember asking Mrs Mulherne, but she just went all tight lipped, said something about these things happening my dear, patted me on the hand and offered me a root beer.

'So what did actually happen?' I asked Jackie. 'Why was it all this "house of cards"?'

'Well, you know . . .' she said.

'No,' I said, hating to admit that I didn't.

'Well, you know, they didn't own any of it.'

'Any of what – the house you mean?'

'*Any* of it – the house, the factory . . .'

'No, I didn't know that, why would I?'

'It was all on loan from the Festinis,' she said.

'By "the Festinis" you mean Uncle Sally and Aunt Bea?'

'We've always used their last names. Mom still refers to them always as "The Festinis".'

'They always seemed very kind . . .'

'Mom said they never got in touch after Dad died – but then maybe with what he'd done to them – with the factory and everything . . .'

'Yes?' I said. 'The factory?'

'Well, that would piss anybody off, wouldn't it?'

So then I had to come out with it – confess that I'd never known, never got a satisfactory answer. M. had tried writing to Aunt Bea after Dad died and had got nowhere – a subject definitely seen as off invisible limits.

'But you knew he'd lost the factory – you had to know that?'

'Not "lost" exactly,' I said. 'He didn't seem to be going there to work when I was at Point Harbor, but then I assumed he was always with you and Lynn at the hospital. How *do* you lose a whole factory?'

'In a crap game – he lost the whole of Festini's Flavoricious in a crap game.'

'Not even he would have bet a whole factory on a throw of the dice, surely,' I said, 'and if it was all the Festinis' anyway, surely it wasn't his to gamble with, was it?'

'No it wasn't – I guess that's where Uncle Sally might've gotten a little mad, don't you? Because by then the whole thing was leveraged against all these different loans Dad had taken out, that he shouldn't have taken out because he didn't own the factory in the first place. But the money to pay for all those dreams had to come from somewhere. Houses at Point Harbor didn't come cheap – neither did suites at the Algonquin come to that – and then, when it turned out he'd gambled the whole thing away, well, the Festinis just wanted to cut us all loose. I guess you can't blame them for that – and then there was the accident – because that's what made people think that maybe it wasn't – '

'Wasn't an accident?'

'You do know about *that*?'

Well, I did – but in a veiled kind of way. Lynn did write once to my mother and told her the police were involved, and she must have hinted at suicide. His car had driven off the Point Harbor bridge, the one I used to take to get down to the Mulhernes every day. It was a sharp left turn, but even so – unless of course he'd been drinking?

'The police cited it as an example years later, we heard,' said Jackie, 'when Chappaquiddick happened – it was the same kind of thing, only they said it looked as if Dad's was deliberate. Nothing wrong with the car's brakes or anything, no reason to veer off to the right like that – and when they found him the next morning there was no sign he'd tried to get out or anything. It was just as if he was exactly where he wanted to be.'

I stared down at the river, absorbing this, not all that surprised, realizing I'd somehow known all along. Jackie suddenly leaned towards me. 'Are you hungry – shall I go get us something?'

'We both could,' I said.

'Might lose our seats.'

'Right, of course – well, yes, I'd love a Coke or something – an ice cream maybe?'

'Can't promise you Festini's,' she said. She was laughing.

'I didn't imagine you could – do you see it on sale anywhere?'

'Are you *kidding* – of *course* – they've got franchises all over – you've never seen one?'

'They haven't made it across the Atlantic,' I said. 'We've got Häagen-Dazs and Baskin Robbins, but that's about it I think.'

'Ben and Jerry's?'

'Never heard of it.'

'Well, Festini's is really kind of fancy. It's on the move – we've even got one opened up in Jackson Hole. Festini's Flavoricious is really something – the bee's knees, like you'd say. Kind of makes you sick doesn't it?'

'The ice cream or the irony?' I said.

'Mom says he'd have done anything for this – if he'd known it was going to take off like this. He was always hunting for the great American food idea – and it turned out it was right there, under his nose – only to make it work it had to be Italian, and that's what he was always trying to escape. Changing his name – our name . . .'

'That was something I did ask him, that summer – why did you change your name – and he said he didn't want to be pigeonholed, whatever that meant . . .'

'Mom always said he didn't want to feel he was carrying immigrant baggage around with him – and she'd tell him, "But honey we're *all* immigrants, unless we're Indians, and look what a raw deal they've gotten, for mercy's sake" – but he wouldn't have it.'

'But you changed your name back?' I said.

'Couldn't be prouder to be a Festini – well, of course I *could* be prouder, if I got a percentage out of every gallon of Flavoricious that gets sold. You too, huh? We'd be multi-millionaires by now.'

'Who does own it?' I asked.

'It's part of Magna Foods – humungous. So what's it to be – Coke and a hot dog?'

'Sounds very fourth of July to me – perfect,' I said, and watched her squeeze through the crowd towards the stairs.

While she was gone we passed the Statue of Liberty, over on the other side of the boat. I hoped she'd be able to see it down at the bar or wherever she'd gone; that she wasn't missing it, as this trip had been her idea. I craned round to peer over heads and take it in, looking up at Green Liberty's Green Crown, seeing the minute dots of people's faces peering down from it, and recalling how hot and breathless Dad had been when I made him climb the endless clanging metal staircase to get up there: how he'd confessed to vertigo once we got down again. We'd felt like a pair then – we belonged together, just for a while. When I, too, had been one of those tiny faces, I had thought it was only the beginning of something huge in my life – and not what it turned out to be, merely the briefest interlude.

She came back, balancing hot dogs across iced cups of Coke, with a bag of potato chips clamped under her armpit. The guide was telling us about South Street Seaport and the Brooklyn Bridge as we ate. I sat there, feeling exhausted with all these family revelations, letting the guide's information wash over me while I held the icy paper cup to my cheeks, willing my body to cool down, absorbing thoughts of Dad, trying to make it all fit in. Jackie had fallen silent too and was leaning forward, concentrating on the trip for the moment as we came out from under the Williamsburg Bridge heading north up the East River. The guide was urging us not to miss the great Fourth of July firework display there'd be at dusk, pointing out the big flat barges all ready for the show.

*

'Does your mom know we're seeing each other?' Jackie asked suddenly, sitting back. So she, like me, was not in fact engrossed in the skyscape. Her mind, too, was busy turning it all over.

'No – not yet,' I said.

'Me neither. I'll tell her though – she knew I wasn't coming straight home, so she'll ask what I was up to.'

'How is Lynn?' I asked, realizing as I said it that I should have asked earlier.

'Pretty good, very busy. She's looking to retire from the restaurant business once she hits fifty-five – that's her goal.'

'She's always worked?'

'Had to – it wasn't a choice – but I guess she likes it. She's still in partnership with Sadie's daughter. They all came out there with us. The business grew out of my grandma's steak house.'

'Is that close to you?'

'About ninety miles north, not far . . .' which made me smile. Ninety miles being a considerable old distance back home. 'Not where we come from – Montana's big sky country you know. I'm down south from her.'

'And you've got your own business – you've done well.'

'Me and my partner. I've always loved horses – so has Mom, come to that. With Big Horn Appaloosas we're looking to rule the world – the Appaloosa world that is. Maybe not that big a world, but it sure is satisfying to know you're doing the best.'

'Business partner or more than that?' I asked.

'Business and life.'

'Tell me about him,' I said.

'Not a him,' she said.

'Tell me about her,' I changed – stupid assumption on my part.

'She's called Rosemarie – and she's what it's all about. Isn't nothing can break us down.'

'Does Lynn approve?'

'What's there to approve? Mom doesn't go in for judgements

304

like that. She's always been a very life-affirming kind of person – go out there and tell the world you're just swell – go out and get it all. I mean, maybe it's been kind of embarrassing sometimes, like at school – you can imagine – but there isn't anything she hasn't thought was there for the taking if you've earned it. Mom taught me to reach for the sky, but then, once you'd got there, that maybe the sky wasn't anything like far enough.'

'Lucky you,' I said, 'that's not a bad philosophy to grow up with,' and I was thinking of us as I said it – of Gran and M. and how they'd seemed to be pre-programmed for disappointment, and drew me along in their wake.

We were passing the United Nations building now, like an elegant box of matches up on end – iridescent bluey gold in the afternoon light.

'What about you?' said Jackie. 'You got divorced way back didn't you?'

'Oh yes,' I said, 'Paul swanned off with his bit of totty when Nat was barely two.'

'"Totty"?'

'Bit on the side? The other woman?'

'Oh, right.'

'Not that my mother didn't think I got everything I deserved. I met him on that voyage you know – originally – only we didn't make much of a connection then. It was just chance really – fate does keep funny tricks up its sleeve, doesn't it, because I so nearly went to Newcastle for my degree. I only plumped for Edinburgh at the last possible moment, on a whim, and voilà, we bumped into each other again. I was already half-way through my History of Art BA when he turned up as a junior don in the Anthropology Department – and, you know, it was the back end of the sixties by then, and we tended to let it all hang out – literally. My mother was disgusted with me – that I was having an affair with a married man. She'd sacrificed so much precisely *not* to do exactly that – and there was her own daughter, as she thought, chucking it all back in her face. Only in my case Paul left his wife and married me – bad mistake as it turned out. Serial marrier is Paul. My mother had a hard job not to say, "I told you so", in fact she did say it. And it hasn't been easy, bringing up three kids alone . . .'

'And your Mom – is she okay now?'

I told her about M., still running her gallery after all these years. How she had managed to grab hold of Mrs Croxton's meanly held carrot at last – and doing very well – not a single dead animal, not a feather or a wispy bit of grass or corn in sight, of course. The moment Mrs Croxton was safely on her way to Golders Green Crematorium, M. had changed the gallery's name to Croxton Metropolitan – specializing in architectural engravings, the more urban the better. She could even be sniffy about Adam or Soane originals if their subject was country houses. And so far, I don't think she's ever been back to Norfolk.

'Sounds as if she's doing just great then?' said Jackie, which brought me up short. It wasn't the description I'd have chosen myself; the phrase 'doing great' not being in my own personal thesaurus. And yet, I thought of M. – old, dogged, unbending, still defiantly alone – and I had to concede, grudgingly, that it suited her. So, 'Yeah . . .' I said, 'you could say that . . .' catching myself smiling. 'Yeah . . . she is . . . doing great.'

Some time about now we lapsed into silence. The boat had passed Roosevelt Island and was well on its way up towards Harlem. The humidity had all of us in thrall. Jackie wasn't leaning forward any more, she'd slumped back on the bench; she was dozing. I wondered whether to wake her – if she was wasting her precious trip – but I let it go. Let her sleep. For the first time in a couple of hours or so, I thought about work again and the muddle with Customs and Garivelli's, only somehow now it didn't seem so important. Here were the two of us – the products of that man whom we scarcely knew, who had obviously held such an unwieldy position in our lives. We are each half the product of his genes, each having had to forge our way more or less in spite of him, but with the backing of undaunted women: something I'm having to do for my own children now.

I didn't doze. My mind was clicking and sorting. This was why I'd felt that sinking feeling when Jackie had telephoned that day. I'd known instinctively that it would all have to heave and churn to the surface. The guide was telling us about Riverside Drive now and the park, and we were moving towards the passenger piers. I leaned out to look as we passed the end of the Cunard docks, empty today. Presumably the *QE2* still used them, occasionally, for now to sail the Atlantic was something of a curious, luxurious treat, something people did for the sake of it when they needed an extra holiday, often en route for the Caribbean, and nearly always, as Dan had teased, flying back in Concorde or a Jumbo. And the *Queen Elizabeth* herself was, I supposed, still lying on the bottom of Hong Kong Harbour. There were those sad pictures we'd all seen on television, of the great ship, already in the process of transformation by her new Chinese owner into a floating university, but instead mysteriously catching fire and listing slowly on to her port side, where she lay as a dying, rusting hulk. A whole era washed away in the swell.

Jackie woke up as soon as we docked, amused at herself, slightly cross with herself. We walked along West 43rd street, and then grabbed ourselves a cab, found us a bar, found us some booze, told us our stories again. Two women – two sets of black button eyes – one dear dead impossible Dad.

It was me who suggested the fireworks. I'd got into this sister thing now, and didn't want it to end – not yet. So we got ourselves back to the UN building, on dry land this time, seeing ahead of us a vast throng of people gathered on the Plaza. There were plenty of pretzel sellers too, and drinks carts doing a roaring trade in the humid night air. It was Jackie who spotted it first. I, of course, wouldn't have recognized one unless I'd known to look: a smart dark green cart with an awning and flags a-fluttering –

Festini's Flavoricious. Jackie was howling with delight, so of course we had to line up, fight our way to the front through the scrum – twenty varieties on offer, just a fraction of their whole range, but even so, how to choose, where to begin? And all so Italian we might have been in Naples, with this stream of American voices calling out their orders of *Cassata*, *Dolcecannella*, *Mandorla*, *Fragola*, *Nocciola*, with as much easy familiarity as if it were Mom's apple pie. Jackie and I were at the head of the queue by then, and I was struggling to make a choice. Jackie was already ordering *Crema della nonna* (Nun's Cream was the translation on the label underneath). And me? Well – *Variegato amarena* – not much of a contest was it? Not once I'd seen it was Sour Black Cherry. I walked away, linking arms with my new-found sister, the huge cone dripping over with its pink custard, gleaming with morello cherries half-submerged and luscious, as in the darkening sky to the south of us the first rockets pumped their conjuror's glitter into the city night.

Acknowledgements

For information on RMS *Queen Elizabeth* and Cunard *circa* 1964, I am particularly indebted to the Special Archives Collection at the University of Liverpool, where the staff were kind beyond the call of duty in helping me winkle out the facts I needed. I also had a wonderful time amongst the ex-stewards and stewardesses at the *Queen Mary* Anniversary Convention in Southampton, especially Bobbie Bedford, Eileen Newton, Jean Washington and most particularly Frieda Collins, who later gave me so much of her time sharing her experiences and vivid memories.

Gratitude must also go to Terry Wong-Lane for his excellent advice, not to mention a very inspiring vintage *Queen Elizabeth* postcard which was stuck to my computer for the writing duration.

Thanks are also due to the worldwide membership of the Globetrotters Club – very helpful via the Web in my search for the precise amount of the British Sterling travel allowance *circa* 1964, when no amount of studious research could provide me with a definitive answer. Not even Her Majesty's Treasury nor Customs and Excise could provide the solution – in fact the latter came up with five different possibilities in a hilarious letter I shall always keep to make me smile in times of angst. If readers think I've still got it wrong then please accept my apologies – as you see, I did try.

Every writer's family has a lot to put up with, not least in the occasional pillaging of vocabulary and anecdote: so to those members of my family who may recognize a certain turn of phrase, I ask forgiveness and send my love.

*

Thanks too must go to my agent Simon Trewin for his wisdom and good humour, and of course to Louise Moore, Harrie Evans, Sarah Day, Chantal Gibbs, Jane Opoku and all the team at Penguin.